IN STRATEGIC LOCATIONS AROUND THE GLOBE, TANTALUS BEGINS IN ONLY TWO WEEKS. . . .

"The Committee" has masterminded a fiendish, far-reaching plot, a malignant conspiracy rooted in the highest corridors of power. Code name: Tantalus.

Tantalus—all the more daring because it is so obvious—strikes at the very lifeline of humanity. Its aim is enormous, horrible, and unknown even to the superpowers.

Only one man, Christopher Locke, an unsuccesful college professor, can expose the trail that begins with the brutal execution of every person in an obscure South American town.

Everywhere Locke turns, someone is trying to kill him. Some are his enemies. Some are his friends. The only way to stay alive is to stop the Committee's sinister plan.

From Washington, D.C., to an ancient castle near Vienna. . . from the mountains of Colombia to the north Texas prairie, Christopher Locke fights his way through a maze of deception and blackmail, torture and assassination, in a shattering race to stop Tantalus.

LABYRINTH

Jon Land

FAWCETT GOLD MEDAL • NEW YORK

A Fawcett Gold Medal Book
Published by Ballantine Books
Copyright © 1986 by Jon Land

Library of Congress Catalog Card Number: 85-91236

ISBN 0-449-12954-3

Manufactured in the United States of America

First Edition: February 1986

For Camp Samoset

ACKNOWLEDGMENTS

All my books are, in a sense, collaborative efforts, for the knowledge, expertise, and patience of many others are duly tried and given. Listing all is not possible. The names that follow are the most select who deserve far more than this simple mention. Any mistakes that appear in *Labyrinth* are wholly mine.

For assistance in the scientific realm, thanks once again to John Signore and especially to Emery Pineo, who never fails to solve even the most impossible problems.

For help with the economic end, thanks to Robin Dumar.

Thanks to the *real* Colin Burgess for his help with England's landscape and geography.

For technical assistance on the names and capabilities of World War II fighter planes, I am especially indebted to Martin Caidin for his excellent book, *Ragwings and Heavy Iron* (Houghton Mifflin, 1984).

For advice on things medical and for providing moral and editorial support, I owe a special debt to Dr. Morty Korn, the only reader to have suffered through all my works.

I am also ever so grateful to a superb editor, Daniel Zitin, and to Ann Maurer for her creative genius along the way.

As usual, my deepest appreciation to a miraculous agent, Toni Mendez, who puts everything together.

And last, an extra special thanks to Elmer Blistein, a man who believed I could do it when no one else did even after weeding through a dismal first novel for my senior thesis at Brown. Enjoy your retirement, Professor, you've earned it!

PROLOGUE

Lubeck held the binoculars up to his eyes. Sweat from his brow coated the glass with a thin mist, forcing him to swipe at the lenses with his sleeve. The South American sun beat down on his exposed dome. He could almost feel his flesh shriveling but paid little attention. Resting the binoculars again on the bridge of his nose, Lubeck wondered if the men near the trucks might be watching him as well.

He turned the focusing wheel and the picture sharpened. Three trucks now, one obviously having been abandoned, left behind for the sun to broil. The troops from the abandoned truck must have crowded into the others. The complement of men and weapons was just as it had been in Florencia.

The men stood with rifles slung over their shoulders, passing cigarettes and gulping water. Lubeck ran his tongue along the parched inside of his mouth, fingering his canteen. He had precious little water left, none to be wasted on a whim. Down below men in green army garb swished gallons around their mouths and spat them out near their combat boots. Lubeck's flesh crawled.

It was a miracle he had found them. His jeep had given out some ten miles back. Walking straight across the land without rest, he had somehow managed to meet up with the convoy again. His shoes held a pair of feet blistered raw beyond pain, while the sun had stripped him of his bearings. He knew he was still in Colombia, though, probably near the southeastern tip where the country joined Peru and Brazil not far from the Putumayo

River. Just what an armed convoy representing no particular country was doing there, Lubeck couldn't figure. It made no sense, just another fragment of a story that contained only parts and no sum.

One of the men below seemed to gaze up at him. Lubeck hunched lower on his elbows, squeezing the binoculars with both his right hand and the steel pincers he had instead of a left. Amazing how well the things worked, an absolute wonder of modern science. The accident had kept him out of Nam but not out of intelligence and later the field. He became the best because people underestimated him, pitied him. His was a cripple's lot, although he never considered himself a cripple. If anything, his substitute hand was a plus, the pincers when pressed together forming a deadly weapon always ready and waiting.

Always.

Lubeck recalled the first time he had made them work, years ago—fifteen maybe—in Brussels. He was sitting across from an Eastern Bloc agent in a bar discussing terms for a turn. The man was quick with a gun, one of the best. The conversation had not gone well. The tone and timing were off. Lubeck sensed something was wrong even before the man's eyes froze and his hand started for his famous lightning draw. Lubeck realized he had been set up an instant before he jabbed his pincers across the table, digging into the legend's throat before his gun had cleared its holster.

The pincers cut flesh like butter. Lubeck mastered their use, became the best at fighting in close. Guns, knives, hands—nothing rivaled his pincers. His mind had drifted back to the damn accident that had led to their insertion in the first place, when the sight of the troops squeezing back on their trucks snapped him alert again. The engines rumbled in protest, shook, then finally caught.

The trucks were on their way.

The going was slow there along a road barely wide enough to accommodate their passage. Lubeck found himself almost able to keep pace if he trotted. But he tired quickly in the wrenching heat, drained some of his water and resigned himself to just

2

maintaining eye contact with the convoy until it reached its destination.

It had started in London with a routine security assignment that had bothered him for its very banality. When you reached Lubeck's level, your superiors couldn't very well pull you out of the field cold turkey. They had to ease you out, get you used to the inevitable before it happened. Retirement was nonexistent. Instead of a gold watch, you got to be station chief in some lush, tropical country with lots of rum where no one could get to you and you couldn't get to anyone. For Lubeck, London promised to be the start of the easing process. Trouble was, he didn't think he was ready, which meant he had something to prove.

Then the Colombian diplomat had come to him with an incredible story. Lubeck started digging, uncovered a trail filled with dead ends and detours, his only signpost being a shadowy phrase that held no substance:

Tantalus . . .

Lubeck would have been laughed out of the section if he called in the reserves based on what he had. So he'd followed the trail that led to South America and eighty fully equipped combat soldiers. He had picked up their movements in Bogotá and had followed them across Colombia in the jeep that had died under him hours before. Soon he would know why they had come and the pieces would fall together. He was getting close to the answer; he could feel it.

Lubeck shifted his pack from the left shoulder to the right. Thank God the radio he'd obtained at the Bogotá station was small, compact, microchip-based. He had checked in there and remained vague about his purpose. The station chief had listened intently, obliged his whim with a promise he'd be standing by, and had gone back to his rum.

Down below, the trucks shifted about uneasily on the dirt road. Its unevenness forced the drivers to slow to a crawl, and Lubeck drew up with them. He might have used the radio then had he known his position. He knew this area of the country was dotted with small, backward towns whose people were mostly farmers out of a different age. Why, then, the troops? Lubeck's nerves were starting to get to him. He wiped his brow again but his sleeve was so thoroughly soaked the effect was negligible. The sweat stung his eyes. His steel pincers ached with phantom pain.

The trucks rolled around a corner out of sight. Up ahead, the hillside he'd been traveling on swerved in the other direction, meaning he would have to descend now and take his chances on level ground. Lubeck stepped up his pace, wanting to check the convoy's position before he made his move. Fifty yards ahead he drew the binoculars up to his eyes, holding them with only his pincers.

The trucks had stopped. Men who must have been the leaders were conferring. A battered sign with rain-ripped letters was nailed to a post on the side of the road: SAN SEBASTIAN.

The wood was rotting, the name faded, but Lubeck made it out clearly enough. A small farming town obviously. Could this be the convoy's destination?

A jeep hurtled down the road from the town's direction, carrying three passengers. Lubeck turned his binoculars on them. The driver was just another soldier dressed the same as the rest, but the man to his right looked to be more, though he too wore the same uniform. The man's hair was long and neatly styled, his features dark with a pair of liquidy black eyes. The man had an air of authority about him Lubeck could feel even from four hundred yards away.

The jeep pulled to a halt near the trucks, facing them. Lubeck moved the binoculars onto its third occupant and felt his blood run cold. The man stepped out from the back of the jeep, shadowing the steps of the dark-eyed leader. He was a giant, nearly seven feet tall, and wide as well. He wore a white suit that looked totally out of place with the temperature stretching over a hundred. His eyes were narrowed into almond-shaped slits; an Oriental, obviously—the biggest Lubeck had ever seen. The giant's hair was slicked straight back behind his ears. His flesh was rich brown; Chinese, Lubeck guessed. He wore a thin mustache across lips held in a perpetual half smile.

The dark-eyed man moved toward the troop leaders with the giant right behind. Nods were exchanged, not handshakes or salutes. Lubeck tried to focus on the dark-eyed man's lips for

4

reading but the distance was too great. The leaders were listening intently to him, nodding their acknowledgment. The exchange was brief. The dark-eyed man headed back to his jeep, the leaders to their trucks. The jeep's driver swung the vehicle back around to lead the convoy forward. The trucks started on their way again.

In the back of the last one, Lubeck could see men checking the clips of their weapons. He felt the pull of fear now, and welcomed it, for it would give him the edge he needed to keep going.

The trucks had slowed to a walking pace. He descended to level ground and hung a few hundred yards behind them. He flirted with the idea of radioing the Bogotá station but dismissed the notion until he had something concrete to say.

Lubeck climbed another hillside and moved parallel with the convoy. The town of San Sebastian came into view. Dust whipped up from the poorly paved street and blasted the shuttered windows of the town's buildings. A church steeple dominated the town's center, and a bell could be heard chiming softly as windblown pebbles cascaded against it. Lubeck reached for his binoculars.

More military-style vehicles dotted the dusty street. Men in uniforms held their weapons tight and paraded freely, all watching the trucks entering the town's perimeter. But where were the townspeople?

The grip of fear held Lubeck tight. Something was very wrong here all right. San Sebastian, a simple farming community . . . His mind kept coming back to that.

The trucks squealed to a halt. Troops piled from the back of all three, arranging themselves in groups, fanning out. The dark-eyed man was barking orders in heavy Spanish. Enough of his words traveled in the wind for Lubeck to string them into context.

"Check the houses! I want them emptied! Lofts too and outhouses! Check every room, every inch! Get to it! Get to it!"

Three quarters of the troops started off.

"Watch for stragglers!" the dark-eyed man shouted after

them. He nodded to another phalanx, which moved for the church.

Lubeck let the binoculars dangle at his chest and started running, trying to better his angle. His mouth was dry and he knew all the water in Colombia could do nothing about it. He sensed now what was about to take place, but the why still eluded him.

He stopped on a hill even with the church. He was just a hundred yards from the town now. A group of soldiers was unloading large silver cans from each of the trucks and packing them onto the backs of jeeps. When ten cans had been loaded on them, the jeeps tore off, a man at the back of each working on the cans' spouts. Lubeck swung his binoculars back around.

The church was emptying. People, virtually all clothed in tattered white rags, swept into the wide street. Soldiers poked their rifles forward, herding the people into a tight mass, keeping them still. The mass swelled. Lubeck saw young children cowering against mothers, teenage boys trying to stand brave by fathers. Older people tripped, fell, were yanked brutally up by the soldiers and tossed forward. Even from a hundred yards away, Lubeck could hear the muttered cries and pleas to God for help. Some of the people were wailing with knees pressed to the ground and hands grasping for the sky. Rifle butts quickly silenced them. Through it all, Lubeck made out one word above everything else:

¿Porqué? . . . Why?

Several of the other soldiers were returning now with stragglers from the surrounding houses. Perhaps they had been hiding. Perhaps they had simply been missed in the original roundup. It didn't matter. They were tossed into the mass now and the mass absorbed them. Two hundred people, Lubeck calculated, at least a third of them children.

The soldiers poked at the mass with their rifles until it was impossible to tell one person from the next. No space to breathe, let alone move.

The dark-eyed man shouted an order.

The soldiers backed up into a semicircle and raised their automatic weapons.

The people screamed, cried, begged, tossed their hands about in desperate circles, shoving to find safety when there was no place to go.

Above the screaming, Lubeck heard the dark-eyed man's one-word command:

"Fire!"

In the drawn-out instant that followed, Lubeck wanted to drop the binoculars from his eyes but couldn't. The soldiers aimed their rifles straight into the mass and fired without pause. Smoke belched from the barrels, flashes swirling together into a single bolt.

Some of the soldiers changed clips.

The bullets kept coming.

The screaming curdled Lubeck's ears. Still he couldn't put the binoculars down.

The first wave of red and white collapsed down and in, the second atop it, clearing the bullets' path for the next. By the end, there was no place left to fall, and punctured, bloodied bodies stood supporting each other until the wind tumbled them over into the heap.

Lubeck's steel pincers sliced through the frame of his binoculars. He leaned over and vomited.

Lubeck gazed back down. He didn't need his binoculars to see the blood spreading outward from underneath the pile and soaking into the dirt street. A young boy rolled off the top of the pile, into the scarlet pool.

Lubeck vomited again.

Down below, soldiers were soaking the bodies with the contents of the same steel cans that had been loaded into the back of the jeeps from the trucks. Lubeck's mind snapped back to reality, forced out the sickening carnage he had witnessed. He grabbed his pack and was off again.

He stopped a hundred yards farther across the hillside, too close to the town for his own liking. He had to report this, but what precisely could he report? The Bogotá station could never respond in time for it to matter. Time was not the problem. His right hand was trembling and he realized his steel pincers were as well. He pulled his broken binoculars back to his eyes.

7

Across the town on another hillside there was a brief flash, sun meeting something metallic. Another person obviously, another witness to the massacre. Lubeck wondered who. Then he saw the jeeps with the silver cans. They were speeding over prescribed stretches of land with one man holding the cans' spouts open, draining them of a clear liquid, which sank into the ground.

The land! Where were the damn—

"Oh, my God," Lubeck muttered.

It couldn't be but it was. He grabbed the radio from his pack, switched to the proper frequency, yanked up the antenna, and raised the plastic to his lips.

"Come in, Bogotá station. Come in, Bogotá station." He fought to hold the transmitter steady. "This is Field Mouse. Do you read me, Bogotá station?"

"We read you, Field Mouse" came a male voice between splotches of static. "But you're broken up. Can you move closer in range?"

"Negative!" Lubeck roared half under his breath. "No time. Just listen. Are you recording this transmission?"

"Affirmative, Field Mouse. It's standard—"

"I don't give a fuck about standard anything. Don't interrupt me. Just listen. I'm broadcasting from San Sebastian. The whole town's been taken out." Down below troops were splattering the buildings with more of the fluid from the cans, drenching the insides as well. "Everyone's dead, massacred. . . ."

"Field Mouse, did you say—"

"I told you not to interrupt me! It's on tape, goddamnit! I haven't got time for a full report now but I think I know why this town can't exist anymore." Lubeck grabbed for the binoculars with his pincers and held them against his eyes as best he could. They were going to burn the whole town, he knew now, and with good reason. "As soon as I complete this transmission forward the tape stat to Washington under sterile cover. Use gamma channel. Tell them I will follow as soon as I can with all the details."

8

"Acknowledged."

Lubeck swept the area with his binoculars. Yes, it was starting to make sense now. "San Sebastian was a farming community. I'm in a position overlooking the fields now. It appears that—" Lubeck's eyes froze. He tried to refocus the binoculars but couldn't manage it with his pincers. "Oh, my God," he breathed into the transmitter. "This can't be! *It can't be!* I'm looking out at—"

Lubeck felt the presence behind him in time to duck but not in time to avoid the blow. It crunched down on his collarbone, snapping it. Lubeck howled in pain and rolled away. The transmitter flew aside.

"Field Mouse, do you read me? Field Mouse, what's going on there?"

Lubeck looked up into the grinning face of the giant in white. Chinese for sure, he decided. Weaponless, the giant approached him making no effort to be subtle.

Lubeck struggled back to his feet, hunching to keep the pain of his shattered collarbone down. The giant was going to try to finish him with his hands. Fine.

Because Lubeck had his pincers.

He held them low behind his left hip, out of the giant's sight. By the time the big man saw them, they'd be carving up his midsection as easily as the plywood Lubeck used for practice. Lubeck hunched over further, backpedaled, made himself an easy target.

The giant kept coming, pace steady and unvarying. Lubeck baited him further, faked a stumble, readied his pincers.

The giant came into range and reached down for him.

Lubeck swung his pincers forward and up in a blur of motion. His target was the midsection, though by the time he yanked his deadly steel out it would have reached the Chinese giant's throat.

The giant was still grinning when the pinchers reached him. Lubeck felt them bang into something, and at first thought it was an illusion caused by the swift entry into flesh. But they hadn't entered at all. Lubeck's entire body trembled with the force of impact, the steel pincers meeting something harder.

Lubeck tried for the giant's midsection again but the strike

9

was halfhearted and the results the same. As he pulled the pincers back, the giant latched onto them and yanked.

The pincer apparatus came free with a pain Lubeck couldn't believe existed. His teeth sliced through his tongue and blood filled his mouth. The world was a daze before him and he was only slightly conscious of the Chinese giant's open hand crashing into his nose, splintering his brain with the shattered bone.

The last thing he saw was the giant's grinning face.

"Field Mouse, please acknowledge," the transmitter continued to squawk through static. "Field Mouse, please—"

The giant silenced the transmitter with one crunch of his heel, while down below flames had begun to swallow the corpse of San Sebastian.

PART ONE

WASHINGTON,
MONDAY AFTERNOON

CHAPTER 1

BRIAN CHARNEY LOWERED HIS GLASS OF CHIVAS REGAL ON THE rocks to the coffee table, neglecting to use the coaster. Leaning forward off the couch, he grabbed the cassette tape and fingered it.

Its contents held the reason for one man's death. Its existence almost surely held the basis for a second's. Charney had been part of that death sentence, and the Chivas couldn't change that no matter how smoothly it went down.

Charney drained the glass anyway.

He had walked back to his brownstone apartment from the State Department, hoping the walk would clear his head. Instead it only clouded it further. He had turned on only one light in the brownstone and didn't raise the shades, keeping the early-spring sun beyond the windows so he might lose himself in the dimness. But the dimness did not blot out the effect of the apartment. It was expensively and exquisitely furnished. Charney much preferred the house in Arlington, but the divorce settlement had given that to Karen and their two boys. He saw them on alternate weekends. Sometimes.

Charney refilled his glass and ran the events of the day through his head yet again. Of the two best friends in his life, one was dead and the other had been chosen to follow him. Charney had come home early because the job was everything and the job had made him do it. God, how he hated the damn job, but he had to admit he'd be lost without it.

He had waited outside Undersecretary of State Calvin Roy's

office for only ten minutes that morning before being ushered in. Roy was his liaison in affairs of intelligence.

"I hope this is important," Roy said in his southern drawl, offering Charney the usual seat before his cluttered desk.

"It is," Charney assured him.

"I cancelled a full block of appointments to see you, son. There'll be some people mighty upset over that. They came a long way to see me."

"So did this," Charney said, producing the tape.

Roy rose slightly out of his chair to look at it. He was a diminutive, balding man with a wry smile that expressed his uncompromising, often cynical approach to his position and politics in general. He would probably never rise beyond the post he held now, nor did he aspire to. Working behind the scenes suited him just fine, providing room to maneuver and breathe. A native Texan who had grown up amid much wealth but enjoyed little himself, Roy owed no one anything—a trait rare enough in Washington to make him a man to be both respected and avoided. He had nothing to lose. Stepping on toes didn't faze him, even if it meant crushing them.

"It contains Alvin Lubeck's last report," Charney continued, popping the cassette into the recorder on the edge of Roy's desk. "Rather incomplete but interesting all the same."

Charney pressed PLAY. Lubeck's voice filled the room, intermixed with static. The fear was obvious and, in his final words, the panic.

"San Sebastian was a farming community. I'm in a position overlooking the fields now. It appears that . . . Oh, my God, this can't be. It can't be! I'm looking out at—"

Charney pressed STOP. "That's it."

Roy's face had sombered. "You mind tellin' me where San Sebastian is?"

"Colombia. Deep in the southeast."

"So Lubeck transmitted this to the Bogotá station. They send someone in after him?"

"Yes, but the team couldn't get into San Sebastian or even close to it. The whole area's on fire and all they can do down there is pray for rain."

14

Roy nodded. "So whatever it was Lubeck saw ain't there no more."

"That's right," Charney acknowledged.

"What do you make of that, son?"

"Somebody started the fire to cover something up. And they took Lubeck out for the same reason."

"Lubeck wouldn't go out easily," Roy muttered nervously. "You mind tellin' me how he ended up at a giant barbecue in a South American piss country?"

"Following a trail he picked up in London."

"What trail?"

"We assigned him to run interference for the World Hunger Conference scheduled for two weeks from now in Geneva."

Roy considered the words. "Sounds like he was addin' manure to a fallow field."

"He was past his prime," Charney said painfully. "We wanted to ease him out, but he wasn't ready to go."

"And set out to prove you wrong. Looks like he did a pretty decent job. You boys gotta let me in on your methods for personnel evaluation." Roy hesitated, shook his head. "God damn, what'd he find down there that was worth murderin' a whole town over? He file any other reports?"

Charney shook his head. "This was the first we heard from him officially. Wanted to be sure, I guess. If he was onto something big, he wouldn't want us to pull him off or send in the cavalry."

"Whole mess stinks to high heaven," Roy muttered. Then his eyes sharpened. "We gotta find out what he saw down there, son, gotta find out what he knew."

Charney nodded.

"But you didn't go to Langley with this, you came to me. Musta had a reason."

"Lubeck was working out of State on this assignment. I figured you should be the first to know."

"Don't bullshit a bullshitter."

Charney took a deep breath. He hated himself for what he was about to do. "I don't think Langley is the way to go with this. I want to keep all the three-letter people out of it for a while."

"Got your reasons, I suppose."

"Plenty of them. To begin with, we don't know where to start a full-scale field case with what we've got. We send the Company or NSA out on Lubeck's trail and all of a sudden the trail disappears. It's happened before. I don't think Lubeck changed the plans of whoever took him out in San Sebastian. I think he just hit on something and was killed for it. So the opposition has no call to change their plans and cover their tracks unless we give it to them by sending in the troops. The problem is time. We've got to figure that whatever Lubeck was on to has something to do with the hunger conference that begins in two weeks."

"You sound pretty sure of that connection."

Charney swallowed hard. "Lubeck and I went back a long time. He was a pro all the way, by the book. Never strayed from his assignment. We sent him on a goddamn throwaway mission and he came up with something."

"So what do we do?"

"Send one man to retrace his steps. Maybe we'll get lucky."

"Son, I don't fancy anything that depends on luck."

"It's a random factor just like everything else."

Roy's eyebrows flickered. "So it's a one-man game. What players are available?"

Now it was time. "I want to stay away from the pros altogether. I want to use an amateur."

"Son, you're talkin' crazy to me."

"I don't think so. Let's look at some obvious ramifications of San Sebastian. Whatever Lubeck uncovered is big and whoever's behind it is big—organized too. They'd make a pro in no time. They'd know Lubeck put us on to something and cover their tracks."

"So?"

"So let's assume they're not even sure Lubeck got through to Bogotá or transmitted anything we could make sense of. They would stay in their original pattern, the pattern Lubeck uncovered and a pattern an amateur would fare far better in picking up again."

Roy regarded Charney with a taut smile and a slight squint in his eyes. "Back where I come from, they say you can always

16

tell when a bull's got somethin' on his mind, even though he don't say much. You got it all figured, don't ya?''

Charney leaned back. "You know about Lubeck's steel pincers?''

"Never would arm wrestle with him. . . ."

"Ever hear how he lost his hand?''

"Crushed or something, right?''

"The circumstances, I mean.''

"Not that I recall, son.''

"Then let me tell you a story, Cal." Charney squirmed in his chair, fighting for comfort. The upholstery seemed to be tearing at him. "Twenty years ago, I went to college with Lubeck. Brown University up in Providence, Rhode Island. We met during freshman week. Both of us were football players. There was a kid who tried to make the team as a walk-on but couldn't. He did end up as our friend, though, and for much of the next four years the three of us were best friends.''

"Should I get out my handkerchief for this one, son?''

"His name is Christopher Locke and at present he's an English professor at Georgetown.''

" 'At present'?''

"Flunked his final tenure hearing. This is his last semester.''

"You checked.''

"I checked.''

"I suppose this is all leadin' us somewhere.''

Charney's expression looked pained. "Locke was responsible for Lubeck losing his hand. It was an accident. Happened at the Academy six months into our training; we all joined up together, you see. The Three Musketeers," Charney added cynically. "Anyway, the details of the accident don't matter now.''

Roy wet his lips. "Then this Locke's not an amateur, after all. . . .''

"He dropped out of the Academy a week after it happened. The ironic thing was that he was the best in our class. As far as skills went, there were none better. But something was missing even before the . . . accident. Locke had the stomach; he didn't have the heart.''

"You think that's changed now?''

"One thing hasn't: his guilt. Locke ran away from the Academy into academia and he's been running ever since. Georgetown isn't the first school he's quit or been released from. The accident with Lubeck seemed to set a tone for his entire life, a string of failures and incompletions. I guess he never got over it. Whoever said that time heals all wounds was full of crap. It didn't heal this one." Charney paused. "We can offer to help him heal it now."

"By sending him into the field?"

"By sending him after the men who killed Lubeck."

Roy hedged. "He's still an amateur, son."

"And the only thing that stopped him from becoming a pro and a damn good one was that he lacked motivation, a clear sense of why. He'll have that now. Flushing out Lubeck's killers will more than provide it. Locke could never face the Luber because those damn steel pincers wouldn't let him. That's not a problem anymore. Lubeck's dead. Finding out who did it will give Locke a chance to finally finish something, maybe the most important thing he never completed and ran away from: his friendship with the Luber . . . and me. The guilt's been bottled up in him long enough. We can give him a vent for it."

"How generous of us. . . ."

"Locke's the human option," Charney continued. "In this case, infinitely preferable to any other that presents itself given the time frame."

"And how much do we tell this human option of yours?"

"As much as he needs to know." Charney paused. "That includes nothing about the massacre."

"So we just drop him blindly in the field and tell him to run."

"I'll be his contact, his eyes," Charney said softly. "I'll shadow him everywhere he goes. The relays, the codes, the contacts—he drilled with similar ones before. All in an afternoon's work. When the time comes, Langley's only a phone call away."

"You've thought this thing out."

Charney nodded.

Calvin Roy's eyes wandered briefly. "I come from farm country, son, and still I didn't understand why you needed shit to make things grow until I got to Washington. This hasn't been easy for you, has it, Brian?"

Charney just looked at him.

"One of your buddies is dead, son. You could leave it at that. You could turn the whole mess over to Langley."

"You want me to do that?"

Calvin Roy sighed. "Nah, I suppose I don't. But Lubeck was a pro and what he found out there ate him up alive. And I don't care 'bout Locke shinin' brighter than a baby's backside at the Academy twenty years ago, none of that's gonna get him very far against what Lubeck came up against."

"It'll get him far enough."

Roy nodded deliberately. "You got the ball, son. You're the one who's got to live with this in the long run."

Now, drinking his third Chivas Regal, Charney ran Roy's final words through his mind. He could live with himself, he supposed; he couldn't like himself any less anyway. He was doing what had to be done, what the job demanded of him. Maybe that was the problem; he had been in Washington too long, had let his role consume him until it deadened his conscience. Locke was the best man for this assignment, so he would make the offer too tempting for Locke to refuse. Charney was good at that.

He recalled his earliest impressions of Locke at double-session fall football practice at Brown. No one hit the bags harder, took the tires faster. Locke was a kid driven to make that team. In the end numbers had done him in. Faceless men had posted his name and that was that.

Charney shuddered at the thought he had become one of the faceless men, playing with numbers and making cuts of a different variety. He didn't relish that power but accepted it. It was part of the job and the job was him. He glanced at the phone on the coffee table in the gloomy room. One call and the wheels would be in motion, irrevocable from that point.

Christopher Locke had a wife and three kids. Charney wondered why Calvin Roy hadn't asked about that. Then he realized. Roy didn't want to know. The less said, the better. Charney glanced again at the phone. The choice, the decision, was his.

He leaned back and squeezed his eyes closed, fighting back the pain that had started in his temples, only a dull throb now but certain to grow into a pounding ache.

I'm looking out at—

What had Lubeck seen?

Christopher Locke was the man to find out, Charney told himself as he poured another glass of Chivas.

CHAPTER 2

"IN THE NEWS THIS AFTERNOON—"

Christopher Locke turned the radio off. Traffic was backed up all the way along 16th Street and the LTD's air conditioner was on the blink as usual, leaving him a victim of the sweltering spring air.

Locke hit the horn out of sheer frustration.

The news from the tenure hearing shouldn't have surprised him. He'd seen it coming for months now. The signals were all there. The department chairman didn't like his methods, and popularity with the students didn't count for anything. Of course he was popular, they told him, his courses regularly produced the highest percentage of A's in the entire English department. Locke never cared much for grades. The academic pressure at Georgetown was sufficiently high without his adding to it. He wanted students in his classes to relax, to be able to learn and enjoy without worrying about their grade point average. So he was an easy grader, albeit a consistent one who never passed papers to his graduate assistants for marking.

But that apparently didn't help his cause with the tenure board. His philosophy was the exception, not the rule, and so he was out of a job again. He would certainly have time now to work on his novels. Why kid himself, though? The truth was that all the time in the world couldn't salvage them. He was a failure as a novelist and now, apparently, a failure as a professor as well.

A horn blared to his rear. Locke realized traffic was moving again. He waved an apologetic hand behind him and gave the LTD a little gas. His shirt was sticking to the upholstery now.

In the end, he thought, everything came down to security. You worked your whole life to reach a stage where worry was nonexistent, where the rudiments of happiness were available and, with a minimum of unpleasant effort, attainable. What would happen to that security now? Without the Georgetown salary and benefits, how would his family survive? Much of his savings would have to go toward the kids' educations, and there was still the mortgage on their home in Silver Spring to consider. The bills came in piles Chris just barely managed to lower with the help of the check his wife had started bringing home from her real estate job. It was life on a shoestring and now even that was about to be severed.

And how was he to tell his family of his dismissal? His wife Beth, he guessed, would calmly remind him of all the times in the past she had urged him to go into business. He had always shrugged her off, saying he preferred the academic life. Practical as she was, she could never really understand his refusal even to consider leaving college for a "real" job. His oldest children, a seventeen-year-old boy and fifteen-year-old girl he knew less and less everyday, would brush the news off casually, becoming concerned only after considering how the dismissal might affect them. Only his youngest son would show Locke the love and support he so sorely needed. Just past twelve, Greg was the pride of his life. Chris wanted to freeze the boy just as he was, keep him forever from middle adolescence when hugs disappear and soft smiles are replaced by impatient frowns.

Locke would like to have been a better father, just as he would like to have been a better writer, professor, and husband. It was easy to see how people could live their lives for their children: It blotted out their own failures and missed opportunities. But Locke wasn't going to fool himself. His oldest children were strangers and he couldn't expect to hold on to the youngest forever.

Those thoughts had tied a knot of anxiety in his stomach by the time he pulled into the driveway of his Silver Spring home.

He lingered briefly before moving from the car. His heart was thumping crazily against his chest.

"Hi, Daddy!" Whitney greeted him with an affectionate hug as he stepped through the door, leaving the phone dangling by the front hall stairway.

"Hi, beautiful."

She seemed not to hear him. "You're not gonna believe what happened to me today! I was asked to the prom, the *junior prom*! Do you believe it? And the guy is absolutely gorgeous, definitely tops in the whole junior class. I can't believe he asked me. Of course, I knew he liked me 'cause Marcia knows someone who sits near him in study period and she overheard him mention my name. . . ."

Locke looked closely at his only daughter as she moved back toward the phone, still jabbering away. She was wearing faded jeans and had tied her flowing blond hair atop her head in a bun. There was a naturalness about her beauty. It wasn't hard to figure out why boys drooled over her. But she was only a freshman. Could she handle it? Locke wanted so much to discuss that issue with her but knew he'd botch things if he tried.

Whitney held the phone against her shoulder. "I'll have to get a new gown for the prom, you know," she said softer, as tentatively as she could manage.

"What about the one I bought you for the Christmas dance?"

"That old thing? Daddy, be serious, you can't wear the same dress to two formals. Nobody does."

"Maybe they just trade off so nobody notices."

Whitney frowned, impatient to get back to her phone call. "Be serious, Daddy." She whispered something into the receiver, then looked back up at Locke as he sorted through the mail. "Can I eat at Debbie's tonight?" she asked.

"What does your mother say?"

"This is Monday, Daddy. Mom works."

How could I not know that? Locke asked himself.

"Okay." He shrugged.

"Thanks, Daddy!" Then, without missing a breath, Whitney was back in her conversation.

Still shuffling through the mail, flinching at each bill, Chris moved into the kitchen, realizing suddenly how thirsty he was. He found Bobby sitting in one chair with his feet up on another sipping Coke and scanning the latest rock magazine.

"What do you say, Pop?"

Locke sighed on his way to the fridge. He had never gotten used to Bobby calling him "Pop." Somehow the word seemed demeaning. He grabbed a Diet Coke and joined his oldest son at the table.

"How was school?"

"Okay, I guess," Bobby replied with his eyes still on the magazine. "Usual shit."

"Give any more thought to that talk we had?"

" 'Bout college, you mean? Not yet. I will for sure. But the band's just starting to get it together and I just haven't had time. We've got two gigs scheduled. Not much money but it's a start. Things are really beginning to happen for us."

"I'm glad," Locke said lamely, and realized Bobby wasn't wearing the usual bandanna tied around his forehead. Its absence allowed his sandy hair to fall almost to his eyebrows in tight curls that hung perfectly. He had never been much at sports, and as he grew older had never grown out of his boyish prettiness. A must for rock stars, Locke figured, as was the earring that dangled from his left lobe. Bobby's jeans were thin and faded with the ragged bottoms tucked partially into a pair of battered high-top sneakers. His ever-present jean jacket was just as faded, barely blue anymore, stuck here and there with pins that Chris thought might be holding the material together. On the back was sewn an embroidered eagle, symbol of some band Bobby had once been fond of.

Bobby looked away, eyes down. "I've been thinking about taking next year off, really giving the band a full shot."

Though not a complete surprise, the announcement jolted Locke. A son of his not going straight to college? It was unthinkable. Still, he kept himself calm. React too aggressively and Bobby would just storm away from the table. *Give him a chance*, Chris reminded himself.

"Got any specific plans?" he managed to ask.

Bobby hedged, seeming almost as if he was looking for

support or approval. "I was thinking about going out west. That's where all the action is—records, I mean."

"What would you do for money?"

Bobby leaned forward in his chair, looking surprised the conversation had gotten this far. "I got it figured this way, Dad," he said, and Locke knew at once what was coming. The only time Bobby called him Dad was when he wanted something. "Even with the load Georgetown takes off the tuition, college has gotta cost you five thou easy. I figured if you advanced me that much, like a loan, I'd have enough to get started."

"Five thousand wouldn't even pay the rent out west."

"I'll live cheap. Besides, there's a bunch of us going out together. That'll really cut the cost."

"And what happens after a year?"

"We'll be big by then. Everybody says we got the stuff. Everybody says—"

The slamming kitchen door broke off Bobby's words. Beth stormed in with Greg trailing behind in his baseball uniform. She glared at Bobby.

"You tell him?" she demanded.

"Tell me what?" Locke asked.

"Tell him!" Beth shouted.

Bobby said nothing. Beth swung toward Locke.

"Our proud firstborn over there was suspended from school today."

"*What?*"

"They caught him smoking in the parking lot."

"I thought cigarettes were allowed."

"Not cigarettes—pot! Marijuana!"

"Oh, Christ . . ."

"The assistant principal called me at work. I had to interrupt a meeting with some clients. It was so damn embarrassing. So I take him home and tell him we'll deal with this later 'cause I've got to get back to the office." Her raging eyes swung back toward Bobby. "And I leave him the car with instructions to do one simple thing: Pick up his brother at baseball practice."

"Mom," Greg started, "it was no big deal. I could have walked. Or hitched."

"Hitched?" Back to Locke now. "You hear that, Chris? You hear that? So of course he doesn't go pick his brother up like he's supposed to and I get another call at the office from Greg's coach telling me that practice is over and nobody's there to get him. Then I have to borrow Sally's car and rush to the field and I'm already late for another appointment." Beth's finger thrust forward violently enough to make Bobby shrink back. "I have had it with you, young man, just had it! Maybe a prep school's what you need after all. . . ."

At ten grand a year, thought Locke.

"I'll tell you, Chris, we've got to talk about this. I can just see all the wives whispering at the next faculty lunch."

Locke almost told her that wouldn't be a problem anymore.

"I'm really fed up with all his nonsense." Beth was already starting back for the door. "We'd better talk as soon as I get home. I've gotta run now. I'm late for that appointment and Sally needs her car."

The door closed behind her.

Sighing, Locke turned slowly back toward Bobby, dredging his mind for the right response to his oldest son's misbehavior. But the boy rushed out of the kitchen and up the stairs before Chris had a chance to say anything. Seconds later the roar of rock music, speakers on full, started pounding the walls, forming a barrier between Bobby and the rest of the world. Chris had never been much good at breaking such barriers down.

"Turn that shit off!" Whitney screamed from somewhere.

Locke sank down at the kitchen table and smothered his face in his hands.

Greg's hand grasped his shoulder. "You all right, Dad?"

"Tough day, that's all."

His youngest son frowned. "Mom's pretty mad."

"Yeah."

"You mad too?"

Locke reached up and touched Greg's cheek, smoothing his wind-whipped hair, which already showed the first sign of the

26

sun's bleaching. "Not at you. Hey, it looks like it's just you and me for dinner."

Greg returned his father's gesture, sliding down Chris's face a small hand dominated by the Little League championship ring he wore proudly even to bed.

"McDonald's?" he posed hopefully.

"You talked me into it."

Locke ordered his usual two Quarterpounders with ketchup only and barely finished one, while Greg gobbled up his Big Mac and fries, washing them down with a giant cup of Coke with Ronald McDonald's smiling face etched all over it. The boy had gotten braces in February and Chris hoped they would stay on forever, for as long as he wore headgear and had to sneak gum, Greg would be a boy and Locke didn't want to let go of that.

It was Greg's turn to pay tonight and pay he did, peeling a bunch of worn, rolled-up bills from his jeans, dodging the buttons of his baseball uniform top as he fiddled for the right change, just making it. It was a game they played. Greg liked to pay when they went to McDonald's as an assertion of his independence. And Locke encouraged him. Later in the night he would sneak into the boy's room and replenish the sock where Greg hid his funds from all except his father. Maybe the boy was on to the game. Maybe he wasn't. Chris kept playing either way.

Locke had stowed the station wagon in the garage when he heard the phone ringing, hurried inside and grabbed the receiver, certain the caller had given up.

He hadn't.

"Chris, it's Brian Charney. . . ."

CHAPTER 3

THEY CHOSE THE TOMBS FOR LUNCH, AN EARLY ONE SINCE TUESDAY was Locke's seminar day and he would be tied up all afternoon. Since seating at The Tombs with its prestigious political clientele was difficult after twelve, the eleven-thirty meeting was probably the best thing anyway.

Locke arrived first and was ushered to a table at the very rear of the main floor, away from the chatter of other diners in an area usually reserved for more distinguished patrons. He hadn't seen Brian Charney in six months and then only briefly at a reception at Georgetown. Their conversation had been strained. There was too much to catch up on and no sense in trying.

Brian Charney stepped into The Tombs, picked Locke out immediately, and started toward him. Chris rose, impressed as always by Charney's appearance. The years had treated him well, left him with a fine physique and all his hair. There were lines under his eyes to be sure and something alien about those eyes, but for the most part Brian Charney looked a decade younger than his forty-two years.

For himself, Locke had managed a regular three workouts per week at the Georgetown athletic center. It was a constant battle, though, just to stay even and not fall back. His muscles didn't respond as they used to and ached plenty for the effort.

"Good to see you, Bri," Locke said, trying to mean it.

Charney took his extended hand with a faint smile. "You too, Chris. It's been a while."

Silently both men took their seats.

28

"I hope the table is to your liking," Charney opened. "I figured we could use the privacy."

"You arranged it?" Locke said, not bothering to hide his surprise. "You must pull some weight here. Government's been good to you, Bri. What is it, still CIA?"

"Hasn't been for years," Charney said.

"But you told me—"

"I never told you anything. I just nodded and made lots of evasive answers. You drew your own conclusions."

"So who do you work for?"

"It's too complicated to explain. I'm sort of a liaison between the State Department and various tiers of intelligence. The Company is one of them. Basically, I'm just a simple bureaucrat."

"Simple bureaucrats don't get corner tables reserved for them in The Tombs."

"This is the city of bureaucracy, remember?"

A waitress came over and took their drink orders. A Perrier with a twist for Locke, gin and tonic for Charney.

"So how are you doing?" Charney asked.

"You want the truth, Bri?" And suddenly their souls touched like best friends again and Locke felt his guts starting to spill. "Things aren't too good and that's an understatement. I've got two kids I don't even know and a wife I have to get to show me a house if I need to talk to her. I've got two novels boxed in a closet and that's probably as much circulation as they're ever gonna get, not to mention the fact that I'm not exactly on best terms with the Georgetown administration." Locke held the truth of his dismissal back. Admitting failure in his personal life came easier than admitting failure of a professional nature to someone of Charney's status. "There's something wonderful about passing into the great decade of your forties, Bri. For the first time you realize you can't go back and start all over but that doesn't stop you from trying; not me anyway."

"It's called a midlife crisis," Charney said lightly.

"Screw that. My midlife crisis started when I was twenty-five. This is worse."

Locke said that with a smile and Charney smiled back slightly. This was still the same person who had been his best friend in college. They shared both a room and their lives. Charney had thought he'd be able to put all that behind him. After all, twenty years had passed and all the change that went with them. Essentially, though, the two of them hadn't changed. They were still the same people at the core, and that would make his mandate all the more difficult. Charney had sent men to their death before but never a friend.

"I know about the tenure review board," he said suddenly, seizing the advantage. He had to take charge now if he was going to go through with it.

"You what?" Locke exclaimed.

"I read their complete report last night."

"It's supposed to be confidential."

"And it is."

"Yet you read it."

"The need was there. Need overrides confidentiality."

"Speak English, Bri. This is about to become the shortest lunch ever."

The waitress arrived with their drinks.

"This isn't a social call," Charney told Locke, sipping his gin and tonic.

"I'm beginning to get that impression."

"I need your help, Chris, and in return I think I can help you."

"You've piqued my interest. Please continue."

"The Luber's dead."

Locke's mouth dropped. He felt a numbness in his brain. The glass almost slipped from his fingers but he recovered in time to place it on the table. He wanted to say something but there were no words. The grim finality of Charney's statement had shattered any possible response.

"He was killed last weekend," Charney elaborated.

"How?"

"We're not sure."

"Eliminated in the course of duty?"

"That's the indication."

"Where?"

"Colombia. That's South America, not District of."

30

"Oh, God." Locke ran his hands over his face, letting the light of The Tombs back in slowly. "Why there?"

"Why not? It would have probably been his last assignment in the field."

"The Luber wouldn't retire."

"We were retiring him," Charney said.

"I can't believe it. . . ."

"He was the same age as you, Chris. Think back to what you just said to me about your life; all the questions, all the doubts. You're starting to see shadows. So was Lube. Only in our business, shadows will get you killed, sometimes other people too. It was in the training, Chris," Charney noted, meeting Locke's eyes and understating his words just enough. "We went thought it together, the three of us."

"Lube must not have learned that lesson very well."

"No," Charney said without hesitating. "He just couldn't accept it in his own case. He knew what was coming and wanted to prove us wrong. The easy life in the sun wasn't for him, never was. He latched on to something and followed a trail. It led him to something big, all right, but he never got the chance to tell us precisely what."

"Why are you telling me all this? I assume it's classified stuff and a man in your position wouldn't just be exorcising guilt."

"I want you to take his place."

Locke was thrown back. "You're kidding!"

"Hardly. We think whatever the Luber was on to has something to do with the World Hunger Conference, which is scheduled to start in thirteen days. That doesn't give us much time. They'll cover the trail if we send out the pros. I think—*we* think—you could slip by them."

"Because I spent six glorious months at the Academy?"

"Because you've got a personal interest. Because Lube was your best friend. Because you . . . owe him."

Locke flinched, stung by the comment. His face reddened. From somewhere down deep came a memory of the Luber pulling him from a crevice in the earth as the sides squeezed together, threatening to crush him.

"If you're trying to make me mad, you're doing a pretty damn good job of it" was all he said.

"I'm trying to make you anything that will convince you to help us."

The waitress returned and took their luncheon orders: two Tombs special turkey clubs, though neither man felt much like eating. Charney opted for another gin and tonic.

"Lots of tonic this time," he instructed. Then, back to Locke: "We wouldn't expect you to work for nothing, of course."

"Can you put my life back together for me?"

"Professionally I think we can. We could promise you a tenured position at the university of your choice."

"That's quite a piece of work."

"There's more, Chris. Those two novels you've got closeted—there are several hardcover publishers that would be glad to bring them out with large advances and a substantial sum up front for two more."

"You're trying to buy me, Bri."

"Who's kidding whom now, Chris? What person isn't bought, hasn't sold out in one way or another? It's part of life. But there are levels of everything. I'm talking about helping you get your dream back."

"You didn't say 'we' that time."

"I still have personal initiative."

"And apparently a great deal of power."

"It's all in knowing how to use it."

"That must have been the part of the training I missed." Locke hesitated, suddenly unsure. "How much else did I miss, Bri? How in the hell am I supposed to remember anything after twenty years?"

"We won't be leaving you alone. I'll be shadowing you myself every step with the cavalry only a phone call away." Charney waited as his second gin and tonic was set down before him. "I'm not asking you to act independently. I'm just asking you to run interference for two weeks at most, flush out the bastards who got Lube."

"I was never good at running interference. Remember my

32

brief football career? . . . You're asking me to take a pretty big risk, Bri.''

"I can't deny that.''

"I don't know, old buddy, I just don't know.''

Charney had one more argument to put forward, one he had hoped to avoid. "You weren't born in this country, Chris.''

"I don't make any secret of that.''

"Your father brought you over from England during World War II. Your mother, the papers said, was killed in a German *blitzkrieg*.''

Locke sat silent, waiting for Charney to continue.

Charney's eyes went cold. "I know the truth. I know she was German-born and was a spy for Hitler all along. I know your father fled England in disgrace when her cover was blown.''

"Fuck off!'' Locke shouted, rising.

"Sit down. I'm not finished. She walked out on you and your old man and tried to make it back to Germany. The British caught her and hanged her.''

Locke was still standing but he hadn't gone anywhere. We completely changed our identities.''

"You can't bury the truth, Chris. It's always there if some-body's willing to dig deep enough for it. You know that.''

Locke sat back down on the edge of his chair. He held his fingers taut on the table, fighting back the urge to fly across and choke the life out of the man who had been one of his two best friends. And he knew he could do it. That part of the training had never left him. Maybe none of it had. He wondered if Charney had enraged him just to illustrate that.

"Why'd you bring this up?''

"Because you owe this country something, Chris. Your mother got a lot of people killed, and some of them were Americans. Then you came over and started fresh with no hard feelings, so let's say I'm calling in a debt.''

Locke felt the guilt swimming in his stomach like a shark—no, two sharks: one for a horrible accident that had cost a friend his hand, another for the crimes of a mother he barely knew. It was too much for him.

He tapped his fingers nervously against the table. "If I play ball with you, Bri, it'll be to help nail the bastards who took out Lube. That's all. I want you to know that."

And Charney knew he had won. "Whatever you say."

"You still haven't given me any idea what the Luber was onto."

"It's sketchy. The only connection seems to be food."

"Food?"

"He was working on the hunger conference, remember? And the village he died in was a farming community." Charney stopped, reminding himself not to mention the massacre for fear of frightening Locke off. "He was looking at something in the fields during his last report and it scared the hell out of him. I'll play the tape for you later."

"And you don't know what it was?"

Charney shook his head.

"Why don't you go down there and find out?"

"We're . . . trying."

Locke regarded him closely. "There's something you're not telling me, Bri."

"Only what it's better for you not to know."

"Your food connection's a little thin."

"It's all we've got."

"Then what exactly am I supposed to do?"

"We've pieced together the trail Lube took en route to Colombia. We even have an idea of the people he spoke with. We're going to have you retrace his steps. The details and specifics can be worked out later."

Locke's features hardened. "But there's one thing we'd better get straight right now. If I retrace *all* of the Luber's steps, I'm gonna end up joining him by the Pearly Gates, and I don't fancy that much. Please don't insult me by bothering to deny that possibility exists."

"Well . . ."

"So what I want is some provisions made in the event I don't return. I want my family taken care of."

Charney nodded. "Enough said."

"I don't think so. I want a treasury check in the amount of

five hundred thousand dollars delivered to my lawyer in an envelope to be opened if I don't make it back.''

"Sounds like you don't trust me, Chris."

"You haven't given me much reason to."

The club sandwiches came but neither man started his.

"I'll take care of it this afternoon," Charney promised. "The money will be tax-free, of course."

"I wouldn't have expected anything else."

"They'll never have to see it, Chris. You'll be coming back."

"I'm doing this for them, Bri, and for the Luber, not for you and whoever the hell it is you work for. I just wanted you to know that." Locke rapped the table hard, then pulled the toothpick from the center of one of his sandwich quarters. "Now, when do I get started?"

"You leave tomorrow night for London," Charney replied softly, pushing back the pang of guilt struggling to rise inside him.

CHAPTER 4

THE NEXT DAY WAS A HECTIC ONE FOR LOCKE. THERE WERE SO many affairs to settle. To begin with, his passport had expired and obtaining a new one with twenty-four hours' notice had proved impossible. Charney said he'd straighten things out. Just bring in a small picture and he'd take care of the rest.

With that behind him, Locke was left to deal with the massive Georgetown bureaucracy to obtain an emergency leave. He owed them nothing now, so he felt not the slightest compunction about taking off for two weeks in the middle of semester. If there was any regret, it was for his students. The classes would be taken by his fellows or canceled altogether.

Locke explained the leave was for medical reasons, refusing to elaborate further. He didn't have to, as stated in the contract that come May was being yanked from under him. He smiled at them all, feeling suddenly powerful. Brian Charney could get him his job back or obtain him an even better position elsewhere.

As the day wore on, Locke found himself increasingly excited, even ecstatic. Charney was giving much in return for two weeks of his time, and Locke wasn't worried about the danger. Risk plainly could not be much of a factor, or no government branch would allow an amateur to take the job. Charney was giving him the things he wanted most, and going after the Luber's killers wasn't so bad either. He could never express his sorrow and guilt when his friend was alive. Maybe he could make up for it now that he was dead.

Later in the afternoon, Locke found himself focusing on how

to tell his family. Considering he hadn't yet told them about his dismissal from Georgetown, it would all be quite a shock. But this might be good if it served to block their questions. He decided to tell Beth first and approach the kids after.

For the time being, he would say he was leaving Georgetown of his own accord, that they had made life unbearable for him there. Other offers had already come in and now he was going to Europe for two weeks to get his head straight and sort things out. He couldn't tell his wife the entire truth. She wouldn't understand; Locke wasn't even sure he did.

On the way to Charney's office in the State Department, he stopped off at his lawyer's to learn that, incredibly, the envelope had arrived. Locke opened it, found the contents to be satisfactory, and then sealed the check in a fresh envelope along with a letter he had typed out before leaving his Georgetown office. The letter to his family was purely technical and advisory in nature, as he fully expected to return in one piece after his mission was complete.

Charney was waiting for him when he arrived. They sat down opposite each other in a pair of chairs before the desk, all of the small talk and personal fronts gone.

"We're still piecing together Lube's last days," Charney explained. "He started in London where he met with a diplomat from the Colombian embassy named Juan Alvaradejo."

"Colombian," Locke echoed, noting the connection with where Lubeck had been killed. "Any idea why?"

"They'd worked with each other before and Alvaradejo was his country's representative at the hunger conference. The Luber probably just wanted some background and ended up with the beginnings of something much greater."

"And that's what I'll be after from Alvaradejo."

"Just find out exactly what he told Lube. We've got to fit this thing together."

"Where to after that?"

"Liechtenstein, then Florence."

"Christ, Lube was a busy man. . . ."

"But we're not sure yet who he met with anywhere but

London. That's all you have to worry about for now. I'll deliver the rest of your itinerary to you there with the names. You'll be staying at the Dorchester.''

"Wow, you guys go all out."

"We try. Besides, it fits your cover."

"I didn't know I needed one."

"You probably don't. But we're going by the book here. You'll be playing yourself on a research tour for your next book."

Locke nodded. "Should be easy enough. You mean no codes, secret meetings, and all that?"

"Just one." Charney crossed his legs. "We need a system whereby you can contact me at all times, so I'm going to give you a number where I can be reached. Call it if you need me, leave your number, and I'll get back to you within two minutes."

"You mean you won't be watching me?" Locke posed a bit anxiously.

"All the time? Impossible. If someone else becomes interested in the trail you're following, putting someone on your tail would be a dead giveaway that you're working for us. The danger factor ends up rising substantially. No, this is a far better way to go at things. Help is just a phone call away. Just make sure you know how to use an English call box."

"I've been back. I know how."

Charney had almost forgotten. "I'll have your tickets and spending money with me when I drive you to the airport. What are you going to tell your wife, by the way?"

"I haven't decided yet."

"Don't say too much. If someone tries to trace you, we don't want her inadvertently aiding their cause."

"You're scaring me, Bri."

"Just precautions again. We don't know who or what we're dealing with here and until we do we play everything safe. You're going in under deep cover. Recall the term?"

"Vaguely. But how do I convince this Alvaradejo to see me?"

"Just mention Lube and you should be in. He'll want to set all the terms—time, place, all that sort of stuff. Let him. He'll be playing it safe too.''

"Do I mention my connection with you, your people, I mean?''

"It shouldn't be necessary. He'd probably prefer not to know.''

The next ninety minutes passed with Locke asking increasingly technical, professional questions drawn from his six-month intensive tenure from twenty years before. Charney answered them all with a small smile playing on his lips. His friend was recalling the lessons. The afternoon had become a refresher course and Locke was taking full advantage. Charney was impressed.

Chris kept his words and gestures mechanical and impassive, anything to hide the conflicting emotions clashing within him. It felt as though he was back at the Academy with Bri and Lube, another training exercise about to be undertaken. Only the last one he'd been on had ended tragically, and during the ride back to Silver Spring the brutal memories of the accident Chris had suppressed for so long rose once more.

It had been a standard exercise for agents of the advanced, field operative level. A session of survival training in the Academy's Disneyland, a huge wooded complex filled with obstacles promising very real danger. The object was to negotiate the serpentine paths safely with as little incident as possible, the point being to teach agents of Locke and Lubeck's caliber an acceptance of risk. Instincts had to be honed. In the field there would be no second chances. The survival training drilled this home.

Three days into the exercise, Locke chose a path that formed a shortcut through part of the complex. The quicker they got out, the quicker the exercise would end. Lubeck resisted, urging caution. Locke was hearing none of that and started down the path, alert and ready, he thought, for anything.

The ground split beneath him thirty yards later, a ragged crevice that shook and rumbled. Chris managed to hold fast to the surface only to realize with horror that the crevice was closing, threatening to crush him. Then Lubeck was reaching down for the collar of his jacket, lifting with incredible strength as the vise continued to tighten. Locke's breath had been squeezed away but at least he was rising, safe, he thought, until the vice closed on the lower portion of his leg.

He screamed in agony as Lubeck's meaty left hand reached lower to free his jammed calf and foot. The crevice continued to close, jagged halves starting to meet once more. Only his foot was still trapped. Chris jerked it free with the last of his strength.

Another scream punctured the woods, Lubeck's this time. His left hand, the one that had saved Chris's life, was wedged in the crevice an instant away from locking tight once more. Locke fought frantically to free the Luber's hand, though there seemed no space left to yank it through. He found a gap in the crevice wall and pulled with all his might.

Lubeck's scream bubbled his ears.

The hand came free, a sickening mass of crushed bones and flesh, painted red from areas where the skin had receded altogether. Chris covered it immediately with a spare sweater. Lubeck slipped into shock and then passed out, regaining consciousness only sporadically in the day and a half that followed as Locke carried him through the mazelike woods, skirting obstacle after obstacle. Lubeck was rushed to a hospital from the base camp. Doctors saved his life but not his hand. Chris quit the Academy a week later, his drive gone, indecision and guilt replacing it.

He plunged back into the unvarying, uncomplicated world of college and academic rigors to pursue his masters and later his doctorate. Ivy-covered walls were as good a place to hide behind as any, insulated from the outside world if nothing else. A series of teaching positions followed, Chris never quite finding what he was looking for and inevitably moving on or being forced to.

He met Beth when she was a senior and he was coming to the end of his third teaching position. Chris married her two months after graduation and life had been relatively simple at first. The three children had come. Then something had started to turn their marriage stale and perfunctory, something Locke couldn't put his finger on. They drifted apart slowly, not in leaps and bounds but in small strides neither took much notice of. Eighteen years had passed and they were both vastly different people from the two who had met in an American literature class. They were virtual strangers to each other now. The facade was convincing enough, though, making it easy for them to live the lie quite comfortably and to feel fortunate for that much.

Still, Locke had to admit that no matter what the situation of their marriage at present, it had been Beth who'd settled him down and helped him find the discipline and persistence required to win the position at Georgetown. Whether he ever really loved her, he couldn't honestly be sure. But he knew she had brought warmth to his life at a time when the cold threatened to consume him. If he hadn't loved her, he had at least desperately needed her, and when you came right down to it, wasn't that the same thing?

Beth's car was in the driveway when Locke swung his LTD in. The children were away.

"We have to talk," he said to Beth. She was sitting comfortably on the living-room couch studying a brochure featuring the latest designs in kitchen cabinets.

"I'm due at work. Can it wait?"

"No, it can't." Chris paused. There was no sense holding back. "I'm leaving the university."

She looked up at him dumbfounded. "You can't be serious."

"Never more so." Locke sat down next to her. Amazing how you could live with someone so long and know them so little. "The administrative pressure's become too much. They created an impossible situation for me."

"And now you've gone and made it even more impossible."

"Hear me out for a while. I've had other offers." He paused, collecting his thoughts, trying to appear convincing. "I've known this was coming and I've prepared for it. Other universities have already expressed interest."

"Where? Where are these universities?"

"All over."

"Not Washington, though. We'd have to move, uproot the whole family. God, Chris, think of the kids. Is it fair to them?"

"Other kids adapt. Why can't ours? They're perfectly normal."

"We should have talked about this."

"We're talking."

"What about me? I have a job too, you know."

"They've got real estate in other states."

"You're using this as an excuse to move, aren't you?" Beth snapped out suddenly.

Locke knew his strategy was blown. He had to let on more. "We might not have to move at all really. There's new interest in my novels and if things work out, I think I'll give up teaching for a while, maybe check out George Washington for a part-time position."

Beth eyed him curiously. "I thought they were still in the closet."

"I mailed out fresh copies."

"Who's the publisher?"

"I don't want to jinx myself by telling you until things are definite." Locke took a hefty gulp of air. "But I will say that this publisher has expressed enough interest in me to finance a two-week trip to Europe."

"Really!" Beth's face brightened. "When?"

Locke had failed to consider Beth's assumption she'd be coming along. "They're, er, just sending me," he stammered, "this time, that is. It's just a two-week preliminary trip anyway. Very bookish. Sightseeing oriented. Gotta find new locales for number three."

"I never realized locales were so important in your books."

"They are if the books are going to keep improving. This is a golden opportunity, Beth. I don't want to blow it."

Beth's eyebrows flickered and Locke thought he could read her mind. Being married to a published novelist of potential acclaim—she'd like that.

"When do you leave?" she asked.

"Tonight."

"Tonight?"

"Things developed rather suddenly. I've got a seven-thirty flight."

"But you'll be gone two weeks" Beth moaned. "We've got an important dinner a week from Friday."

"Please express my regrets."

His wife shrugged. "I suppose it's for the best."

"I *know* it is."

For a long while neither said a word, only tension passing between them. Somehow Locke wanted her to question him more, to demand an explanation more substantial than the obviously thin one he had come up with. The fact that she hadn't indicated how little she knew him . . . or cared how far apart they had grown. It had been months since they had been lovers and Locke had come to accept life without sex. It was life without love that was bothering him.

"I could drive you to the airport," Beth offered limply.

"Someone's picking me up" came Chris's reply. "Thanks anyway."

Locke finished carrying his bags down the stairs just as Brian Charney pulled up in the driveway.

"Need some help with those?" he asked when Locke opened the door.

Chris checked his watch. "Absolutely. It's almost six thirty. We're running late."

"The plane will be held if necessary."

"You never cease to amaze me."

When Charney opened the trunk, Locke noticed the absence of his friend's baggage.

"You won't be coming along?"

"Not on this flight, Chris. Too risky. I'll follow you out on a later one. We've got to avoid any even remotely direct links once in London. If the opposition's good, they'll know the Luber worked for me, which means they'll be watching. That's why I couldn't pick up the trail myself."

"Then I'll be on my own for a while in London."

"Proceed just as we discussed. Check into the Dorchester and call Alvaradejo immediately. Then call the contact number and leave word about the meet. I'll be in just hours after you." Charney hesitated. "Believe me, it's for your own good."

Dulles Airport was crowded with early-evening traffic. This

was a comfort to Charney, who much preferred crowds to open spaces. As soon as the bags were checked through, he wished Locke luck and took his leave, appearing to be merely one friend dropping another off.

Locke had started for the gate, toting a single piece of carry-on luggage, when a man wearing a plaid sports jacket stepped up to a pay phone and dialed an overseas exchange.

"He's on his way," the man said simply and hung up.

PART TWO:

PARIS AND LONDON, THURSDAY MORNING

CHAPTER 5

ROSS DOGAN'S GAZE SHIFTED RAPIDLY AS HE STROLLED IN THE PLACE du Tertre trying to appear as much a tourist as possible. The Russian had wanted a public site for his defection, and Dogan had chosen this place because it was certainly public, but reasonably confined as well.

The tables of several sidewalk cafés sat on the ancient cobblestones of the square. Artists sold their work from makeshift stands. Some had arrived at sunrise to assure themselves of a choice spot near a tree or storefront. Others created on the premises, adding a new and unique tourist attraction. But the Place du Tertre was no modern outdoor mall. The charming demeanor of the shopkeepers and sidewalk vendors provided the quiet feeling of a place where people could linger over their food and drink, soaking up the sun and the air. No one hurried.

Dogan found Keyes seated at one of many tables covered with red tablecloths. He took a chair across from him.

"Everything set?" Dogan asked.

Keyes looked at him deferentially. "Yes, sir."

"Don't call me sir."

"Yes, everything's set." Keyes touched the miniature walkie-talkie in his lapel pocket. "All units in place. I've stationed four men at both the front and rear of the street, so we should be covered from there. And I've spread another dozen out in the general vicinity of the meet."

"Here," said Dogan, glancing at the tables cluttered around him.

"Here," acknowledged Keyes. Fifteen years Dogan's junior, he represented the new breed of Company agents, the first full generation of field men who hadn't used Southeast Asia as a training ground. Langley had tried to take up the slack with various entanglements in South America and Africa but the media was keener now, so efforts had to be curtailed. Field men were nonetheless cockier than ever. The CIA had become fashionable again.

Dogan ordered café au lait and surveyed Keyes. Six feet tall, perfectly built, able to kill efficiently with any weapon or his hands. What the Company's new recruits lacked in experience was made up for in training. Or so they thought. Dogan had no patience for men like Keyes. The only way to understand the field was to give a little, but these new recruits seemed to have no give in them at all. Everything was black and white. And the desire to score points with the brass had become an overriding goal that clouded the true nature of the job. Keyes was like all the rest and Dogan despised them all.

Without Nam, it had fallen on senior field agents like Dogan to field-train under actual conditions recruits for the Company's Division Six, the rather mundane equivalent to MI-6's fictional double-0s. Extraordinarily few recruits were considered good enough for Division Six. Keyes was one of them. Dogan had his doubts. The kid had too many edges, from the way he wore his short-cropped black hair to the way his tautly coiled fingers flexed into fists and then opened again. Keyes's vision was narrow. Dogan would have to break him of that.

"Do you mind if I ask you something?" Keyes asked him suddenly.

Dogan's eyes stopped sweeping the end of the Place du Tertre where the defector would be making his approach. "Go ahead."

"You know anything about this Russian?"

"Weapons division research chief, I heard. Bringing with him a microfilm of all sorts of drawings and schemes. I try not to listen much. Doesn't help the job."

"You don't seem impressed."

Dogan's eyes bore into the younger agent's. "Son, I've been at this a long time and seen us get hurt by defectors more than anything. We lose more than we turn. The Russians are just better at this sort of thing than we are. Use the photocopying machine over there without clearance and you lose a finger or two and end up with a one-way ticket to Siberia. Most of the defectors we get are plants.''

''This one?''

''Won't know that until the debriefing.''

Keyes hesitated. ''Can I ask you something else?''

Dogan glanced around him. ''We've got time.''

''Your code name—Grendel—did you choose it yourself?''

''It was chosen for me.''

''Grendel was the monster who ate human flesh, right?''

''And terrorized countrysides,'' Dogan elaborated. ''People lived in fear of him. Nobody dared to cross him.''

''And that's the way it is for you?'' Keyes asked, mugging up to Dogan like a Little Leaguer would to Dave Winfield.

''That's the way it's got to be. Intimidation is everything. The opposition is afraid to send their guns after you because failure means you'll send your guns after them, and that's too high a price to pay. No one wants escalation, people killing each other over personal things. Above all, men like Vaslov and me, we're professionals.''

''Vaslov,'' Keyes muttered. ''I've studied his file.''

''A fine gentlemen. My opposing and equal number for the Soviets.''

''You sound as if you like him.''

''Respect is closer to it. He's been at this as long as I have, maybe longer. We're both anachronisms. I'd bet he feels the same way about me.''

''Ever talk to him?''

Dogan looked Keyes over again. Big, strong, and smart. Yes, the Company was choosing well these days, but Dogan wasn't ready to entrust the country's safety to men like him. There was something missing in men like Keyes, a genuine regard for what they were doing and an understanding of the total picture— something like that. Dogan couldn't put his finger on it.

Keyes's walkie-talkie began to squawk.

''I'll take it from here,'' Dogan said, and the youth handed the box over reluctantly with an "I wanted to do it myself" stare. Dogan lifted the plastic to his lips. "This is Grendel."

"Grendel," a voice boomed. People at neighboring tables looked over.

"Don't talk so damn loud!" Dogan ordered in a whisper.

"Grendel," the voice started, softer, "subject has entered Place du Tertre from Sacré-Coeur side."

That would be the front from his vantage point, Dogan calculated. The speaker was thorough.

"Is he alone?" Dogan asked.

"Affirmative."

"Clothing?"

"Black overcoat, unbuttoned. Tan suit."

Damn! thought Dogan. It was eighty degrees and the Russian bastard was wearing an overcoat. Must have thought he was still in Moscow. That would make him stand out. A shield was in order.

"Detach two of your team to his rear. Understood?"

"Understood, Grendel. They'll be in his shadow."

"No! Not too close. If we spook him he'll stand out even more. I don't want him to know they're there."

Sweat slipped down Dogan's back and stuck to his shirt. He felt sticky. Something was wrong about this, all wrong. His eyes swept the area around the Place du Tertre, the street bordering it across which lay a row of shops and stores. Everything looked routine.

"What's the matter?" Keyes asked. "Do you see something?"

"Shut up!" Dogan barked. His eyes kept sweeping. Artists with paintbrushes in hand doodled across canvas as they talked nonstop to wide-eyed tourists hoping to turn them into buyers. A mailman bicycled down the street. A blind beggar stuck his cup in the faces of approaching tourists. A single car with an old woman driving crept down the neighboring street, stopped to let two men wheeling baby carriages pass, and then stalled. The woman fought to restart it. Behind her, horns honked.

"Where is he now?" Dogan asked into the walkie-talkie.

"Halfway down the street" came back the voice. "Should be in your view now."

"Is anyone else following besides us?"

"Negative. Do you want me to move the rest of my team in?"

"Absolutely not!" Dogan ordered. "Stay where you are until you hear different from me. Keep your eyes and your men on the *head* of the street. We're not home free yet."

Dogan glanced down the *place*. The man in the black overcoat was shouldering his way through the crowd, the agents at his rear much too obvious in their attempt to keep up. The defector reached one of the artists' booths and stopped.

The men with the baby carriages, dressed like butlers, had started toward the red-clothed tables.

"We move," Dogan told Keyes.

The younger agent looked frazzled. "That wasn't the plan."

The baby carriages squealed closer.

"Take him!" Dogan shouted at Keyes and into the walkie-talkie at the same time, already propelling himself from the table.

The baby carriages were just behind him. The walkie-talkie squawked.

Dogan threw himself at his targets, the move perfectly timed. An instant later he had both men dressed as butlers pinned on the ground, holding them to make extracting a weapon impossible.

One of the baby carriages teetered on half its wheels, spilled over. A baby slipped out, crying more from surprise than hurt.

Dogan looked down at the butlers. Their eyes showed fear. They were babbling in French.

"Grendel, come in! Come in, Grendel! . . . I'm taking my team in. Repeat, I'm taking my team in!"

"NO!" Dogan screamed as if the man at the head of the street could hear him, lunging off the butlers back to his feet. Where was the damn walkie-talkie? How had he dropped it?

Dogan spotted it next to the closest red tablecloth. He jammed it to his lips, the plot suddenly clear to him.

"No! Do you hear me? Stay where you are! Repeat, stay where you are. We've been had. Stay where you are!"

There was no response. The man had already moved his team in.

"Damn!"

Then Dogan was running, hurdling one table and slithering between tight groups of people. By the artist's booth, Keyes and others were hustling the man in the black overcoat away.

"Follow me!" Dogan shouted as he passed him.

Keyes hesitated only slightly, then took off. He had almost caught up with Dogan when the man with the walkie-talkie sped by them and screeched to a halt.

"Assholes," muttered Dogan, shoes clip-clopping atop the cobblestone.

The head of the Place du Tertre was in sight with the dome of the Sacré-Coeur basilica in the background. But so was a white-haired man who might have been a twin of the one agents were holding at the booth forty yards back, except he wasn't wearing an overcoat. Dogan watched helplessly, still too far away to respond, as a well-dressed man grabbed him on either elbow and spirited him toward a waiting Peugeot. The real defector resisted only slightly before giving in. The car sped off.

Dogan's eyes locked on the blind beggar who had somehow gotten fifteen yards ahead of him and apparently was no longer blind. The man tipped his cap.

Vaslov!

In spite of himself, Dogan made the semblance of a wave. He didn't even consider going for the pistol in his belt.

Keyes roared to a halt just in front of him and digested the scene, eyes blazing.

"That's Vaslov!" he screamed. "Vaslov!" The man dressed as a beggar was strolling away from the Place du Tertre, drifting into a crowd. "You're letting him get away!"

Keyes rushed forward, drawing his pistol. A goddamn cannon, Dogan saw.

"Let him go!" Dogan ordered. "Let him go!"

Keyes was hearing none of that. He sped into the street and angled for a shot into the crowd the blind beggar had become a part of. The young bastard was violating a direct order and you just didn't do that to Grendel. Sure, the kid was a pro; he had recognized Vaslov from file pictures, after all. He was good, far better than Dogan had estimated. But he was too green to understand.

Passersby saw Keyes's cannon and started screaming. Dogan crashed into him and shoved him aside but the kid pushed back, still aiming the gun, ready to fire.

"I said let him go!" Dogan repeated, and something in him broke. He grabbed the younger agent's wrist at its weakest point and twisted. There was a snap and Keyes howled in pain. He started to swing his free hand at Dogan.

Dogan's defense was just as fast. He blocked the strike effortlessly and crashed a set of rigid fingers under the youth's jaw. Keyes's head snapped backward and he went down, eyes dimming. His jaw would probably never work right again and his days of bare-hand kills and quick draws were finished as well. All in ten seconds of Dogan's wrath.

The rest of the agents had caught up with the scene by this time, two still holding the imposter Vaslov had planted. Passersby stopped, crowding together to observe two men huddled over an unconscious third.

"Get an ambulance," Dogan ordered.

There'd be hell to pay for this, he knew. Keyes represented a substantial investment on the Company's part and he had ruined it just like that. Probably did them a favor, but they wouldn't see it that way.

He walked away from the crowd disgusted, wondering if Vaslov was still watching.

CHAPTER 6

LOCKE FOUND HIMSELF UNABLE TO SLEEP DURING HIS FLIGHT. HE WAS going back to England, his place of birth but never his home.

His memory of those days was sketchy. So as the 747 streaked across the Atlantic, he patched the story together for the thousandth time in his mind, taking what he remembered and mixing it with the bits he had been able to pry out of his father as the years wore on. The old man had died at eighty just the year before in a Virginia rest home.

It was in his last days that the old man became most lucid about their years in London and flight to America. He rambled on and on, jumping from year to year with the passing of a minute and making no connections. It was left to Locke's scholar's mind to string events together and put them in context.

Locke's father was an English diplomat assigned to Germany in the mid-thirties. He knew in a matter of months what was coming, and his reports were listened to but not acted upon. He married a young German girl and spirited her back to his homeland when channels of diplomacy broke down and Hitler's war machine started to roll.

Their son, Christopher, was born in London in 1942 amid the turbulence and despair of a battered country. By then his father had become an advisor to Churchill's cabinet, disappearing for long days at a time without contact, always to return to the loving arms of his wife. Charles worshipped her and the feeling seemed mutual, for Chris's mother, Rosa, was forever grateful for being saved from Hitler's wrath. Chris could vaguely recall the lingering hugs his parents shared.

In his final ramblings, the man who became Charles Locke when he reached America told his son tearfully of the pain memories of those hugs evoked, because any love his wife ever showed him was part of her cruel disguise. For years Hitler had operated a remarkably successful spy network within England capable of betraying British plans to the Fatherland almost as soon as Churchill passed them on to his subordinates. All members of the British Cabinet and ministry were urged to take special precautions against the possibility of someone close to them being a turncoat.

Those last days in the nursing home had brought back to Charles Locke all the agony of his subsequent discovery in cruel, vivid strokes. He told his story to his son as if to purge himself. He talked of suspicions arising from the peculiar number of walks Rosa took late at night when she thought he was asleep. He spoke of waiting outside their house one night after pretending to rush out for an emergency Cabinet session and watching his wife emerge into the street dressed in dark clothes. He had followed her to a warehouse where he watched in horror as others arrived, all apparently subservient to her. The meeting was held in German, and although Charles Locke was too far away to pick up details, it was obvious that his beloved Rosa was the head of a subnetwork operating in London not two miles from their home!

Charles Locke returned home that night and loaded his gun, fully intending to use it first on his wife and then himself. It was the sight of his son sleeping peacefully in his crib that changed his mind. The boy could not grow up an orphan, especially amid war. Nor could he grow up in the shadow of a man who had killed his mother for whatever reason. Charles Locke doubted anyway that he could have shot his beloved Rosa. He still loved her too much, but he also loved his country. The choice was excruciatingly simple: Ignore what his wife was or turn her in. He couldn't see himself living with either alternative, but a choice had to be made. When Rosa returned hours later, much surprised to find him waiting in his study, Locke told her he was going to call the proper authorities and would give her a two-hour headstart. There were no tears, no pleas. Just hushed whispers exchanged as Rosa packed one small suitcase. They were professionals, after all. Charles waited the promised two hours, made the call, then cried well past sunrise.

The worst thing of all, he told his son from his deathbed, was that Rosa hadn't as much as kissed Chris good-bye. Her love for him was nothing more than a facade to better enable her to perform her role as spy. Charles had hoped nevertheless that the headstart would be sufficient for her to escape the country. The British authorities, though, responded quickly and apprehended Rosa even as a German submarine was approaching to pick her up. She was tried, sentenced, and hanged all in three days. Charles was the only one who attended her funeral, not bothering to argue over the lack of a headstone. She was above everything a spy who had betrayed his love and his country. He felt the pain of emptiness, of losing something he never truly had.

Through no fault of his own, Charles lost the trust and confidence of his peers and compatriots. Eventually higher powers arranged for new identities for him and his son and shipped them to America, where they might start afresh. But Charles had left too much behind. He was never able to adapt to his new life, nor did he seem inclined to. He withdrew inside himself, leaving his son to grow up without affection or security, apart from financial. He started swallowing Scotch and ultimately it swallowed him, stealing his liver and kidneys long before his heart failed. Charles Locke lived in pain the last ten years of his life but he seemed to prefer it. And only in those last days in the hospital did Chris feel anything but bitterness and alienation toward his father.

He had long before resolved to be a different kind of father to his children. He wanted them to trust him as he had never trusted his father. He wanted to be everything to his family that Charles Locke had never been to him, and in the process tried too hard and seemed to screw everything up. *You don't get second chances* had been a lesson from the Academy, and he had done a nice job of botching up the only chance he would get.

Chris felt himself thrown forward as the 747's tires grazed the runway, bounced, then settled finally as the pilot applied the brakes. One last opportunity to grasp an impossible second chance—that's what had made him accept Charney's offer. The money was nice too but it wasn't the major thing.

Locke started coming out of his daze as the stewardess went through yet another series of perfunctory instructions. It was early morning in London, near seven-thirty A.M. and Locke was bone tired. Still, there was Customs to negotiate and luggage to retrieve. The details seemed endless, as did the line at the British Customs station. Grimly he took his place in line.

"Mr. Locke?"

The sound of his own name shocked him and he swung to his right, to find himself facing a man in a perfectly tailored blue Customs uniform.

"Mr. Locke?" the man repeated.

Locke shook himself from his daze. "Yes?"

"The name's Robert Trevor, sir," the man said in a British accent, extending his hand. Then, lower. "I've been sent to expedite matters a bit."

"Oh?"

"Mr. Charney thought you'd appreciate the courtesy."

"Of course," Locke said, and allowed Trevor to lead him to the right, bypassing the long Customs entry procedure for a single, isolated room. The Englishman closed the door behind them.

"If you'd be good enough to show me your passport," Trevor requested. Locke obliged. The Customs official stamped it twice. "I'm having your luggage brought in first and set aside. I've also hired a car to take you to the Dorchester."

"How thoughtful . . ."

"You have Mr. Charney to thank again. He's very thorough. The Dorchester has your suite all prepared."

"Suite?"

Trevor nodded. "And there's one last thing Mr. Charney asked me to provide you with. Quite irregular but understandable." The man from Customs unlocked a drawer in the windowless office and slid it open. "I believe you are qualified with this," he said, extracting a .45-caliber pistol, standard army issue.

"It's been years," Locke said, not reaching for it.

"But you're qualified," Trevor repeated.

"Yes," he admitted, and reluctantly accepted the pistol. Charney had mentioned nothing about guns. What had changed?

"Simple precautions," Trevor explained, seeming to read his mind. "Mr. Charney didn't want to unjustly alarm you before. He wants you carrying a bit of protection until he arrives."

"But carrying guns is illegal over here."

"Officially, yes. But exceptions are made for men with legitimate needs. We have worked with Mr. Charney often in the past. His requests are always well founded and never refused. Please carry it until he advises otherwise."

Locke stuck the .45 in his belt, made sure his jacket covered it. "Fits rather well," he said, not quite comfortable with all this. Brian would not have issued him a gun unless a chance existed that he might have to use it. Something was wrong here; new factors were being tossed into the game. It was too late to turn back so Locke had to play along. Still, delivering a gun under these circumstances through a subordinate didn't seem like Charney's style. Then again, he was full of surprises, and Locke knew that if guns had been mentioned in the States, this mission would have ended before it began.

"Let's collect your luggage and get you on your way," Trevor said, handing him back his passport and ushering him toward the door.

They reached the claim area, and sure enough, a porter had already loaded his luggage on a pushcart. Trevor tipped him, then pointed Locke toward a waiting cab.

"I'll be moving on now," he said, grabbing Locke's hand in a firm handshake.

"Thanks for everything."

Trevor smiled, tipped his cap. "Enjoy your stay in London, sir."

Locke started for the taxi.

The ride to the Dorchester from Heathrow took longer than he expected, and Locke passed it off to impatience and anxiety. He wanted to get to his room, get settled and refreshed, perhaps grab a short nap before contacting Alvaradejo at the Colombian Embassy.

At quarter-past eight he was ushered into a newly redecorated suite, the rooms lushly done in browns and apricots. There was a fully stocked dry bar in the living room's far corner and beneath it a refrigerator packed with mixers. Locke pulled the blinds open to let in what little sun the morning had to offer. It was a dreary day, the temperature not yet fifty and promising to go little higher. The weather was typical for London in the springtime. All sun was a bonus.

Locke plopped down in a plush chair, feeling like a boy with a new toy. It was all very exciting to him, being treated like royalty in one of London's finest hotels. He was too charged up to sleep and chose a shower instead, hoping that by the time he had redressed in a new suit of clothes, Charney would have arrived at the contact number.

He turned on the water as hot as he could take it and waited until the bathroom was filled with steam before stepping under the jets. He soaped up quickly and then stood with eyes closed under the warm stream, washing all the travel fatigue from his weary muscles, feeling himself come alive again. He switched off the water after twenty minutes, totally refreshed. He toweled himself dry and inspected his face to see if a shave was in order, found it was, and pulled his travel razor from the bottom of his suitcase.

The task of unpacking seemed monumental, and Locke had barely half finished when he grew bored and decided to put the rest off until later. He pulled Charney's contact number from his memory and punched it out on the phone in the bedroom.

"Your message?" a male voice asked simply.

"I, er, Brian Charney please," Locke stammered.

"Your name and number." Stated flatly, mechanically.

"Christopher Locke." And he proceeded to read off the Dorchester's number along with that of his room.

"Mr. Charney is unavailable."

"I'll call back soon."

Locke hung up the phone. Even though Charney hadn't yet arrived in London, he felt more secure. The shadowy phone number made him feel less alone, as if he was part of something greater. Reassured that larger forces were backing him, he felt ready for his next move. Charney had been specific about not waiting for his arrival before calling Alvaradejo. It was almost nine o'clock now; the embassy would surely be open. The hotel operator put the call through for him.

"Colombian Embassy," a receptionist answered in Spanish-laced English.

"Juan Alvaradejo, please."

"Whom should I say is calling?"

"Christopher Locke. He won't know me but I have important business with him." Locke hesitated. "A friend said I should call."

"One moment."

A pause.

"This is Juan Alvaradejo speaking" came the diplomat's voice. "What can I do for you, Mr., er—"

"Locke." Chris recalled Charney's instructions. Get right to the point. "I need to see you, Mr. Alvaradejo. It concerns your meeting with Alvin Lubeck."

Silence filled the other end of the line, broken only by sporadic breathing—nervous breathing, Locke thought.

"Mr. Alvaradejo? Are you there?"

"Yes, *señor*. You wish to see me."

"As soon as possible. I've traveled a long way."

"And you were an associate of Lubeck?"

"A friend."

"Where are you staying, *señor*?"

"The Dorchester."

Another pause. "Are you familiar with London?"

"Somewhat."

"Meet me by Achilles Statue in Hyde Park in one hour."

"How will I know you?"

"Just stand by the statue, *señor*. I will know you."

"One hour," Locke repeated. "Thank you. I'll be—"

But Alvaradejo had already hung up.

The Dorchester overlooked Hyde Park, the sprawling grounds that had once been used by Henry VIII for hunting boar. It was a short walk to the statue, fifteen minutes at most. That gave him forty-five minutes to kill, so he ordered a light breakfast from room service. It arrived just as he had finished dressing in fresh

60

clothes. He gobbled up the croissants quickly and waited until the last possible minute to try the contact number again.

"Your message?" the same male voice droned.

"I'm calling Brian Charney."

"Your name and number?"

Locke gave them.

"Mr. Charney is still unavailable."

"When he comes in, tell him the meeting is set and I'll report on it soon. Oh, and thank him for the . . . gift."

"Acknowledged."

The phone rang off.

CHAPTER 7

It was cold enough outside to warrant an overcoat, which made Locke's .45 totally inconspicuous. In his mind, though, every person he passed knew he had the gun and he found himself glancing down regularly at his left hip to make sure the bulge wasn't showing.

Of course it wouldn't be. They had taught him how to tuck a pistol into his belt so it wouldn't be seen even if he had only a sweater to cover it.

My God, how did I remember that?

Locke stood for a few seconds outside the Dorchester before inspecting the bleakness of the morning. Whatever hope there had been of the sun appearing was gone. A mist had risen, and Chris turned up his collar as he started across Park Lane for Hyde Park. Park Lane was actually composed of two different streets, running one way in opposite directions. Locke made it to the median strip separating them and had to wait for upward of a minute before a traffic light permitted him to dash across onto one of the many paths that crisscross Hyde Park.

He followed the path to Serpentine Road, the largest of all routes in the park, and swung left toward the Achilles Statue by the famed Carriage Road. Locke leaned against the base of the statue and checked his watch. He was right on time but there was no one else in sight. He rubbed his hands together, wishing for a pair of gloves, then stuck them in his pockets. The air was raw. The minutes passed.

Still no sign of Juan Alvaradejo.

Locke felt his nerve strings tugging at him. His life in academia revolved around order, precise and unvarying. Everything was scheduled. He had grown accustomed to minutes passing just as they should. Alvaradejo had chosen the time and the place, so where was he? Locke's uneasiness grew.

"I knew you'd come, *señor*." Alvaradejo's voice came from the right side of the statue, the Carriage Road side. "I knew they'd send someone."

Locke turned with a start, the sudden appearance surprising him. "Mr. Alvaradejo, I'd like to—" Locke stopped when he saw the pistol in the Colombian's hand.

"¡Carniceros!" he screamed. "Butchers! Animals! You will pay! You will all pay! The souls of San Sebastian will be avenged!"

Alvaradejo started to raise the pistol.

In that drawn-out instant, a thousand thoughts ran through Locke's mind but none pushed forward. Instinct born of long-ago training took over. Drills, incessant and repetitive, came back to him.

Move and keep moving! An elusive target creates a panicked shooter. . . .

The Colombian's pistol spit once, twice, bullets splintering cement where Locke's head had been only an instant before. He hit the ground hard and rolled twice, trying to use the statue's base for cover.

More cement showered over him.

"Bastards!" Alvaradejo ranted. "Killers! *¡Asesinos!*"

Locke ripped the .45 free of his belt. At that moment, survival was all that mattered. There was no time to consider what he was doing.

He rolled away from another blast onto the grass. Alvaradejo charged at him, still bellowing.

"¡Ases—"

Locke pulled the trigger. The gun went off with surprising ease, the kickback easily controlled. He fired three shots in rapid succession, the motions of his finger automatic. The first bullet pounded into the Colombian's stomach, the second blew his chest apart, and the third missed him altogether as he was hurled backward.

Locke struggled back to his feet, every inch of his flesh trembling. He moved as in a dream to the Colombian whose feet and hands were twitching in death throes. The whole scene seemed unreal to Locke, impossible in its implications.

A man had tried to kill him and he had killed the man. . . .

Impossible!

Locke tried to shake himself awake.

Alvaradejo stayed dead, the ragged chasm in his chest pouring scarlet, mouth open wide and spilling blood.

Locke looked up suddenly, senses alive again. Footsteps pounded the pavement toward him. Alvaradejo had tried to kill him. What if he hadn't come alone?

Reflexively, Locke jammed the .45 into his overcoat pocket and started running away from the footsteps toward the Carriage Road. He crossed it quickly, glancing back only once, heart lurching in his chest. He cut a diagonal path toward the traffic sounds of Park Lane. There was safety in numbers, camouflage anyway. Another lesson.

An unoccupied taxi stood at a stand.

Locke glanced back again. If there were others, he couldn't see them. He had to get back to the Dorchester fast, had to get out of view, had to call Charney.

He sprinted for the taxi, lunged into the backseat out of breath.

"You all right, mate?" the cabbie asked him.

"Just drive."

The cabbie started the meter. "Where to?"

"Just drive!"

The cabbie did just that.

Locke tried to control his thoughts in order to steady his panic. His breath still eluded him. He was hyperventilating. It had all been too much and now the reality was beginning to hit him, the cloak of shock starting to dissipate.

The gun was still in his pocket, still hot. He had killed a man! No training could have prevented the sick feeling lodged in the pit of his stomach. But the Colombian had tried to kill him; he had to remember that. His own life had been at stake.

Madness!

Charney would get him out of this. Thank God his friend had sent him the gun. Otherwise . . .

"Take me to the Dorchester," Locke instructed the cabbie.

"We just passed it, mate."

Locke flipped him a five-pound note. "Go back."

The man grabbed the bill. "Cheers, mate."

Something about the cabbie's voice disturbed him, a distant ring of familiarity, but what?

Cheers, mate.

The accent was not quite British, it was laced with something more like . . .

Locke went cold. The man's accent was Spanish!

Chris leaned forward and searched for a cabdriver identification form, found none. This wasn't New York or Washington, after all. He had no way of knowing if such cards were required in London, where even the damn steering wheel was on the wrong side. Maybe he was letting his imagination run wild. The shock had been too much for him. A Spanish-speaking man had tried to kill him and now he was hearing Spanish accents everywhere. He tried to settle back but couldn't.

The cabbie inched up the Hyde Park side of Park Lane away from the hotel. His eyes flirted with the rearview mirror. Locke sensed them watching him. He looked up and the eyes moved back to the road.

Stop it! Locke commanded himself, but something just wasn't right. His defenses had snapped on. He felt for the .45 in his pocket.

The cab came to a halt at a red light. Locke glanced behind him and made out the Dorchester's sign clearly four blocks back. Jump out, that was it, jump out while the cab was still stopped.

Chris tried the door. It was locked!

He searched for the knob. It had been cut off. He was trapped!

Locke felt the engine idling. He looked up. The cabbie held the steering wheel with only his right hand, his left was by his side.

65

The light turned green. Locke saw the cabbie's shoulder shift suddenly and sensed what was happening. He threw himself forward over the seat, crashing his forearm into the back of the cabbie's head. The man's face snapped into the steering wheel. The car lurched crazily through the intersection and started to spin.

Locke saw the pistol in the cabbie's hand, struggled to reach his wrist. He felt a set of rigid fingers smash the bridge of his nose. Pain exploded through his head. His eyes watered and blurred. He lost sight of the gun, forgot his own, grasped desperately about.

The pistol was coming toward him. Locke projected his entire frame into the front seat, trying to pin down the gun-wielding hand.

"Killer!" the cabbie screamed. "*¡Carcinero! ¡Asesino!*"

The same words Alvaradejo had used.

The car continued to spin, hopelessly out of control now. It slammed into a bus, bounced off, and crashed into a light pole. Locke was tossed forward into the windshield, his back striking first. The cabbie's head snapped hard against the dashboard, recoiled crushed and bloodied. The door had blasted open on impact. Locke pushed himself toward it. The horn was blaring. Chris rolled out of the car onto the sidewalk where people were starting to approach.

Then he was being helped to his feet, his legs unsteady, his knees wobbly. It seemed his feet weren't receiving signals from his brain. There was a throbbing pain in the back of his head and neck but, miraculously, no agonized sharpness indicating something had been broken or torn.

"There he is! There he is!"

The words were shouted in Spanish, and he could hear footsteps approaching from where he had just come. How many of them were there? First Alvaradejo, then the cabbie, now . . .

With a motion as desperate as it was sudden, Locke broke free of the men supporting him and rushed down the street. Behind him he heard orders being shouted in Spanish and men taking off after him. Pain racked his head and shoulders. His feet thumped against the sidewalk, sending jolts of agony through his entire spine. He was dizzy but knew he couldn't stop. He didn't dare look back, nor was there reason to, for he knew what would be there: men following, undoubtedly with guns. Alvaradejo had had a gun, the cabbie too. Chris could only hope the crowded street and abundance of witnesses would stop them from firing. He crashed through pedestrians, certain all eyes were upon him.

He sprinted down the sidewalk back toward the Dorchester. There would still be several streets to cross, and he would be an easy target all the way. He knew he had to keep moving in spite of the raging pain that made him want to give up. He thought of reaching for the pistol and making a stand here.

The .45 was gone! It must have fallen out during his struggle with the cabbie.

Locke heard more shouts in Spanish and swung back to see men—three, he thought—following in his path. He sped past the Dorchester, wind giving out and legs cramping.

Then he saw the red double-decker bus squealing to a halt at the corner of Park Lane and Curzon Street. He rushed toward it, nimbly dodging through fast-moving traffic. He prayed the small line of passengers would linger long enough for him to make it.

For an instant, it seemed they wouldn't. Then a woman dropped her handbag and bent to retrieve it as the driver waited to close the doors. Locke reached the bus just as the woman lifted her handbag from the steps. He leaped in, the doors hissed closed, and the driver pulled the double-decker away.

Locke rode the bus for almost an hour. The exact time eluded him because his watch had been broken when he smashed into the windshield. The time allowed him to calm down and collect himself, letting his muscles loosen and the pain subside. So far as he could tell, all his injuries were minor, limited to a few cuts and bruises, the worst of which lay over the bridge of his nose where the cabbie's fingers had landed.

Finally Chris saw a red call box up ahead and rose tentatively, reaching for the hand signal. His muscles responded sluggishly but without pain. He climbed out the middle set of doors and stumbled when his beaten legs reached cement. He staggered to the box and settled himself. Luckily he found the proper change in his pocket.

The number! What was the damn number?

Locke searched his scholar's mind and found it.

"What is your message?" The drab male voice was more welcome than any he'd ever heard.

"Charney," Locke muttered. "I need to reach Brian Charney."

"What is your name and number?"

"Christopher Locke." He read the man the call box's number.

"Wait by the phone."

The line clicked off. Chris replaced the receiver immediately.

It rang seconds later. Trembling, he jammed the plastic to his ear.

"Brian!"

"Chris, I've been trying to reach you. Where the hell have you been and what's this about—"

Locke found his voice. "I killed Alvaradejo."

"You *what*?"

"Brian, he tried to kill me! I let him set up the meeting just like you said and he tried to shoot me. If it wasn't for the gun you left for me, I'd—"

"Wait a minute, what gun?"

"A man from Customs issued me one at the airport. On your orders, he said."

"I never sent you a gun."

"Then how—"

"That was the gift you mentioned in your message," Charney realized. "Oh, God, and you shot Alvaradejo with it. . . ."

"Because he tried to shoot me!"

"Take it easy, old buddy, I believe you. I'm just trying to put this thing together. Someone set you up."

"I need help, Brian. You've gotta get me out of here. There was another man with a gun too, a cabdriver, and others chasing me, all screaming in Spanish."

"Do you remember anything they said?"

"It was all pretty much the same. They kept repeating the words 'butcher,' 'killer,' and 'animal'—singular *and* plural. And

68

Alvaradejo said something like the souls of San Sebastian would be avenged."

Silence filled the other end of the line.

"You there, Brian?"

"Yes, Chris. You're sure he said San Sebastian?"

"Of course I'm sure. Does it mean anything to you?"

"It might."

Locke looked around, feeling uncomfortable at staying in one place for so long. His shoes kicked nervously against the sidewalk.

"What do we do from here, Brian? They'll still be looking for me. I might be able to make it back to the hotel if—"

"No!" Charney instructed. "It's the first place they'd expect you to go. They'll have a man waiting. Stay clear of it, do you hear me? I'll meet you someplace else."

"Where? When?"

"It'll be a while. I've got to make some calls, sort things out. Say five P.M."

"That's five hours from now!"

"Four and a half. Believe me, it's necessary. I've dealt with these situations before." Charney paused. "Do you know St. James's Park?"

"I've been there."

"The bridge that cuts across the Chinese-style lakes?"

"I know it."

"Be in the center of it at five P.M. That'll give me the time I need."

"To do what?"

"Call in the cavalry."

The tall man saw his target swing away from the call box and stand there frozen against it, either relieved or exhausted. They had missed him in the park, missed him again in the streets. Those failures were about to be corrected.

The tall man quickened his pace. His hand felt for the butt of the revolver hidden under his jacket.

He had killed before, often and mostly well. This kill would be simple, and especially satisfying since others had failed.

The target moved from the call box.

The tall man started to pull the gun out. He would brush up against him, fire one neat shot that would be muffled against the target's body, then escape. As simple as that. The tall man drew closer.

A woman with long blond hair smacked into him from behind, spilling the contents of her shopping bag. Annoyed, the tall man had begun to shove her aside when he felt her fingers grasp his elbow, pinning his gun hand to his side.

Then he saw her knife. It whipped up and across so fast that the tall man thought, incredibly, she had missed. Until he felt the warm blood spilling from the tear in his throat where her knife had found its mark. He crumpled to the sidewalk, dead an instant after he struck it.

The woman with lond blond hair left him there amid her spilled shopping and walked away.

CHAPTER 8

LOCKE HUNG UP THE PHONE STILL NERVOUS, BUT NOT AS FRIGHTENED. Charney had gotten him into this mess and Charney would get him out. For now, though, he had time to kill.

He moved away from the call box and joined the sparse flow of pedestrian traffic, forcing himself to walk along. He was on Vauxhall Bridge near the Thames River. He wanted to get back to the commercial district where crowds abounded and he would stick out less. Walking was out of the question and he'd had his fill of taxis for the day. That left only one safe alternative by Locke's count. He saw an entrance to the London Underground up ahead and moved toward it, taking the steps slowly.

It took him awhile to figure out the way the lines ran, but he was in no rush and the crowds comforted him. He grabbed the northern line and climbed to street level at the Soho Square station. The mist had given way to a raw drizzle and Chris found himself shivering. Killing four hours in the outdoors was unthinkable. The minutes were already taking forever to pass.

He walked past the collection of shops and restaurants, finding himself on Oxford Street with his head pounding, and saw a large marquee not far away that provided his solution. Just before Oxford gave way to New Oxford Street, there was a row of cinemas. Locke knew at once how he would spend the next four hours before his meeting with Charney: two movies would do the job nicely. He purchased tickets to the movies in advance to avoid having to stand in line again. The titles of the films were meaningless; he wouldn't be paying much attention to them.

Sitting down in the darkened, nearly empty cinema, Chris felt his breathing return to normal. He stretched his legs and massaged them, then tried to do the same with his neck and shoulders. Finally he leaned back and squeezed his eyes shut. Fatigue swept over him. He found himself dozing, snapping back awake occasionally with a jolt forward. Between shows he purchased a pair of Cokes for want of coffee, hoping the caffeine might recharge him. As he revived, he found himself ravenously hungry, so he left to buy three portions of prepackaged popcorn. A short time later, he checked the damage to his face in a men's room mirror, afraid his injuries might make him too recognizable. Fortunately the swelling was minor and a cup of ice obtained from the refreshment stand took much of it down.

By four thirty he felt reasonably alive again. It was time to head for his meeting with Charney. Soon all this would be over. Chris had known from the start there was some risk involved, but never did he imagine his life might actually be threatened, that he would have to become a killer to survive. The possibility, even probability, of that had been dealt with in the training. They tried to desensitize you. Guilt was the real enemy, they had said, not bullets. Guilt made you slow, hesitant. But Locke hadn't accepted the desensitizing process. In fact, it was around that time he had quit.

The memories were uncomfortable, so Locke turned his mind toward piecing together all that had happened. He found himself with only questions. If Alvaradejo had helped Lubeck, why had the Colombian tried to kill Locke when all he had done was raise his dead friend's name? It didn't make sense. And if Charney hadn't provided the gun, who had? More madness.

And what of San Sebastian? What in hell was it and where did it fit in? Most of all, who were the men that were trying to kill him?

Locke would leave the questions for Charney. He rode the underground to the St. James's Park station and arrived at four fifty, according to a clock in the terminal. He took his time departing from the station and found the bridge with little trouble. He strolled around briefly before moving to its center at precisely five o'clock.

Charney was nowhere in sight.

Locke's heart started pounding again. Panic rose in him. The steady drizzle soaked his jacket and his hair. The mist had developed into a fog and St. James's Park seemed totally deserted.

Then he heard the footsteps coming from the northern side. He turned swiftly, letting go of the wooden railing.

Brian Charney approached routinely, a man out for an afternoon stroll, no spark of recognition in his eyes. Locke was about to say something, then thought better of it. Contact was up to Charney. He would take no chances.

Charney leaned over to tie his shoe when he reached Locke.

"Start walking," the man from State instructed. "Keep your pace steady. I'll stay about six feet behind you."

"What?"

"Just do as I say. Walk leisurely and don't look back. You hear me, don't look back! I've been made."

Locke started walking, hand gliding across the wooden railing to convince anyone watching of the leisureliness of his pace. His fingers trembled.

"I lied to you, Chris," Charney said softly, almost too soft, pulling to within six feet of him. "I lied to you from the beginning. You were meant to be a decoy, a sacrifice. We—I— never expected you to make it back."

Fury flared in Locke's cheeks. "How could—"

"Turn around, goddammit! Don't look at me. I'm trying to save your ass . . . and mine. It's bad, real bad, a thousand times worse than I ever imagined."

"What is?"

"The massacre was the key. I should have seen that before."

"What massacre?"

"San Sebastian."

"You didn't tell me anything about—"

"Turn your goddamn head around and keep it that way or I'll save our friends the trouble and blow it off your shoulders."

"Where are they?"

"I don't know. Close, though. I couldn't lose them."

"What about the cavalry?"

"There is none. Not for us. At least not here. I don't know whom to trust, how deep it goes."

Locke made out the panic in his friend's voice. He felt his own trembling increase. "Brian—"

"I can't talk anymore. Go back to your hotel and wait for me there."

"But you said it wasn't safe."

"Nothing's safe. It's the best we can do. They're after you and they're after me and there's no one in the middle."

"*Who's* after us?"

"Not now. Get back to your room. Wait for me inside. Don't turn the lights on. If the phone rings, don't answer it. I'll try to lose them and meet you there. Be ready to leave in a hurry."

"Just say the word."

They had reached the end of the bridge.

"I'll veer to the right here. You stay straight. Find a crowd, lose yourself in it, then get back to the hotel."

Locke started to twist his shoulders.

"Keep your fucking eyes forward. I'm trying to save your life! Just do as I say and don't ask questions!"

Charney veered away. Locke didn't stop to think, just kept moving at the same unaffected pace onto the mall heading straight into Piccadilly. It was all a nightmare and it was getting worse. Charney had spoken in shadowy, desperate phrases that told him nothing. His life was clearly still in danger.

The drizzle had given way to a steady rain. Locke might have been the only person walking without an umbrella. That made him stand out. He swung onto a smaller, less crowded street and aimed for the Dorchester. He reached it in fifteen minutes, being as sure as he could that no one had followed him.

He stood under the marquee to the right of the hotel's entrance for a few minutes, getting a fix on the lobby.

Two men stood just inside the revolving doors, surveying every man who came through. Just the men. Locke couldn't make out their features but their intentions were clear enough: They were looking for someone and it was probably he.

Wasting no time, Locke followed the arrows to the hotel's

parking garage and walked down the ramp, ignoring the old sign prohibiting entry on foot. A car screeched up at him, headlights shimmering and tires screaming. Chris spun out of the way and pressed hard against the wall. The attendant behind the wheel shouted something at him. Locke started down the ramp again.

A minute later he had found the elevator and was inside. Forty seconds after that he was stepping out watchfully on the eighth floor.

The hallways were vacant. Locke started for his room, flinching each time he reached a break in the wall or a partition sufficient to hide the frame of a man. Finally he was at his room, pushing a now-steady hand into his pocket in search of his key. He jammed it into the lock and turned the knob without hesitating.

His suite was a shambles. Clothes were scattered everywhere, the mattress from the bedroom was upturned and torn, drawers had been ripped out and emptied of whatever contents he had managed to unpack. His suitcase was torn to shreds, all the lining ripped out in search of hidden compartments.

What had they been looking for?

Locke swung the door closed, pulled his hand away from the light switch just before he hit it. Terror gripped him as he stepped about the room, kicking aside remnants of his clothes and possessions. They had spared nothing. Even the bathroom had been ripped apart. In the corner of the living room, the desk had been pushed on its side. Chris rushed toward it.

His passport and extra money were gone!

Outside the drenching rain battered the windows. Night descended on London. Locke pressed his shoulders against the wall, afraid someone might be watching him through the glass, someone with a rifle perhaps.

The phone rang, maddeningly loud, insistently repeating its double ring.

Locke lowered himself and crept toward it, again pulling his fingers back at the last instant. Charney had told him not to answer it. But what if something had gone wrong and Brian was trying to call to alert him? No way to be sure. The original instructions had to be observed, the limits adhered to.

The phone stopped ringing.

Locke stayed huddled on the floor, lost in panic. His muscles cramped up and he stretched them out slowly, as if any sudden motion might betray him to whoever had ransacked his suite. The men in the lobby watching the entrance perhaps, or their fellows.

Who were they?

Animals! . . . ¡Carniceros!

Accusing words screamed at him by Alvaradejo fluttered through Chris's mind. What did the Colombian think he had done?

The souls of San Sebastian will be avenged!

What was the connection?

Locke stayed frozen. Minutes passed. Time ceased to have meaning.

Brian, where are you?

Outside the window, night was firmly settled in the London sky. The darkness of the room was broken only by lights from the city's skyline dancing madly across the walls.

There was a barely audible knock on the door. Locke crept across the carpet, his movements painfully slow. He raised his eye to the peephole.

Brian Charney stood outside, body pressed against the door frame. His knock came again. Locke opened the door.

Charney collapsed against him, breathing in heaves. Locke eased his friend down and managed to get the door closed.

Then he saw the blood. It was all over him, all over Charney. His friend had been shot, several times by the look of it. His lips were parched, trembling. Blood dribbled from the sides of his mouth. His face was ghastly pale, his eyes were darting. Charney was dying.

Locke took his friend's head in his lap.

"I'm sorry, Chris" came the raspy mutter. "Oh, God, I'm sorry."

"Don't talk." Locke could think of nothing else to say.

"I know how . . . bad I'm hurt. There are more important things now. Lubeck knew. It's why they killed him." Suddenly Charney grabbed Locke's lapel. His eyes blazed. "They must be stopped!"

"Who?"

"They're everywhere, everything. Lubeck saw. Lubeck knew. The world will be theirs if they're not stopped."

"Who?"

Charney's eyes drifted. His grasp slipped from Locke's coat, his fingers dangled in the air. "I set you up, old buddy, and then someone else did. Alvaradejo had to die, the other . . . links too." Charney coughed up a stream of blood. "Oh, God, my kids! What about my kids?"

"I'll go the American Embassy and tell them everything. I'll tell them everything!" Locke promised.

But Charney's eyes flashed alive and his grasp tugged tight again. "No. Mustn't. Trust no one. Don't . . . know . . . how deep this goes. They murdered a whole town so no one would know."

"Know what?"

It was obvious Charney was incoherent and rambling. What was giving him the strength to go on, Locke couldn't imagine.

"Liechtenstein," he muttered, breath failing. "Felderberg was Lubeck's next stop, Felderberg the broker. Find him, find him!" Charney shifted slightly. "My pocket . . ."

Locke pulled a bloodstained sheet of paper from his dying friend's jacket. He could make out writing.

"Go to Cornwall. Find Burgess. He'll . . . get . . . you—"

That was it. Charney died. The last of his breath poured out in a wisp, as if a vacuum had sucked him dry. His eyes locked open and sightless. Locke eased his head onto the carpet. He wanted to collapse and cry for himself as well as his friend, give up and just sit for a while. But he couldn't. Whoever had killed Charney was close, in the hotel by now almost surely, coming to the room perhaps. Locke had to act fast but his mind wouldn't cooperate.

It was too much. Memories of the horrible accident twenty-two years before filled his head, of watching helplessly as the doctors lifted an unconscious Lubeck onto a stretcher and tore away the field dressing to reveal the mangled remains of his hand. It was a nightmare he couldn't wake from and now the nightmare had returned. He had seen one friend crippled and another killed. Both were dead, and he was so goddamn alone. . . .

But he had to act! Survival called out to him, Brian Charney called out to him, the training from long before called out to him.

They're everywhere, everything. . . .

Who had Charney been talking about?

Locke's mind craved release. He focused on escape, on survival. He had no passport, little money. All he had was an address.

He looked at the tattered, bloodied sheet of paper Charney had given him and read it quickly: Colin Burgess, Bruggar House, Cadgwith Cove, Cornwall.

Chris struggled to recall his knowledge of English geography. Cadgwith Cove was located on a stretch of land called the Lizard at England's southwesternmost tip. Accessible easily by train. First he would need a cab to get him to the station.

He was getting ahead of himself, though. His clothes were bloodied and demanded changing before he set out. He stripped off the ruined ones he had on, grabbed a fresh set from the floor and changed quickly, tucking all his remaining money in a pocket along with Charney's paper. He started for the door, glancing at his friend's corpse one last time. There should have been something else he could do for him. Letting him lie there didn't seem right, but he had no choice.

Locke stepped into the corridor and advanced slowly. He reached an intersection and stopped, wary of proceeding. He could turn right or keep straight. Which way? He hesitated, but not for long because up ahead two men had just turned onto the hallway. The men from the lobby! Locke ducked to the right and starting running down the adjacent hallway. He had no idea if the men had seen him. Either way, there would be others around.

A diversion, he needed a diversion. Confusion had to be created into which he could disappear. But how?

The answer lay before him at eye level on the wall. Locke hit the lever hard and yanked.

The fire alarm began to blare instantly. At this relatively early hour of the evening, most guests were in their rooms preparing for dinner. In seconds the corridor was lined with milling bodies moving unsurely but rapidly, searching for someone to follow as they tested the air for smoke.

The elevators had shut off automatically. Eight flights of stairs had to be descended, and the unnerved guests clustered toward the nearest exit. Locke let himself be swept up in their momentum, slowed at each descending level as they caught up with more figures and more clutter. By the fifth floor he realized there was no one shoving toward him from the rear. He was breathing easier when he reached the lobby to find people gathered everywhere, the overflow spilling into the street.

Locke joined the spillover, staying among the crowd as he searched for a cab, breaking away only when he was certain the chaos had him totally shielded.

Trust no one. . . .

Locke wanted to go straight to the American Embassy and dump his story on the ambassador's desk, but Charney's command prevented him. Who knew how deep this mess went? In Washington, Charney had said there was an army supporting him, reinforcements only a phone call away. Then where were they when he had needed them? Why hadn't then responded? No, his friend had encountered forces he had not expected and was ill equipped to deal with. And if that were so, what chance would Locke stand against them?

Trembling, he walked further into the night.

CHAPTER 9

DOGAN HAD BEEN EXPECTING A CALL FROM THE COMMANDER ALL day, so when it came he was more relieved than surprised. Best to get things over with. Operatives of Division Six seldom fucked up, and when they did there was hell to pay. And Dogan had fucked up big time.

The Commander requested a nine P.M. meeting at his favorite outdoor café on the Champs-Élysées. Dogan was ready for a typical chewing-out session. He would grit his teeth and nod his way through it.

The Commander was waiting for him at an isolated table for two in the sidewalk café's rear corner. He looked more French than American with thinning hair, rimless glasses, and a thick mustache sliced off well before it reached the edges of his mouth. As always he was reading a newspaper. His tone would be indifferent; his eyes would seldom leave the print. Funny thing about the Commander, he could chastise you without ever meeting your stare, as if you didn't even merit the recognition. How he had risen to the position of chief of Division Six's affairs in Europe was beyond Dogan. Then again, much had been beyond him lately.

"Good evening, Grendel," the Commander said, not looking up from his newspaper. "Please sit down." Dogan did as he was told. "A most unfortunate day."

"I've had better."

"And not many worse, I should hope. I've just received the

medical report on Keyes. He'll be manning a desk for the balance of his career, thanks to his wrist.''

"It's the best place for him."

"We invested a lot of money believing otherwise."

"You were wrong."

"A report would have more than sufficed. An assault was totally uncalled for.''

Dogan felt his anger rising. "I gave him a direct order. He disobeyed it.''

"Yes, Grendel," the Commander responded. "I've read the boy's report on that. You ordered him to let Vaslov go, correct?''

"Correct."

"The most wanted number from the KGB and you ordered him let go. Keyes claims he had the Russian dead on target.''

"The shot wasn't clear. People were everywhere. If I had let that kid start blasting, innocent bystanders would have been dropping everywhere.''

"Along with Vaslov perhaps?''

"Possibly, but the risk was not acceptable," Dogan explained, trying to justify his actions, though the truth was much simpler: Vaslov had beaten him and deserved to walk. "Shootouts are a thing of the past, Commander, you've told me that yourself on more than one occasion.''

The Commander glanced up briefly. "That's not the point and please don't talk to me about procedure. You didn't just stop Keyes from firing into a crowd, you shattered his wrist and made holding a telephone painful for him for the rest of his life. He's not happy and neither is the department.''

"You're not expecting me to deny this, I hope."

"There would be no sense in that. You violated a major rule of the field this morning: You let anger get the better of you."

"Not anger, Commander, frustration. You gave me a bunch of wet-eared kids who couldn't follow orders on a simple pickup operation.''

"The operation was yours, Grendel. So is the responsibility for bungling it.''

"And I'm not trying to pass that off. Except the operation wasn't bungled. It was clean and well conceived.''

"The results seem to indicate otherwise. . . ."

"Because Vaslov and the Russians beat us. They played a better game. They're superior to us because their agents know nothing about ego gratifications. They have a job to do and it gets done. Simple."

"So they planted a fake defector and you took the bait."

"Yes, Vaslov planted a fake defector but he also planted a half-dozen other diversions to throw us off the track. A stalled car, a pair of baby carriages, a blind man—all his work."

The Commander flipped the page of his newspaper. "Tell me about the setup."

"The defector reached us through his contact with the place and the time. He was impatient. He'd been holed up in Paris for almost two weeks waiting for his chance."

"Then I must assume Vaslov knew something of the plan himself."

"Probably only shadows but they proved enough. The defector's contact must've had a big mouth. So Vaslov planted a fake defector to draw us off. When we lunged at the bait, his men were the only ones around to pick up the real defector. We got beat, just like I said before."

A cool night breeze ruffled the Commander's paper. His eyes grasped Dogan's for the first time. "I don't see it as that simple. Perhaps, Grendel, you are becoming too predictable."

"Given the limitations of what I have to work with, I do the best I can. The men who beat us today were strictly professional." A pause. "The way we used to be."

"I see," the Commander noted, flipping to the back section.

Dogan grasped him firmly at the elbow. The older man flinched but didn't bother trying to pull away. Annoyance swam in his eyes.

"No, I don't think you do, sir," Dogan charged. "Let me try to explain. Men like Keyes can't read between the lines, can't estimate their opponent's next move based on simple instinct. Everything has to be cut and dried for them. In the field, though, it's anything but that, which means losing to the Russians is something we better get used to."

"An interesting depiction of your failure this morning."

"Call it whatever you want."

"Now I would kindly ask you to remove your hand from my arm." Dogan complied. The Commander straightened his sleeve. "And as long as you're explaining things, take as your next subject, Grendel, the reason why you chose to take out a fellow Division operative instead of Vaslov."

"We lost. There was no need to press the matter further. Besides, at least I know what I can expect from Vaslov. That's not always true anymore about those on my own side."

The Commander lowered his newspaper, actually *lowered* it. "That's one hell of an accusation."

"Take it for what it's worth. Just make sure you understand something else along with it. If I had let Keyes take Vaslov out today, the Russians would have replaced him and I'd have to deal with a new, unfamiliar network. Considering the bureaucratic overtones, Division would have been set back by such an action more than the KGB. I know Vaslov. Finding out the means and methods of some KGB replacement is a chore I can do without."

"Knowing Vaslov didn't help you this morning." The Commander sat motionless on the other side of the table, making no effort to still his newspaper in the breeze. "This morning's fiasco has escalated far beyond an embarrassment. It's won the qualification of incident. Congratulations, Grendel."

Dogan said nothing.

"I'd like to say I'm bringing you up before the review board," the Commander went on, cold eyes digging into Dogan and startling him with their stare. "But of course, we have no such board or any precise procedures to follow. You have accused the Company and the Division of losing their professionalism. Perhaps you have lost yours. Times have changed. The days of the lone wolf are over. You're not a team player, Grendel. You just don't fit anymore." The Commander hesitated. "Pick a country, something warm and tropical perhaps."

"Carrying a gold watch in your hip pocket, Commander?"

"You know the procedure, Grendel. A most generous one, I might add."

Dogan felt the rage building within him. The Commander's

right hand disappeared under the table, for a gun perhaps. No matter. Limits were everything and Dogan knew he could tear the man's throat out before he could pull the trigger. The thought comforted him, and the knowledge was in his eyes. The Commander's hand came back up and started to dog-ear the pages of his newspaper.

"Uh-uh," Dogan said simply. "I'm not ready for the country yet."

"I wasn't offering you a choice."

"But you've left yourself one, haven't you, Commander? How many men are watching us now? What weapons are they holding on me? They're waiting for a signal from you, of course, which you'll give if I don't agree to your reassignment and go quietly." Dogan leaned back. "Give the signal, Commander. You know there's no way they can kill me before I kill you. Think of it, we'll pass into eternity together, but in different directions, I suspect."

The Commander swallowed hard.

"Of course, you could let me go and have them deal with me later. Who knows, they might even succeed. I'm not too worried, though. They're all like Keyes and I'd slice a limb off you for each one of them you forced me to kill. There's not a dozen of them who could get me before I got you and you know it."

The Commander removed his rimless glasses and wiped the lenses. "I withdraw my offer. You're out, Grendel, plain and simple."

"Without a going-away party? My, what's the world coming to?"

The Commander was shaking his head. "You could have had it easy, Grendel. All you had to do was accept the desk we offered you. A man should know when his run is over."

Dogan stood up. "I'll know," he said simply and walked away, leaving a huge chunk of his life behind. He had known he'd face this day sometime; it had been inevitable. But he came away wondering if there was something he might have said to make the Commander change his mind. The field was everything to him. Without it there'd be no purpose. Free-lancing was always possible and quite lucrative. But such mercenary work denied your identity, and Dogan had been around too long to lose his now.

He knew the Commander would have him followed and took immediate steps to lose his tails. He never saw them but knew they were there all the same. He probably had trained many of them, but a good teacher never passes on all of his lessons. Losing them proved effortless. Dogan toyed with the notion of leaving one bound and gagged in the Commander's bed that evening.

He wandered about until he reached the Place de la Concorde, stopping at the spot where Louis XVI was publicly guillotined. The large fountain shot majestic bursts into the air. The water was colored by the night lights of Paris, a kaleidoscope of vitality, awesome in its beauty. But Dogan didn't care much about beauty tonight. His life was the Division and now the Division had been taken from him. And there was no one above the Commander he could plead his case to, even if he had a case to plead. The old man was the only one he was answerable to. To other Company men, he was simply a name on a restricted file card. Dogan glanced up at the naked marble figures basking in the fountain's spill and wondered how Louis felt the moment the cold steel spit his head into a wicker basket. He thought he might know. He sat down on a bench and focused on the symmetrical perfection of the layered brick surface of the Place de la Concorde. An anachronism of construction, just as he was.

"Mind if I join you, comrade?"

Dogan looked up to find Vaslov standing before him. Somehow he had been expecting this.

"Be my guest."

Vaslov sat down next to him on the bench. He was wearing an elegantly tailored French suit that emphasized his finely chiseled frame. His hair was neatly styled, also western, and his eyes were bright and alive.

"How'd you find me?" Dogan wondered.

"I followed you, of course. Marvelous job of losing your tails, by the way."

"I didn't lose you."

The Russian shrugged.

"You witnessed my meeting with the Commander, no doubt," Dogan assumed.

Vaslov nodded. "And it wasn't hard to judge from your physical responses—body language, I believe you Americans call it—that things were not going well. I'm not surprised. You should have let that young man kill me this morning."

"Not in my book."

"Any regrets?"

"Only that I didn't crush the prick's vocal chords."

Vaslov leaned back and laughed easily. "Look now at how we find ourselves, two cold warriors sharing the fine French landscape. If only I had brought wine . . ."

"We could toast the success of your mission today. You had a clean escape coming to you."

"You used a similar ruse against me in Prague with similar success. When was that, seventy-seven, seventy-eight maybe?"

"Seventy-nine. Winter."

"You remember?"

"I remember the cold." A pause. "You spared my life then just as I spared yours today."

"And with good reason, comrade. When the nobility is gone from our profession, we become nothing more than simple assassins instead of knights jousting for our country's pride."

"How romantic. . . ."

"Indulge me, comrade. I look forward to the rivalry between us because it forces me to challenge myself, to reach for perfection. I could have had that defector collected and returned to Moscow yesterday or even the day before, but that would have prevented another match in our ongoing tournament."

"You took quite a risk."

"But well worth it. In the end, what do we have besides each other? Today I won. Tomorrow may be different."

"For sure. Tomorrow you'll be the only one playing."

Vaslov sighed. "They pulled you, comrade?"

"I forced the issue."

"This morning?"

"And tonight."

"They are fools, comrade, little different from my superiors in the Kremlin. Only sometimes I think those in the Kremlin know they are fools so they leave me to run things as I wish.''

"You're lucky, my friend." Strangely, addressing Vaslov as "friend" didn't come at all hard for Dogan. This was the longest conversation they'd ever had, but through the years they'd shared things far more important than words.

"Of course, I knew the sanction you would face, comrade," Vaslov said in a more somber tone. "I knew you would have plenty of time on your hands, and I have a project that might command some of it."

"Working for you?"

"Not exactly. What if we had a common enemy, an enemy that could devastate all the ideals we fight for along with our countries?"

The breeze toyed with Dogan's thick brown hair. "You're on to something?"

"Just talk now, random pieces of information that together make no sense. Something is in the air, that's all I know. Our countries are strong, but vulnerable to another who knew what to look for."

"Another country?"

"I don't think so." Vaslov hesitated, crossed his legs. "Have you ever heard of the Committee?"

"Just rumors. No one's sure they really exist."

"Which is their greatest strength. No one believes in them, so no one bothers to stand in their way."

"We thought their existence was tied to disinformation on your part."

"Just as we thought about you, comrade. With both of us chasing our own tails, they could operate unhindered right before our eyes. True enough?"

"I suppose."

"Then tell me what you *have* heard of the Committee."

"The best I've been able to gather is that it's an international organization dedicated to bringing control of the world to the private sector through economic manipulation."

Vaslov nodded. "Their *own* sector, actually. It all comes

down to vulnerability again. If they understood ours sufficiently, they could use it against us with greater results than any bomb.''

"That would certainly fit the pattern. The Committee, some say, has bankrolled terrorist and other subversive activities in the hope of destabilizing governments and weakening their economic structure. Then they move in and take over the marketplace. Eventually they control the entire country.''

"And the rest will tumble, one at a time. Like dominoes, comrade?''

"Doubtful. Assuming the Committee really exists, they would have found the process too long and unfulfilling. You can't take over the world a little piece at a time because the little pieces don't mean shit.''

"Ah, but what of the big pieces? What if the Committee had discovered a means to successfully cripple the countries it needs to the most?''

"The United States and the Soviet Union?''

"Precisely, comrade. The Committee is patient but you're right, dominoes do take a long time to tumble. The world is changing fast these days. Something might fall in the path of the dominoes and block them. So the Committee had to find a way to strike at our nations directly.''

"You just switched to the past tense.''

"Because I believe they have already found this way.''

"Why?''

"There is talk. People have been disappearing conveniently. Funds, massive funds, have been mobilized. Money is changing hands in amounts too vast to contemplate. And all of this I think has to do with a simultaneous strike against both our nations.''

The breeze caught part of the fountain's spray and whipped it out at the two men. Dogan didn't bother to wipe his brow.

"Nuclear?'' he posed.

"To provoke a war between us, Grendel? No, a war-ravaged world would not be what the business-minded people who make up the Committee would want. Their ideals have been shaped in the marketplace. They seek to control the world by controlling its resources. That is where the weapon will come from.''

"Which doesn't tell us a whole hell of a lot.''

Vaslov thought briefly, choosing his words carefully now. "Whatever strike they are about to initiate will be against something we hold in common, something that can damage us both equally. The two superpowers are what truly stand in their way. If they are to obtain global domination, our power must be neutralized. We are not vulnerable militarily, either of us. The way to strike is economically, where our shortsighted leaders have opened the door to any number of strategies."

Dogan found the inside of his mouth was dry. "Hell of a scenario. But everything's too vague."

"That is how the Committee works, comrade. This time, though, they may have left one of their stones turned up. It will lead us to them. Our weapon will be exposure. Once in the open, they cannot function."

"Where is this stone?"

"Colombia. A town called San Sebastian."

PART THREE:

CADGWITH COVE,
FRIDAY MORNING

PART THREE

CAIRO WITHOUT COVER:
FRIDAY MORNING

CHAPTER 10

THE TRIP TO CADGWITH COVE AND BRUGGAR HOUSE, THE RESIDENCE of Colin Burgess, took Locke a good part of the night and left him exhausted. After leaving the Dorchester, he had found a cab, which took him to Paddington Station. There he boarded a train traveling south for the English countryside. The journey was long to begin with and the train's many stops—at Reading, Somerset, Taunton, Exeter, and Newton Abbot—had Locke's nerves even more frazzled. Rest was impossible, especially during the rocky segment between Exeter and Newton Abbot as the train passed into the wilds of Dartmoor over ancient track beds. Finally it arrived in Plymouth, where Chris boarded another train for Cornwall, disembarking at the station in Truro. A single cab waiting outside then took him the final hour-long stretch through Helston onto the Lizard and ultimately into the remote village of Cadgwith Cove.

It was two A.M. when the taxi rumbled up the pebble drive of a stately, ancient manor known as Bruggar House. Locke could hear the hard sea breaking on the rocks below and could smell the thick, salt air as he climbed out of the cab and paid his fare. The man drove away and a chorus of barks started up immediately inside the house.

Locke headed toward the front door, feeling as if he were stepping back in time. Bruggar House had been erected several centuries before. It was a massive, granite-stone structure rising majestically over the cliffs with a single center tower poking up at the night sky.

Locke could only hope that the worst part of his journey was not yet to come. What if Burgess, a perfect stranger, turned him away? Worse, what if Burgess wasn't at home?

Locke reached the front door. He rapped three times with the heavy brass knocker. Angry snarls and barks followed, then the sound of the dogs rushing at the door. He had lifted the knocker to rap it again when he heard the latch being undone inside. The door creaked open.

"Yes?" came a crusty, tired voice. Locke could see a hulking body just beyond the crack.

As it had turned out, the rest had been easy. All Chris had to do was mention Brian Charney's name and the door was opened wide. Flanked by growling dogs at every angle, he started his story still standing in the foyer. He didn't say much but it was enough to convince Burgess of his desperation brought on by the brutal murder of their mutual friend. The burly Englishman refused to hear more until morning. Locke was exhausted to the point of being incoherent. A good night's sleep was in order. In the morning, things would seem more clear.

Locke fell asleep as soon as his head struck the pillow, a deep rest that ended with the barking of Burgess's dogs as the mail arrived late the next morning. Chris rose, climbed back into his only clothes, and descended the staircase. The massive house was filled with the smell of strong coffee.

"I thought I heard you milling about," Burgess greeted. "Trust you slept well."

"Incredibly, yes."

"Not so incredible, lad. The body knows best what it needs. Take it from an old soldier."

"I owe you a great debt."

The Englishman's face grew bitter. "And I owed Brian Charney an even greater one."

Locke figured Burgess to be in his midsixties. He had a thick crop of white hair and a face creased by experience as well as time. There were several scars too, the most prominent of which ran down his forehead through his left eyebrow. His fingers stroked it constantly. They were huge fingers, coated with a crust of farm dirt, yet they possessed a gentleness Locke could feel in Burgess's ice-blue eyes as well. They were the eyes of a man who had lost his youth but none of its ideals. His frame had sagged, though only slightly. He must have once been a mountain of a man, Locke reckoned; was still a mountain, but one that had weathered many storms. His great bulk covered the chair he sat in. He rose slightly to pour the American a steaming cup of coffee, then settled back down. His eyes were hard yet sad as well.

"Whoever got Brian will hear from me, laddy. I can promise you that much."

"He was my friend too."

"Then we'll hunt the bastards down together, we will!"

"Right now all I want to do is get home."

"You mentioned Liechtenstein last night."

Locke sipped his coffee. It was astonishingly refreshing.

"Liechtenstein is where I'm headed first," he said. "Brian thought you could help me get there."

"If the country's still on the map, lad, I'll get you in. Bring you right to the damn border and kill anyone who gets in our way, I will. But I'd like to know what you're on to, the thing that Brian died for."

"I wish I could tell you. I'm just not sure."

"You know more than you think, lad. It's just a matter of putting things together in the proper order. Let's talk things out, shall we? Tell me what got you into this."

Locke told him everything: from accepting Charney's offer, to the encounter with the bogus Customs agent, to his meeting with Alvaradejo, which had ended in death and its equally bloody aftermath in the streets; from his desperate rendezvous in the park with Charney, to his friend's murder and as many of his final words as Locke could recall.

"Does it make sense?" Chris wondered at the end, confused and frustrated once again.

"Enough, lad, and the sense it makes is not pleasant at all."

Locke hesitated, feeling the need to purge himself further. "He would have sacrificed me. That was his plan from the beginning."

95

"It wasn't his plan, just a risk he undertook. He had faith in you, laddy. You went through the training."

"Twenty years ago and I never finished."

"But what you knew came back to you yesterday, didn't it? Pros like Bri and myself, laddy, pride ourselves on being able to size up a man's capabilities. The fact that you made it here shows Brian was a pretty good judge of yours. He was just doing his job, lad, and it doesn't make him any less of a friend. I worked with Bri all through the seventies. Never met a man who loved his country more." Burgess swabbed at his watery eyes with a shirt sleeve. He cleared his throat. "Now let's try to put together the events of yesterday from the beginning. The man from Customs issued you a gun, you say."

"On orders from Brian, he claimed. Except Brian knew nothing about it."

"And this Colombian was your first contact and your friend Lubeck's first contact."

Locke nodded. "Alvaradejo was the first step of the trail."

"And Lubeck died in Colombia."

Another nod. "A town called San Sebastian." *The souls of San Sebastian will be avenged.* . . . "Lube witnessed the massacre."

Burgess shook his head, squeezing his lips together. "We are dealing with true animals here, lad, men who have nothing to lose and obviously much to gain."

Locke flinched. How often had he heard the word "animal" shouted at him yesterday?

"The people of San Sebastian were witnesses to something," Burgess went on, "and had to die to keep it secret. Lubeck was killed almost surely for the same reason." His eyes flashed. "Did the diplomat initiate contact with Lubeck?"

"I'm not sure."

"Let's assume he did then, lad. Obviously he knew something, had heard something, and alerted Lubeck to whatever it was that took him to Liechtenstein. The animals knew he had followed a trail to San Sebastian but they didn't know what it was. Then you ventured into the scene, lad, assigned to pick up that very trail."

"Wait a minute," Locke interrupted. "How could they have known about me? My assignment was deep cover."

"Such assignments must go through channels, lad, and all channels have leaks. These animals seem capable of anything." Burgess leaned forward, resting his huge forearms on the table. "You venture in and the animals see a marvelous opportunity to fill in the trail Lubeck uncovered by using you as the shovel. Somehow they leak word to the Colombian that the men who butchered this town and killed Lubeck are on to him and are sending a killer."

Locke nodded. "Me."

"Then these animals of ours arranged for you to be given a gun, knowing you would be forced to use it in self-defense."

"And Alvaradejo obviously thought I was part of something bigger because he addressed me in the plural. But what if I had failed?"

"Then you'd be dead and the animals would have dealt with the Colombian themselves and devised another way to come up with the rest of Lubeck's trail."

Locke thought briefly. "But Alvaradejo must have been part of something bigger too. The men who chased me spoke Spanish as well, shouted the same phrases and accusations he did."

Burgess fingered his scar. "Then they must be organized. The bit with the taxi driver was not an easy stunt to pull off."

"So we're dealing with two forces here."

"At least, lad, but the animals are our prime concern. These others—Alvaradejo's people—are dangerous yet not nearly as professional; professionals do not shout in the streets."

"And what about Brian?" Locke asked with a lump in his throat.

The Englishman's stare went rigid. "Between your desperate phone call and meeting in the park, he went searching for answers. Apparently the answers found him first."

They're everywhere, everything. . . .

"He said they were everywhere, that the world would be theirs unless they were stopped," Locke muttered. "Christ, they could have killed me at any time."

"But instead they chose to use you, lad. Your friend Lubeck

uncovered a trail that died with him. But it can still do the animals great harm if someone else uncovers it. Alvaradejo was the first step, Liechtenstein the second. By following you, they cover their tracks.''

"Then who was waiting for me in the hotel?"

"More of the Colombian's friends probably. It was the animals that killed Charney, though, because he got too close to them.''

Locke drained a hefty gulp of his coffee. The caffeine was recharging him, but as Burgess dug deeper into his story, his fear deepened along with his sense of helplessness.

"So by going to Liechtenstein," he concluded, "I'll be aiding the cause of those Brian said had to be destroyed."

Burgess shook his head. "Before, maybe." He tapped his still-massive chest with an index finger. "But now you have me. I'll show you what you need to know to stay one step ahead. They will keep you alive so long as you fill a need. We must use that to our advantage, lad. Also they have no idea now where you're headed next. Time is on our side and we must take advantage of that too." Burgess leaned back and crossed his arms. "You said something about Brian drawing a connection between the events."

"It wasn't much." Locke sighed. "He felt the key was food."

"Food?"

"Lubeck was investigating the World Hunger Conference when Alvaradejo met with him. And Lube died in Colombia because he saw something in the fields. His last words dealt with it."

"Words he never had a chance to finish," Burgess completed. "Now tell me what Brian said about Liechtenstein."

"Only that I was supposed to go there and find a man named Felderberg."

"Felderberg!" the Englishman bellowed in obvious surprise.

"You know him?"

"Everyone in our line of work does, knows *of* him anyway. Let me tell you something, lad, don't believe everything you hear about Switzerland being the financial capital of the world. People might still keep their money in Swiss numbered accounts because they represent the ultimate in privacy. But when they want to move that money around, they go to Liechtenstein. Deals are arranged there, funds large enough to boggle the mind are transferred there. And all of it carried out with the utmost discretion, kept secret from governments . . . and tax services. Claus Felderberg is the leading middleman of them all, a power broker who controls the flow of money when certain parties don't want anyone to know its true origin. He consolidates funds or spreads them out. Discretion is maintained above everything else.''

"And Lubeck saw him," Locke said, almost in a whisper. "The next link in the chain . . .''

"Leading us where, I wonder, lad. What does an international power broker have to do with the massacre of a Colombian town?''

"Only Lubeck could tell us that.''

"Then we'll have to find out for ourselves, won't we? You came to the right place. I owe Brian Charney this much and more.''

Burgess finally asked Chris if he was hungry and proceeded to put together a giant breakfast of steak and eggs, toast, sausages, and more coffee. As they ate, the burly Englishman told his own story and Locke found himself fascinated.

He had enlisted at the very start of World War II at the age of eighteen, ending up at the German front where he was three times decorated for bravery. Twice he was wounded and twice he returned to battle, refusing to be sent home. He hated the Germans with everything he knew, wanted to kill as many of them as the army would give him bullets for. Though exact counts were never kept, it was more than possible that Colin Burgess killed more Nazis than any other single infantryman in all of England's vast regiments.

It was the third wound that got him sent home. Burgess couldn't argue; he was in no position to. A German grenade had torn a measure of his stomach away and sunk so deeply into his leg that some of the fragments were impossible to reach.

"Thought I'd be shitting into a bag for the rest of my life, lad," Burgess recalled.

His recovery was miraculous but his days at the front were

finished. The shrapnel had left him with a slight limp and most sudden motions were impossible. So the British command found something else for him, a task far more important and even more satisfying than his work at the front. Burgess was assigned to the OSS detail responsible for ferreting out German spies in England. Burgess loved the role because it allowed him to deal with the men he hated most face to face, not from across a battlefield.

After the war he took his sharply honed skills to MI-6, the British counterpart of the soon-to-be-formed CIA. He spent thirty years in the field, meeting up with Brian Charney on one of his final assignments, which took them to East Berlin. Things did not go well. They walked into a trap and Burgess took two bullets in the side. Charney killed his assailants and then half-dragged, half-carried Burgess three miles to a rendezvous point at the Wall with KGB agents in hot pursuit. Charney and Burgess never lost contact with each other after that night, the older man becoming a father figure to the boy-wonder of the American intelligence community, teaching him all the tricks the classroom had neglected. When Burgess retired from the field, Charney still consulted with him often and referred to the big Brit as his true mentor.

"He was like family to me, lad," Burgess said bitterly. "I'll get the bastards who killed him all right."

Locke felt something sink in his stomach. "What about my family?" he said rapidly. "We've got to reach them and secure them from danger!"

Burgess thought for a moment. "Leave that to me, lad."

"But Charney said there was no one I—we—could trust."

"In his government, not mine. I'll call some people I know in the British intelligence community, free-lancers mostly. Everything will be unofficial, a few favors called in. Within eight hours I'll have your family under watch and guard. You'll have nothing to worry about from that end."

Locke shook his head slowly. He stared across the table as though in a daze. "I don't know if I'm up to this, Colin, I just don't know. . . ."

Burgess's expression became tight and sure. "I do, lad. You see, Brian Charney was not a man to leave things to chance. He contacted me this afternoon and said there was a possibility I'd be hearing from you and if so it would mean he was dead. He read me a portion of your file he knew would be of . . . interest to me. That portion convinced me that you had it in you to complete the mission for him, that you could uncover the implications of what's already happened and prevent what might be about to. You see, it's in your blood.''

And then Locke realized. ''You know about my mother.''

''More than that, lad,'' Burgess said with no emotion in his voice. ''It was I who captured her.''

CHAPTER 11

"WHAT WE GOT HERE, GENTLEMEN," CALVIN ROY SAID, "IS A MESS that stinks worse than a corn pasture 'round planting time."

The Undersecretary of State leaned over his desk and faced the two men seated before it: Louis Auschmann, deputy National Security Adviser, and Major Peter Kennally, director of the CIA.

"The autopsy on Charney just came in," Roy continued. "Some bastard shot him four times and we can't find hide nor hair of the man he put in the field."

"I should have been consulted about that," Kennally said dryly. "You don't send amateurs into the field without proper clearance and cover."

"Sprinkle your manure somewhere else, Major," Roy snapped. "Charney had full clearance to do whatever he damn well pleased whenever he damn well pleased. He answered only to this department and I approved of the human option deployment, as did the Secretary himself."

"And now your human option is the subject of a manhunt in London. Killed a Colombian diplomat and damn near killed a cabdriver."

"Yeah, well, I'm sure he had his reasons and I'm betting Charney's death confirms them."

"Unless he killed Charney as well. He could have been a foreign all the time. We've got to consider the possibility that this whole scenario was set up by him."

"The bullets that killed the Colombian don't match up with the ones that killed Charney," Auschmann pointed out.

"Standard procedure dictates he wouldn't have used the same gun twice," Kennally said.

"Screw your standard procedure up your asshole, Major!" Roy's face was furious. "I asked you here to help me figure out what in hell is going on, not to recite chapter and verse from the spy manual. You read the report I sent over summarizing what Charney thought he was on to?"

Kennally nodded. "And all I could draw from it was that he wasn't on to anything concrete."

"Not then anyway, but it looks plain to me that whatever it is seems to be hardening real fast and I'd like to find out what before someone else gets buried, maybe a whole mess of people. Charney was pro, Major. He worked for you long enough for you to know that."

"All the same, he placed a lot of credence in Lubeck's report."

"You heard the tape. You blame him?"

"You're saying there's a connection between Lubeck's death and Charney's. . . ."

Roy feigned shock. "Man, oh, man, move that boy to the head of the class."

"So where does Locke fit in?"

"Right now, Major Pete, nowhere we can find him."

"And San Sebastian?"

"Fire stopped last night. Just got the first report from the team that went in. Nothin' within twenty miles that'll tell us a damn thing. Lots of human bones, though, roasted clean through. Whole town's been burned to a crisp."

"Obviously someone went through great pains to cover their tracks," Auschmann concluded.

"When I want the obvious stated, Louie, I know I can always turn to you. Now how 'bout telling me something less obvious, like what in the hell happened to Charney?"

"What do you mean?"

"He didn't call nobody, that's what I mean. Instead of using the regular channels and making an emergency report, he gets himself killed trying to deliver it to our Professor Locke."

"There's no record of his having requested backup at any time yesterday," reported Auschmann. "Also no contact was made with our people at the embassy."

"Charney was never the solo type," noted Major Kennally.

"So what made him change?" Roy wondered. "Maybe he didn't cross the usual channels 'cause he was afraid they might collaspe under him."

"A leak?" from Kennally.

"Maybe." Roy paused. "Or maybe something worse than a leak."

"Like," Auschmann said, "discovering that certain forces in our government were part of what he had uncovered."

"Yup, Charney must have found that the shit on somebody's shoes led right back to our doorstep."

"He wouldn't have called in because the wrong person might have answered," added Auschmann, a dapper man in his early thirties with a Harvard degree and high aspirations. "Time was probably a factor. He had to go it alone."

"But he went to Locke," said Kennally.

"The only one he knew he could trust when they started closing in."

"When *who* started closing in?" Roy asked loudly. "What I got, fellas, is one dead agent and one college professor running around England wanted for murder."

"Has Scotland Yard been of any help?" asked Kennally.

"Dumb bastards couldn't find a pile of shit if they were standing knee-deep in it. They threw a net over the Dorchester and Locke slipped through it. Didn't even realize he had until they decided to plant a man in his room and found Charney's body and evidence our professor had just left. The trail was still hot but before they could follow it, somebody set off the damn fire alarm."

"Locke maybe," Auschmann said.

"In which case he's a lot more resourceful than we gave him credit for, unless you cover such things at the Academy, Major Pete."

"And now he's alone," said Kennally.

"Maybe not," said Roy. "Charney would have sent him to someone. Poor guy didn't drag himself all the way up there with four bullets in him just to die on the plush carpeting. No, he told Locke something, a whole lot more than we know now."

"The solution's obvious," said Kennally. "We find Locke." The major leaned back. "Only where do we start? Charney could have sent him anywhere."

"No," countered Auschmann, "not anywhere. Since Locke hasn't made contact with any government branch or foreign embassy yet, it's safe to assume Charney steered him away from us."

Roy nodded, interlacing his fingers. "Pull Charney's file, Louie, and go over it with a magnifying glass. Brian had lots of contacts in England. Find the one he would have sent Locke to."

"Why England?"

"Because Charney was a pro and he knew Locke wasn't. Distance would be a factor, travel something to be avoided at all costs."

"And since Locke didn't come in," said Kennally, "it's possible, even probable, that Charney used him to replace himself."

"Which would win him the benefit of Charney's killers . . . and Lubeck's," added Auschmann.

"Unless we find him first," said Roy, "and that, fellas, is just what we're gonna do."

The one-eyed man walked into the bar quietly, doing his best not to be noticed. It was difficult. He was large and powerfully built, with dark features, black hair, and a pair of eyes that were sharp as steel. People moved out of his way, stealing a brief extra glance, as he walked toward a table in the rear occupied at present by a single dark-haired woman chain-smoking over a glass half full of melted ice cubes.

"We lost him," the woman reported.

"So I gathered," said the one-eyed man. He sat down. "Something confuses me about your report. You say the American came *alone* to the park?"

"Yes."

"That isn't right. They should have sent others."

"There was only Alvaradejo, they thought. Hardly the need for others."

The one-eyed man pulled his chair in closer. "You also say the American rushed from the park. Would you describe his motions as panicked?"

"Desperate perhaps. That's what our man in the cab said." She added, "He's going to be all right."

"Professionals aren't desperate. The American should have discarded his gun in the bushes and walked calmly away. Instead he ran, as though surprised by the unexpected."

"Alvaradejo had a gun."

"He should have allowed for that possibility."

"The American's aim was perfect," the woman persisted, lighting a fresh cigarette.

"From an extremely close range. Doesn't mean a thing."

The woman hesitated. "He could have known about our ploy with the cab or guessed it. The panic might have been a facade meant to take our man's guard down. Apparently it succeeded."

The one-eyed man wasn't satisfied. "Yet he still waited until our cabdriver had gone for his gun before he acted."

"He could be a showman. Americans have always gone in for the quick draw, cowboy stuff. Besides, he did quite a job on our man when it was called for."

"But he was left alive. A professional would have killed him. A professional wouldn't run from the chaos creating more."

"Unless he was baiting us. And the trap worked. Arturo walked right into it. His fingers were still locked on his gun handle when they found him. Only a professional could have moved so fast."

The one-eyed man shrugged. He waved away the smoke. "That is another thing that doesn't fit. So thorough a killing with no witnesses . . ."

"As I said, the work of a professional," the woman reiterated, pressing her cigarette out so not to annoy the man.

"Undeniably," he said. His face twisted uncomfortably. "The American called for the meeting with Alvaradejo?"

"Just as we discovered he would. They sent him on Lubeck's trail to kill all those Lubeck contacted, those who knew too much."

"A college professor . . ."

"With six months of CIA training," the woman said. "They say he dropped out. It was the perfect cover for his present employers."

"Then why mention such training in his dossier at all?"

"It doesn't matter. Obviously Locke leads a double life. His teaching allows him ample time for his second vocation. And no one raises questions if a teacher travels frequently. The cover is perfect. And Georgetown University, a coincidence he chose a college in Washington, you think?"

The one-eyed man said nothing.

"Everything fits," the woman declared boldly. "This Locke is the worst kind of professional, one that is unpredictable, whose motions seem random when each step is actually cunningly thought out." The woman paused. "I saw Arturo's corpse. It was not an amateur's blade which tore his throat. The problem now is that we have exposed our existence to Locke. He will be expecting us and he is good. Our advantage is gone."

"Maybe not. Where did Alvaradejo send Lubeck?"

"Claus Felderberg in Liechtenstein."

"Then it's time to alter our strategy a bit. . . ."

The shock of Burgess's words hit Chris like a slap in the face. *This was the man responsible for his mother's death!*

"I caught up with her on a beach just before dawn," the big Brit continued. "There was a submarine surfacing a half mile off shore. They saw us and went back under. Your mother didn't put up a fight. She knew it was over." He sought out Locke's eyes and hesitated. "A professional understands such things."

"It's a small world, isn't it, Colin?" Chris asked with a calm that surprised him.

Burgess nodded. "And not a very pleasant one. You have the right to be angry with me, lad."

Chris looked at him. "I can't. I can't feel angry. Part of me wants to but it's not a big enough part. Brian's dead. You're all I've got. The past is finished.''

Even as he spoke, Chris knew it wasn't quite true. For while events had shrunk down to memories, the past remained tightly woven into the present. He was there now partly because of his mother, and he found some reassurance in thinking his course had been charted long before. But when Burgess said, "Experience makes orphans of us all," Chris knew that would have to be the truth for now.

The burly Englishman took his leave soon after but not without first obtaining Locke's measurements. New clothes were needed. Locke would be doing a lot of traveling. There were arrangements to be made, information to be obtained. Claus Felderberg was a powerful man. There was no way Locke could simply call and make an appointment as he had with Alvaradejo. A cover was needed, a means of entry. And speed was of the essence.

That last thought made Locke shudder. Lubeck would have done everything he was doing and more, yet they had gotten the Luber. Could Chris realistically expect anything different? He had been lucky in London. So much depended on his luck holding up.

Locke tried to calm down, even nap, but couldn't. Being faced with his mother's treachery again after pushing it successfully aside for years added to his strain. He also had to face his own vulnerability. He was no longer just a piece in the game; he was a major player whose moves were his own, or would be once he reached Liechtenstein.

Before Burgess left, Chris begged to be allowed to contact his family.

"Not smart, lad," the Englishman told him firmly. "Lines are too easily tapped these days. You might give away your location . . . and your advantage."

"What about a safe line?"

"Around here they're impossible to set up."

"My family will be expecting a call," Locke persisted. "When I don't make it, they'll get panicky. Then they'll start with their own phone calls, maybe get themselves in trouble. I don't think I can live with that.''

"Then don't think about living, lad, think about dying, because that's what will happen to you for sure if you take unnecessary risks. Give it a few more days. After Liechtenstein maybe.''

Locke reluctantly agreed.

Four hours later Burgess's return was signaled by the happy barks of his dogs. Chris watched him approach from an upstairs window and met him at the front door.

"How did it go?''

The Englishman sighed and sat down in the first chair he saw. He looked tired and worn.

"I'm not used to this anymore, lad.'' He moaned. "Too old, I suppose.'' He leaned back and breathed deeply. "I got what we need to set you on your way but it wasn't easy. Too many people had to be involved, which means there are too many chances for the information to slip into the wrong hands.''

"But you got it.''

Burgess tapped his jacket pocket. "All in here, including a new passport for you. I've got a suitcase full of clothes and toilet articles in the car. I still know all the tricks, lad, and God knows we'll need them if we're going to win.'' He paused. "You leave for Liechtenstein tonight at nine. There was no time to arrange for private passage and most often it causes more attention than it's worth anyway. Your transportation will all be public, and a hectic schedule it is, lad. Changes will be frequent. People will be looking for you. We must keep them off balance.'' Burgess paused. "My sources tell me the entire country is being scoured for an American wanted for the murder of a Colombian diplomat.''

"What? It wasn't murder!''

"It can be made to look like anything certain powerful forces want. The animals do not want you to have your own government as an ally. In fact, you're also wanted for questioning with regard to the shooting of an American State Department liaison.''

"Brian . . .''

"Before much longer they may have his death pinned on you too.''

"But I—"

"It doesn't matter, lad. If our enemy is as strong as you've made me believe, they could have representatives in high places everywhere. Investigations are easily redirected. The point is that lots of people are looking for you and we can't send you on the straightest route to Liechtenstein. You'll be taking the boat train into France and will make your way to Paris by rail. From there you'll fly to Geneva, making two plane changes, and then travel to Liechtenstein by train. You arrive at approximately noon tomorrow."

Locke sat down in the chair opposite Burgess. "And once I'm there?"

Burgess pulled the fresh passport from his pocket and handed it to Locke. "You check into your hotel as American business-man Sam Babbit coming to the country to make some rather large financial transactions. You have chosen Mr.Felderberg for his discretion and willingness to operate on short notice. At a rather exorbitant fee, I might add."

"Which I'll need if the cover is to hold."

Burgess nodded. "A man like Sam Babbit must be seen passing big bills freely. He would not have come to Liechtenstein if he was one to spare expense. Have no fear in this area, though. I have the money for you, roughly seventy-five hundred pounds."

"From where?"

"Nothing more glamorous than my bank account, lad." Burgess stopped and his face tightened. "Brian was a good friend. You can't put a price tag on what I owe him. In any case, you will arrive in the community of Vaduz tomorrow in plenty of time to check into your hotel before meeting with Felderberg. He will be waiting at a restaurant near Castle Vaduz at four P.M. The mountain is steep and the only access to the restaurant is by tram. Once you reach it, the rest will take care of itself."

"What do I tell Felderberg?"

"I'm afraid that's up to you, lad. He will know soon enough that you are not who you claim to be; an international financier is usually quite adept at sizing up his clients. Be direct but don't reveal too much at once. Remember, it's conceivable Felderberg is working for the enemy."

Locke's mouth dropped. "I hadn't thought of that. . . ."

"Then don't bother worrying about it, lad. It's unlikely anyway because Lubeck never would have made it all the way to San Sebastian if Felderberg was one of them."

"He has bodyguards, of course."

"Oh, several of them. But the Hauser restaurant always holds a private room for him. He meets his clients inside alone—discretion, again. But his guards will be right outside. You will be alone with him only until he directs otherwise." Burgess's eyes bored deeply into Locke's. "I won't lie to you, lad. There's danger in this, quite a bit, in fact. But Felderberg's the key for us now, the key to what your friend Lubeck uncovered. I hate sending you out alone into the field but . . ." He shrugged. "Remember, though, I'll only be a phone call away."

"But you don't have a phone."

"The number I'm going to give you belongs to a young lady who can reach me in a matter of minutes. If an emergency arises, call her and say that you wish to speak with Uncle Colin."

"Then what?"

"One of two things. Either the girl will ask for your number and call back immediately to take your message, or she will say Uncle Colin has gone fishing, which means they got to me and you're on your own."

"And what about after the meeting with Felderberg?"

"You go wherever he sent your friend Lubeck, lad. The next link in the chain."

Dogan received the Commander's message late Friday night. At first he rejected the meeting because he owed the bastard nothing. But the night quickly turned sleepless and Dogan couldn't help wondering if his superior might have reconsidered his decision of Thursday. Not that Dogan would be ecstatic about returning to Division Six. The terms would be different now, his entire essence redefined; he knew that. So why bother?

Because, simply, he had nothing better to do. His life was his work; the field, the code he shared with men like Vaslov. It was in his blood and no transfusion could clear it.

He didn't set the alarm or request a wake-up call but arose at seven all the same and walked to the Champs-Élysées after a quick shower. The Commander was at his usual table. He didn't so much as look up from his newspaper as Dogan approached, and seemed to take no note of him until Dogan sat down across the table and blocked out the sun.

"Glad you made it," the Commander said.

"Just happened to be in the neighborhood."

A brief glance up, squinting his eyes against the sun. "Breakfast, Grendel? Some croissants perhaps?" He pointed to a basket covered with a checkerboard napkin. "Café au lait?"

"Sure."

The Commander poured him out a cup, then peered briefly across the table.

"There's been a change of heart" was all he said.

"Concerning?"

"Don't be coy, Grendel. It doesn't suit you." A pause. "Your reinstatement is being strongly considered."

"And what have I done in the past thirty-six hours to deserve such an honor?"

"It's nothing you've done. It's something you're about to do."

Dogan felt confused. He waited for the Commander to go on.

"Simply stated, we want a man killed, taken out with a minimum of fuss."

"Why not call on one of your new superstars, maybe another from Keyes's graduating class?"

The Commander hesitated, flipping nervously to another page of his newspaper. He didn't appear to be reading very carefully today.

"This assignment," he began finally, "requires a rather . . . tactful approach. Nothing can be done officially, nothing can exist that leads back to us."

"So since I'm no longer in the Division, I'm the perfect man for the job."

"As I said before, do this job for us and that condition becomes temporary."

"Any guarantees on that?"

"None that would make you any less suspicious. The Division needs you. You've really made your mark."

"Which could end up as my epitaph if this turns out to be a suicide mission against some crazy Third World leader. Kaddaffi maybe? Or Khomeni?"

The Commander shook his head and raised his eyes. They looked small behind his glasses. "Someone far more mundane, I'm afraid. A State Department intelligence man named Brian Charney was killed yesterday by an agent he was running who's turned rogue. The man is looking for buyers of certain information, *sensitive* information he possesses that can do us extreme harm if it falls into the wrong hands. Of course you can see the need for immediacy here, as well as tact."

"I'm sure you have a file on this target."

The Commander nodded and pulled a manila envelope from his lap, placing it on the table. "His name is Christopher Locke."

"Any idea who's running him now?"

"No, but it doesn't matter. We want him put away quick. What we do know is that he's headed for a meeting in Liechtenstein. You're to be on the next available plane."

"I haven't accepted the assignment yet." Then: "Why is he going to Liechtenstein? Who is this meeting with?"

"Claus Felderberg. I've written all the details down. No reason to go over them now." The Commander slid an envelope across the table.

"Felderberg," Dogan said, "the financier. A broker in dollars, not information. Seems strange this Locke would be heading for him."

The Commander nervously cleared his throat. "No questions, Grendel. Do you want the assignment or not?"

Dogan tore a croissant in half and stood up over his untouched coffee, picking up the envelope. "I'll send you a postcard from Liechtenstein."

PART FOUR:

LIECHTENSTEIN AND AUSTRIA, SATURDAY AFTERNOON

CHAPTER 12

LOCKE FOUND GETTING TO LIECHTENSTEIN A MORE DIFFICULT CHORE than he had expected. Burgess's itinerary got him to Geneva right on schedule but the train he boarded there, the Arlberg Express, made no stops in the small country. So Chris took it as far as the border station at St. Gallen, where he found a taxi for the fifteen minute trip to Vaduz, Liechtenstein's capital. He was surprised to find there were no checks at the border and also relieved. The less he had to expose himself, the better.

Still, Locke could not help but be taken in by the country's beauty. The thin road taken by the driver curved comfortably through the fertile flatlands of the Rhine Valley, which was just beginning to show its spring blossoms. He could see mountains in the north layered with snow and the temperature barely broke fifty. Locke longed for a warmer coat but the sights kept his mind off the cold.

The taxi deposited him in the storybook town of Vaduz in front of the Sonnenhof Hotel at two thirty. Locke paid the driver with some of the Swiss francs he had obtained in Geneva and included a generous tip. A doorman came over and grabbed his suitcase, beckoning him toward the hotel entrance. Locke hesitated a moment to look up beyond the hotel at the sprawling, majestic structure of Castle Vaduz. Directly below it he made out a dark shape nestled amidst the lush greenery—the Hauser restaurant, where his meeting with Felderberg would take place in just over an hour. The tram leading up to the restaurant from ground level would be hidden by the trees from this angle. There would be plenty of time to locate it later.

Finally he moved toward the entrance of the Sonnenhof. The same doorman who had taken his suitcase held the door for him, and Locke tipped him handsomely as well. He had to play his role to the fullest by passing sums of money and being noticed for it. Felderberg would be asking about him, perhaps even had people watching. Any reservations the financier entertained about Sam Babbit had to be laid to rest.

Locke stopped at the front desk, flinching just for an instant when he registered under his assumed name. There had been no time for Burgess to obtain a credit card for him, so he left a deposit in cash. The clerk was friendly but methodical, finally handing Chris his key and signaling for a bellboy. Five minutes later, after another exorbitant tip, he was inspecting his room to find it tastefully and elegantly appointed in light colors corresponding to the lavish grounds beyond. There was a terrace off his bedroom, and Locke collapsed there on a chair facing the sun. The wind chilled him but after the long, confined journey he needed the open air and space. It was almost three o'clock now; an hour to go until his meeting with Felderberg.

Chris suddenly found himself uncomfortable. First he passed it off to the long, sleepless trip, but there was more. He was in a foreign country registered under an assumed name about to meet with a man who was somehow part of a monstrous conspiracy. It might have been comic if someone else had put it to him that way, and he found himself more distressed than ever. Lubeck had seen Felderberg . . . and Lubeck had died.

Chris moved back inside his room, closed and bolted the sliding door behind him. He picked up the phone and had the hotel operator connect him with the number Burgess had provided. He had last checked in hours earlier in Geneva.

Uncle Colin has gone fishing. . . .

Please don't let it be those words, Locke prayed.

"Hello," came the friendly female voice with the sharp British accent.

"I want to speak with Uncle Colin."

"Your number, please."

Chris gave it to her.

"Stay put, sir. Be right back with you."

Locke hung up. The phone rang three minutes later.

"Yes?" the girl said.

"I have another message for your uncle."

"Go on."

"Tell him I've arrived at Vaduz and all seems to be well. I'll be meeting with Fel—"

"Please mention no names," the girl interrupted.

"The meeting will go on as scheduled." Locke hesitated. "Is there any way I can reach Colin directly?"

"I could have him call you at this number but it'll take a while."

Locke knew he'd have to leave for his meeting with Felderberg in a half hour at most. "No, it's all right. I'll call again after the meeting?" Then: "He's okay, isn't he?"

"Fine, sir, and taking all necessary precautions."

"Good."

Chris replaced the receiver as soon as the conversation ended. Something was nagging at him. What precautions had the girl been talking about? Did Burgess know someone was on to him? Locke couldn't bear the thought of being totally alone again. Burgess was his only hope now. If something happened to the big Brit . . .

Locke stretched out on the bed and forced his mind to other considerations. London had taught him that hotels could not always be regarded as safe refuges. Unexpected happenings on the mountain could conceivably make a return to the Sonnenhof impossible. So he needed a safe locale for some fresh clothes and other basic necessities, including his passport. He wasn't comfortable carrying it on his person, nor did he want to leave it in the hotel room. He reached deep down into his memory for an effective strategy. It had been covered in the training, repeated over and over again.

Use a public place, somewhere crowded, as a stash. A train or bus station, perhaps an airport, would be best. Use a locker.

There was a good-sized rail station on the outskirts of Vaduz. Certainly there would be lockers inside.

119

It took him ten minutes to change into a new suit and another five to pack a tote bag with two changes of clothes, a razor, and other toilet articles, along with his passport. In addition there were several implements Burgess had obtained in the event a disguise might be needed. Locke had the doorman get him a cab forty minutes before his appointment with Felderberg and headed for Vaduz Station. Then he told the driver to wait outside for him.

As it turned out, there were indeed lockers inside the station, a whole bank of them. But keys had to be obtained and deposits left at a central desk, which meant exposing himself to more attention. Locke weighed the situation only briefly before determining that obtaining the locker was worth the risk. The clerk was courteous, had thick glasses, and spoke very poor English. The cost of a locker was fifteen francs per day. Locke received one key. A master that was also required to open the lockers was always present at the desk, available once the customer had paid up his account as noted on the card Locke was issued. It all seemed far more complicated than a simple coin system, but he went along with it because he had to.

The driver dropped him at the tram at the base of Vaduz Mountain fifteen minutes before his meeting was scheduled to begin. The ski season had ended, so there was little activity about. A lift operator sold tickets to the few tourists who wished to take in Vaduz from an aerial angle. Another helped seat them in the small enclosed cars that looked like miniature diving bells. Chris straightened his tie, purchased a ticket, and was ushered into one of the green compartments. The door closed tight. The lift began to pull him up the mountain, taking him farther and farther from the ground. The cable squeaked and trembled every time a connecting tower station was passed. Halfway up the tram, Locke could clearly make out the Hauser restaurant, a small but stately building that seemed to be a small imitation of the castle standing above. It might once have been a carriage house by the look of it, or a guest lodging for visitors of Liechtenstein's royalty in days of old. It was simply a restaurant, though, constructed in the sixties to capitalize on the tourist trade.

The restaurant was located up a path from the tram's unloading platform, and Locke had started to walk toward it when a man appeared in front of him flanked by two others.

"Mr. Babbit?"

"Er, yes."

The man's eyes were ice blue. He had wavy blond hair and a neck as wide as his head. "We have been sent to escort you up to your visit with Mr. Felderberg. You have come alone?" the man asked, eyes darting back toward the tram.

"That was the arrangement."

"We are merely confirming. Precautions, you understand."

"I understand."

There was a suppressed tension about the man, Locke noted, something coiled in him ready to spring at an instant's notice. He didn't smile; there was no expression whatsoever on his face. He seemed somehow familiar to Locke and it wasn't until they reached the entrance to the restaurant that he realized why. He had known a hundred others like him twenty years ago at the Academy. The man had the capacity to kill without hesitation. Felderberg was taking no chances.

The blond man led Locke into the Hauser, which was dimly lit and almost deserted but impressive in its furnishings all the same. The designers had done their best to create the feel of a seventeenth-century inn with thick wood tables and several functional fireplaces. A large bar dominated the central floor, huge beer mugs with Liechtenstein's coat of arms displayed proudly on shelves suspended over old-fashioned wine bottles. Few of the tables were occupied and only three seats at the bar were taken, one by a thick-haired American-looking man whose eyes held Locke's briefly as he passed. When Locke glanced back, the man's attention had returned to his stein of beer.

"This way," the blond man said, and Locke followed him with the other two men bringing up the rear.

They moved down a corridor where two additional bodyguards waited in front of a wooden door with a brass knocker.

"We will search you here," the blond man told him.

Chris felt himself being eased gently against the wall. Then a pair of powerful hands slid over him checking for concealed weapons. Satisfied, the hands slipped off and Locke turned around to find the blond man lifting the knocker. He opened the door without waiting for a reply and signaled Locke to enter.

"Thank you, Peale," came a voice from the room's rear, and Chris found himself looking at Claus Felderberg. "Leave us."

Peale headed back out the door. Felderberg stood up and started out from behind a table. Locke met him halfway across the floor.

"Nice to meet you, Mr. Babbit."

Locke took Felderberg's extended hand. The grip was cold and clammy. Felderberg was overweight, with bulging jowls and a triple chin. His blue suit was perfectly tailored and what remained of his thinning brown hair was pulled from one side to the other to make it seem he had more. His mustache was his most outstanding facial feature, mostly because it was embroidered with strands of red. Felderberg breathed hard and noisily through his nose.

"Thank you for seeing me," Locke said.

"My pleasure. Come, please sit down."

"I mean, I know how busy you are. I appreciate your time."

Almost on cue, Felderberg pulled a gold watch from a chain in his vest pocket and checked it as he returned to his seat.

"And little time I have, Mr. Babbit. Economies are booming everywhere. Many people have money they wish resettled."

Interesting choice of words, Locke thought as he waited for Felderberg to take his seat before he followed. The financier eased his bulk down and then pulled his chair under the table, which had been set for two. Locke sat down opposite him.

Felderberg settled his legs under the table. "As I said, Mr. Babbit, my time is short, so please excuse me for dispensing with formalities. My right foot is presently resting on a button which the slightest pressure would activate, sending a signal to my men in the corridor telling them I need them immediately. They will respond fast and rashly, Mr. Babbit. That is what they are paid for."

"I understand."

"No, I don't think you do. In my business precautions are everything, Mr. Babbit. Personal safety is maintained above all

122

else. I am going to ask you a question and if the response doesn't satisfy me, I will press my foot down and have my bodyguards deal with you." Locke made out the fear in Felderberg's voice. The financier's eyes bore into him. "Who are you?"

"Sam—"

"Not satisfactory. You are not Sam Babbit and your presence here has nothing to do with desiring excessive financial resettlements as I was asked to believe."

Locke felt numb. The ruse was up. No sense trying to continue it. "I congratulate you on your intuition," he managed.

"Investigation was more like it," Felderberg told him. "I had you watched at the hotel. Your tipping was impressive but no man in your alleged position would pay for a hotel room in cash. You also have no credit cards in your wallet—Peale signaled me to that fact when he entered the room. The men I deal with invariably carry a flock of them. I also understand that you made a stop at the train station on the way here."

Locke leaned back. "I'm impressed with your thoroughness."

"I have many enemies. Hired killers have shown up here before."

"But you don't consider me one," Locke said.

Felderberg hedged. "My foot is on the button," he said as a reminder. "But you're right, I don't believe you came here with violent intentions. Your cover was too thin, too shabby. Killers always come with impeccable credentials and qualifications. Peale always picks them out in an instant, and he's quite good at dealing with them."

"I'm not surprised."

"Every move you made was contrary to what a man who had come in quest of my life would make, starting with a rather bizarre arrangement for this meeting."

"Then why did you agree to see me?"

"Curiosity, I suppose. Since I knew you couldn't be one of my enemies' hired hands, I had to ask myself who you were and what bit of desperation led you to my door."

"Desperation's as good a way to describe it as any. . . ."

"Who are you?"

"My name is Christopher Locke and you're absolutely right:

123

I'm no professional killer. I'm no professional *anything*. I used to be a college professor. Now, to tell you the truth, I'm not sure what I am."

"But you haven't come here to quiz me on ways to finance your retirement."

"Right now my major concern is just making it to retirement. A friend of mine didn't. His name was Alvin Lubeck and he met with you last week, I believe."

Felderberg's heavy breathing stopped all at once. He wet his lips. Locke noticed they were trembling.

"I'm here to find out what you told him," he continued.

"On whose authority?"

"Or who's 'running me'? That's the popular spy phrasing, isn't it? Doesn't matter. The answer's no one. I'm here on my own authority. There was someone else until two days ago but he was killed too, and there are quite a few people out there who'd like nothing better than to make me number three on their list."

Felderberg's breathing became even heavier. His brow was sweating. "Who was this someone else?"

"A State Department intelligence man who was once my best friend. He put me in the field to follow Lubeck's trail because he figured I'd have the best chance of digging up what he discovered. Well, I dug part of it up all right and it buried him. He sent me to you and an English colleague of his made the arrangements to get me here."

"You must tell me everything. From the beginning."

Chris obliged as best he could, taking almost twenty minutes from beginning to end, almost laughing a few times at the incredibility of his story.

"Does any of this make sense to you?" he asked at the end.

"Some," Felderberg replied. "Enough. I have no knowledge of these Spanish-speaking killers of yours but the others pulling the strings behind the scenes, the ones your friend calls 'animals,' they are what Lubeck came to see me about."

"How did he get to you?"

"Through Peale, interestingly. He and Lubeck had worked together a few times before Peale came to work for me. He had

124

met with that Colombian diplomat who tried to kill you and the meeting had raised certain questions he felt I could answer.''

''And could you?''

''Somewhat.'' Felderberg leaned forward, interlaced his fingers tightly over the table. ''The diplomat was his country's delegate to the World Hunger Conference. When he learned that Lubeck was running a routine security check, he contacted him with the claim that someone powerful was plotting to sabotage the conference . . . and that same someone had by some shrewd manipulation become the virtual owner of Colombia.''

''An entire country?''

''Why are you so surprised, Mr. Locke? What else is a country besides land? And land can be bought in virtually any quantities for the right price. You think it's any different in your country? See where Arab money is going these days. Land is by far the greatest investment, the only one guaranteed never to depreciate or be affected adversely by inflation or recession.''

''But Alvaradejo must have put Lubeck on to something far greater than clever investments.''

''Most certainly. What I said about some powerful force becoming the virtual owner of Colombia is a bit misleading, Mr. Locke. The force is only interested in great chunks of arable land, suitable for farming if not ideal. This may amount to only twenty to twenty-five percent, but much of the rest is arid. Control that twenty-five percent and you control the country.''

''Why?''

''Because all development, all industry, and all wealth will be centered there.''

Locke nodded. ''And Alvaradejo sent Lubeck to you because you were the broker who sealed all the Colombian land deals for this . . . unknown group.''

''Yes,'' Feldererg admitted. ''But it wasn't just Colombia. Every arable nation in South America has been affected. The pattern is always the same. Exact instructions are provided as to how to resettle massive funds stretching into the billions, subdivide and spread them out to make it impossible for anyone to realize that one party was behind it all. It is the kind of work I have done for twenty years, Mr. Locke, but I've never seen anything that even approaches the scale of this before."

A soft knock came on the door.

"The waiter," Felderberg told Locke. Then, in the direction of the door: "Yes?"

It opened and Peale escorted a man in white shirt and black bow tie inside.

"Some wine before our meal, Mr. Locke?"

"Thank you."

Felderberg ordered a certain year and vintage, which the waiter jotted down on a pad before leaving. The door sealed shut again.

Locke felt a tremor in his stomach. The scope of what he was facing was finally taking shape.

"And the common denominator of all the countries and all the deals you completed was arable land," he concluded.

"Much of it was still undeveloped, you understand. South American nations are seldom very good at utilizing their resources. But the potential for farming the lands was there. Hundreds of soil analyses from hundreds of regions in perhaps a dozen countries crossed my desk—another common denominator."

"So your client is buying up farmland."

"Yes." Felderberg regarded him closely. "Obviously that interests you."

"Charney thought food was the key to this somehow. Lubeck too."

Felderberg nodded, leaning back. "And it all started with Alvaradejo. The Colombian contacted Lubeck and sent him to me."

"Because he feared someone was buying up his country?"

"Not exactly," Felderberg said. "Because he feared someone was going to destroy it."

CHAPTER 13

"DESTROY?" FELDERBERG'S RESPONSE HAD HIT LOCKE LIKE A SWIFT kick to the gut.

"Not physically, you understand. Alvaradejo's fears were rooted in the belief my client was turning his country's people into slaves, forcing them off land they believed they owned and leaving them destitute."

"I told you about San Sebastian," Locke said. "It fits."

"What fits?" Felderberg demanded. "I apologize for my impertinence, but in my position control of the situation is everything and in this case I've lost mine. You described a massacre to me, hundreds of people murdered for no reason."

"Unless they saw something, knew something."

"Which your friend Lubeck also stumbled upon. . . ."

"The fields," Chris said. "It all comes back to his rantings about something in the fields. The townspeople were witnesses to it and then Lubeck became one too."

"But what did he see? What did the townspeople know?"

"Your client was doing something on that land. Testing a new weapon, something like that."

"Which was then burned in a fire?"

"The fire covered the effects, that's all."

Felderberg shook his head. "No, the key is land and by connection food."

"An entire town wasn't massacred over food."

"Unless, Mr. Locke, something about that town made it a microcosm of a much greater picture."

127

"The rest of South America . . ."

"At least those portions my client had purchased."

Locke hesitated. "Did Lubeck come to any of these conclusions?"

"No. He had only shadows when I saw him. San Sebastian had not yet occurred and that, I'm certain, is somehow the key."

"Along with food." Locke ran his hands over his face. "But where does food tie in? Where does its importance lie for your client?"

Felderberg looked at him with mild shock. "Fifty percent of the world's population goes to bed hungry every night and many, many of these suffer from true famine. A country as powerful as the Soviet Union can bargain with the United States to keep a sufficient grain supply flowing. When oil was the crisis, engineers simply built cars that used up less. When food reaches such a crisis, similar steps cannot be taken with the stomachs of man."

"You said 'when,' not if."

"Because the crisis is inevitable. A few bad Soviet harvests back to back, wars in other agricultural-producing nations, a change in the political climate of your own country—all or any of these could lead to a crisis like none the world has ever seen, ultimately bringing on a global revolution of catastrophic consequences."

"I fail to see how—"

"Of course you fail to see!" Felderberg roared, jowls flushed with red. "Everyone fails to see, that is the problem. You think plutonium is the world's most valued resource, or gold, or diamonds, or even oil? Hardly. Food is by far the most crucial commodity, and yet it is subject more than any other to gross mismanagement and unconscionably bad planning. Your own country is ruining its own topsoil by rushing crops in and harvesting them too fast. It takes nature anywhere from a hundred to a thousand years to create one inch of top soil. But in America's frenzy to squeeze more food from the land, she is destroying on average an inch of topsoil every forty-five years. It is no wonder my client may well be planning for the crisis to come."

"By buying up unused farmland in order to become an agricultural power. . . ."

Felderberg frowned. "Except that would not explain the covert nature of their activities, nor the need for such haste. Growing crops in the abundance required for export take months, even years of effort and hard work. The motives of my client remain bathed in shadows. What are they after? What is worth the investment of literally billions of dollars?"

Neither man had an answer. Tension passed across the table between them.

"It might help if I knew who this client was," Locke ventured tentatively.

Felderberg chuckled, but there was no trace of amusement in the sound. "You think in a situation such as this they would reveal their true identity? No. Everything has been concluded through middlemen, mostly lawyers, and mailings. The arrangements have never failed to be in order and because my commission is always paid promptly, the need has not arisen for questions."

"But you must still pose them, Mr. Felderberg. You went through great pains this afternoon to have me checked out. I have to believe that is the rule for how you operate regularly."

"Within certain limits. The force behind the South American land deals and the massacre at San Sebastian has gone through great pains to keep its identity secret." He paused. "But there are clues, hints. They add up to little but still . . ."

"I'm listening."

"All my commissions were paid out through the Bank of Vienna."

"Interesting."

"But not terribly conclusive. The Bank of Vienna is known for its willingness and ability to handle exceptionally large financial arrangements."

"Going through Swiss institutions is more the norm, isn't it?"

"Not so much anymore. Political pressure from abroad has forced the famed Swiss banks to become less accessible and secretive. Accordingly, persons seeking large transactions have had to look elsewhere." Felderberg cleared his throat, fingered the stem of his wineglass. "The problem then became determining how long my client's account had been active at the Bank of Vienna. I had the account number and knew there had to be a means to gain the information I sought."

"But most banks take steps to make that impossible."

"To a point, yet they must at some stage bow to procedures made necessary by the computer. There had to be a code in the account number, something in sequence the computer could use as a key. It took much time and money, but careful analysis of this account number and comparison with others whose origin I knew led to the discovery that the account in question had been active for some seventeen years."

"Any chance of the account number leading back to its bearers?"

"Not through any means I'm aware of."

"So all we're left with is the probability that your client is based in Vienna, at least Austria, and has been for some time."

"And something else. One memorandum I was issued held the traces of a stamp on its bottom. Only the top half and quite light, as if someone had stamped another page with the memorandum protruding from beneath it. I had the stamp blown up and hired detectives in Zurich to trace it down. Their report led back to my own doorstep: the Sanii Corporation in Schaan, not more than eleven miles from where we sit now."

"What is Sanii?"

"High-tech experiments and development."

"Weapons?"

"I suppose."

"Then we're back to San Sebastian again, what the people saw down there before they were killed."

"That had nothing to do with a weapon, Mr. Locke. The key remains food. Sanii is part of an American conglomerate, but ownerships can be shielded just as funds can be."

"Then whoever's behind the corporation is behind the land deals, San Sebastian, everything. That's an awful lot of power."

"Indeed," Felderberg agreed. "And at first I thought it was being wielded by an emerging nation with a plot somehow related to food. But everything was done too covertly. Organiza-

130

tion and single-mindedness of the extent no country could possess. And then there was the account in the Bank of Vienna to consider. No, my client is someone from the private sector."

"But the plot still exists."

"And the best means for determining precisely what that plot is would be to uncover who's behind it." Felderberg hesitated. "I sent your friend Lubeck to the Dwarf."

"Who?"

"I broker large financial transactions, Mr. Locke. The Dwarf brokers large transactions of information. He maintains a chain of spies and informants across the world any intelligence service would be jealous of. His fees are often even higher than mine. Nothing of the magnitude we are discussing could escape his attention."

"You could have contacted him already yourself."

Felderberg smiled. "Such things aren't done. Our interests often conflict. We maintain respect for each other but we are hardly allies. No, it is you who must seek him out, just as Lubeck did. He resides in Florence. You can find him by—"

Felderberg was interrupted by a knock on the door. "Come in."

The waiter entered holding a bottle of wine. Peale followed him in and watched with arms crossed as the waiter rested the bottle on the table and pulled the cork out, handing it to Felderberg for approval.

"Excellent," said the financier after sniffing it.

He poured a small amount into a glass and Peale stepped over, taking the glass from his employer. He held the contents in his mouth for a few seconds, then swallowed, nodding deliberately after a brief pause.

Peale and the waiter took their leave.

Felderberg poured out two glasses of rich red wine.

"So Peale also serves as a wine taster," Locke quipped.

The humor was lost on the man across from him. "He was checking for poison."

"My God!"

"I demand loyalty from my men, Mr. Locke. There are risks involved but they are paid exceptionally well for taking them."

131

Felderberg sipped his wine. "Now, as I was saying about the Dwarf, you can reach him by—"

Felderberg's face puckered. His mouth dropped and he gasped for air like a man choking on a piece of food. Locke was already out of his chair moving toward the financier when a violent convulsion shook the fat man backward, then forward to the table. His wine spilled across the tablecloth. The cork went flying.

The cork! Locke realized. *There had to be some sort of poison he had inhaled from the cork!*

Locke lifted Felderberg's head up. His flesh was purple. His eyes bulged, veins and arteries rippling across his forehead. His whole body shook, spasmed, stilled. His breathing stopped. His eyes froze open.

Locke shook the financier in disbelief and was about to start administering CPR when one last spasm shook through the man's legs, activating the emergency button beneath his right foot. Chris was tilting Felderberg's head back for mouth to mouth when the door burst open and Peale rushed in with the other bodyguards behind him.

Chris hadn't even had time to start an explanation when the blond man grabbed him with the strongest hands Locke had ever felt and flung him against the wall. His head hit first. The light in the room flickered, faded. Seconds passed, how many Chris didn't know. Men were standing over him.

"He's dead," a voice said near Felderberg.

"Shit," Peale muttered, drawing closer to Locke.

Then Chris felt himself being hoisted to his feet. The room was still spinning.

"Who sent you?" Peale demanded. "Who hired you?"

Locke opened his mouth but no words emerged. Peale hit him hard in the stomach and pain exploded everywhere. His wind was gone and he felt bile struggling to rise. He wanted to vomit, and had started to double over when Peale lifted his head up and smashed him in the gut again.

"I want to know who you're working for!"

"Not . . . me." Locke gasped. His eyes searched frantically for the cork to offer as proof. "The cork, the wai—"

Peale hit him again, under the chin this time, and Chris slipped toward oblivion.

"We'll take him down to the office. We'll get the information out of him there no matter what it takes," Peale ranted as two men hoisted Locke up again.

He tried to stand on his feet but balance eluded him. "It wasn't me," he muttered, fighting for words and wondering if any of them could hear him. "Find the waiter. It was the waiter. . . ."

"What is he saying?" Peale asked.

"Can't make it out," the man on Locke's right replied.

"We'll have plenty of time to hear him once we get him out of here," said Peale. "An eternity. You two take him to the office. The rest of us will take care of the boss." The final words were spoken with true regret, spoken bitterly by a man not used to failure.

Someone was going to pay for this, Chris knew, and it was probably going to be him. Peale was the kind of man who took things personally.

Locke found his feet finally but didn't show it, just let himself be dragged along, hoping he might surprise the men holding him when he chose his moment of escape. Pressed close against them, he could feel their pistols beneath their jackets, reminding him that breaking free of his captors was not enough; he also had to disable them.

The two men continued to drag him along when they reached the main floor of the restaurant, oblivious to the stares of the Hauser's few customers. Chris met the eyes of the thick-haired man seated at the bar again and could have sworn there was more in them than just surprise and shock. Then he was outside, yanked down the path back toward the tram. He had to act fast. Once on the way down the mountain in the enclosed compartment, his slim advantage would be gone.

Think!

No, he reminded himself, thinking slows you down. The training, remember the training. . . .

React! Respond! Seize the moment and make it work for you!

They reached the wooden loading platform and started to

move for the next available car. A single man was at the controls.

Then Locke was in motion. He wasn't sure what triggered the action, probably the sight of the tram car swaying toward him. He shoved the man on his right forward into its path so that the steel frame struck him square in the back of the head and drove him into the wall. In the same instant Chris pushed hard against the man on his left, jamming his hand against the holster beneath his jacket to make drawing the gun impossible.

The man shook off his shock and went for a countermove. Locke felt a fist blast his stomach. Then the man went for his pistol, tying up both his hands and giving Chris time to recoup. He grabbed for the man's face and shoved him viciously backward until his head smashed against the platform's frame. The man tried futilely to pull away, but Locke slammed him backward again and blood smudged up on the dark wood. Chris slammed him one last time and let his body slide to the floor. Then he leaned over and yanked the man's pistol from its holster. Holding it tight, he swung quickly around.

The other man was still slumped against the far wall, his head partially supported and eyes closed. The tram controller had grabbed a red telephone and was pushing a series of buttons. Locke rushed across the floor and tore it from his hands, holding the revolver up to his head.

"Is this the only way you can communicate with the base of the mountain?"

The man, face smeared with grease, hesitated, then nodded.

"Is there any way you can stop the mechanism from up here?"

The man nodded. "Emergency switch. O-o-over there," he said, pointing to a steel fuse box on the wall over the first of the downed men.

Locke ripped the receiver right out of the phone box. Then he hurried to the emergency switch and found three wires running to it. Two yanks and they had come free. His eyes darted back to the path leading from the restaurant. Peale and the others could appear at any time. He had to get out of there.

After stealing one last glance at the engineer, Locke pulled himself into the next tram car as it swung by, then settled himself in and closed the door behind him. As the car began to descend the mountain, Chris watched out the rear window. The engineer rushed up the path toward the restaurant. Peale and his men had not yet appeared on the platform, which passed out of sight as the car dipped sharply and continued its descent.

Locke started to breathe easier, trying to collect his thoughts. He had escaped, but was no less vulnerable, for all of Felderberg's allies would be after him. His meeting with the financier had been fruitful, yet would he live to share his information with Burgess or anyone else?

Someone in Austria was behind everything and somehow they were connected with the Sanii Corporation in Schaan. Then there was the Dwarf, an information broker in Florence—the man who might be able to add the final pieces to this puzzle. Chris would have to find him somehow, but first there was Schaan to investigate as soon as he was off this mountain and out of Vaduz.

He was halfway down the mountain. Squinting his eyes, he thought he could make out figures on the platform above moving about, perhaps climbing into another car. No matter. At least fifteen yards separated one car from the next and Locke had a headstart of fifteen cars, maybe twenty. And with no way to stop the tram from there or call down to the mountain's base, he should be home free. He fingered the pistol wedged in his belt, happy he wouldn't have to use it.

He would call the contact number in Falmouth and, in order not to stay in one place for any extended period, he would tell the girl to have Burgess standing by for a second call in thirty minutes. That would be the professional way to handle matters. The burly Englishman would approve.

The tram car squeaked past a connecting station and ground to a halt.

Locke felt a flash of fear. He could only hope this was some standard procedure, and that it would be only a brief pause.

But the tram did not start up again. All the cars remained at a dead stop swaying in the wind. Locke glanced back up the mountain.

Three figures were descending on foot, following the grass

directly beneath the tram line. Obviously there had been another mechanism to stop the trams from the platform above or a means to contact workmen at the base platform. Chris was trapped! A sitting duck waiting for three armed men to come and finish him. He gazed beneath him; a fifty-foot drop at the very least. It was hopeless.

Then it came into his mind—his means of escape. It was a drill he had practiced dozens of times on a wire suspended between trees or over water at the Academy. He didn't have the proper equipment, but he had a . . . belt. Yes, that was it!

Chris unfastened his leather belt and yanked it from the loops. He stuck it between his teeth. Wasting no time, he opened the door to the stalled car and pushed himself forward, swinging the car toward the connecting station pole. Once, twice, three times . . . Finally he grabbed hold of the wood and pulled himself onto the pole from the car. His feet dangled in midair, then came to rest on a pair of spikes driven into the pole. He looked behind him.

The men had drawn to within a hundred yards. One stopped to raise and aim his gun. Chris wasn't sure which came next, the sharp crack or the explosion of wood chips not a foot from his head. There was no more time to waste.

He pulled the belt from his mouth and strung it across the heavy cable just above him, grabbing each end with a tight hand around the leather. He bent his knees to provide a cannonball effect, then pushed off.

The results were dizzying. Wind rushed past him as he slid down the cable, helped along by the grease that eliminated any friction from leather scraping against steel.

Another car came up fast and Chris knew there was no way he could steer past it. He slammed into it feet first and absorbed the rest of the shock on his thighs and stomach. His breath exploded out and his left hand started to let go but he recovered in time to grab the belt at the buckle, steadying himself on top of the car.

More bullets, a whole series of them, rang out, clanging against steel, whizzing past his ear.

Locke lowered himself down and placed the belt over the wire again, pushing off. He kept his speed lower this time and learned quickly how to manipulate body and belt to slow his pace before reaching each of the cars. He negotiated the next one easily and required barely any time to climb over it and continue on. The next one came even easier. That left eight more to go. Peale and his men were still racing down the slope beneath the tramway but Locke was holding his lead now.

With three cars left and a thirty-foot drop beneath him, Chris's hands became his greatest enemy. The flesh had turned raw and sweat made a sufficiently tight grip impossible. Each pass between cars became a maddening exercise in nerves as his fingers started to slip down the leather, flirting with the tips as the next car came near. He couldn't afford to slow down, couldn't afford the time to even wipe his hands dry. Peale's men were too close, their bullets even closer.

After the last car came a long forty-yard segment during which the line leveled off before reaching the base platform. He tried to gather up enough momentum to make it all the way but felt himself slowing still quite a way from his target. His hands could take no more. They finally slipped off the belt with fifteen yards left to go, when the drop was twenty feet. Chris tried to tuck into a roll as he landed but one of his legs twisted and he tumbled out of control down the hill toward the loading platform. The sky had clouded up, so there were few tourists at the base.

Locke's roll finally came to an end and he struggled to his feet, coming up lame on a right ankle full of knifing pain. He limped forward, tripped and fell, then rose with a glance to his rear to find his pursuers just fifty yards back and closing.

Chris dragged himself forward, doing the best he could to run with his bad leg like a ball and chain behind him. Bullets rang out. The pursuers were almost on top of him. He dove to the ground, turning as he tore the pistol from his pants. From his prone position, he fired a pair of shots.

Three figures sprawled for cover twenty yards away. He knew where they were now. That was something. The deserted platform was just ahead but too difficult to climb onto. Chris made it back to his feet, ducked low to use the wooden rise and steel supports as cover, and hustled around the outside of the tram complex.

Please God, let there be a cab!

Locke swung around the front corner of the building. Cement chips exploded just over his head.

A cabdriver, frustrated by the lack of fares, was inching away from the zone in front of the building.

"Stop!" Chris screamed, and then scampered into the street, fueled by the last of his adrenaline.

The taxi continued on for a few yards, then its brake lights flashed.

Locke made it to the door just as Peale and his men cleared the corner. He hurled himself inside before they could take aim.

The driver started away before speaking, accepting Locke as just another crazy tourist.

"Where to?" he asked in poor English.

Chris almost said "Out of this nightmare," but settled for the train station.

138

CHAPTER 14

LOCKE HAD THE DRIVER DROP HIM AT THE STATION BUT HE DIDN'T enter. Felderberg knew he'd left something there, which meant Peale did too. They'd be watching for him. He needed a plan. He saw a cab of a different make and color waiting at the head of the line and limped over to it.

"Drive around for a while," he instructed the man behind the wheel, flipping him ten Swiss francs.

The man grunted an acknowledgment.

Chris leaned back and hunched himself low so his head was out of sight from outside the cab. His ankle was throbbing and swelling too, but he could tell that the sprain was relatively minor.

Locke again tried to make sense of what he had learned from Felderberg. He was certain now the key was food. Somebody was buying huge masses of arable land in South America for a reason that Lubeck had stumbled upon in San Sebastian. The party behind it was based in Austria, and somehow the Sanii Corporation's high-tech plant in Schaan was connected.

They're everything, everywhere. . . .

Charney's words rang more prophetic than ever. They had killed Felderberg ingeniously with a poisoned cork, but not before he had the opportunity to pass on Lubeck's next stop: the Dwarf in Florence. They had set Locke up to kill Alvaradejo in London, allowed him to reach Felderberg only so they could kill him as well. Now they would follow him to Florence and the Dwarf.

Chris told the driver to stop at the next bar where there would be a phone. He needed to share his thoughts with Burgess. Five minutes later he found himself going through the complicated procedure of making a long-distance call halfway across Europe. Depositing the proper amount of change would have aroused too much attention, so he charged the call to his credit card number.

"How long will it take to get your uncle to the phone?" he demanded, after the girl answered.

"Thirty minutes. A little more maybe."

"Say thirty. It's an emergency. I'll call back then. And tell him to be careful, tell him nothing's safe."

Locke replaced the receiver. He left the pub with a package of ice purchased from the barman. He reclined as best he could in the taxi's backseat with his head pressed against the left door and his ice-covered ankle propped up against the right.

"Take me on a tour of Vaduz and the surrounding area," he told the driver. "Try not to pass down the same road twice."

"In Vaduz, that will not be easy."

Chris settled back to think. The ice was already numbing his ankle. The decrease in pain helped him clear his mind. The train station was his next logical stop to retrieve his passport and call Colin. Peale's men, though, would be everywhere by now, and a long phone conversation in an exposed booth was out of the question. He would just have to drive around for the next thirty minutes and call Burgess from another pub. Then he could make his way to the train station, which, at midevening, would probably be crowded.

Beyond the taxi, the sky had lost its brightness, and Locke noticed passing cars had their lights on. By the time he reached the Vaduz Station it would be dark, which would also work to his advantage. If not for the mandated retrieval of his passport, he could have taken the taxi all the way to Schaan. The strategy that earlier in the day seemed the safest route had ended up only complicating matters. Chris cursed himself for electing it.

They had moved into the countryside beyond Vaduz and Locke had the driver pull up to a mountain inn that was isolated enough to suit his purpose. Almost a half hour had passed since his call to the girl. He stepped inside and addressed himself to an elderly woman behind a counter.

"A room, sir?" she asked hopefully.

"How much do they cost?"

"One hundred twenty francs for three days."

Locke pulled fifty from his pocket. "This is only to let me use a room for the next few minutes. I need to make a phone call. I'll give you fifty more to dial the number direct and absorb the charges."

"You are officially our guest," the woman said, taking the bill Locke had slid across the counter and handing him a room key in its place. "Room eleven right down the corridor, one of the few with its own phone."

"Thank you."

"Please visit us anytime."

Locke chained the door to room eleven behind him. It took five minutes to find a free long-distance line and dial the girl's number.

"Is he there?" Locke asked without returning the girl's greeting.

"Yes, hold—"

Then Burgess's heavy voice took over. "Chris, what the hell's gone on there, lad? Why the need to roust me from my fortress?"

"Felderberg's dead."

"Christ . . . Not by your hand again, I trust."

"No, but his bodyguards think otherwise. . . ." Locke went on to relate that part of the story.

"With a bloody cork, you say? I'll be damned. Clever bastards, these are. We've got our work cut out for us, lad."

"And a place to start, Colin. The Sanii Corporation right here in Schaan."

"Never heard of it."

"High-tech firm. Lots of futuristic stuff probably. They're connected to this somehow. I'm sure there are answers to be found there."

"In which case getting in will be a chore, lad, and a risk you'd be wise not to undertake."

"I've come this far."

141

"Luck pressed is usually luck lost, lad. Remember your family."

"I haven't forgotten them, Colin. But Charney was right, this is big, bigger than either of us imagined. If I pull out now they won't get me tomorrow, but there's always the next day or the day after, and one of those times they *will* get me." Locke paused. "They got Felderberg and he was better protected than I could ever be. My only chance to survive is to expose them, and I'm the only one who can." Forming those thoughts for the first time into words sent a shiver through Locke he couldn't suppress. Finally it stopped on its own, leaving behind only a trembling in his fingers.

"Was Felderberg helpful in any way?"

"He confirmed that food is the key. Somebody's buying up huge quantities of farmland in South America."

"Colombia," Burgess said. "San Sebastian . . ."

"Exactly. It's only part of the story, but at least we've got something to follow now. Felderberg said Lubeck's next stop was in Florence. Someone known as the Dwarf. Ever heard of him?"

Burgess chuckled. "Heard of him? If MI-6 had him on the payroll, we'd never have lost a single defector. The man's an information warehouse. This might be right up his alley."

"Why do they call him the Dwarf?"

"Because that's what he is, lad! Little bastard doesn't stand more than four feet high and most of it's in his head. What a magnificent brain, the best in the world at what he does. But finding him won't be easy. I can't help you much there."

"I'll find a way and I'll be careful."

"Being careful won't be enough, lad, not against the forces you've described." Burgess took a deep breath. "I'm going to give you the address of this young lady who's been relaying messages between us. If anything happens to me and you need to come in, use her place as a safe house. Got something to write with?"

"No. Give me the address. I'll memorize it."

"Two-oh-five Longfield. Falmouth, Cornwall. Got it?"

"Easy enough. I'll call in tomorrow."

"Cheers, lad."

"Colin, wait. My family, I-I've got to speak—"

"I've got a friend in the States monitoring them," Burgess interrupted. "Calling your house now would be the worst step you could take. The bastards behind all this might believe you'd passed something on to them over the line. We can't have that. Your family's fine, lad. Trust me."

The phone clicked off.

Chris fought back the almost irresistible temptation to get his wife on the phone. He fought back too the urge to sprawl out on the room's big bed and succumb to exhaustion. His ankle felt better now but his head had taken over the throbbing. He glanced at the phone for a long moment and came ever so close to lifting the receiver before he forced himself to his feet and left the room. He deposited another fifty francs at the front desk and returned to his taxi. It was dark outside now, a clear, crystalline night that would see a rapid drop in temperature. It was time to return to the train station.

Locke gave the driver a fifty-franc tip and headed into the Vaduz Station. It proved to be far more crowded now than it had been in the afternoon. So far as he could tell no one was waiting by the lockers for him to extract his bag. If there was surveillance of any kind, it was well camouflaged.

Chris bought a paper and sat down on a wooden bench with the front section in front of his face. He had to wait things out, look for something that looked wrong before he made any move. A man sat down next to him holding a crumpled newspaper. Their eyes met and the man, who looked to be about fifty with a solid day's beard growth, smiled. Suddenly Locke had an idea.

"Do you speak English?" he asked the man.

"English!" the stranger exclaimed. "Is like a secoont langooge to me. I iv studied long and hart." He smiled proudly.

"I need a favor. Would you like to make some money?"

"How mooch?"

"A hundred francs."

"What can I dooth for you?"

Locke reached into his pocket, pulled out a card and key, and

143

handed them to the man. "Take these to the service desk and say you wish to get into your locker. The clerk will—"

"I know the proceese."

"There's a small bag inside the locker. Bring it to me on track two." The next train to Schaan would be leaving from there in fifteen minutes.

"That ese all?"

"That and no questions."

The man nodded. "You have mooney?"

Locke handed him the hundred francs.

"I go now," the man said and stood up. He looked down and winked. "You in trooble, eh?"

"A little."

"Wooman?"

"No questions, remember?"

"I une-der-stand. I weel help you."

The man walked away.

Locke rose quickly and moved from the bench with a measured pace, trying to match that of the people who shuffled around him. By the time he had reached the track entrance, the man was leading a clerk to the row of lockers. No sooner had he stuck his key in the slot then out of nowhere a herd of men converged on them from every corner of the station. The man was grabbed and wrestled to the floor. The clerk was escorted roughly away. Now the man was being spirited off too, screaming at his captors to no avail.

It was the distraction Locke had hoped for. He couldn't get his passport or clothes now but at least he could escape. He turned quickly.

An old hag, dressed in tatters, grabbed him at the lapel with one bony, filthy hand.

"American, you got money?"

Chris shoved her aside, eyes darting about feverishly to see if he had been noticed.

The hag poked him from behind.

"I know you got money. Give some to me. I not eat in three days. Please, American, please!"

Locke had swung to push her away again when he felt something hard jab into his ribs from beneath her bulky sweater.

"Don't say a word or I kill you here."

Locke started to speak. The hag poked him harder with her pistol.

"Walk forward to the track," she whispered.

Chris obeyed, moving toward the knot of people waiting near the track for the next train to Schaan. He might be able to knock the hag's gun aside and neutralize her there but in doing so would draw too much attention to himself. The building would still be crawling with Peale and the others after him for Felderberg's murder. He couldn't risk alerting them.

"Keep walking," the hag instructed, the steel beneath her ancient sweater never moving from his ribs.

Who had sent her? Locke wondered. Obviously not Felderberg's people, or she'd be leading him back to the station lobby instead of away from it.

They moved beyond the crowds and down into a tunnel where a sign warned NO PASSENGERS BEYOND THIS POINT in five languages. The air was dark and sooty, the only light provided by ceiling lamps strung irregularly. Locke knew the woman was taking him to his death now, but he dared not moved against her until he was sure they were out of earshot from the loading platform.

The hag slowed her pace, eyes searching for a closed-off spot to finish him.

That was Locke's cue.

He whirled backward in a blur, grabbing the barrel of the gun and forcing it away from him through the sweater, shredding the material. He went for the hag's throat with his other hand but she slithered backward, still trying to pull her gun free, and sank her teeth into his palm. Locke opened his mouth but managed to suppress a scream that would have drawn attention to their struggle.

The hag sank her teeth in deeper and clawed for his face with her free hand. Chris felt her nails find flesh and begin to tear as he threw himself sideways against the wall. His left hand lost the barrel briefly, then regained it. A shot rang out, kicking up dirt and cement chips behind him.

Locke yanked his hand from the hag's mouth and smashed her hard across the face. She winced, bellowed, and came at him again, free hand tearing for his eyes. Chris deflected the fingers and grabbed them, jerking the bony hand back over. The hag howled in pain and started kicking wildly out with her scrawny legs. Locke's shins and ankles bore the brunt of the assault as he pedaled sideways, trying to tear the pistol free from beneath her mangled sweater. But the hag's grip was iron. Her eyes were bulging with rage.

He let go the fingers he was certain he had snapped and pounded her nose hard. The hag screamed again and blood gushed from both her nostrils. The hand he had snapped backward before shot forward and down. Chris felt the pressure on his groin like a vise closing and lost his breath. The hag shrieked as she squeezed as tight as her hand would let her. Locke tried briefly to pry the grip off but the fingers had taken hold like a pit-bull's bite.

Finally, with the pain stealing all his breath, Chris latched his right hand over his left and pulled. The hag's pistol came free and tore through her ragged sweater. Her eyes swelled with shock and she clamped her fingers harder over Locke's groin in a grasp born of desperation.

This time it was Chris who found the breath to scream in agony as he brought up the pistol and smashed it across the hag's face. She pitched to the side with a grunt. Blood poured down the side of her face.

Locke slid down the wall, his mind holding onto consciousness through the horrible pain in his groin. Holding the pistol tightly in both hands, he leaned over and puked his guts out.

The hag rushed him from her knees.

Chris turned the gun on her, cocked its hammer.

She stopped. Locke pushed himself to his feet.

"Who are you?" he demanded.

The hag spit at him.

"I'll kill you slowly," he threatened. "A bullet here, a bullet there. I owe you a lot of pain."

She spit again. "Hah! You have all caused enough pain for a lifetime, you bastard."

"All? What are you—"

"Their souls scream out for vengeance. You *killed* children! You are the scum of the earth!"

Then Locke realized. "The people who tried to kill me in London sent you!"

The hag spit a third time. "San Sebastian will not be forgotten. All of you will pay."

The tunnel rumbled with the approach of a train.

"Kill me," she ranted. "It doesn't matter. Another will take my place. We are many and we will see you all burn in hell!"

The train roared closer.

The hag struggled to her feet, ignoring the blood that covered her face. Locke moved toward her. She stepped backward, keeping her distance.

"Who are you people?" he asked her. "You've got to tell me who sent you! Who do you think I work for? Please, you've got to tell me."

"You will all die! San Sebastian will be avenged!"

The train thundered forward, catching them in the spill of its front lights.

The hag glanced at it and smiled.

"No!" Chris screamed, already in motion, reaching for her with his free hand. "Noooooooo!"

It was too late. With a horrible wail the hag leaped off the platform directly into the path of the onrushing train. The train hurtled by, leaving nothing.

Chris leaned over and vomited again.

Kill me. It doesn't matter. Another will take my place. We are many and we will see you all burn in hell!

The hag's people wanted him dead because they thought him part of the very force he was fighting. He was, incredibly, on their side. But they didn't know it. And he didn't know who *they* were.

Everywhere he turned he found new pieces that didn't fit the puzzle. Chris started back toward the platform, limping again.

It was time to head to Schaan. Maybe the Sanii Corporation had some answers.

Peale waited in the shadows across the street from the Schaan Station. There was only one exit from the small building, so he knew exactly where his target would be emerging. He tightened the silencer around the Browning's barrel and steadied it over his left arm, squeezing one eye closed to check his aim.

Peale knew Locke was good and also knew from a tape recording of his conversation with Felderberg that he would be headed for the Sanii Corporation there in Schaan. Peale never bothered to question Locke's motives or aims. He had killed the blond man's employer and that was all that mattered. Peale had never lost a man he was protecting before. The score had to be settled, and his soldier's mind did not seek additional complexities. Life was easier that way.

People began squeezing from the station and Peale waited for his target. He had spoken barely thirty minutes ago with his people in Vaduz to learn that Locke had eluded them at the station there. Peale had expected as much. He held the pistol tighter, hunching lower in the darkness.

Locke emerged from the station, eyes nervously searching for a taxi. There were none to be found immediately. He started walking. Peale noticed his limp, glad for it because it would assure him of more than one shot if needed.

Peale focused his eye, ready to pull the trigger.

There was a scratching sound behind him and he swung quickly. A dark figure whirled before him. Something glimmered and Peale felt a tingle in his wrist as he spun away and tried to refocus in the darkness.

Long blond hair danced before him.

God, it was a woman!

Peale started his gun up to finish her, found it was gone, and looked down to see his hand was . . . gone too.

He realized the tingle had been the sensation of a blade slicing through his flesh. He screamed horribly as it came for him again. He dodged but it ripped into his shoulder on the side already missing the hand.

Now his mind accepted death as inevitable, but the woman had to be taken too. She came at him again but he rolled free, noting that she actually held two knives, one in each hand. They were *Kukhri* blades, weapons of the Gurkha soldiers from India.

Peale's roll had taken him to his lost gun, still clenched in his severed hand. He tore it free and lurched to his feet, screeching to fuel his fury and deaden his pain.

The *Kukhri* knives came down together, meeting in his chest and carving it in two before he ever found the trigger. Peale's last sight was of his killer, blond hair waving about the coldest eyes he had ever seen.

He took their memory with him into eternity.

CHAPTER 15

THE MEETING STARTED LATE, MUCH TO THE DISTRESS OF THE PARticipants who had traveled far and wished above all not to have their absences from the places they were supposed to be noticed and recorded.

They had come from several corners of the globe to the small Austrian village of Greifenstein on the bank of the Danube. From there they were driven up the narrow mountain road to Kreuzenstein Castle, which had been bought and refurbished several years before by the woman who was their leader. The ancient castle had become their symbol, its regal towers and steeples reminding them of the nations they represented and sought to destroy. Kreuzenstein had stood for eight hundred years and had needed to be rebuilt only once, after being destroyed by the Swedes during the Thirty Years War. It had weathered many storms and sieges, had been a refuge from the Black Death and a strategy center in World War II when bombs had exploded everywhere but within its walls.

The members of the Committee looked on that as divine providence. The choice of the castle as their headquarters had not been random.

There were four of them present that day, all members of the executive board, with only the British representative missing. They met in a huge room that years before had been used by kings and princes for lavish balls to entertain visiting royalty. The hard oak table, easily long enough to accommodate the Committee's one hundred direct representatives, was being used that day because the woman who had orchestrated the most daring operation they had ever undertaken preferred it for reasons of tradition.

They had been speaking quietly among themselves for nearly twenty minutes after the sun had set beyond the windows when the double doors opened and Audra St. Clair strode majestically in. The four men rose out of respect as well as etiquette.

Audra St. Clair was past seventy now but she looked a full twenty years younger. Her silver hair was styled traditionally, and the gray hat she wore was a perfect complement to the tweed dress that elegantly covered the fine lines of her body. Her face was remarkably free of wrinkles and other marks of age, as if her power could overcome time along with nations.

"We have much to discuss, gentlemen," she announced, taking her customary seat at the head of the table. "I apologize for my lateness but I've just received a report from the agent I dispatched to Liechtenstein to clean up the mess Mr. Mandala has gotten us into. Let us begin today's agenda by considering this poorly handled threat to our security."

Mandala leaned forward. His features were strikingly dark, as though perpetually tanned. His hair was combed neatly off his forehead to cover the tops of his ears, and his long, radiant teeth sparkled like daggars. It was his eyes that were most striking, liquidy black and piercing.

"I was simply doing as ordered, madam" came his response. "I offer no excuses."

"And I'm not looking for any," St. Clair snapped. "Excuses are meaningless to the Committee."

Mandala leaned back and held his tongue. He was not used to being chastised. Men, as well as women, had died for far less than the old bitch's words. But at this point he didn't dare cross her. His time was coming. He flashed the smile that had won him friends, influence, and women, suggesting his acceptance of St. Clair's criticism.

"I also believe your handling of San Sebastian was rash and overdone," the Committee's chairwoman continued. "You jeopardized everything for the elimination of that town."

"All the same," began the American representative, a silver-haired man who, with the Committee's help, had risen to an extremely high position in U.S. government, "if it wasn't for the unexpected presence of the American agent, the massacre wouldn't have become a factor."

"The fact is that it happened," said St. Clair, "and it forced us to realign our strategy."

"For the better in many ways, I think," noted Werenmauser, the German, a large, heavy-lipped man with bulging cheeks. "Thanks to San Sebastian, Locke was drawn in. And thanks to Locke, we are eliminating the only holes left in our very long trail."

"In addition to encountering our mysterious enemy face to face for the first time," added the curly-haired Russian, Kresovlosky. "An enemy who has been doing its utmost to subvert our efforts in South America for some months."

"Not exactly face to face," said St. Clair. "We still don't know who they are."

"The identity of the man your agent disposed of in London should help us find out."

"He carried no identification," the chairwoman reported. "No papers or clues of any kind. We will learn nothing from his corpse, I'm afraid. We must rely on Locke at this point to lead us to them."

"But leaving Locke alive presents too much of a risk," argued the American nervously. "He has become too dangerous to be considered an asset any longer."

Audra St. Clair leaned over the table. The flickering light from the chandelier danced and darted across her face. "He is simply a puppet on a string we pull. We can direct him any way we desire. Cutting that string now would be a gross error."

The American shook his head. "I don't think you understand my position. For the rest of you membership on the Committee is a simpler matter to conceal than it is for me. My movements are scrutinized constantly. I am taking a terrible risk by being here now. If Locke slips from our grasp and gets too close, I'll be the first one exposed."

"Apparently it's you who doesn't understand, Mr. Van Dam," the chairwoman said firmly. "Locke is the only thing standing between us and a rather significant force potentially capable of bringing harm to Tantalus. We will continue to monitor his movements, filling in the holes he shows us, and ultimately he will lead us to our unseen enemy."

"Where exactly is he now, can you tell me that, madam?" Van Dam said sharply. "Well, there's a man named Calvin Roy in the State Department with the nose of a bloodhound. He authorized Locke's deployment in the first place, and sooner or later he might sniff out our puppet and yank him beyond our reach."

"It would have to be quite soon, Mr. Van Dam. Tantalus will be activated eight days from today." Audra St. Clair turned to the Russian. "Mr. Kresovlosky, your report please."

The Russian cleared his throat and opened a manila folder on the table before him. "Production of canisters will be completed on schedule by the middle of this week. Arrangements have already been made for shipping to Target Alpha for dispersal. The canisters have been fitted to the exact specifications Mr. Mandala requested."

"I am in the process of retaining all necessary equipment and personnel." Mandala picked up on cue. "To guard against the possibility of early discovery and potential countermeasures, I have also retained a rather large and well-equipped security force. Everything will be in place plenty of time before final activation."

"And the timetable for appreciable results?" St. Clair asked Kresovlosky.

"Based on data collected from our experiments in San Sebastian, I would say four days for Area Mary, a week for Areas Peter and Paul, ten days for Mark and Matthew, and up to two weeks for Luke."

Audra St. Clair simply nodded. "Let us turn now to Mr. Werenmauser."

The German rubbed his huge cheeks. "We are ready to go at my end. Final experiments are taking place in Schaan this week to determine optimum packaging. I estimate shipping can begin to Targets Delta, Gamma, Sigma, and Zeta within ten days. I expect no difficulties or complications."

153

"What about our crews?" the chairwoman asked.

"We would be best off not to move them in until after the effects of Tantalus have begun to surface in America. We can use the resulting chaos as camouflage for the sudden influx of personnel into South America that might otherwise cause a stir and lead to many questions. By the time the true answers are made known, we must be sure Tantalus has reached its full effect and the world is powerless to do anything about the follow-up portion of our plan."

St. Clair settled back in her chair. "It appears, gentlemen, that from a technical standpoint, matters are proceeding very smoothly indeed. My concern now is for security." Her eyes dug into Mandala's. "What conclusions have you reached regarding our unseen enemy?"

"They are organized, but not powerful or overly strong in number" came Mandala's precision reponse. If his own plan was to work, he couldn't risk becoming the target of the old bitch's wrath . . . and suspicions. "They must not represent any government or accepted body of another sort. Otherwise they would have exposed us instead of engaging in this foolish cat-and-mouse game."

"The game may be foolish," the chairwoman told him, "but it has brought them closer to us than any other group has come in a generation."

"A problem soon to be rectified. I could accomplish this just as easily without Locke. I suggest we take him out while we are still in control of his movements."

"No," Audra St. Clair ordered staunchly. "Locke is to be kept alive until I direct otherwise."

"That seems to me to be a clear violation of your own security precautions," Mandala said, "as well as the Committee's."

The chairwoman leaned forward over the table, eyes narrowed into slits of anger. "Do not lecture me on Committee policy, Mr. Mandala. You are a killer and little more. We have existed for more than twenty-five years by steering clear of your kind and choosing more subtle measures."

"And look where those subtle measures got you, while mine have put you on the brink of achieving your greatest goal."

154

"You are a soldier to us, a mercenary, nothing more."

"It took a soldier's insight to make operational a great plan you could only conceive in raw form." Mandala glanced around at the elegantly appointed conference room and smirked. "You call me here and expect me to be overwhelmed by your furniture and paintings? Hah! While you were holding meetings in air-conditioned rooms all those years ago, I was sweating in fields that stank of death, fighting to destabilize the world you wanted to control. Then when you needed someone to carry out your plans in the field, you came to me. And you have turned to me repeatedly whenever you didn't want to get your hands dirty. Fine, but don't criticize me because mine are not clean."

"We tolerate your methods, Mr. Mandala," St. Clair said in a softer voice. "We do not accept them."

"Let's not be naive, madam. We have thus far discussed Tantalus only up to its activation and immediate effects. What about after? The world will be at its most vulnerable. That is the time to increase destabilization and disruption strategies. We can bring the entire world to its knees, not just the United States."

"People cannot reach bank tellers' windows on their knees, Mr. Mandala. We are an economic body, not a political one. Politics is useful to us only when it functions as a vehicle for our economic plans. Tantalus *will* bring the U.S.—and the world—to their knees. But we will leave them able to regain their feet, with our assistance."

"Power lies in controlling people, madam, not their bank accounts."

"People *are* their bank accounts, Mr. Mandala."

"We have the capacity to create total chaos and turn ourselves into the sole voice of order."

"Precisely what we are doing. Economically."

"Politically we would be far more effective and far reaching."

"You're missing the point," St. Clair told Mandala. "Economics and politics are inseparable. People respond based solely on how full their wallets are. Tantalus will give us the ability to control that factor as we see fit."

Mandala just nodded. It was not the time to say anything that

155

might make the old bitch suspect the plan he was about to undertake.

The people in the room were used to silence. Meetings were often dominated by it.

"Let us return to the issue of this Locke," Van Dam said finally. "If we are not going to kill him, we must have a backup means for controlling him ready should anything else go wrong."

"I am in the process of arranging just that now," Mandala said.

"And what if it isn't good enough?" Van Dam demanded. "If Locke reaches someone powerful without our knowledge, what then? I believe Charney discovered my identity. He may have told Locke or left him some clue. Every minute he's allowed to live increases the chances of my exposure. You must understand my position," he pleaded, mostly to the woman at the table's head. "I-I didn't realize how important he was to our plans. I thought he had completed his usefulness. I couldn't take the chance. I couldn't!"

"What have you done?" St. Clair asked him.

"I ordered a man sent to erase Locke."

The chairwoman's features sank. "Recall him, you fool."

"It's too late," Van Dam said.

PART FIVE:

SCHAAN,
MONDAY MORNING

PART FIVE:

SELASA,
MONDAY MORNING

CHAPTER 16

"WE ARE NOW PASSING INTO THE SECTION WHERE SANII TECHNOLOGY has discovered new ways of taking soil samples from other planets," the tour guide's voice droned as Locke's eyes wandered.

Saturday night he had found an unpretentious mountain inn where a room was available. Chris's first thought was to pay someone to go out and get him some new clothes, but the sight of the desk clerk gave him another idea. The man was just a little smaller and stouter than he was. His clothes wouldn't be a great fit yet they'd certainly pass, and he accepted Locke's cash with no questions. A bit more money gained Chris bandages and antiseptic for the hand chewed by the hag, and a hearty dinner. And, since on Sunday the offices of the Sanii Corporation would be closed, he had an entire day for much-needed rest and healing.

He slept past noon on Sunday. He found out from the desk clerk that regular tours of the Sanii Corporation plant began Monday at ten A.M. Sanii was one of the very few major corporations to have large facilities in Liechtenstein and was thus quite an attraction. It specialized in futuristic high tech, which meant there would surely be an agricultural experimentation section. There he might find a clue to what lay behind the South American land deals Felderberg had been a party to.

"It is now possible," the tour guide explained as the group peered through glass at miniature displays of bizarre machines working on soil, "to program robot probes to travel millions of miles away and actually *land* on foreign bodies to collect samples and then return home. Sanii scientists have discovered a means to . . ."

Locke's eyes wandered again. He was in the right area, he could feel it. This section dealt with soil. Agricultural experimentation couldn't be far away.

He had arrived there in plenty of time for the tour and was impressed by the size of the Sanii site. There were four separate buildings: one giant one that ran across almost the entire length of the site, a smaller one near its right flank virtually hidden in the shadows, and a third at least half the big one's size extending beyond its end to the site's far left. The fourth was a mirrored building that probably contained offices. The tour began in the giant structure, which announced SANII in huge red letters on its sloping roof. The roof did have one large flat spot, and Locke could hear the exhaust from powerful compressors that would regulate atmospheric conditions for the experiments inside.

The tour guide had completed her description of collecting soil samples from foreign bodies when Chris raised his hand.

"Yes?"

"I am curious about agricultural experiments closer to Earth. Are any conducted here at the plant?"

The tour guide looked puzzled. "We do have a very standard agricultural section but it's located in the smallest building and contains little of interest. Now, if you'll all follow me . . ."

That was it! Locke had his answer, at least a place to start. When the tour group swung around the next corner he slipped away and made his way back to the entrance. The security guard quizzed him and he complained of nausea, saying he needed some fresh air. The uniformed man wished him well, took back his guest pass, and held the door open for him.

Glancing back only briefly, Locke left the building and swung to the right and then quickly to the left. The smaller agricultural wing ran parallel to the mother building, and he moved toward it as quickly as he could, hoping not to attract any attention.

The entrance contained a sign warning AUTHORIZED PERSONNEL ONLY, and two guards were poised inside to enforce it. That ruled the entrance out. Locke kept walking.

Around the other side of the building, two huge garage bays

160

had been opened and men were unloading hundred-pound bags of something into a large warehouse. Locke remembered the clothes the clerk had provided him with were those of a workman, not a tourist, and he wasted no time. He joined the line of workers lifting bags from the truck and piling them inside the warehouse.

No one seemed to notice him. The Sanii workers probably thought he was part of the trucking crew and the trucking crew must have thought the reverse. Just in case this changed, Locke kept the bags he hoisted up in front of his face and avoided the eyes of those around him. Once the pile of bags inside was high enough, Locke slipped behind it and moved through the rear of the warehouse without hesitation, opening the first door he saw and stepping inside the building.

He was in a long, white, brightly lit corridor.

A moving person may attract attention but a person standing still attracts even more.

Locke heeded another memory from his training and started walking before he had any idea of his bearings. The corridor was deserted, fortunate but probably only temporary. He reached a junction in the corridors and studied what was up ahead in both directions. A locker room was to the right and he steered toward it, hoping to find something inside that might help his charade.

The locker room was typical in design, banks of lockers fronted by benches with the sound of showers and the smell of steam not far off. Two men passed him as he entered without giving him a second look, and Chris found himself thankful for the multitudes of people Sanii employed. There had probably been close to 750 cars in the parking lot. He had gotten another break in that midday was fast approaching, which meant time off for lunch. The locker room was crowded. Locke moved quickly into the bathroom, bolting a stall behind him.

He sat down on the toilet and fought to steady his breathing. Nerves would give him away faster than anything. A calm exterior was the best disguise of all.

Disguise! That was it!

The two men Locke passed in the doorway had been wearing simple white lab coats. If he were walking the corridors in one of

161

those, no one would accost him. Locke's memory sharpened. The coats had badges pinned to their lapels, picture badges. He would have to take his chances that no one would look closely. He flushed the toilet and moved out of the stall, stopping between two men shaving before the row of sinks, and washed his hands. Moving routinely back among the lockers, he grabbed the first white lab coat from the first open locker he saw. Tossing his arms through the sleeves, he started back toward the corridor.

The coat was a poor fit—much too short in the arms—and the picture on the ID looked nothing like him. Same color hair, though, and that might prove enough to get him through. Locke kept walking and a minute later found himself about to enter a giant greenhouse. Men in similar white coats were everywhere, checking gauges and readouts and making notes concerning plants of virtually all varieties. He was in a section apparently devoted to insuring that no plant species became extinct. He walked through it and on until he came to a pair of double doors, just wide enough to accommodate their warning label: CLOSED SECURITY SECTION, NO ADMITTANCE EXCEPT BY RED BADGE.

Locke glanced down. Miraculously, his badge was red. He started moving through the heavy doors but they wouldn't budge. Then he noticed the steel slot on the wall to his right. A special ID card was required for entry. He started to search his pockets on the wild chance the coat contained one.

"Problems?"

The voice came from behind him. Locke swung to see a mustachioed man about his own age.

"I'll say. Damn slot won't accept my card. It must have bent in my wallet."

"I was going in anyway," the man said in excellent English, apparently the official language of the corporation. The machine swallowed his card, then spit it back out. There was a buzz and Chris heard the door snap mechanically open. "See." The mustachioed man smiled, holding the door open for him. "Nothing to it."

"Thank you," Chris responded, moving to the right as the man veered to the left.

He had surprised himself with the way he'd handled the

situation. Nothing had been planned. It just came to him like an actor's lines and he didn't question his actions further.

Locke passed a plate-glass window looking into a room twenty feet square lit up with fluorescents strung over strange-looking green shrubs. An iron clipboard was hanging on the wall, attached to the plaster on a light chain. Chris pretended to be studying it briefly to make sure no one was approaching, then ripped it free, holding it in his right hand as he started walking again. Where, though, was he going? He had made it into the high-security section but there were still dozens of hallways, hundreds of rooms.

Other technicians were moving past him regularly now, none giving him a second look. The labs came one after another, all with different announcements printed on their doors.

Then he saw the door up ahead with no markings at all, just a security guard watching intently. Something fluttered in Chris's stomach. He had to get inside that room. He bent over a water fountain and took in as much water as he could hold. When he stepped back he saw a group of scientists advancing steadily down the corridor. They drew closer and Locke noticed all wore red badges with black crosses drawn through them. His own lacked a cross, but he joined the group.

"Good morning, Professor," the security guard said to the bearded man at their lead.

"Good morning."

The guard held the door, allowing the entire team to pass through, and nodding at each one. Locke turned his shoulders around to hide his badge and held his breath as he passed, but the guard made no move to stop him.

The door closed with an echo. Chris drifted away from the group. He was in a giant terrarium lined with four rows of different crops. He made a quick inventory and found they were labeled corn, oats, wheat and barley. But their sizes! Some looked ready for field harvest. Others were barely sprouting from their soil boxes.

Locke started up one of the rows, studying the white cards placed at floor level. He skimmed their contents, afraid to stay in one place too long with so many people in the room. He knew

163

there was something in the white cards he was gazing at, some pattern, but he couldn't think clearly enough to pin it down. He had reached the end of the row and was standing before the highest stalks of wheat when it struck him. He reread the notation on the white card six times to make sure he wasn't seeing things.

Planting date: March 26.

It couldn't be! These wheat stalks had attained a year's worth of growth *twenty-one days from planting.* Mesmerized, Chris walked back up the row.

Each boxed section, approximately ten feet square, represented a different stage of growth divided into seven three-day periods. If the information on the white cards was accurate, the crops' growth rate had been accelerated at a phenomenal clip. The implications of this would be enormous. He tried to think about the relationship between what he had just seen and what Felderberg had told him at Vaduz. But it was no use. He couldn't concentrate until he was safely out of this place.

Chris reached the end of the row and turned quickly. The bearded scientist blocked his path.

"Who are you? I don't know you." His eyes fell on Locke's badge. "Wait, you don't belong . . ."

Chris was already moving in the other direction, breaking into a trot.

"Stop him! Stop that man!"

Another scientist lunged in his path. Without hesitating, Chris raised the steel clipboard over his head and smashed it down hard into the man's face. The scientist crumpled to the floor.

Locke dropped the clipboard and darted into part of the miniature wheatfield. In seconds his feet found tile again only long enough to project him forward into the oats, then the corn. The door was just up ahead, but so was the security guard fumbling to yank his gun from its holster.

The pistol had just come free when Locke crashed into him with a shoulder block. The guard dropped the gun as he fell backward.

Chris sped into the corridor. He could hear the feet pounding after him only until the security alarm started wailing. He ran down the hall fighting for his bearings, trying to recall the placement of the nearest exit door. He charted how much ground he had covered by counting glass windows of the lab rooms. At the next larger corridor, he turned.

A parade of guards charged from the opposite direction. Locke squealed to a halt and swung to the right. It must have been nearing lunchtime because a number of white-coated figures were moving leisurely about in this smaller hall. They formed his cover. All he needed was an exit to take him into the parking lot. There he could mingle among the workers long enough to seal his escape.

He spotted a red emergency exit sign over a door at the end of the corridor. His heart lurched against his chest as he continued slithering through bodies, gaining precious ground on the men behind him. He reached the heavy steel door and crashed through it into the bright sunlight. He had to squint and half cover his eyes with his hand but he kept moving. The guards would not be far behind.

Luckily, the timing of his exit had been perfect. The end of one shift and lunch for another had brought a flood of bodies pouring from inside the plant, too many people for the guards effectively to sift through. Chris kept his pace steady, not too fast and not too slow, doing nothing to make himself stand out. He headed toward the main parking lot hoping for a taxi, a bus, even a ride from a fellow worker. He was hurrying now, giving in to impatience, afraid to look back in case the Sanii guards were closing on him.

Suddenly a figure appeared before him, big and thick-haired, with gun drawn.

The man brought his pistol up from his hip in a blur of motion.

"No!" Chris screamed, knowing it was too late.

The man fired.

Locke had started backward, tensing for an impact he knew must come. There was a grunt followed by a thud behind him. Chris turned and saw the prone figure of a security guard grasping his bloodied shoulder, a pistol lying on the cement just out of reach. Then people were yelling, scattering, calling for help.

And the figure with the still-smoking gun was beckoning to Locke.

"Let's get out of here!" the man screamed. "Now!"

CHAPTER 17

SATURDAY NIGHT DOGAN HAD ARRIVED AT VADUZ STATION IN SEARCH of his quarry but found someone else. At first he didn't recognize the man with a newspaper in his lap smiling at him from the wooden benches. As he drew closer, though, he found himself smiling too.

"Ah, Grendel, I've been expecting you. What brings you to Liechtenstein, comrade?"

Dogan sat down next to the Russian in the all but empty train station. "Business. I'm here to kill a man."

"Yes," Vaslov said knowingly. "Christopher Locke."

Dogan didn't bother to hide his surprise. "You never cease to amaze me."

"Our intelligence was quite accurate on the subject," Vaslov continued. "I came to Liechtenstein to make sure you did not complete your assignment. You're being used. It's not your own government that wants Locke dead, it's someone in the Committee."

"What are you talking about?"

"Locke is the key, comrade. Remember I told you about San Sebastian? We intercepted a taped transmission sent by one of your side's agents, a certain Lubeck. We believed he was on the Committee's trail. When the agent was killed along with the rest of the town, Locke was recruited to take his place and retrace his steps."

"My God, you know all this from intelligence *within* my government?"

"The bits and pieces, yes. The rest is conjecture but most accurate in this case, I believe. The exact agenda of Locke's trip eluded me. I learned he was in London only when a report surfaced accusing him of the murder of a Colombian diplomat."

"I wasn't told anything about that."

"Because it would have raised questions on your part. You were told only that Locke had killed a State Department attaché. In fact, that man was running him. It was the Committee who arranged the attaché's elimination. They needed Locke isolated so they could control his movements. None of this made sense to me until I learned who Locke was to meet here."

"Felderberg?"

Vaslov nodded. "Recent intelligence all but confirms that he is the financial middleman for the Committee."

"*Was.*"

"That's right, comrade, you were there. And yet you did not carry out your termination order even when the opportunity presented itself."

"Something smelled about this from the beginning," Dogan told him. "I was being used and I didn't like it. The scene at the Hauser just didn't play right if Locke had really come there with something to sell. After Felderberg's bodyguards escorted him out, I made a fast check around. Someone killed him with a poisoned cork and the logistics ruled out Locke. . . ."

"Yes," interjected Vaslov with a slight smile, "I've used that method several times successfully myself. The Americans tried it with Castro, only to find out he drank beer exclusively."

"Locke was set up," Dogan continued, "which means I was set up too."

"And Felderberg's killing was made to look as if Locke were responsible, once again orchestrated by the Committee. They are using him to reveal the pattern uncovered by your agent in San Sebastian, so they can eradicate it."

"But why would they want to eliminate their own middleman?"

"One question at a time, comrade. Felderberg became expendable because he had outlived his usefulness to them, in which case their latest plot must be nearing completion." Vaslov sighed. "I had hoped to turn Felderberg to our side myself."

168

"And now he won't be able to tell us anything."

"Another man can, however."

"Locke."

Vaslov shifted his legs, slid the newspaper to the bench beside him. "So you can see why we must take him alive. We not only have confirmation of the Committee's existence now, but also proof that they are about to activate an important operation. And Christopher Locke is the only man who may know what it entails."

"He may just as easily know nothing."

"How long was he inside with Felderberg, comrade?"

"Thirty minutes, maybe thirty-five."

"Plenty of time for the financier to pass at least as much as he passed on to your agent in San Sebastian. Yes, Locke has data. What he lacks is any real knowledge of what's involved."

"Which we possess."

Vaslov nodded again. "But I'm afraid there's a complication, several, in fact. To begin with, the actions of the Committee are not consistent. They killed Locke's control in London so Locke would be forced to do their bidding. Their next move is to retain you to eliminate Locke."

"Maybe someone got nervous."

"My thought exactly. Someone panicked over Locke being allowed to roam free. The Commander received an order from a higher level. It follows."

"What about the other complications?"

"The second's a bit more involved, I'm afraid. Earlier this evening, one of my men saw Locke being led away from the train platform by an old woman who's a known free-lance assassin. He didn't intercede because he was under strict orders just to observe. By the time he reported back to me, traces of the old woman's body had been found on the front of a train."

"Locke killed her?"

"She was obviously trying to do the same to him. And if Felderberg's people had hired her, she would have led Locke back toward them, not away from the platform."

"So someone else wants our college professor dead. . . ."

Vaslov's eyebrows flickered. "A third party, Grendel. And to find out who, we must trace the woman's contacts. They are well known to me. I used the old hag a few times myself. I'll initiate the tracing procedures as soon as we part."

"And the third complication?"

Vaslov hesitated. "Perhaps the most confusing of all. Someone seems to want Locke alive as much as others want him dead." Vaslov noted Dogan's questioning stare. "After ridding himself of the hag, Locke left for Schaan. Felderberg's top security man was found outside the station there with his chest torn in two."

Dogan nodded. "Schaan's quite lovely this time of year."

"Locke must feel the same way."

Dogan stood up. "I'd better start hunting."

Vaslov pulled a blue gym bag from under his legs. "When you find Locke, give him these belongings. His passport is among them, and he may have need of it."

"But how did you—"

"He paid me a hundred francs to open a locker for him." Vaslov shifted his aching shoulders. "Felderberg's people made me feel my age, but I was happy to be of service to Mr. Locke."

The stranger led Locke to an Audi parked halfway up on the grass strip separating one row of cars from the next. They jumped inside and screeched away, Chris studying the stranger's face trying to recall where he had seen him before.

"The Hauser!" he exclaimed as the Audi tore off the Sanii grounds. "You were at the Hauser! Who are you? Why'd you save my life back there?"

Dogan's eyes darted between the road and the rearview mirror. "One question at a time. The name's Dogan, Ross Dogan of the once-proud CIA."

"Wait a minute, if you were at the Hauser you must have been following me all along."

"If I was following you, Locke, how in the hell could I have been waiting *inside* the Hauser before you arrived? Six months at the Academy should have taught you enough to figure that out."

Locke felt his mouth drop. "You know that much about me?"

"Mostly because I was sent to Liechtenstein to kill you."

"*What?*"

"Don't worry. A careful analysis of the situation back in Vaduz mandated a change in plans."

The Audi thundered down the two-lane highway. Dogan reached an intersection and screeched into a right-hand turn.

"But why did the CIA send you to kill me?"

"It's not the CIA specifically, but a subgroup called Division Six. Don't let it confuse you. The Company's got more hidden compartments than a rich widow's mansion. The story was you killed a State Department man named Charney."

"No! He was the one who pulled me into all this but I didn't kill him. Somebody else did!"

Dogan nodded. "A friend of mine filled me in on that. Charney must have been getting too close to them. His execution not only eliminated a threat but also served to isolate you."

"*Who* was he getting close to?" Locke asked.

"Later," Dogan replied flatly. "What brought you here to Liechtenstein and Felderberg?"

"Charney's last words."

"Was Felderberg Lubeck's second stop as well?"

"Wait a minute, how did you know about Lubeck?"

"What I know doesn't matter. It's what you know that counts, what Felderberg told you."

Locke breathed deeply. "Brian told me the key was food and Felderberg confirmed it. Someone is buying land in South America, millions and millions of acres, and all of it arable. Billions of dollars were exchanged. Whoever these people are, they're attempting to gain control of the entire continent. But even Felderberg didn't know why."

"He sent you to Sanii," Dogan concluded.

"He discovered a connection between the plant and his elusive clients. The answer was there all right, in the top-secret agricultural wing." Locke paused. "They've got wheat, corn, oats, and barley crops there that have reached full maturity in *only three weeks*!"

"Genetic engineering," Dogan muttered. "Our scientists have been working on it for years with no breakthroughs whatsoever."

"Apparently the force behind Sanii has made plenty. Who are they, Ross?" Locke asked, surprised at how calm he felt.

"They call themselves the Committee." Dogan's hands tightened on the wheel. "We've all heard stories about small groups of fanatics plotting to take over the world—usually they're products of someone's paranoid delusions. The Committee's the exception. They're real and they've been out there for God knows how many years looking for a way to gain control of the world economically. But its members don't operate above the surface. Only shadows emerge. The Committee functions apart from any government. Its members come from many races, nationalities, and countries. They hold high positions, which allow them to gain accurate intelligence as well as affect policy to the Committee's benefit."

"You're talking about a sublayer of control all across the world." Locke controlled his shock at the enormity of what he was hearing.

"And governments have no way of knowing to what extent this sublayer has influenced their policies. The Committee's manipulations are felt by everyone. Remember the gas lines of seventy-two? There are those who say the Committee, through a complicated series of maneuvers, was behind the whole embargo. Control oil and you control the world was the common belief back then. But America rallied and the emphasis had to be shifted."

"To food. . . ."

"It's the one resource that cuts across all barriers. You can't control the distribution of water and air, but you sure as hell can manage the flow of food."

"But developing all this land in South America won't go far toward *controlling* this flow. It'll just expand things a bit, widen the circulation and toss a new major supplier into the market."

"No," Dogan countered, "that's not how they work. What I said about the Committee seeking to run the world wasn't an exaggeration. But it's pretty difficult to run a world with two

172

superpowers bookending everything in the middle. Their first thought has to be how to neutralize the U.S. and the Soviet Union.''

"What about undercutting us in the market, slicing into our share of the farm exports?''

Dogan shook his head, keeping his eyes steady on the road. "No, that's too chancy and conservative. Also, I doubt they would be that naive. Our allies aren't stupid. They know that a major item we export is food. If they buy from someone else, we—our dollar—gets hurt, which means they get hurt.''

Dogan glanced again at the rearview mirror. The view was clear behind them, and they'd been driving long enough now for concern over immediate pursuit to wane. The Swiss border would be coming up shortly. Once across it, he would head straight to Zurich and temporary refuge.

"The Committee craves power,'' Dogan continued. "They've got something far worse up their sleeve than simple entry into the market, you can bet on that.''

Chris studied the man next to him briefly. His face was determined. When he wasn't speaking, he clenched his teeth tightly. Locke was astounded by the aura of strength he projected and felt as if he was seated next to a volcano about to erupt.

"How is it that the Committee has never been investigated?'' he asked.

"They have. Unofficially. The problem is nobody knows what to investigate, even less where to start. The Committee never leaves a trail.''

"Until now.''

"And a lot of people have died already who were part of it, starting with San Sebastian. Felderberg revealed part of what's going on and Sanii clarified it. But a part is still all we've got.''

Locke recalled more of the financier's words. "Felderberg sent Lubeck to Florence, to someone called the Dwarf.''

Dogan nodded, a slight smile on his face. "It figures he might be involved in this somehow.''

"Felderberg said he brokered information.''

"Along with weapons, blackmail, extortion—just about any-

173

thing for a price. I've dealt with him before. Sneaky little bastard, and it's my bet he'll have gone into hiding by now. There are ways to reach him, though."

Locke thought quickly. "There was another man, an Englishman named Burgess. He was an old friend of Charney's and Brian sent me to him. He helped me get to Liechtenstein. Should we contact him?"

"I doubt there's anything he can do to help us," Dogan said suspiciously. "You'll have to fill me in on the details of this later. He could be a Committee plant."

"Impossible logistics," Locke said. "He's clean."

"Then I wouldn't want to be his insurance company. The Committee will get him before long."

"He's one tough son of a bitch. He takes precautions."

"Precautions mean nothing to the Committee. They can get to anyone anywhere. It's how they operate."

"That doesn't say much for our chances."

"Not entirely true. To begin with, we're on the move. More important, though, they aren't even aware of my involvement yet and they want very much to keep you alive to continue uncovering Lubeck's trail for them." Dogan hesitated. "One of Felderberg's men was waiting to kill you in Schaan Saturday night. Someone cut him up like candy."

"But there are other people who want me dead."

"An old hag in the train station in Vaduz among them?"

"Yes! Yes! But how did you know? How *could* you know?"

"It doesn't matter. The old woman was a known assassin, quite proficient in her trade. You're lucky to be alive."

"I was lucky two other times as well." And Chris went on to relate the details of his deadly meeting with Alvaradejo and the bloody chase that followed it. "Whoever's behind these killers must have been the ones who used Alvaradejo to alert Lubeck in the first place," he concluded, "which means we're actually on the same side. My—our—problem is that they don't know it. It looks to them like I'm being controlled by the Committee so they're going all out to eliminate me."

Dogan was nodding, a bit shaken by Locke's conclusions.

"That presupposes that this mysterious third party knows what the Committee was up to in San Sebastian. Then, why did they attack the problem through Lubeck? Why not expose the truth themselves?"

"Fear of retaliation perhaps."

"No, that doesn't wash. Otherwise they wouldn't have exposed themselves so much in trying to take you out. What was it that the old hag in the train station said?"

"She said it didn't matter if I killed her because another would take her place. She said there were a lot of them and they would see us all burn in hell."

" 'Us' meaning the Committee."

"That's the implication, yes. But she didn't have a Spanish accent."

"Interesting. The reach of this third party obviously extends beyond a few Spanish fanatics. Individual teams are being called up, or just individuals, available for suicide missions."

"I'll repeat the question: then why bother using Lubeck at all?"

"You tell me, Locke. What did Lubeck offer them?"

"Legitimacy?" Chris replied.

"I think you've hit on it," Dogan told him. "These allies of ours who don't realize they're our allies can't risk exposure any more than the Committee can."

"So we're dealing with another sublayer here."

"One that picks and chooses its times to rise above the surface. We'll know who's behind it soon enough. That friend of mine is tracing down the old woman's channels. Find out who hired her and we'll have our answer."

"Just one of them, you mean," Locke corrected. His voice grew distant. "Lubeck saw something in the fields of San Sebastian before he died, something that terrified him. It all comes back to land . . . and genetic crop growth."

"Lubeck saw a lot more than just crops in those fields, even if they sprouted right before his eyes, and we've got to find out what. It's the key to this whole mess."

The car crossed over into Switzerland. Both men breathed

easier, though the security they felt in passing the border was fleeting. If the right connections had been made swiftly in Schaan, no border could protect them.

"You never explained how you found me," Chris said suddenly.

"I put myself in your position," Dogan explained, "and made a quiet search of all Schaan lodges and inns I'd have chosen if I were you. It wasn't until early this morning that I found the right one. I followed you to Sanii and shadowed you on the outside, ready to lend my services if it became necessary."

"Lucky for me. . . ."

Dogan glanced over at Locke. "Charney was a bastard for drawing you into this."

"He was only doing his job."

"Bullshit. We don't involve amateurs. We never involve amateurs."

"I had six months of training, remember?"

"And most men with a lifetime of it wouldn't have stuck this out like you have." The car stopped at an intersection. Dogan's eyes bore into Locke's. "Running would have been the normal reaction."

"No, Ross, I had to see this thing through," Chris said softly. "I'd love to say it was out of patriotism, but I can't. These bastards killed the two best friends I ever had and that's part of it, a great part, but there's something deeper that's kept me going: fear. I've been scared all my life but the fear was never something I could overcome, because it was never tangible. Now I can see it, feel it. It's out there and it's alive and it's monstrous. And maybe if I can look it in the eyes and not be stared down, all the other fears won't mean so much and I'll be able to look myself in the eyes too. Being a failure isn't so bad; it's realizing you're one all of a sudden at forty-two."

Dogan said nothing. He understood how Locke felt, better than he could admit to anyone. They were both trying to stop running. But to respond to Locke's words would have been too difficult, so he turned back to the subject immediately at hand.

"When we get to Zurich, I'll make the necessary arrangements to get you to Florence. The Dwarf will see you; he owes me lots of favors."

"And what about you?"

"There's only one place with all the answers, Chris, and that's where I'm headed."

"South America?"

"San Sebastian."

CHAPTER 18

"GOOD EVENING TO YOU, COMRADE."

"It won't be good after you hear what I have to say."

Dogan made contact with Vaslov after settling in at the Staadhof Hotel in the center of Zurich.

"Your voice sounds tired," Vaslov noted.

"And scared. I caught up with Locke."

"I never expected any less. . . ."

"His meeting with Felderberg was even more informative than we had hoped." And Dogan proceeded to outline the information Locke had passed on, stressing those parts dealing with food, South America, and the experiments underway at the Sanii plant. "Your fears have been substantiated," he said at the end. "The Committee is after both our countries and the key is food. The only remaining question is precisely how they plan to strike."

"They couldn't have picked a better target, though, could they, comrade? Food, the ultimate resource to control. We are dependent on your supplies and you are dependent on your exports. But I agree that far more must be involved here than merely the crop genetics Locke discovered at Sanii. The problem is finding out what."

"Locke learned the Committee was based in Austria. Will that help us?"

"Austria is a rather large country, comrade, but I'll start digging tomorrow. KGB computers should be able to obtain information pertaining to repeated trips into the country by certain individuals, perhaps some of whom are notable. This will eventually lead us to a list of potential Committee members."

"Sounds like a lengthy process."

"Too much so, I'm afraid," Vaslov acknowledged grimly. "And time is short, very short. There is one thing your report to me excluded: the World Hunger Conference, which will begin in a week."

"I didn't think it was important, just a random coincidence."

"Unfortunately it's anything but. Let us say all our speculations about the Committee launching a massive strike against both our nations are true. What would be the worst turn of events for them?"

Dogan thought through the silence. "Some sort of pact between us, I suppose. But that's inconceivable."

"Militarily perhaps, but not economically. From the intelligence I've recently been able to gather, that's where the purpose of the hunger conference lies: to announce a trade agreement between our two nations, the likes of which have never been seen before. Your President has determined quite accurately that the way to avoid war is through the stomach. Trade is being opened up for everything except your most advanced computer equipment. The Soviet Union is being granted favored-nation status in exchange for several political concessions, including a gradual pullout from Afghanistan."

"Food and politics—a potent mix."

"The best is yet to come. At the conference, delegations from our two nations will deliver a joint memorandum on plans to deal with feeding the world's starving people. Working together, our leaders believe we can accomplish anything, and in this case they might be correct. New supply lines will be made available, fertile land developed and cultivated where no crop has grown before."

"Which would totally negate the Committee's plans for South America."

"But as we know, comrade, far more is brewing here. The Committee did not choose their moment to strike at random. The hunger conference is the cue for them."

"And a unified front presented by the U.S. and Soviet Union would prove catastrophic to their ends."

"We cannot be sure of that until we are aware of all their means."

"But disruption of the conference might be part of their plan."

"They have used terrorism before. The daring message of this conference cannot be allowed to gain worldwide publicity. It does not suit their goals."

"The Committee's goals, yes, but what about the goals of our mysterious third party? Did you learn anything from the old hag's contacts?"

Vaslov sighed. "Not enough, unfortunately, and what I did learn is even more perplexing. The channels used to retain the old woman originated in South America."

"What about names, places?"

"Nothing specific. But the channels were ones used primarily by terrorist groups."

"You're saying a terrorist group based in South America is behind the repeated attempts on Locke's life?"

"I'm saying nothing. But the pattern is there. Everything fits." Frustration laced the Russian's voice. "Still, it makes no sense. My people in Moscow are experts in terrorism, originators of several of the groups behind it, and they assure me that no known group is behind this. The checks have been made. Nothing."

"Checks that would be superfluous if the group wasn't part of the international terror network."

"True. But where does that take us?"

"It takes me to the place where all this started: San Sebastian."

"The town has been obliterated."

"Someone must have seen or heard something. The answers are down there. I leave for Colombia later tonight."

"You're fishing, comrade."

"I'm desperate."

"We're all desperate but you are more so." Vaslov hesitated. "You are overdue by days with your report. Your superiors who so graciously reinstated you are no doubt aware that you have

180

totally disregarded your orders. And soon they will learn that you are aiding the very man you were supposed to take out. What do you suppose they will do about that, Grendel?''

Dogan didn't venture an answer.

The emergency meeting of the Committee's executive board began at ten o'clock at Kreuzenstein Castle.

''You have landed us in a terrible mess, Mr. Van Dam,'' Audra St. Clair snapped at the American representative.

Present in the dimly lit room were the same five people who had been at the table on Saturday. In addition, the sixth chair, which had been vacant at the last meeting, was today occupied by the the British representative.

Van Dam's lips trembled. ''I had to consider my own security.''

''And now you have violated all of ours,'' the chairwoman said. ''Mr. Mandala, please give us an appraisal of the damage.''

Mandala leaned forward, eyes consciously avoiding the American's. ''Locke arrived at Sanii as we expected. The plan was to have him captured and then allowed to escape so he might lead us to the Dwarf. But a man later identified as Ross Dogan, known in the field as Grendel, rescued him.''

''He was the one sent out on the sanction, Mr. Van Dam,'' St. Clair said.

''How should I know? I merely gave the order. How it was handled, who was sent out, I don't know.''

''I was not phrasing it as a question. Grendel *was* the man sent out, and we are all aware of his rather unique reputation. There is only one reason I can see to explain why Dogan would have disobeyed his assassination order, and that is he somehow learned that Locke was part of something greater. This is bad for us, Mr. Van Dam, very bad, and you are to blame. Locke is now allied with a top intelligence man and carrying with him all the knowledge we allowed him to obtain thinking it could only end up back with us. That scenario has been altered considerably. We can no longer control Locke's movements or even chart them. Grendel has replaced us as his guide.'' St. Clair turned to the British representative. ''How much would Felderberg have passed on?''

The Englishman shrugged. ''Information pertaining to our

181

land deals mostly. Nothing that Locke will be able to string together into any coherent pattern and no hint whatsoever as to the existence of Tantalus.''

"And what of Grendel? Remember, he now possesses every bit of information Locke does. He could be extremely dangerous to us.''

"Only if he were aware of our existence," the Englishman pointed out. "All he has to go on are rumors and vague conjecture.''

"He will piece the truth together," St. Clair said. "It's what men like Grendel specialize in. But it's not the damage he could personally do to us that concerns me. It is the possibility his suspicions might reach forces high up in the United States government.''

"That can be dealt with," Van Dam noted. "I can use Dogan's failure to obey orders as the basis for a quarantine order. He'll become an untouchable. That should prevent him from doing us any harm.''

"Elimination is the only way to assure that," said Mandala.

"If I make the quarantine order restricted, it will provide sanction for precisely that. Quite unofficial, you understand.''

"Yes, I understand, and your assurances mean nothing to me." Mandala's eyes darted from one Committee member to the next, locking finally with the chairwoman's. "Grendel's reputation and prowess will prevent any average agent from taking him out or even daring to try. He's extremely resourceful and he likes to kill. I suggest we go along with Mr. Van Dam's restricted quarantine strategy. I will insure the elimination is handled at the earliest possible time." Then, with a slight smile: "I have the perfect man for the job.''

"Of course, we'll have to find Dogan first," St. Clair said. "Any ideas on where to start?''

"Switzerland," the British representative suggested. "Dogan has many contacts there and its proximity to Liechtenstein makes it a logical refuge. But he won't stay in one place long. Locke's information will send him searching for answers.''

"Then perhaps we can get him through Locke," Mandala noted. "Finding our college professor should prove a far easier matter. I have the means to insure he cooperates with us fully and knowingly. Once his contribution has been made, I can have him eliminated as well.''

"Not a wise move," St. Clair said firmly, "for we must learn if he has contacted anyone else. We will learn nothing from Grendel, even if we are able to take him alive. Therefore, I want Locke kept alive and brought here. Is that understood, Mr. Mandala?''

Mandala nodded as convincingly as he could manage. He had no intentions of following any of the old bitch's orders unless they suited his plan. Her reign over the Committee was drawing to a close. His was about to begin. Mandala suppressed a smile.

"All right, then," St. Clair continued, addressing herself to all the men before her. "Bring all our intelligence forces to bear. Put out the call to all our contacts in the field, especially Switzerland." She paused. "It's a small world, gentlemen. Our quarries will not be out there for long."

Calvin Roy pressed his fingertips into his forehead, as if imprinting ten small permanent marks might relieve the frustrations of the past five days.

"Goddammit, Major Pete, that's not a whole helluva lot to go on. You're tellin' me all we got's the shit we started out with.''

"Liechtenstein was slow in responding, but we know now that Locke used his credit card number there to make a long-distance call. He dialed a number in England—Falmouth, to be exact. We've got the line tapped and the house under watch."

"Any more calls from our renegade professor?''

"Not a word.''

"What about to his home?''

Kennally shook his head. "I've covered Liechtenstein with agents. If Locke's still in there, we can't find him.''

"You ever walk across a plowed field at night, Major Pete? You can smell the shit something awful, but the idea is still not to step in it 'cause there's more places where it ain't than where it is. But those places where it is, they get ya every time. Same thing with Locke. We just gotta follow his trail.''

"He didn't leave one, Cal.''

Roy seemed not to hear him. "You find any strange occurrences in Liechtenstein immediately preceding Locke's phone call to England?"

"There was a murder," the CIA chief reported, "but the details are sketchy."

"Sketch 'em for me."

"A financier named Felderberg was killed. The Liechtenstein authorities aren't saying much but it's a safe bet there's nothing to link Locke with the murder."

Calvin Roy smiled and scratched his bald dome. "Right now, Major, I got the feeling that Locke and Felderberg are tied tighter together than bull's balls. What I don't get is how."

"Locke started out following Lubeck's trail," Louis Auschmann noted. "And we know Lubeck was in Liechtenstein at some point before San Sebastian. What if Locke's still following the trail? That would explain why he hasn't come in yet."

"But without Charney to run him, he would've needed help for that, Louie. What about our check of Charney's contacts in England?"

"A total blank."

"That ain't right. Makes no sense I can see. The connection's gotta be there. Still got the file, Louie?"

"In my office."

"Bring it over when you get a chance."

"You think we missed something?"

"Maybe," Roy replied. "We got any notion of where Lubeck went after Liechtenstein?"

"Florence, if he's following Lubeck's trail. But we have no way of knowing who he's going to meet there."

Roy nodded. "Throw our primary field forces into Florence, Major Pete. *Heavy* concentration. That's where Locke's headed."

"If he's still alive," from Kennally.

"Least his family still is. You pull them out like I ordered?"

Kennally hesitated. "There was a . . . complication."

Roy frowned. "Clean the shit off your shoes, Major, and tell me all about it."

*   *   *

184

The woman climbed into the backseat of the idling car and faced the big man with the black eyepatch.

"Our efforts to find Locke have led nowhere," she reported in Spanish.

"The old hag's reputation was excellent."

"The bastard Locke will pay," the woman spat out. "He'll pay for her death too."

"Self-defense," the one-eyed man offered, "is understandable."

"Why are you defending him? You of all—"

"Something isn't right here. It hasn't been from the beginning. I was never comfortable about London. Alvaradejo got off four shots before Locke took him out. And the cabdriver said that Locke was helped by a car crash more than anything else."

"Pablo's throat was cut ear to ear."

"You didn't read the autopsy report. The slice was delivered from low to high by a person barely five-and-a-half-feet tall. Locke is six one."

"A helper?" the woman asked, flustered.

The big man shook his head, fingered his eyepatch. "That doesn't fit. If Locke was as good as he must be to have been given this mission, others would be superfluous . . . unless it has all been an illusion."

"I don't understand."

"We were set up. Locke is nothing more than a decoy. We must act fast. It may already be too late."

"You think they know who we are?" the woman asked fearfully.

"Once they discover our identity, they will destroy us."

"The corpses, none carried IDs."

"They have been using other methods to flush us out all along. They have dangled Locke on a string and pulled him back when we got close. They have distracted us enough to buy themselves time. If they learn who we are, time won't matter. We will become the hunted."

"God . . ."

"We aren't finished yet," the big man insisted, his one eye narrowed. "Our base in Spain is secure, our remaining soldiers

185

safe. We will turn our attention to the conference and strike at them there."

"And then?"

"If we fail, there will be no 'then.' Not for us," he told the woman. "And not for South America."

The Commander laid his newspaper on the table at his regular café on the Champs-Élysées as he addressed the man across from him.

"You have made an admirable recovery."

Keyes grunted an acknowledgment. Words came hard for him. The ruined cartilage along his voice box smothered them before they could emerge. Syllables gurgled from his lips as if he had a mouth full of water, and each one burned the linings of his throat.

"I would like to give you an assignment," the Commander told him. "Are you up to it?"

Keyes nodded.

"The hand will not impede you?"

Keyes glanced down at the black glove pulled tight across his ruined hand to hide the twisted damage Dogan had done. Only time could help him now, the doctors told him. Fuck time, Keyes thought.

He shook his head.

"I want you to find Grendel and kill him. He has become an outcast and we wish to be rid of him." The Commander hesitated, relishing the perfect match of the man to the assignment. Word had been passed that a restricted quarantine had been placed on Dogan. But the Commander knew that was not quite sufficient. "I felt you would appreciate the assignment," the Commander resumed. "Of course, everything is unofficial, no reports to be filed or anything so trivial. Such things aren't done every day. Thus you will not have to provide explanations for any actions undertaken during the course of this assignment. Do whatever is necessary but do it fast. Understood?"

Keyes smiled.

PART SIX:

FLORENCE AND SAN SEBASTIAN,
TUESDAY AFTERNOON

CHAPTER 19

LOCKE COULDN'T BELIEVE IT WHEN DOGAN PRESENTED HIM WITH HIS passport Monday night.

"A Russian friend of mine retrieved it from the train station at Vaduz" was all he said. "Without it, travel at this point would prove extremely difficult."

"I thought you guys had contacts all over the world who could whip one up in no time."

"And all of them are being watched hoping I'll do just that."

"So I remain Sam Babbit."

"Felderberg was the only one who knew you under that name so it should be safe to keep it."

"Burgess knows about it too," Locke reminded him. "He set the identity up, and you expressed reservations about him before."

"But from what you've said, I doubt we have anything to fear from him. Besides, we haven't got much choice."

"Then maybe I should call the contact number and fill him in."

"No. By now someone has probably linked him to Charney, which means they'll be watching him. You'll only throw Burgess into more danger and risk exposing yourself at the same time."

Locke lowered his eyes to the ceramic floor of his room's balcony. "I suppose the same can be said about contacting my family."

"Even more so," Dogan said softly, trying to comfort Locke as best he could. "They would ask questions you couldn't answer, ask for reassurances you couldn't give. Worse, contacting them could place their lives in jeopardy."

"And what if that's already the case?" Locke demanded suddenly. "The Committee stops at nothing—you said that yourself. My family are sitting ducks for them."

"Only as leverage against you, leverage they didn't think they needed until yesterday and leverage that means nothing since they have no idea where you are. The Committee stops at nothing, true, but none of its motions are wasted. You can count on that."

"Excuse me if I don't." Locke sat down wearily. "God, this is crazy. A week ago I hated my life. Everything was falling apart and I would have grasped for anything just for the sake of change. That's probably what drove me to accept Charney's offer more than anything else. Now I find myself trapped in a labyrinth, and everywhere I turn there's another wall. This may sound nuts, but all of a sudden I realize maybe I didn't have it so bad. Maybe my problems at home weren't worse than anybody else's."

"I know how you feel."

"Do you? Do you have a life back in the States that you'll probably never make it back to?" Locke challenged, feeling guilty even before the hurt appeared on Dogan's face.

The agent looked away. "A family never meant much to me, just something to tie me down. We can't have that in my profession, can we?"

"Brian tried. It didn't work."

"It seldom does. The profession has to be everything." A bitter tone entered Dogan's voice. "Especially for me because I was the best. But the only thing being the best does for you is set you up as a target, for the opposition and for your own people. And it's your own people who are the worst. When you're too good, they start to fear you've gained too much control. That's when you become expendable. You work your whole career to attain something and then they take it away because to them you're just a machine; no, less than a machine—a number, a number they can delete from the central computer with one touch of a key. Then you don't exist anymore because maybe you never did in the first place."

Dogan was breathing uncharacteristically hard. Locke found himself smiling.

"Is this the moment we cry on each other's shoulders?"

Dogan chuckled, then checked his watch. "Not if I want to make my plane. It leaves for Bogotá in an hour and yours leaves for Rome tomorrow morning. After landing, you'll enjoy a scenic train route north into Florence. I've already contacted the Dwarf's people. He's expecting you."

"So I just walk right into his office and tell him you sent me. . . ."

"Hardly. Something seems to have spooked the little man rather badly and he's gone into hiding. You can bet it won't be easy to get into see him. He'll have you checked out carefully. It may be a long afternoon."

"I've heard Florence is beautiful this time of year."

"That's good because you might be seeing a lot of it. Standard procedure in this situation dictates you'll be run around a bit to make sure you're alone. Just follow their instructions. The Dwarf takes precautions, but if you cooperate, you'll see him."

"And then?"

"Back to Rome and the Hilton Hotel, where a reservation for you has already been made. You'll stay put there until you hear from me. We'll set up a contact code through the hotel manager. I've worked with him before and he's very reliable. If he doesn't present a warding-off signal, I'll know it's safe to come in. I don't expect to be in San Sebastian long anyway. I should be in Rome by late Wednesday with any luck."

"We haven't had much yet."

"We're alive, Chris, and that's a start."

Calvin Roy finished going over Brian Charney's file for the sixth time. The feeling that something was missing was still very strong in him. His eyes tired and bloodshot, Roy started his seventh survey.

What he sought was there, he felt certain of that. The problem was to find it. Proof positive that a high-security file had been tampered with could confirm his, and Charney's, greatest fears:

Whatever was happening had deep roots in the United States government.

Roy kept reading.

Charney would have sent Locke to someone in England, a person who had to be present in the dead agent's file. The key was there, the answer sure—

Roy's eyes froze. He went over the section a second time, a third. He flipped the page over and studied it closely.

He had found what he was looking for!

The file had been tampered with, all right. The evidence was quite clear. The question was why? And by whom? Something was very wrong here and somehow an innocent college professor had been thrust into the middle. Roy reached for his phone and hit one button.

"This is Roy. Put me through to the Secretary on the scrambler, wherever the hell he is."

Locke's train from Rome deposited him in Florence at four o'clock in the afternoon. The trip had been hectic but, incredibly, nothing had gone wrong. He hailed a cab and gave the driver his destination: the Palazzo Vecchio. Chris felt he was prepared for anything.

The palazzo was a medieval palace in a large piazza. Its single tower rose the length of a football field into the sky and featured a huge, ancient clock. Statues of varying sizes and constructions adorned the palazzo's front, while its insides were dominated by artistic treasures unaffected by the centuries. Locke would not be entering, though. His instructions were to wait outside among the statues, pigeons, and horse-drawn carriages. He mingled with the natives and other tourists. Someone would contact him there. Chris had to make himself seen but not obvious.

He was strolling amid the pigeons, amused by their boldness, when a horse-drawn carriage pulled up near him.

"A ride, mister?" the driver asked in poor English.

"No thanks," Locke said, turning away.

"A ride, mister?" the driver repeated.

"Not right now," Locke said as politely as he could manage.

The driver smiled faintly and moved his right arm over the side of the carriage, holding the reins with only his left.

"A ride, mister?" he repeated a third time.

"Look, I told you—"

Locke's eyes strayed down and fixed upon a tattoo on the driver's right forearm, an impression of a small man standing between two large ones. A very small man.

A dwarf.

Locke looked up. The driver winked.

"A ride, mister?" he offered yet again, and this time Chris climbed into the back.

The horse trotted through the center of the old city, undaunted by the small cars surging past blaring their horns. The horse pranced as if it owned the streets and the machines were intruding. Soon it passed onto narrow streets where automobile traffic was prohibited. The ride lasted just over five minutes and ended in a square before what Chris recognized as the famed Baptistery, one of the oldest buildings in Florence. The driver yanked the reins hard, thrusting Chris forward a little. The man signaled him to get out. Locke reached into his pocket for some of the *lire* he had obtained in Zurich, but the man waved him off and slapped the horse gently with the reins, taking his leave.

Locke moved into the square.

The Baptistery was a striking, octagonal building made of different-color marbles and surrounded by a collection of pilasters that supported its arches. Locke started toward it, watching the numerous pigeons maneuver to avoid his feet without giving up their precious share of ground and breadcrumbs. An old, white-haired woman tossed feed to the birds by the handful, and their movements were dictated by the motions of her fingers.

Chris passed her and felt a batch of crumbs fall against his feet. The pigeons approached tentatively, grabbing their feed but pecking clear of his pants and shoes. Locke looked up at the old woman to find her sauntering away. He looked back down. A rolled-up piece of paper rested between his feet. Cautiously he knelt down and retrieved it, keeping it hidden from anyone close by as he unrolled it. The paper's few words provided his next destination:

Uffizi Gallery, Madonna Enthroned . . .

The gallery was located back near the Palazzo Vecchio in the Square of the Uffizi. It contained some of the greatest art treasures in the world, the *Madonna Enthroned* by Giotto as great as any. As he snared a cab back beyond the Baptistery square, he mused that the Dwarf must be an art lover.

Because it could not use the mall streets and had to negotiate through dense traffic, the cab took ten minutes to get him to the Uffizi Gallery. The gallery was surprisingly empty and Locke had no trouble locating the massive *Madonna*. The painting dominated an entire wall, which Chris had all to himself. He was glancing at the painting, expecting a nudge to his shoulder or note stuck in his pocket, when he noticed a flicker of white sticking out from beneath the *Madonna's* frame. Pretending to inspect the wood, he reached under and snatched it free. An envelope! Glancing around him to reassure himself no one was watching, Locke withdrew its contents.

West side of Ponte Vecchio Bridge. White Alfa Romeo.

The walk across the bridge, past a variety of open-air shops set up along it, took only ten minutes but seemed much longer. The spring warmth of Florence had begun to take its toll on Chris. His shirt was soaked through with sweat and he resisted the temptation to strip off his jacket for fear it might cause the Dwarf's men to lose him. His mouth was dry and he was horribly thirsty. He realized his last drink had been a mouthful of water from a fountain before boarding the train from Rome.

Locke reached the far side of the bridge. An engine kicked on somewhere up the narrow street. Locke swung quickly, senses alert.

A white Alfa Romeo was inching its way into traffic. It stopped right next to Chris, doors snapping unlocked. He couldn't make out the driver clearly through the tinted glass, but he opened a rear door and climbed into the backseat anyway.

"Good afternoon, Mr. Locke. We are satisfied you are who you say you are and that you have come alone," the driver said in decent English. Locke was about to respond when he spoke again. "I will take you to the Dwarf now."

They followed a winding road as it bent around the bank of

the Arno River, then swung right into the hills above the ancient city. They wound up a road enclosed by lavish greenery, cars coming from the opposite direction seeming to miss the Alpha only by inches. Locke flinched with each pass. The driver seemed unbothered. Before long, he turned onto a private road and a sign made their destination clear: FORTE DI BELVEDERE.

The driver disregarded a smaller sign beneath it announcing *Chiuso in Restauro* and continued on until they reached four armed guards at the fort's entrance waiting to meet any tourists who had not heeded the earlier warning. One of the guards spoke briefly in Italian to the Alfa's driver, a chain was lowered, and the car slid forward into an impenetrable fortress built nearly four hundred years before.

The Forte di Belvedere consisted of one large central building surrounded by huge fortified parapets offering a fantastic view of the city below and the hills in which it was nestled. Obviously, though, the Dwarf had chosen it for its strategic advantages rather than its aesthetic ones. The Alfa came to a halt and Locke noticed a makeshift tent set up in the center of the fortress's courtyard. A small man eyed him from beneath it. A giant flanked him on either side.

Locke stepped out of the car and was met by a smiling, tanned man with a rifle slung over his shoulder.

"Welcome to Florence, Mr. Locke. We apologize for any inconvenience our precautions may have caused, but I'm afraid I must now also ask you to submit to a search."

Chris obliged and as the hands ruffled along his body and clothes, he noticed far more precautions had been taken. Stationed on the parapets were a number of armed men. A sandbagged station at each end was occupied by two men and a tripod-held heavy machine gun. The guards were everywhere, including on the roof of the central building and in the bell tower. The Dwarf was prepared to fend off a full-scale attack.

"You approve of my choice of retreat, Mr. Locke?"

The hands holding Chris allowed him to turn round and face the small man behind him.

"I'm happy to be at your service," the Dwarf pronounced, extending a thick, miniature hand.

195

Locke took it and found the grasp surprisingly firm. The Dwarf's features were not twisted or scarred at all. Instead, his face was dominated by a perfectly trimmed mustache and goatee, eyes above it full but somehow tired. He wore gray slacks and a blue sports shirt.

"I'm impressed," Locke said, glancing around him.

The Dwarf followed his eyes. "This structure was originally built to protect Grand Duke Ferdinand I. I appropriated it recently because it remains a superb defensive fortress. You can't be too careful these days."

"Especially with the information you possess."

The Dwarf's eyes dimmed. "I possess much information, Mr. Locke, and every piece of it brands me someone's enemy. In my business there are no friends, only associates. No matter. People have never done anything but disdain me. So I turned to art and history. There I found a refuge where size didn't matter and prejudice never entered in. You should see my villa, Mr. Locke. I make vast sums of money and great portions of it go into the purchase of original art treasures. There are days when I do nothing else but stare at them, trying to appreciate their fantastic beauty. They are timeless and exquisite, a welcome relief from my dealings with men." The Dwarf took a deep breath. "But you have not come all this way to listen to my ramblings. We shall get out of this hot sun. You look thirsty."

Locke kept his pace slow to allow the Dwarf to keep up with him. The little man's legs were turned outward at the knees, and Locke detected a slight grimace with each step. But not a single complaint emerged from his host's lips. They moved into the cool shade provided by the tent and sat down at a table. The Dwarf's guards backed off a little but their eyes remained alert.

"What would you like to drink?" the Dwarf asked.

"Anything cold and nonalcoholic."

"Two iced teas," the Dwarf called behind him. "Bring a pitcher." Then his eyes returned to Locke. "You have nothing to fear from my guards. They are here to ward off any assault on the part of the Committee."

Locke tried to wet his lips, but his tongue was also dry. "You know that's why I've come here."

"Dogan hinted as much but I wasn't sure until I saw the fear in your eyes when I mentioned their name. The Committee is quite good at stirring fear in men's souls, though few live long enough to express it. My compliments in that respect, Mr. Locke."

Chris shrugged his thanks. "Felderberg believed you'd know much about them. He sent me to you just as he sent my friend Lubeck."

"And now both of them are dead. An unfortunate legacy."

"I don't plan on joining them."

"And you won't if I can help it. But first you must highlight for me what you have learned so far."

When Chris finished, the Dwarf was nodding. "You are to be complimented on your resourcefulness, Mr. Locke, and now I will tell you just what I told your friend. But beware of information. It's like an anchor. After you have dragged it from the water, it must be carried on your back."

Strangely, Locke didn't feel frightened, just more determined. "But the weight can be spread out. Knowledge can balance it."

The Dwarf looked impressed. "Spoken like a true scholar."

"A long time ago I used to be a college professor."

"I know," said the Dwarf with a slight smile.

A burly man set down a tray containing two glasses and a pitcher misted with ice. He filled both glasses with iced tea, allowing several cubes to slide out and clink together.

"I was never involved with the Committee in a direct sense," the Dwarf began. "I was one of many middlemen retained by them for a specific purpose, in this case to provide sensitive information pertaining to certain South American leaders."

"For purposes of blackmail?"

"And assassination. Sooner or later the land deals Felderberg spoke of had to be extended beyond paper transactions into active development. At that point governments would raise questions, present barriers, create inconveniences." The Dwarf sipped his tea. "Consider, Mr. Locke, that the Committee is trying to achieve in South America what no one has ever dared attempt before: the fullest development of its agricultural resources. But the land is spread out, much of it isolated. To achieve their full goal of production and export, then, a strong central organization was necessary, apart from and above the governments of the individual nations. They needed *absolute* control.''

"So leaders were replaced.''

"Entire governments were toppled. Check the pattern of communist-terrorist activities in that part of the world. It was too precise, too organized to be random.''

"Organized by the Soviets, most thought.''

"Which is exactly what the Committe wanted people to think. The Soviets were responsible for enough of it to provide the screen, and they deny everything anyway. The Committee has mastered the art of misdirection. That explains how they have survived unnoticed for so long. Much of the unrest in South America was arranged by the Committee to distract attention from what was really going on.''

"And to place puppet leaders in positions where they could manipulate decisions and affect policy.''

"All toward the successful end of the operation you have stumbled upon,'' the Dwarf completed. "Exactly, Mr. Locke. I'm impressed with the degree of expertise you've gained.''

Chris took several large gulps of his iced tea and reached for the pitcher. "Desperation makes a better teacher than I could ever be.''

The Dwarf leaned forward. "And now we come to the greatest lesson of all: What was the Committee to do about North America? Here they were with millions of farmable acres and a means of turning them full of crops almost overnight. Yet the United States presented a seemingly impenetrable obstacle, for how could they possibly hope to compete with the world's greatest crop producer? A factor was missing.''

"Something to do with the U.S. no doubt.''

"Yes,'' the Dwarf acknowledged. "Its economic destruction.''

CHAPTER 20

THE GLASS OF ICED TEA SLIPPED AND TILTED IN CHRIS'S HAND. A pair of ice cubes toppled over the side to the ground below.

"Understand, Mr. Locke," the Dwarf continued, "I have no proof of this, only speculation. But the evidence exists and it is overwhelming. To begin with, the Committee has been moving its vast deposits from U.S. banks for some time now. The process has been too gradual to stand out, but billions and billions have been either withdrawn or divested from U.S. holdings. Much of the money has shown up in Euro-dollar transfers and in new accounts from England to Switzerland. But more has been used to purchase gold, diamonds, silver, even oil resources, along with tremendous quantities of land all over the world."

"All natural resources . . ."

"As if an impending collapse of the dollar-based economy was imminent."

"Inevitable because the Committee made it so. But how?"

"That I don't know," the Dwarf replied. "All I have is a word one of my people stumbled upon in the course of work: *Tantalus.*"

Locke's eyebrows flickered. "Greek mythology . . ."

"Then the term is familiar to you."

Locke nodded. "The Gods punished Tantalus for his crimes by placing him chin-deep in water he couldn't drink. Over his head were fruit-filled branches he couldn't reach. It's where the word tantalize comes from."

199

"Yes," added the Dwarf, "and as I recall the punishment was to last for eternity."

"With no chance for a reprieve. But what does that tell us about the Committee's plan?"

"Their recent financial resettlements indicate a plot to render the United States as helpless as Tantalus was in determining its own fate."

"Food," Locke muttered. "The allusions all come back to food. Food that can't be eaten, lying out of reach for . . ."

"Eternity," the Dwarf completed.

Locke returned to Rome some hours later on a private plane arranged for by the Dwarf. The shape of what he was facing was clear now, and he found himself more frightened than ever.

Tantalus. . . .

The Dwarf's portrait of the Committee painted them as invulnerable. This was the ultimate criminal organization, for its crimes lay less in action than in the ways in which forces around them were manipulated. Those ways were always subtle, the shadowy sublayer behind them hiding their true intentions behind screen after screen.

In the cab from the airport to the Rome Hilton, Locke determined Dogan was probably in San Sebastian by then and his family was God knows where. It was afternoon in Washington. If all was well, Greg would be dragging through the last hours of school thinking about baseball practice, Whitney would be passing notes in math, Bobby would be pounding out guitar riffs, and Beth would be showing a house in Bethesda. Locke prayed that was the way things were because it would mean the Committee hadn't touched them.

He'd know for sure soon enough, because he was heading home. As soon as Dogan reached Rome, Chris would advise him of his plans and refuse to be talked out of them. Charney told him to trust no one. The arguments had seemed valid when the enemy had been merely a shadowy outline. But now that enemy had taken a shape that held terrifying implications. Someone in Washington would listen. Information relayed by the

Dwarf and Felderberg could be confirmed. The Committee would not be allowed to condemn the world to the fate of Tantalus.

Locke checked into the Hilton exhausted, craving a shower and a long sleep with the air conditioning turned on high. He had only the one bag from the Vaduz Station locker that Dogan had returned to him, so he told the desk clerk a bellhop would be unnecessary; the fewer people who saw him, the better.

His room was on the sixth floor, and in his fatigue he neglected to press the proper button in the elevator until it stopped on two. Four floors later he moved thoughtlessly for his room. The key slid in easily, the door just clearing the carpet as he swung it open.

A light was on in the far corner. A shape was seated not far from it.

"Good evening, Mr. Locke," greeted the shape.

Panic seized Chris and blood rushed to his head. He swung quickly back toward the door and found himself facing the biggest man he had ever seen.

The giant stepped forward. Locke moved backward. The giant, a grinning Chinese wearing a white suit, closed the door and threw the bolt.

"We have some business to transact, Mr. Locke" came the voice of the shape, and Locke turned back toward it. The speaker was on his feet now. He was a tall, striking man with perfectly styled jet-black hair and dark eyes. A cigarette in a gold holder danced in his right hand. The man pressed the cigarette out in an ashtray. His features were not American, European, or Oriental but somehow a combination of all three.

"Who are you?"

"Ah." The dark man smiled and Locke felt the giant draw up close to his rear. "The standard question. Who I am doesn't matter," the man continued. "I suspect you know who I represent."

Locke said nothing.

"The Committee is most unhappy with this crusade you've been waging. We thought we'd give you the opportunity to agree to a business arrangement between us. You possess some information we wish to purchase."

Locke held his ground, coiling his fingers into fists to still their trembling. Escape was clearly impossible. His greatest weapon was his calm, *if* he could keep it.

"A purchase implies you have something to offer in return," he said coolly.

"An accurate analysis." The dark man's eyes moved toward the giant. "Show him, Shang."

Locke turned in time to see the Chinese giant pull a handkerchief from his pocket. He unraveled the layers and held it forward for Locke to see its contents.

Chris saw the blood first, dried and purple, and then the object.

Bile bubbled in his throat. The object was a small finger with a—

"Oh, my God!"

—ring still wedged past the middle joint. Greg's Little League championship ring.

"We offer the life of your son," Mandala said flatly.

But Locke had already sank to his knees, opening his mouth for a scream that was choked off by the giant's hand.

The jeep crept down the last of the desolate stretch toward what remained of San Sebastian. Dogan could still smell the residue from the fire in the air, could feel the death it had brought in the hot wind. The closer the jeep drew to the site of the massacre, the more uncomfortable he became.

At the wheel was Marna Colby, a CIA operative who had spent the last four years at substations throughout South America and the six before that working under Dogan at Division Six. There were few women he had ever allowed himself to become attracted to; Marna was one of them because she tempered tenderness with strength. Dogan responded best to strength and a woman who showed it. Marna was as brave and skillful an operative as he'd ever worked with, and he had genuinely lamented her reassignment, both for her talents in the field and in bed. For Dogan, sex had seldom proved fulfilling. Marna provided an exception. But sex was the furthest thing from their minds now.

The jeep had behaved like a loyal animal, pushing past or climbing over debris tossed into the road by the fire. One mile before they reached the remains of the town, the vehicle met its match in a series of huge branches charred black as charcoal. They climbed out and started walking.

"Why so much interest from Division over a dead town?" Marna prodded Dogan. "I know we're the last to hear things down here but if San Sebastian's important, I should have been informed."

"The interest isn't Division's, it's mine. And the interest comes from the hope that the dead might be able to tell me what the living can't."

"It's good you're not expecting to find anyone alive. The fire got them all."

"Something else got them all. The fire was just a cover."

Dogan's grim tone silenced her as much as his words. They continued walking, and with each step Dogan felt his heart thudding harder. Death was something you never got used to, and he could feel the agony of those butchered in the hail of bullets Lubeck had described. Maybe their ghosts walked the charred land. Maybe they could tell him what the hell it all meant.

Finally they reached an empty piece of land marked with pieces of San Sebastian. What was left of a church bell lay half embedded in the ground, the crude foundations of collapsed buildings were now graves. Dogan moved past the church bell into the center of town and stopped with Marna lagging several yards back. The authorities had already stripped the ground free of bones but it didn't matter. The feeling was still present.

"It happened here," he said absently. "The massacre happened here."

"Massacre? What are you talking about?"

If Dogan heard her, he didn't show it. He drifted about slowly, kicking at the dirt with his feet, occasionally lifting a charred piece of wood as if expecting a survivor to lie beneath it. He glanced around him.

"Lubeck must have been sitting on one of those hills, probably with his back to the sun so it would be in the eyes of anyone who looked up in his direction. He watched them all shot. He saw it all."

"Shot?" Marna swallowed hard. "I wasn't told anything about that. Christ, you're talking about a town of two hundred and fifty people. I thought you said Division wasn't interested in this."

"They're not."

"Then why—"

Dogan swung toward her, the intensity of his stare making her break off her words. "Listen to me, Marna, this is part of something much bigger. All of South America might be at stake."

She regarded him strangely. "You sound like Masvidal."

"Who?"

"Masvidal. He's the one-eyed leader of a bunch of terrorist Robin Hoods. They see themselves as the saviors of the continent."

"Terrorists?" Dogan said softly, and suddenly everything fell into place. He had found the mysterious third party who had been trying so desperately to kill Christopher Locke. "Who are they?" he demanded. "What's their name?"

"They call themselves SAS-Ultra. The SAS stands for South American Solidarity. They're dedicated, or claim to be anyway, to freeing these countries from any foreign intervention whatsoever. The Carter Doctrine was prime fuel for their fire, but they've got a gut hatred for the Soviets and Cubans as well. I guess you could say they choose their enemies without prejudice."

"But they're not part of the international terror network?"

"No," Marna acknowledged, "they're the ultimate revolutionary isolationists. They even loathe publicity. I only know about them from some investigations I was pursuing on the destruction of oil fields in Paraguay. It turned up more questions than answers. I haven't even got enough to file a report on them yet."

"What about Interpol or the CIA data banks?"

Marna shook her head. "Nothing. Officially, SAS-Ultra doesn't exist."

No wonder Vaslov found no trace of them, Dogan realized. The wind swirled through the town, its howling sounding too much like the screams of a child. Dogan suppressed a shudder. Marna wrapped her arms about herself.

"But a group that wide in composition," Dogan started, "would take one hell of a central organization."

"Masvidal is mostly to blame for that." Marna's eyes swept the dead town. "But you can forget about his troops having anything to do with what happened here. The people who were killed in this . . . massacre are the kind SAS-Ultra's been fighting for, not against, if I've got my signals straight."

Dogan thought briefly. "But how do you suppose they'd react if a group as powerful as any nation moved in and started . . ." He grasped for a way of accurately describing the Committee's methods. ". . . manipulating things? Displacing people and taking over huge acres of land for their own benefit?"

Marna didn't hesitate. "I think they'd go at them with everything they had."

It made sense, Dogan figured. SAS-Ultra was not part of San Sebastian but they were tied directly to the larger picture.

Kill me and another will replace me.

The threat the old hag in Schaan had shouted at Locke. Yes, SAS-Ultra possessed an inexhaustible supply of fanatical manpower, if not their own, then hired out from across the globe. The Committee had been using Locke all along to flush them out, and SAS-Ultra had responded by repeatedly trying to kill an innocent college professor made to look like their enemy. Sooner or later, the Committee would find and destroy them.

Dogan looked beyond the edge of town to huge patches of dust between a pair of hillsides, a graveyard for the crops that had burned along with the people who nurtured them. Wordlessly he started walking, and Marna followed. Dogan moved right into the center of the dust patches, squinting his eyes against the wind. The ground was hard and parched. He felt a softening in his stomach. Here lay the key to everything, the missing piece of the puzzle. If only the ground could tell him what horrible things had been done here before the massacre.

Suddenly Marna was at his side, grasping his elbow.

"Up there, high on that hillside."

Dogan held a hand over his eyes to shield them from the sun.

He made out what looked to be a small shack camouflaged among what remained of the flora.

"An old shack," he noted. "Why the sudden concern?"

"Because it wasn't there last week."

CHAPTER 21

"THIS DOESN'T HAVE TO BE DIFFICULT," MANDALA SAID CALMLY AS the giant Chinese lifted Locke onto a chair near a round table in the back of the room.

The balcony's glass doors were slightly open and a cool breeze slid through, awakening him to the madness.

They've got Greg! Oh, God, they've got Greg!

Thoughts of the severed finger, ring and all, sent a shudder through him. He couldn't stop shaking.

Mandala nodded to Shang and the giant started for the door, grabbing something from the dresser on the way. Mandala showed his gun. Locke noticed all lights in the room had been turned off except for a powerful pole lamp directly over him.

"You have turned into quite an inconvenience for us," Mandala said evenly. "But you can make up for that now. Your son will be released. You as well. All you have to do is answer a few questions."

Locke looked away from the dark man, flirted with the notion of jumping him while the giant was still gone, but dismissed it quickly after considering the gun. The man held it tightly, just out of range of a quick lunge. He was a professional and not about to be taken by a fool's act.

"Come now, Mr. Locke, you don't want to make things any more hard on yourself than they already are. Why bother resisting? It is too late for you to do us any harm. We are unstoppable now. Only a few holes remain to be filled and we need you to point them out for us."

Locke remained silent.

"Do you want further reassurances that your son will be released? I can't give them. All I can give you is the promise that his finger might be only the beginning. If you don't cooperate with us, we will cut him apart piece by piece."

The door opened and Shang returned with a white plastic bucket in his hand. Mandala returned the pistol to his belt. The giant's presence was a better deterrent than bullets.

"You see, Mr. Locke," Mandala proceeded, "your son is being held by a team of Shang's persuasion—experts in torture. They can remove any limb without the subject even passing out. Amazing, isn't it? Tricks of the dreaded Tong Society, which was Shang's first employer."

The giant lowered the plastic bucket to the table. It was filled with ice. Locke kept himself calm but left the fear plain on his face. He had to convince them he would give in. His chance would come, an opening to be taken advantage of. To create that opening, he had to make his captors underestimate him.

The giant grinned.

"Shang is quite an expert at torture himself, Mr. Locke. In fact, he quite enjoys it. But sensible men like ourselves are too civilized for such base undertakings, aren't we? Simple answers to simple questions and Shang will stay just as he is." Mandala settled himself in the chair across from Locke. "Now let us begin. You visited the Dwarf in Florence. Where is he hiding?"

Locke swallowed hard, said nothing.

"Where is he hiding, Mr. Locke?"

Still no reply.

Mandala shook his head as if disappointed. "We know you met with the Dwarf, Mr. Locke. Where can we find him?"

Locke bit his lip to stop it from trembling."

"Shang!"

In an instant the giant had leaned over Locke's shoulder and grabbed his left hand, still bandaged from the wounds inflicted by the hag's teeth in Schaan. Shang ripped the dressing off and grabbed the left pinky in one massive hand, clamping the other over the back of Locke's hand.

"Pain, Mr. Locke, is a great persuader," the dark man said

softly. "It is most effective when the level starts relatively low and is then increased gradually. I believe you must be given a sample." He nodded.

Shang bent the pinky finger back viciously until it snapped at the joint. Agony exploded through Locke's hand and his teeth sliced through a section of his tongue. He had started to scream when the giant's hand covered his mouth and forced back his breath. Blood bubbled in his ears. His left hand was trembling horribly. His pinky was bent at a sickening angle. The pain remained intense. Locke steeled himself against it as best he could.

"As I said, Mr. Locke, just a sample," the dark man explained. "It gets much worse from here." He grabbed Locke's battered hand almost tenderly and lowered it into the bucket of ice, covering the mangled pinky with cubes. The numbing started almost immediately, the pain retreating. "Relief is that simple. The comfort can continue in place of the pain. Just answer the question. Where is the Dwarf?"

Inside Locke wanted to answer but he couldn't let himself weaken. He focused on Greg and what they had done to him to maintain his rage, and thus his strength.

"Very well, Mr. Locke, I will give you the benefit of the doubt on that one," Mandala said patiently. "We will turn our attention to more important matters. Where is Grendel?"

Locke stayed silent.

"Where is the man you know as Ross Dogan?"

Chris wet his trembling lips.

"He is meeting you here soon, isn't he? All we have to do is wait and he will come walking in."

Locke looked away.

I'll kill you for what you did to Greg. Somehow, someway . . .

"No," the dark man continued, "he has gone somewhere, hasn't he? He is looking for evidence to tell him what is going on. Tell us where he has gone, Mr. Locke, tell us where."

Chris just stared vacantly ahead.

Mandala nodded quickly.

Shang snatched Locke's hand brutally from the ice and slammed it down on the table, clamping it there. The pain returned with a rush, exploding through the swelling portion of his hand. The giant was grasping his ring finger now.

"Where can we find Grendel?"

When Locke stayed silent, the dark man nodded again.

Chris closed his eyes, feeling Shang's hand tighten and lift. The snap sounded like glass breaking. The pain exploded everywhere and a kaleidoscope of colors burst before his closed eyes. He opened them to the sight of crackling silver lights. A scream rose within him, which the giant promptly choked off.

Breathing hard, Locke glanced down at his two ruined fingers, twin distortions cracked clean at the joint. The pain was battering his head. He had never experienced anything like it.

Mandala seemed to read his mind. "Yes, it hurts quite horribly, doesn't it, Mr. Locke? Yet we are at the early stages of our evening. Would you like to hear what follows if you continue to be stubborn? We will repeat this process with two fingers on your right hand, and if you still persist we will be forced to become more . . . persuasive." Suddenly Shang was flashing a knife in his hand. "You have undoubtedly heard of the Chinese torture in which the fingers are severed one knuckle at a time. Shang prefers a cruder version of this. The knife he is holding is a more elaborate version of a kitchen paring knife. He is a specialist in cutting the flesh away *layer by layer* until he reaches bone. One finger at a time. And you will not pass out, Mr. Locke. He will see to that."

Locke shuddered again, seized by a fear greater than any he thought could exist. These men were animals, brutal killers of woman and children, torturers. Dogan had described the Committee as being civilized, organized toward accomplishing their ends economically instead of with violence. Well, perhaps the architects of the Committee held to that credo, but the men they retained as soldiers simply ignored it. Locke knew he had to act while he still retained a measure of his senses. Any further agony might ruin his response and thought processes. He couldn't afford that.

The dark man was lifting his mangled hand back into the ice. It stung his flesh at first but relief came quickly again after his skin grew accustomed to being pricked at by the sharp edges of the ice.

Sharp edges . . . Yes, it might work! But there were two men to consider. If only one of them would leave the room or at least back off. If only . . .

"Where is Grendel, Mr. Locke?" the dark man asked him. "Come now, my patience is wearing thin and so, I trust, is your tolerance of pain. Let us end this stupidity. We will find him whether you help us or not. How can you possibly think you can stay clear of us? We are everywhere."

Mandala paused to let his words sink in.

We are everywhere. . . .

Charney had said that too, and suddenly Locke saw the reality of his situation with stunning clarity. Nothing he could say here could save Greg's life. If the boy was still alive. If he escaped, though, they might need to keep the boy alive to use as leverage against him later. It was time to move. Now!

"Where is Grendel, Mr. Locke? I will ask you one—"

Locke acted. Grasping the rim of the ice bucket as best he could with his twisted hand, he brought it up and over his shoulder, smashing it hard into the giant's face in the hope that an edge might find Shang's eyes. The giant reeled backward.

As the dark man rose and went for his gun, Chris snapped to his feet, left side angling toward him. His next move astounded himself even more than it did Mandala. He used his ruined hand for the assault, not for surprise but simply because it was the closest, chopping hard into the bridge of the dark man's nose. It was hard to tell at impact whose pain was greater. Locke screamed in terrible agony but still managed to tear the pistol from Mandala's hand before the dark man pitched backward. Chris turned it on Shang, who was charging back toward him.

Locke fired into his midsection, emptying the clip, the roar of the bullets sandblasting his ears. The giant slammed into the dresser and knocked it over with him to the carpet.

The dark man was lunging for him. Locke twisted around the table and kicked him first in the stomach and then under the chin as he keeled over, slamming him against the wall. Wasting no time, Chris dropped the gun and scampered toward the narrow

211

opening in the glass doors, ducked behind the curtains, and slid the doors open enough to pass through.

The fresh air sharpened his senses. He had to get off the balcony. The question was how. A leap to one of the neighboring structures was fifteen feet at least; out of the question. A drop to the floor below was at least that much and at a difficult angle to boot. But he could manage it if he could swing himself beneath this balcony properly and work up enough momentum.

Locke gripped the balcony railing with his ruined hand. It seemed to catch fire. The pain brought floods of tears to his eyes and the swelling made a sure grip impossible. He did the best he could, lowering himself until his legs were stretched toward the ground six stories below, hands supporting his entire weight.

The pain in his broken fingers was worse than he could have imagined and he grimaced against it, starting to sway back and forth, trying for enough impetus forward so that when he dropped, the angle would carry him to a safe landing on the balcony below. Incredibly, it seemed to be working, each sweep bringing him closer over his target.

Then a massive hand reached over the railing.

Locke looked up and saw the Chinese giant. Six bullets in the gut and still alive! Black powder burns dotted his white suit jacket but no splatters of blood surrounded them.

Why didn't you die? Locke wanted to scream.

But he couldn't waste the effort. His final swing was almost complete when the giant's hand found his hair.

Chris's legs carried him well beneath the balcony, and out of reflex he let go his hands an instant before Shang's grasp on his hair became firm. Then he was falling, unsure in that drawn-out moment whether his movement had carried him far enough or if he would drop sixty feet to oblivion.

He landed hard on the balcony tile below, breaking the fall with his left side and sending bolts of electric agony right through to his brain. His eyes dimmed and he felt himself hitting a wrought-iron table. But he couldn't give in to the pain or the force of impact, couldn't let himself forget Greg and what they had done to him.

Chris pushed himself back to his feet and staggered to the glass doors of the room directly beneath the one he had escaped from.

They were locked.

He picked up one of the wrought-iron balcony chairs, taking as much of its weight as he could in his right hand, and smashed it against the glass door. It shattered into a spider-web pattern on the first thrust and gave way on the second. Locke reached inside, unbolted the door, and slid it open.

He rushed through it into the darkness of the room without stopping. Shapes were indistinct, and he did his best to avoid them. A footpost of the bed nearly tripped him up and he wondered madly if someone there might be asleep. No matter. He was in the corridor an instant later holding his breath against the very real possibility that Shang and Mandala would smash into him around the next turn.

Footsteps pounded the floor in the corridor immediately ahead of him. Locke turned onto another hall and bolted for the first exit sign he saw. He wasn't sure if his pursuers saw him as they passed and didn't bother thinking about it. Instinctively his feet carried him up to the floor he had just left. They wouldn't expect that. An amateur's move would have been to make a straight line for the lobby and a desperate escape. But he wasn't an amateur any longer. They would still consider him one, and that was the best thing he had working on his side.

He emerged back on the sixth floor with no plan of what to do next. He couldn't stay in the open. The dark man could have people scouring the hotel even now. He would be spotted too easily. A room, he had to get into a room. But how?

If you're in trouble, contact the hotel manager. Tell him you work for the Grendel Corporation and your room isn't satisfactory.

Some of Dogan's last words to him. But to get to a phone he had to first get into a room, which put him back where he started. Locke kept himself moving. There had to be something, some way to—

He saw a maid with a towel cart close a door behind her. She was doubtless on her nightly rounds to turn down beds and replenish bathroom supplies. That was it!

Locke started to tuck his shirt back tight into his pants, briefly forgetting about his swollen hand. The agony bit into him like a sharp knife. He withdrew his left hand from his pants slowly and set about tucking the rest of his shirt in with his right. Satisfied, he started down the corridor whistling, his pace that of a contented tourist.

The maid had just stopped her cart in front of another room and was sliding her passkey into the door.

"What timing," Locke announced buoyantly, pretending to tuck a nonexistent key back into his pocket. "I need two glasses."

Startled, the maid looked at him. She didn't speak English well, if at all.

"Glasses," Locke said slower, pointing to a tray of paper-wrapped ones on her cart and stealing a glance back down the corridor.

The maid nodded her understanding and handed him two.

"Anything else?" she tried to say in English.

Chris shook his head and thanked her, already inside the room and closing the door behind him. He glanced quickly about to assure himself he was alone, then hurried over to the phone. His left hand was still ravaged by pain and he could feel the sweat dripping from his brow.

"Front desk."

"I'd like to speak to the manager please."

"I'm afraid he's busy at the moment. Is there something I can help you with?"

"No. I need the manager," Locke insisted.

"If you leave your name and room number, I'll—"

"This is an emergency, *goddammit*!"

The clerk hesitated. "Hold for a moment please."

Seconds passed with agonizing slowness. Chris's eyes fixed themselves on the door, expecting Shang to burst through it any moment.

"This is the manager" came a male voice in Italian-laced English.

"This is Mr. Locke. I work for the Grendel Corporation and my room isn't satisfactory."

A short pause.

"What room are you in, Mr. Locke?"

214

Chris eyed the number on the phone. "Six twenty-seven."

Another pause, longer this time.

"My records show that is not the room you checked into."

"Circumstances forced me to move."

"Very well. Stay where you are. I'll be up presently."

The phone clicked off. Locke tried to steady himself with a series of deep breaths. The throbbing in his hand was incessant. His gaze fell on his mangled fingers. They made him think of Greg, of what the bastards had done to him.

Show him, Shang.

Locke's mind filled with a picture of the championship ring caked with dried blood. He fell backward on the bed and stared mindlessly at the ceiling. He wanted so much to cry, as if tears might purge his emotions. But no tears came. He was beyond them, beyond everything.

They had mutilated his son!

Chris felt himself about to pass out when the knock came on the door. He swung it open without checking the peephole.

A gaunt man with olive features and dark hair, in his late thirties probably, stepped in. One foot dragged behind the other in a slight limp.

"My name is Forenzo, Mr. Locke," the man said, closing the door behind him. "I am the hotel manager. You must tell me what has happened."

"When I got to my room less than an hour ago, two men were waiting inside. They . . . tortured me in an attempt to gain certain information I possess."

"And you are working with Mr. Dogan on this?"

"Yes."

"What did these men do to you?"

Locke held up his swollen hand.

Forenzo's eyes bulged. "We must have the hotel doctor look at that immediately. There will be time to finish your story later."

Chris shook his head. "No doctors. I've had my fill of strangers for one night."

"Please, Mr. Locke, I have had experience in these matters before. The doctor is a man to be trusted and your hand must be treated. If the bones are set wrong, the damage will be permanent. We have splendid facilities within the hotel. Everything can be handled here, I assure you.''

"The men who did this are still in the building."

"Then you must give me their descriptions and I will have security watch for them."

"Make sure your men carry bazookas," Chris said, still wondering why his bullets had not killed the giant.

"What?"

"Nothing."

Forenzo cleared his throat. "The first thing we must do is get you settled in another room. After the doctor has attended to you, the next step will be to determine how we can get you out of here safely."

"I'm supposed to stay and wait for Dogan."

"To insure your safety, that is out of the question. Where might safe ground exist for you?"

Locke hadn't considered that question yet but the answer was quick in coming. Colin Burgess! England. He would call the contact number and have the girl set everything up. Burgess would take care of him now as he had before. Together they would link up with Dogan again somehow. Maybe the man who had tracked down German spies would be able to track down the bastards who had his son. The big Brit was the answer!

"England," Locke said finally.

"And your passport, should I have it retrieved from your old room?"

"Ye— I mean, no. The people who were waiting for me there must have known the alias I was traveling under. They'll be watching for that name at the airport. Can't you arrange for a new passport?"

Forenzo tried to smile. "I am only a simple hotel manager, Mr. Locke. I possess no such resources on such short notice." Something seemed to occur to him. "But wait. England is your destination, you say?"

"Yes."

"Chartered flights travel several times daily from Rome to London and the Customs officials are sometimes lax in checking passports for charter customers. Random collections and stampings are made to speed up the process so as not to create logjams. We Italians prefer to pass such problems onto you. Yes, I think I can come up with a way to get you out of Rome. The problem is what happens once you reach London. . . ."

"Let me worry about that. Just get me safely to the airport with a ticket and keep me alive for tonight."

"That much I can do. Mr. Dogan is an honored guest of the hotel. Any friend of his . . ." Forenzo's shrug completed his thought.

"Speaking of Mr. Dogan, he said you would provide a warding-off signal if things weren't safe."

"Indeed. When is he scheduled to arrive?"

"Tomorrow evening sometime."

"My eyes will be alert and the proper signals will be in place." Forenzo started back for the door. "Now I better see about arranging for the doctor and getting you moved. It's going to be a long night."

Locke's new room was on the tenth floor. As soon as he had chained the door behind him, he made for the telephone and read the instructions for dialing beyond Italian borders. The line in this particular room was not routed through the hotel switchboard, so no one could trace the call back to him there. He pulled the girl's number in Falmouth from his memory and dialed it properly.

"Hello," she said tentatively.

"I'm in trouble. I need Colin."

There was no response.

"Didn't you hear me? I said this is Locke. I *need* Colin."

Locke could hear the girl's erratic breathing on the other end before she spoke again.

"Uncle Colin has gone fishing."

The phone clicked off and Chris felt the walls closing in around him.

CHAPTER 22

DOGAN AND MARNA MOVED UP THE HILL TOGETHER, KEEPING THE shack always in sight.

"It looks deserted," Dogan said as they moved within killing range for his Heckler and Koch P-9.

"It's not," Marna responded confidently.

Dogan made sure the P-9 was ready for a quick draw, wishing he had taken the Mac-10 machine pistol along instead. Its nine-millimeter, thirty-shot clip would be infinitely more comforting at this point.

They had cleared a ridge thirty yards before the shack when the blast rang out. Instinctively both Dogan and Marna dove to the ground.

"You all right?" he asked her.

"A little shaken, that's all. What did you make it?"

"Shotgun, double-barrel. Whoever's inside isn't much of a shot."

Another blast sounded, apparently aimed at nothing.

"Just trying to scare us away, you think?" Marna asked.

"They would have waited until we were in range if they meant to kill us. Hell, they could have waited till we were right on top of their doorstep the way we were moving."

"Then who the hell is it?"

Dogan was already starting to rise. "There's only one way to find out. . . ."

"Ross!" Marna shouted as loud as she dared.

But it was too late. Dogan was already standing straight up

with his hands held directly over his head and pistol plainly in view.

"I'm throwing my weapon down," he yelled to the inhabitants of the shack. He tossed the P-9 aside. It rolled across the dirt. "I'm unarmed now," he said calmly, still holding his hands high. "We mean you no harm. We only want to ask you a few questions." A pause. "We can help you." Another pause. "I'm going to walk slowly forward. Please signal me if it's all right to keep going."

Dogan started walking, heart in his mouth, ready to lunge to the side at the first sight of a gun barrel. His actions represented a clear violation of every rule in the book. This was the last thing a field agent was supposed to do, but his instincts overruled standard precautions.

Dogan kept walking, his pace slow and measured, until he was within ten yards of the shack and could see that it was haphazardly constructed almost totally of nearly burned wood. There was movement inside, followed by a loud creak. Dogan froze.

The door swung open. Still he could make out nothing inside. He reduced his pace slightly, ready to spring.

When he reached the doorway, he had to bend at the knees to pass inside. His vision fizzled in the darkness. He started to straighten up and something crashed into his back, pitching him down hard to the floor.

"The other one I saw, tell her to come in too!" a voice demanded in broken English.

Dogan looked up. His eyes adjusted to the darkness. Before him was a boy of barely thirteen, dressed in tattered white clothes. His dirty face was all but hidden by his long, scraggly hair. Dogan raised himself to a sitting position slowly, keeping his hands in the air so not to spook the boy who held a shotgun in trembling hands before him.

"I'm going to stand up now. Don't worry, I mean you no harm."

Dogan rose deliberately and moved to the doorway. He could have stripped the gun away from the boy effortlessly at any time but he needed his trust, and that was no way to gain it.

"It's all right," he yelled to Marna. "You can come in. And pick up my gun on the way."

The boy paled at that.

"You can hold it if you want," Dogan told him. Then he heard the others.

They emerged from the shadows of the makeshift shack—two girls and another boy. The oldest girl seemed eleven, twelve maybe. She held the other girl, three or so years younger, from behind at the shoulders. The second boy was the youngest, about four. The small shack stank of dirt, sweat, and above all, fear.

"Ross, are you—" Marna's eyes bulged in shock as she entered the shack. "Ross, who are these . . . children?"

"That's what I was about to find out. How's your Spanish?"

"Better than ever."

"Good. Tell them we mean them no harm. Tell them we're here to help them."

The oldest girl screeched out words Dogan couldn't keep up with. "What did she say?" he asked Marna.

Marna's eyes showed fear. "She said that's what the others said and they killed her town."

"Ask her who the others were."

Before Marna could oblige, the boy with the shotgun spoke in broken English.

"Men, *señor*, many men. Bad men with guns from far away." Dogan could see the tears welling in the boy's eyes. The contrast between the sweaty hands grasping the shotgun and the scared, vulnerable eyes of youth was bizarre. "My papa did not trust them. When the . . . bad things started he sent us away. Now we can *never go back*!"

The gun slipped from the boy's hands and he collapsed to his knees crying. Dogan felt for this boy as he hadn't felt for anyone in years. He moved forward to grasp him at the shoulders.

"We will help you, all of you. We will take you away from here, where the men can't get you. But you must tell us what happened. Can you do that?"

The boy nodded, hiding his eyes as though ashamed of his tears. "But my English, it is not very good yet."

"Speak in your own language. My friend Marna will translate. Try not to get too far ahead of her. My name is Ross."

The boy slid out of Dogan's grasp and backed away until his shoulders struck one of the walls. Dogan sat again on the cold dirt floor.

"My name is Juan, *señor*," the boy said in his best English. "But my *padres* called me John because someday I would go to live in *los Estados Unidos* and live better than they."

"Are these your brothers and sisters?"

"The two girls, yes. The boy is my *primo*."

Dogan looked at Marna.

"Cousin," she said.

Dogan looked the boy warmly in the eyes, trying to reassure him that he was not alone anymore.

"I want you to tell us the story of what happened from the beginning. Take your time."

The words started spilling out in a flood and Marna began translating them into English almost as fast. Locke knew quickly there would be no sense in interrupting the boy to ask questions; that would only break his train of thought. Eventually he would answer all the questions he could anyway.

"It started many months ago, half a year maybe," Marna began, and almost immediately her voice matched the boy's so that his words seemed to emerge in English. "There were only a few of the men at first, but then more came. They said they could help us. They said they had a way to make our crops grow faster, stronger, and more plentiful, so the weather wouldn't affect them as much and they wouldn't need as much water.

"The village elders agreed to let them help us, and more men followed in many trucks with much equipment and bags and bags of special seeds. Our old crops were destroyed and the land tilled over. The new seeds were planted immediately. The crops began to sprout the next day or the day after. They were full grown in—"

The boy kept speaking but Marna stopped.

"What's he saying?" Dogan asked her.

"It can't be right," she said, her face suddenly pale.

"What did he say?" Dogan repeated. The boy was silent now.

Marna took a deep breath. "That the new crops were ready to be harvested in only three weeks."

"Tell him to go on," Dogan instructed.

"But *three weeks*, Ross! Doesn't that—"

"Just tell him to go on."

Marna complied reluctantly and started translating again, her voice nervous now. "The elders started asking about the harvest. In time, in time, the men said. But the crops had reached full growth. Only three weeks, but they were ready for harvest. Everyone could tell. But the men would not allow us to touch them. The village grumbled. Our food supply ran low and there was little to replenish it. We were not even allowed to leave the town. Guards were posted everywhere with big guns. People became angry and scared. Many would sit all day watching the crops that had taken only three weeks to grow to perfection. But we couldn't touch them. It was like a dream. You can see, but not taste or touch. The elders, some of them, protested. They . . . disappeared."

Dogan could see the boy was holding back tears. He could almost hear the youth urge himself to be brave, to act like a man. He had seen enough death for any thousand men, though. He had the tears coming to him.

"More men with guns began to arrive, a whole truck full. Suddenly we were treated like sheep. The entire town was herded into the church and ordered to eat and sleep there. We were allowed to wash or use the toilet only in shifts. They started feeding us well, though, and most people relaxed and stopped worrying. Others, the smart ones, feared the worst was coming." The boy gulped some air and swallowed hard. "My father was one of these. One night he awoke the four of us very late when the crickets' chirp was at its loudest. There were only two guards and neither paid much attention. We crawled across the floor past all the sleeping bodies into a secret room behind the altar. The room had a trap door in it leading into a tunnel. And the tunnel led outside to the hillside on the edge of town." The boy was crying now, not bothering to hold back. "He made us go! We didn't want to but he made us! He said he'd follow as soon as he could but for now he had to stay with the rest of the

222

family. The guards would miss adults, he said, but four children could slip by them."

The boy broke down and smothered his head in his hands, squeezing his knees to his chest. He steadied himself as best he could and spoke again through sobs and whimpers.

"The next morning a jeep arrived carrying two men. One was dressed like a soldier but he didn't look like one. With him was a giant with slanted eyes and a white suit. The giant lifted a steel box from the back of the jeep. The new man talked with the leaders of the troops who had become our jailers. A little after that another man came out of the building dressed like a space-man in a gray outfit that shone in the sun. He was carrying a funny-looking spray gun and he pulled a can from the steel box and stuck it in the back of the gun. Then the spaceman moved off into the fields. He stood where the new crops started and sprayed a gray mist from inside the gun. He sprayed for just a few seconds. Then—"

The boy kept speaking. Once again Marna had stopped.

"Marna," Dogan prodded.

She rubbed her face with her fingers. They were trembling. "I misheard what he said. I'm going to ask him to repeat it."

She spoke to the boy in Spanish. He nodded and did as she told him.

Still Marna remained silent. "I've got to be hearing this wrong," she said finally.

"What did he say?"

"He said a few minutes after the mist was released, the crops started . . . dying, crumbling into the ground. Ross, what the hell's going on?"

Dogan fought back the chill of fear. "What else? What else did he say?"

"They fell row by row, one after another," Marna continued, "like something under the dirt was yanking them back down." Her eyes flashed wildly. "Ross, you've got to tell me what's going on!"

"Oh, my God," Dogan muttered, rising to his feet. It was worse than he possibly could have imagined, much worse. The missing piece had finally been added. Not only had the Committee discovered a way to genetically alter crop growth, they had found a means of killing crops on contact. The boy said the destruction started after only a slight amount of the gray mist had been sprayed. It was incredible. No wonder San Sebastian had to burn. All evidence of what the Committee had done there had to be wiped out. Suddenly the massacre made very clear sense. Everything made sense.

The Committee was going to kill all of the U.S.'s crops and replace them in the marketplace with genetically accelerated crops grown on the South American lands they now owned!

Just considering the prospects brought the chill of fear back to Dogan, and this time he couldn't suppress it.

"Have the boy go on," he told Marna.

"Ross, it's true what he said, isn't it? You've got to tell me what's going on down here."

"Later," Dogan said firmly, sitting back down. "I've got to hear the rest of his story."

The boy was trembling harder but still he went on. "Less than an acre of the crops was still standing when the trucks arrived." His voice became frantic. Marna struggled to keep up with him. "Men climbed off, soldiers with heavy guns. They took them from their shoulders and spread out. The people inside the church were forced outside. I remember seeing them shield their eyes from the sunshine. I tried to pick out my parents but everyone was dressed almost the same. I tried and tried. It was so important to me but I couldn't find them.

"More of the soldiers came down the street pushing the townspeople who had wandered off or tried to hide maybe. People were screaming and crying. It was horrible, horrible!

"The soldiers fired their guns over and over again. All I could hear were gunshots. The people kept screaming but the screaming made less and less noise as they fell dead and the blood ran everywhere. I wanted to cry but I couldn't. It felt like I was forgetting how to breathe. They left the bodies piled on top of each other. Some of the bodies fell off the top, and it was then that . . ."

The boy stopped suddenly. His eyes grew glazed and distant. When he continued, his voice had turned maddeningly calm.

". . . I saw my parents. They were lying next to each other, their arms touching. Their eyes were open but they couldn't see me. I made myself be brave like my father would have wanted and took the others far up the hillside, as more of the soldiers soaked the fields and the town. They were going to burn everything, I knew it, so I led us high up into the wind so the fire would stay away. It burned for three days, turning our skin red and hot. But then the rains stopped it and we built this shack farther down the hill so we could see the place where our town had been." He took a deep breath, started shaking all at once. *"Their eyes were open but they couldn't see me!"*

The boy's voice had turned hysterical and so loud that Dogan barely heard the gunshot fired through an opening in the shack. It splintered wood just above his head and he spun quickly toward Marna, thinking of his pistol still tucked in her belt.

She already had her own gun out and was firing from a crouch when three bullets pounded into her, shredding her chest and turning her face into pulp with a huge crater where the nose and eyes had been. She rocked backward to the floor, writhing in death throes.

Dogan felt a scream of rage rising in him as he dove across the room, reaching for Marna's belt and his P-9. A bullet exploded in the area he had vacated and the boy screamed in agony. Dogan feared he was dead too. The other children were screeching now, drowning out the other shots that sent dirt and wood chips everywhere. Dogan gripped the P-9 hard and, still rolling, came up to his knees in firing position facing the area the shots were coming from.

A flurry of bullets punctured the wall, and a large figure smashed through behind them. Dogan pumped three bullets into him. Two more figures rushed forward. Dogan took the first out with a head shot and the second with a bull's-eye to the heart. The two bodies toppled over backward, their blood splattering the walls.

Dogan held the P-9 steady, calculating how many bullets he had left. He stayed there for several long seconds, the exact number he didn't know or care. The children were still screaming. The boy Juan was moaning softly on the floor, a neat red splotch widening on the rag he wore for a shirt, mixing with the dirt. Dogan started to move for him.

The woman crashed through the hole in the wall and fired before her aim was clear. The bullet whistled by Dogan's hair. She was tumbling, spinning on the floor, a blur before his eyes. Dogan might have been able to take her out easily if he hadn't chosen instead to move sideways to shield the boy's body with his own. He got off one shot, a hit but a poor one, and before he could get off another the woman had grabbed the oldest girl and shrank down behind her, using her thin body as a shield.

Dogan raised his gun. The woman raised hers. A stalemate. He could see where she was wounded. Left shoulder, just a nick but she was losing lots of blood.

She backed up toward the hole in the wall, yanking the girl with her.

"You won't get away," she growled.

"You're the last one who can stop me," Dogan said, still trying to figure out who had sent her and the others. Was it the Committee or SAS-Ultra? "Tell me who sent you and I'll let you live."

The woman's response was to squeeze her pistol against her hostage's head. "You're in no position to issue ultimatums."

"The Committee or Masvidal?"

The woman just looked at him, breathing heavily.

"It was the Committee, wasn't it? SAS-Ultra couldn't possibly have known I was here and they wouldn't have reason to—" And then Dogan realized. "Wait a minute, you didn't come here to kill me, you came to kill the children! *You fucking bastards!*"

"More children than these will die," the woman said with strange calm, blood and sweat staining her face. "All the world's children if that's what it takes."

"The Committee wouldn't have much of a world to own then."

Her eyes flickered. "The Committee is changing and there is nothing you can do to stop it. It's too late. You can't fool me with your words. I know they sent you."

Pistol hand trembling, the woman kept inching toward the

226

window, lowering herself even further behind the girl, free hand draped over the child's neck, obviously confident that if the man was going to chance a shot, he would have done so already.

"It's as good as over," she taunted.

"Absolutely," Dogan muttered, and fired the P-9 from his hip.

The bullet ripped into the woman's neck and tore most of it away, pitching her backward through the remnants of the wall. The child she'd been holding cowered screaming on the floor.

Dogan moved back for the boy but his eyes strayed to Marna's corpse first and he felt the tears welling in his eyes.

He was Grendel, named for the monster who ate human flesh.

And he was crying, the rest of the world be damned. . . .

The boy was whimpering now and Dogan hurried over, lifted him gently from the floor into his arms. There was a lot of blood but he judged that the wound had missed all vital organs. The boy might live.

"It hurts! Don't leave me! Don't leave me!"

"I'm here," Dogan soothed, cradling the boy close and wishing he could have been there for Marna as well. "I'm here."

But only for now, he thought to himself. The words of the woman he had just killed fluttered through his consciousness. What did they mean? He was in no condition to figure it out now but there would be plenty of time later. Yes, plenty. Much traveling lay ahead of him. There were scores to be settled, a vent to be found for the anger and rage that swelled within him. Violence would be met with violence.

Death with death.

PART SEVEN:

ROME AND LONDON, WEDNESDAY MORNING

CHAPTER 23

LOCKE BARELY SLEPT ALL NIGHT. THE DOCTOR SET THE CRACKED bones as best he could and used layers of adhesive tape and a pair of Ace bandages to hold his work in place. Without proper hospital treatment, which Chris refused, the doctor said he could not guarantee the fingers would ever work properly again. Locke shrugged him off. He did accept painkillers, but they made little dent in the constant ache that gave way to a blast of pain whenever he moved the hand wrong or put any pressure on it.

He stared at the ceiling in the dark room, flirting with sleep but never quite passing over.

After his fateful call to Burgess's contact exchange, Chris had dialed his home number in Silver Spring. Precautions were clearly useless now. The opposition had Greg. Burgess' protective arm had not been long enough. Chris felt the knots of anxiety tighten in his stomach more with each of the three rings it took before the phone was answered.

"Hello," said a male voice he didn't recognize.

He pressed the receiver closer to his ear.

"Hello?" the voice repeated.

Locke hung up the phone struggling for breath. A stranger had answered his family's phone, a stranger with an American accent. If it wasn't one of Burgess' men, then who was it? In that moment Chris wanted so much for this mess to be over so he could go back home again. But home would never be the same, not ever again. And now he had to consider the possibility that home didn't even exist anymore. The Committee could have his entire family by now. Greg's finger might have marked only the beginning of their madness. Whom could he turn to?

Uncle Colin has gone fishing.

They had gotten to Burgess. The big Brit had proved no match for the power of the Committee. But the girl was still alive, which meant her house in Falmouth might still serve as a refuge for him. As of now, Locke had no other destination available. Once in Falmouth he would begin to make new arrangements. The American Embassy offered an alternative, and what other did he have? He'd make sure more than one man was present in the room when he told his story. Someone would listen, someone would act. The Committee couldn't possibly have gotten to everyone at the embassy, Chris thought, trying to convince himself.

His only other option was to stay in Rome and wait for Dogan. But that was out of the question with the dark man still lurking about. He had to leave the country as soon as possible and make contact with Dogan later, as Forenzo had suggested.

The hotel manager had obtained a return ticket on a charter to London and arranged for a car to take him to the airport in time for its departure the next morning. Forenzo had also given him an American passport with a picture that didn't even resemble his face. It was just something to hand cursorily over to Customs officials in Rome. London would be another matter.

Locke reached the airport with his single bag in tow. The condition of his left hand had made taking a shower a difficult task and shaving not much easier. Accordingly, Chris felt grimy, and the tension that might have unwound in his neck and shoulders beneath the hot needle spray had stiffened into steel bands under his flesh.

He moved rapidly through the international terminal toward the charter's departure gate, as planned with little time to spare. That meant little time to be spotted. But still he was alone, a single man with a bandaged hand easy to pick out of a crowd. En route to the gate he fell in stride with a number of other passengers who apparently were heading for the same flight. Locke tried to mix with them, doing his best to appear part of their conversations without drawing too much attention.

A girl in jeans up ahead was carting too many bags, and one slipped from her hand. Its contents spilled all over the floor, souvenirs by the look of it.

"Damn." She moaned, dropping the rest of her bags in frustration.

She had started to gather up her spilled belongings when Locke drew up even with her.

"Need some help?" he offered, trying to make a much-needed friend for the moments ahead.

"Sure." The girl glanced up. She looked to be in her mid-twenties with sandy hair that danced about her shoulders. She had radiant blue eyes and was stunningly attractive. Chris felt himself taken aback.

He did the best he could at retrieving her souvenirs of Italy with his one good hand.

"Hey, what did you do to yourself?"

"Fell down some stairs," Locke explained, trying to look embarrassed.

"We got insurance for that kind of stuff. It says so in the brochure." She started to reach inside her handbag. "I've got one here somewhere."

"Don't bother, please. It's already been taken care of. Right now the only thing I want to do is get home to my own doctor."

He dropped the last of the souvenirs back into the bag.

"Home sounds like it's America for you too," the girl told him.

"Yes."

"I'm sorry I ever left," she said somberly. And Chris realized he had fallen in quite naturally with her step as she moved for the gate. "Europe sucks. Boring as hell, if you ask me." They had almost reached the perfunctory Customs station. "Hey, what's your name?"

"Chris."

The girl stuck out her right hand and the bag of souvenirs almost went tumbling again. "Chris, I'm Nikki. Got anyone to sit next to on the flight?"

"As a matter of fact, no," Locke said, blessing his luck as he took her hand warmly.

"Glad to hear it." Nikki squeezed her features into a tight mask. "I didn't mean that. What I mean is that since you're not with anyone, we can sit together."

"I'd like that," Chris said.

They passed through the Customs station where a woman was casually checking passports. Locke reached into his pocket for the one Forenzo had obtained for him, along with his ticket.

"Where did I put the damn thing?" Nikki was asking herself, letting all her bags slide to the ground. She gave up on the handbag and tried a pocket in the jeans jacket that was faded the same color as her pants. "Here's the damn thing. God, can you imagine leaving it in the hotel or something?" she asked Locke.

"I've done that," he told her, handing both passports to the Customs woman, "a couple of times."

Boarding came ten minutes later right on schedule, and Chris carried one of Nikki's bags onto the plane as well as his own. Her presence was a godsend to him. A couple, or what seemed to be a couple, traveling together aroused almost no attention whatsoever. If the Committee had people looking for him, their task would be more difficult now.

Once they had taken their seats, Chris's attitude toward her changed. She had served her purpose and he wished now only to be left alone for the duration of the flight. He made himself smile through her constant chatter, occasionally responding just to assure her he was paying attention. It went on like that for some time before his words became terse and impatient. Finally he snapped at her after the drinks were served, and hurt, she became silent and lost herself between the standard set of earphones deposited on each seat.

Chris dozed briefly, awakening suddenly to a horrible thought. What if Nikki had been sent by the enemy? What if the plan was to have her kill him in midflight? Certainly for people capable of using a wine cork as a murder weapon, the means would come easy. He watched her stealthily through partially opened eyes, resolved to keep his vigil for the entire flight. And a weapon, he needed a weapon on the chance that—

No! No!

Locke shuddered inwardly. What was he becoming? Had he

changed so much in order to stay alive? No, people couldn't change that fast . . . unless they had it in them to begin with. Burgess had said he was right for the job because it was in his blood, part of the legacy his mother had left him. Maybe the big Brit was right.

And what of his son? Chris wondered what he could do to save Greg, if the boy was still alive. Just considering the problem, though, formed a knot in his stomach. He didn't even know where to start. Even his mother's legacy did not include sufficient resourcefulness for that.

Locke shrank down in his seat. The effect of the painkiller was wearing off and he didn't want to be dullwitted when he reached London. Greg was beyond his reach, just as so much in his life had been. Barring a miracle, he would have to carry his son's death on his conscience for the rest of his life. Chris wondered about Brian Charney's conscience. How many similar burdens had *he* carried? Not that they prevented him from taking on a few more.

Locke thought of Lubeck dying alone in a godforsaken South American town and of Charney spilling his blood on a thick carpet inside the Dorchester Hotel. They died as they had lived, Chris realized: empty, alone, a vacuum where their morality had once been. They too had been running, afraid to look back, just as he was. So he wasn't alone there, wasn't the only man to suffer through such a crisis. Maybe all men did. Some were just better at the running—and the dodging—than others. You could fool the others but you couldn't fool yourself. The Luber had resisted being retired, because then the running would have to stop and all that lay behind—the truths—would catch up. So he had run to San Sebastian and died there and maybe it was better that way. And Locke had run to London, Liechtenstein, Italy, and now back to London again.

But dying wouldn't be better.

Because he had something Lubeck never had and Charney had lost: a family. His marriage was no better or worse than anyone else's; it just was and he had been a prima donna to believe otherwise. And what kids these days didn't want to break from their parents at younger and younger ages?

235

Locke felt chilled suddenly as his thoughts came back to Greg. Was running to the American Embassy the best way to arrange for a rescue? Or would the Committee keep Greg alive only as long as Chris kept his mouth shut? If he was still alive. There were no answers, only decisions to be weighed and a chance taken either way. No black or white, just gray. Men like Dogan were used to the gray. For Locke it was a new shade.

When the jet came down in London, Nikki gave him one slight smile and moved into the farthest aisle. Chris felt the guilt chew at him. He cursed himself for even considering she might have been part of the opposition when, in fact, it was he who had placed *her* life in very real danger by using her to help him escape from Rome. He wondered if he should call her back and warn her quietly to be on her guard, that he had behaved strangely out of fear. But she was already too far away, still hurt and confused by his treatment of her. It was probably better that way. A thinly veiled warning would have led to questions and to her acting out of apprehension rather than routine. It was safest to leave her ignorant.

Nikki moved down the ramp into the Heathrow terminal ahead of him, never looking back.

Locke's next problem was making it through Customs. The passport that had gotten him out of Rome could never get him past the far more diligent officials in London. During the long flight he had come up with a shadow of a plan but lacked a method to implement it.

A female representative from the airline stood just inside the terminal greeting the disembarking passengers with smiles and well wishes, hoping on behalf of the airline that they had enjoyed the charter and would book it again. Locke's method of implementation was suddenly clear. He approached her straightaway, not waiting for the woman to pick him out.

"A problem, sir?" she asked, her smile dimming.

"Yeah, I suppose having my passport stolen on the plane could be called that."

"Stolen?"

"Somebody yanked it from my jacket while I was asleep."

"Did you inform the stewardess?"

"Yes, and she told me to see you as soon as I was off the plane. Not much help at all really." Locke gritted his teeth. "Hell of an operation you're running here."

The woman's face reddened. This was probably the last thing she'd expected or wanted to hear. "We'd better go somewhere and get this straightened out."

"That would be jolly."

"Follow me."

They moved beyond the regular Customs lines into the same bank of offices where Chris had met Robert Trevor, the man who had given him the gun six days before. Wouldn't it be something to meet up with him again? The woman ushered Chris into one of the small offices and offered him a chair.

"I'll find one of the supervisors and be back presently," she explained. "The airline will represent you every step of the way and will take whatever steps are necessary to expedite matters, Mr., ah—"

"Jenkins, Peter Jenkins."

"Yes, Mr. Jenkins," she said moving for the door. "I'll only be a minute."

When she was gone, Chris sprang immediately from his chair. He had penetrated this part of Customs, but getting into England proper remained the real obstacle. There was only one chance.

Locke stepped out of the office and wandered into an area prohibited to passengers, all the time keeping his eye peeled for the return of the airline rep.

"See here, what are you doing?"

Locke turned to his right and found a man in a blue Customs uniform approaching.

"This is a restricted section," the man charged. "No one's allowed in here without an escort."

Locke made himself look puzzled. "They sent me to the receiving area. My young nephew's coming in on—"

"Well, sir, you've missed the receiving area altogether," the official snapped. "Deboarding passengers don't even pass this way."

"But I—"

"You'll have to exit this area immediately."

Locke sighed, shrugged his shoulders, and started down the corridor with his bag in hand. He had done it! But that gave him little cause for celebration. He still had to reach Falmouth and the safe house. If the girl was a professional, she'd be expecting him. With Burgess dead, this was his only recourse. She'd know that, and Locke felt equally certain that Colin would have left her with detailed instructions on how to proceed. The big Brit must have known they would get him all along. He would have taken precautions.

Chris quickened his pace to a fast walk when he hit the main concourse of Heathrow. Speed remained the paramount concern but a trot would have made him too noticeable. At the exit he talked with three cabdrivers before finding one willing to make the five-hour journey to Falmouth. Chris agreed to his exorbitant fee. His funds were dwindling, but money meant nothing to him now. It was a tool to be used like any other.

The sun had just set when they reached a large housing development a mile from the center of Falmouth. Locke had the driver drop him off around the corner from the girl's house at 205 Longfield, opting to walk the final stretch in case the house was under surveillance. The development's homes were all pleasantly similar, terraced and fronted by small, tidy gardens. Two-oh-five Longfield was colored medium brown, virtually indistinguishable from the rest on the street, except for the lack of a garden.

He scanned the area carefully, passing the house three times before deciding it was safe to approach. Other than the barking of a few dogs and the low hum of music coming through an open window, the dark street was silent and the only cars parked along it deserted. Locke kept his pace steady up the walk toward 205 Longfield's front door.

He rang the bell. Waited. No answer.

He rang it again. Still no answer.

Locke wanted to bang as hard as he could on the door but that might attract notice. He would have called the girl's name had he known it.

He tried the bell a third time with the same results.

Reflexively his hand slipped to the knob and turned it. The

door creaked open. Chris entered without hesitation and closed it behind him. Obviously the girl had gone out, leaving the door unlocked for his expected arrival. Those would have been Burgess's instructions.

Locke moved into the foyer and froze. The girl hadn't gone out at all.

Her naked body dangled from the high ceiling, toes about even with Chris's head, suspended from a light fixture by a rope strung in layers around her throat. Her face was purple and her bulging, crossed eyes seemed focused on the black, misshapen tongue hanging out between her lips.

Locke stumbled backward and fell. His breath had gone and his eyes couldn't leave the girl's corpse. Then the room spun briefly into darkness and he shook himself from the spell.

He had clawed his way back to his feet just as the front door burst open and three men in suits rushed in, tackling him hard. Locke knew he hit the floor but never felt it, nor did he bother to resist. The hands treated him roughly, grasping and pulling. Then he was yanked back to his feet as a fourth man stepped through the front door. He had silver hair and looked tired.

"Christopher Locke, I presume," the man said plainly, extracting an identification wallet from his suit jacket.

Chris just stared as the picture ID stopped inches from his face.

"MI-6, Mr. Locke," the silver-haired man continued. "The name's Colin Burgess and I'd like some answers."

CHAPTER 24

"I'M NOT SURE I FOLLOW THIS."

The Secretary of State lowered his eyes back to the portion of the file Calvin Roy had handed him.

"Simply stated, boss, somebody exchanged mud for manure in Charney's file. Damn thing's been doctored."

"How?"

"It's obvious, ain't it? Six pages detailing all of Charney's field assignments with never more than one month between entries, except here," Roy said, standing up and touching his finger to the section of a page the Secretary was looking at. "Seven months missing, boss, and if that don't tell us somethin' I don't know what does."

The Secretary's eyebrows flickered. "You checked further into the missing seven months?"

"Sure did. Dug up Brian's old travel vouchers from records. Took some time but it was worth it when I got to the bottom of things: Charney was in England for almost the whole period bumped off his file."

"We lost Locke in England."

"Yup, because we checked all of Brian's contacts there except the right one. Somebody wanted to make sure we missed him."

"Find out who it is yet?" the Secretary asked.

"The contact, you mean? Crosscheckin' now, boss. Won't be long till we know but it won't matter much 'cause it's too damn late. Fact is, though, we got snookered good."

"By somebody high up," the Secretary acknowledged.

"And I don't like it one bit. Access to these kinda files goes a long way beyond simple restricted. Only a few fingers in the whole city can call up this kind of info on their boards . . . and erase it."

The Secretary looked straight ahead. "We'll have to find the person behind those fingers, of course."

Roy held his stare. "Already working on that too, boss."

"And Locke?"

"We think he's headed back for England. He called a certain number there from both Liechtenstein and Rome. We handed the info over to MI-6. They got a watch on the place, probably a safe house arranged by Charney's British contact whose name was yanked off his file."

The Secretary sighed. "What in hell did this Locke get himself into over there, Cal?"

"It's what we got him into, boss, and now we gotta get him out. And it's not just over there either. I pulled his family out soon as I could but I missed one. His son's disappeared."

"We're dealing with pros, then."

"We're dealing with maggots, boss. Something superbig's about to go down and lots of people, startin' with Lubeck, have been killed to keep us from knowin' what. Hell, there's bodies all over Europe buried with pieces of what's goin' on, and I'll bet the barn Locke's the only one who can put them together."

"What's your next step?"

Roy didn't hesitate. "I'm gonna trace the snookerin' with Charney's file back to the fucker responsible. When I find him, he'll lead me to the rest of the maggots."

"What about Locke?"

"I've had a man on his phone twenty-four hours a day. So far he hasn't called home. That might mean he's dead already."

"Then you better get to it, Cal. Pull out all the stops."

"That's the idea, boss."

As soon as Calvin Roy had left the room, Secretary of State David Van Dam reached for his phone.

"You're *who*?"

Locke heard himself ask the silver-haired man the question but

241

it didn't register. He felt himself tilting back on his heels and might have tipped over if it wasn't for the men holding him at either shoulder.

The man calling himself Colin Burgess grabbed Locke's lapels and yanked him so close that Chris could feel the heat of his breath.

"Look, you bastard, I'm in no mood for games. I've got scores to settle here and they might as well start with you."

"No," Locke pleaded, "you don't understand. I thought you were dead. But it wasn't you. It was—"

Burgess shook him hard. "What in hell are you talking about?"

"The *other* Colin Burgess. He helped me but it must have been a setup to make sure I'd get where they wanted me to go."

"Make sense, boy!"

"Brian sent me to him—to you."

Burgess's fingers, locked on Chris's collar, almost choked his breath off. The foyer's only light, the sole break in the darkness, danced across Burgess's enraged face.

"Brian *Charney*?"

Locke tried to nod. "He recruited me. He was dying so he gave me your address. Bruggar House in Cadgwith Cove."

Burgess's grip slackened. "I haven't been to Bruggar House since my wife died. That's over a year ago."

"They knew that and used it. You don't realize who we're dealing with here. They're capable of anything. *Anything!* Oh, God, they must have had this all planned out from the start."

"And just who are 'they'?"

"The Committee."

Burgess released his grip altogether. His eyes clouded with uncertainty.

"I think it's time we got this whole thing straight, mate."

They headed through the misty darkness for Plymouth and the Holiday Inn in Armada Way. It contained a restaurant Burgess had used for important meetings in the past. He referred to the establishment as "safe," but Locke new nothing was safe, not so long as the Committee was moving closer and closer to implementing its plans. Their conversation began in the backseat,

242

with two of Burgess's men in the front and two more in a car following.

"They've got my son," Locke said desperately, "maybe the rest of my family too."

"Just your son, according to the latest reports we received. The rest of your family is under government protection. You can speak with them later."

"Oh, thank God." Locke sighed, feeling relieved for the first time in longer than he could remember. "Wait," he said suddenly, alert again. "Latest reports? What are you talking about?"

"Operatives from every major intelligence service in the free world have been looking for you, mate. Man named Roy in the States seems determined to bring you in."

"I'm not going anywhere until I get my son back. You've got to help me. You've got to!"

"In time, in time. My stake in this is personal too," Burgess said grimly. "I'm supposed to hand you over straightaway to Roy's men but first I've got my own questions. Whoever took your son killed Brian. That's the score I've got to settle."

"Then that much is true. You and he *were* friends."

"Far more than just friends, mate. He saved my life in East Berlin. . . ."

"And carried you back to the Wall."

"Your information is rather complete."

"The other Burgess passed it on. The Committee leaves nothing to chance."

Burgess looked away. "You're throwing ghosts in my face again, mate."

"The Committee's no ghost. Nobody can see it because that's the way it functions. But you've heard of it, haven't you?"

"Rumors, just rumors."

"That's the way they want it, damn it! That's how they've been able to go undetected for so long."

Burgess looked back at him. "And what is it they're about to do now?"

Locke hesitated. Burgess seemed to read his mind.

"Wondering why you should trust me, right? What if I'm the imposter and the other Burgess was the real thing? Here, check

243

my ID again. I've got a flashlight somewhere in the front to let you study it letter by letter.''

Burgess started to reach into his jacket but Locke stopped him.

"Don't bother. Fake identifications must be child's play for the Committee.''

"Then I'll have this car take us straight to Whitehall in London, right to MI-6 headquarters. Or would you prefer Downing Street and the Prime Minister herself? Afraid they might have built a replica of her house, mate?''

"I wouldn't put it past them, not after what I've seen and heard this past week. I trust you because everything finally makes sense. They had to be aware of my movements while keeping me isolated at the same time. The other Burgess had to be one of theirs, I see that now. Otherwise, they never could have arranged for Felderberg's death so conveniently and left me holding the bag.''

"Felderberg was connected with this?''

"Indirectly. He acted as a middleman for the Committee without realizing whom he was acting for.''

Burgess was nodding feverishly in the half light. "Yes, yes, that fits. He was killed the same day you were placed in Liechtenstein. Go on. Go on!''

"He confirmed the key to the entire operation was food—crops, to be specific. The Committee was buying up huge amounts of land in South America.''

"Why—''

"I'll explain the details later. What Felderberg didn't grasp was the significance of these investments. He sent me to the Dwarf in Florence. The Committee would have followed me to him as well if it wasn't for Dogan.''

"Dogan!'' Burgess roared. "How does Grendel enter into this?''

"Apparently he was assigned to kill me but realized I was the wrong target. He went to South America to check out a lead that started this whole thing.''

"My Lord,'' Burgess sighed, "what did Brian drag you into?''

"I'm not sure, not of all of it anyway. It's all centered around something called Tantalus, some sort of plot to destroy the U.S. economy."

"Did you say 'destroy'?"

Locke nodded. "And when it's done the Committee plans to replace us as the number-one crop producer in the world. I was at a plant in Liechtenstein where they've come up with a way to drastically speed up crop growth. I *saw* the results."

"And this Tantalus?"

"Still bathed in darkness, unfortunately. But Dogan should be returning soon with more answers." Locke felt his muscles stiffen. "We'll have to get to him. The plan was for him to meet me in Rome. But the Committee penetrated my cover. The other Burgess obviously passed on the false name I was traveling under." Chris held the real Burgess's weary eyes. "All the more reason for me to trust you."

Burgess nodded. "I didn't get myself assigned to this detail for nothing, mate. I knew you held the key to finding Brian's killers. Now we'll bring the bastards down. I'll have the wheels in motion by tomorrow morning, even tonight. Just let me get everything straight."

"You can't destroy them. They're too big."

"Exposure will do for a start. It'll give us time to operate."

"What about Dogan?"

"Leave that to me."

Chris touched his mangled fingers. "They'll spare nothing to find him . . . and us."

Burgess glanced down at the bandage. "Broke your fingers, did they, mate?"

"How did—"

"Simple. It's a crude torture and usually quite an effective one when used on amateurs." He regarded Locke closely. "It seems they underestimated you."

"I got lucky."

"In this business there's no such thing as luck."

They were almost to Plymouth. Locke rested his head against the back of the seat.

"The other Burgess told me he—you—were responsible for my mother's capture. Is . . ."

Burgess nodded. "Yes, mate, it's true. I caught her, all right. Those were difficult times. A man wasn't always able to be a gentleman."

"I understand," Chris said, swallowing the lump in his throat. "She deserved to die for what she did."

Burgess's eyes went blank. "She escaped."

"She *what*?"

"You heard me. We hanged someone else in her place. Too much publicity to do otherwise, you understand. Morale in the country was low enough as it was. We couldn't let on the truth. There were only a few of us who knew it anyway. I authorized the switch. It wasn't a public execution, so there were no witnesses."

"You're saying she escaped England *alive*?"

"No. I'm just saying she wasn't hanged. Our people caught up with her again at a farmhouse the Germans had been using as a pickup point. It was quite a battle. No survivors on their part. We used explosives in the end. Whole house burned. Not a board left standing by the time it was over."

"Her body?"

"Nothing left, like I said. I'm the last one left alive who knew the truth. I figured you deserved to hear it." Burgess closed his eyes. "Those were bad days, awful ones. I thought when they were over I'd seen the worst." The eyes opened again. "Now you've made me wonder."

Locke felt more secure almost as soon as the two cars passed into Plymouth. Somehow returning to a big city comforted him, especially when they approached Holiday Inn's familiar logo. He almost felt at home.

Though not comparable to the Dorchester, Armada Way's Holiday Inn was Plymouth's finest hotel. Burgess explained that Locke would go through an initial debriefing period there. The risk of moving him at this stage had become too great. The involvement of the Committee in what was going on merited a change in strategy.

Two of Burgess's men stayed outside while the other two accompanied Locke and the MI-6 man across the lobby into the hotel's finest restaurant. The lighting was bright and there were plenty of windows looking out at the darkened city. They were ushered to a table against a wall in the rear, similar in placement to the one Charney had chosen in The Tombs a week before. Locke noticed that it was impossible for shots fired from beyond the windows to reach them. And Burgess left two men on guard at the restaurant entrance.

The MI-6 man sat down with his back against the wall and signaled Locke to take the chair adjacent to instead of across from his. Burgess waved an approaching waiter away and leaned across the table.

"I want to hear everything now, mate. From the beginning."

Locke told the story yet another time, sparing none of the details and focusing especially on the information passed on by Felderberg and the Dwarf. Burgess interrupted occasionally with questions, and it was a half hour before Chris had brought him up to the moment the cab had dropped him around the corner from the girl's house in Falmouth.

"Who was she?" Locke wondered as Burgess finally signaled for the waiter to come over and take their order.

"Nobody. Just someone . . . the Committee set in place to back up Burgess's cover, the fake Burgess, that is."

"Why not just use him as the contact?"

"Too direct." Burgess ran a hand through his thinning silver hair. There were bags under his eyes. "They didn't want you able to contact the imposter at every whim because that would have meant more questions, and sooner or later doubts might have sprouted in your mind."

"They protected me for as long as it suited their needs."

"But something made them change their minds rather abruptly, as your hand there indicates. Something unexpected, I would guess."

"Dogan," Locke surmised. "He pulled me right out from under them, in effect replacing Burgess as my guide. They hadn't figured on his presence, or of anyone helping me or believing me for that matter."

Burgess nodded somberly. "That explains it."

"Explains what?"

"Word has been put out—very subtly, you understand—that Grendel is an outcast and not to be trusted. His credibility is gone. His own people have disowned him. In our line of work, it's called a quarantine order, restricted status in this case."

"There's got to be somebody he can go to."

"There weren't many people to begin with. Dogan's assignments were strictly deep-cover field operations through something called Division Six. . . ."

"He told me."

"Well, officially, Division Six doesn't exist and neither does Grendel. If he walked into the CIA tomorrow, no one besides the director would know who he was."

The waiter arrived again and Burgess ordered for both of them, Chris just nodding his acceptance.

"I, on the other hand," Burgess went on after the waiter departed, "have the backing and support of an entire government at my disposal."

"It isn't enough."

"To bring down one criminal organization? Think again."

"The Committee is no ordinary organization. They've remained undetected for this long by eliminating anyone who had the potential to do damage."

Burgess smiled confidently. "They never dealt with the power of MI-6 before, mate. I could have a squadron of Special Air Service commandoes standing by with one phone call."

"And send them where? To do what? The enemy's invisible, a ghost, remember? You can't destroy what you can't see."

"That Chinese giant who ruined your fingers was visible enough and so are the rest. The Committee's just people, and people can be killed. If all else fails, that's what necessity will dictate."

"You'll have to find them first."

Burgess nodded. "You've given us plenty of places to start looking: Felderberg was right about Austria; it sounds like their base of operations all right. We'll just have to narrow things down a bit. The clues will be there. They're probably in your words and I haven't caught them yet." He leaned over closer to Locke. "I'm going to put in a call to London now. An hour from now this hotel will be swarming with my people. We'll begin our assault from here.''

Burgess started to stand up. Locke grasped him on the forearm. "What about my son?"

Burgess shrugged. "That's a tough one, mate. He's the only leverage they've got over you, which should keep him alive.''

"Leverage to insure what?" Locke demanded. "That I don't talk, right? Well, I've done that. I've told you all I know, which means the leverage doesn't mean shit anymore. It's superfluous and so is the life of my son!''

The MI-6 man sat back in his chair. "Calm down. They can't know we've made contact.''

"Unless they were watching the house, waiting for me just as you were. They killed the girl, Colin. They knew that's where I was headed and they killed her. Maybe as a warning, I don't know.''

"You're giving them an awful lot of credit.''

"Brian said they were everywhere. I think I'm beginning to understand him. They've penetrated important levels of governments everywhere and that's just the beginning. *Nothing* is beyond their capabilities.''

Burgess stood up quickly this time, looking shaken. "I'm going to make that phone call now, and I'm going to pray you're wrong. But even if you're right, I know the right people to marshal a force against them. We'll beat them, mate, you'll see.''

The MI-6 man moved from the table, then out of the restaurant into the lobby. His two men held their positions on either side of the door. Locke gulped his water, reached over and drained Burgess's as well. His mind was racing. The Committee could not be destroyed through normal measures but it was vulnerable. Otherwise, the dark man and Shang would not have appeared in his hotel room. The Committee was effective only when its control was total. That, though, was no longer the case. Locke had slipped from their grasp and Dogan had entered the scene, and they certainly seemed scared of Dogan. They *could* be beaten, especially if Burgess reached the right people in

British intelligence. His phone call would not take long. He would be returning shortly and—

Locke glanced up toward the restaurant entrance. The two guards were gone from their posts. He felt the rise of anxiety in his stomach and fought to steady himself. Perhaps they had followed Burgess into the lobby. Their job was to protect him, not Locke. That must be it.

Chris waited. He'd give it another few minutes and then check the lobby himself.

The waiter brought their salads, set Locke's down in front of him and Burgess's before an empty chair. Chris turned a fork through the lettuce. Still no Burgess. He strained his eyes, trying to see further into the lobby, feeling the grip of panic seize him tighter.

Locke lowered his head and massaged his eyelids, trying to keep calm. He opened his eyes again and looked at the restaurant entrance.

A girl was approaching. He recognized her. Blond hair, dressed in jeans. It was Nikki!

"Hey, fancy meeting you here!" she said when she reached his table.

"Look, I—"

"Keep quiet," she said in a suddenly serious tone. Her face had taken on a new expression, which made her look totally different. Older somehow.

"Who are—"

"I said keep quiet. Just listen. Your friend and his men are finished. They got them. But we can still get out if we move fast. Through the kitchen. Don't move until I tell you to."

"Tell me who you are."

"Your fairy godmother. I've saved your life twice already, three times now. You really should be more careful."

Locke felt confusion sweep over him. "But I thought it was the Committee that kept me alive."

"It was."

"Then you're—"

"That's right."

"Why?"

"Long story I can't even start now. Things are changing, crumbling. It may be too late already to set them right again. We've got to act fast. You've already helped us unknowingly. Now you're going to have to with full awareness."

"What makes you think I will?"

"Because we're not your true enemies, not all of us anyway. There's lots going on here you don't understand. You will in time, but for now you'll have to trust me."

"Then you better give me a damn good reason to."

"The life of your son."

Locke almost slipped from his chair.

"Stand up, it's time to move. I said stand up! If you want to save your son, we've got no time to waste!"

Chris started to rise. "You know where they're holding him?"

She nodded. "Our next stop: Bruggar House in Cadgwith Cove."

CHAPTER 25

DOGAN FOUGHT TO CLEAR HIS HEAD AS THE STEWARDESS ANNOUNCED they'd been cleared to land at Leonardo Da Vinci Airport in Rome. San Sebastian weighed heavier and heavier on his mind.

He had carried the boy back to the jeep, then swabbed and bandaged his wound as best he could with the first aid kit. Next came a nerve-racking ninety-minute drive to the next town of reasonable size, the jeep threatening to give out a number of times. He took the boy and the other three children straight to the town doctor and proceeded to make a series of phone calls, trying to reach someone who could help him make sense of what he had learned in San Sebastian.

By late Tuesday night he was sitting in the still stifling heat of an office belonging to a U.S. Agriculture Department representative on temporary assignment to Bogotá as an adviser to the Colombian farming industry. His name was Tom Halloran, and the assignment seemed to have both bored and disgusted him. He was fair-skinned and had done his best, though futilely, to avoid the South American sun. His flesh was burned red, his nose peeling off in layers. Sweat poured from his brow in a steady stream as a ceiling fan sliced through the hot, thick air. His freezer made ice cubes, which turned back to water almost as soon as they were lifted from their tray. Dogan could barely find a trace of them in the glass of soda Halloran handed him.

"Christ," the agriculture expert muttered when Dogan had finished highlighting those parts of his story directly related to

Halloran's expertise. "No wonder you want to keep this off the record."

"It never happened, right?"

"Oh, sure," Halloran said with a wink. He guzzled half his cola down, then held the still-cool glass up to his cheek. "I don't want to get involved anyway. You ask the questions."

"The mist that wiped out the crops," Dogan started. "What could it have been?"

"A fungus, most likely. They reproduce like crazy, exist purely to grow."

"But I doubt even an ounce of the mist was released. What had to be a hundred acres of crops were . . . gone in less than an hour."

Halloran waved his forearm, already wet from swiping at the sweat on his face. "This fungus is obviously some sort of hybrid. The mist released millions of individual fungi spoors which produced toxins as they divided. The toxins are what killed the crops down wherever the hell you were. As more spoors were created, more toxins spread. It's a geometric progression. The fungus gets stronger and stronger as it goes along. Picture billions and billions of tiny eating machines doubling in number with each bite. That's what you've got here."

"Then that explains why they burned the fields," Dogan concluded. "The spread of the fungus had to be stopped."

Halloran's gaze was noncommittal. "Fire would have knocked most of the spoors out by denying them a food supply, but these little bastards are smart. They travel with the winds in weather systems. There had to be something more." He thought briefly. "This town you've described, was it surrounded by mountains?"

"Yes, on all sides."

"There's the rest of your answer," Halloran said. "Mountains in these parts can block winds plenty long enough for the rest of the spoors to die for lack of food supply—that is, of course, because so few of them were released in the first place. A little more of that mist and the stuff would be all over South America by now."

"That fast?"

"Four to six days. Winds and weather systems, remember?"

"Oh, Christ . . ." Suddenly the room felt even hotter to Dogan. He reached down for his cola to find that he had drained the glass without realizing it. The ceiling fan swirled noisily above. He gulped down some stale air. "And what if this same . . . fungus was released in the United States?"

"How much?"

"A lot more."

"If the logistics were right, there wouldn't be a damn field crop left in the whole country within ten days, two weeks at the outside." Halloran paused. "This part's just theoretical, right?"

"Sure. What happens next, after all the crops are gone?"

"To begin with, lots of people will go hungry for more reasons than one. The United States controls more than sixty percent of the world's exportable grain and other foodstuffs basic for human existence. We maintain more of a monopoly on food exports than all the OPEC nations combined have over oil exports. So if we lost our crops, it's not an exaggeration to say our balance of trade wouldn't exist anymore. We'd suddenly have to become a food-*importing* nation. And, even given the vast stockpiles we keep, the first impact of that would be staggeringly inflated prices for all farm-based products. Before long, white bread will end up costing more than caviar."

"But wouldn't it get better once the imports started coming in?"

Halloran shook his head. "Coming from where? The reserves of other food-exporting nations aren't nearly as strong as ours, and what little they could get to the U.S. would be subject to the equally pressing problem of distribution. We're just not set up for that. What criteria are we going to use to decide who gets the food and how? If you leave it to a market of drastically inflated prices, only the rich will be able to eat. Americans will starve, Ross, lots of them."

"With no relief in sight?"

Halloran's cheeks were dripping with sweat now. "The worse would be yet to come. Remember, we're not just talking about farmers here. What about the dairy and poultry industries, not to mention beef ranchers? The quantity of field crops animals require is staggering. Cut back on their food and you end up with less meat, less chicken, and less dairy products. And don't forget that field crops are actually grasses, so we're also looking at the loss of all grazing land. Need I tell you the results?"

"Massive price rises in all food-related areas," Dogan replied softly. "People would be priced straight out of eating."

Halloran nodded, licked the sweat from his lips. "And inflation would continue to skyrocket as supplies continued to diminish. The farm belt states would face immediate bankruptcy. Defaulting on loans would cause panic and runs on banks that could not possibly meet the demand for cash. The government would be forced to step in with massive stopgap spending measures, which would push inflation off the board. Under these conditions you can forget all about Washington's capacity to provide long-term relief."

"Depression," muttered Dogan. "But it would be temporary, right? I mean, the farmers would just have to start over from scratch."

Halloran dabbed a rumpled piece of notebook paper against his face. "Nope, that's the clincher. Soil that cannot sustain crops will erode immediately. It would be useless for a hundred years or more. Much of the middle U.S. will literally become a giant mud slide and will end up being washed down the waterways. The effect of this hyperfertilized water packed with lingering pesticides rushing into the Ohio, the Missouri, and especially the Mississippi River would be an oceanic algae boom in the Gulf of Mexico. Hundreds of square miles of ocean would be turned into a sludge of green, choking off the direct oxygen needed to sustain marine life. Our coastal fishing industry would become virtually nonexistent, worsening the food scarcity all the more."

"I imagine the rest of the world won't be faring much better," Dogan said lamely.

"Even worse, if you can believe that. Without us to supply them with food at drastically reduced prices or through direct aid, developing and Third World countries will be *totally* unable to feed their people. England, France, and Japan won't be far behind either, nor will the effects be limited to our allies. Last year we exported fifty million tons of grain to the Soviet Union and another twenty to other Warsaw Pact nations. People starve just as quickly behind the Iron Curtain as in front of it."

"But say someone else was able to supply them—and us—with crops."

"What do you mean?"

"What if a powerful force was able to organize all of South America into a vast food-exporting consortium? What if they had discovered a means to genetically increase crop growth enough to turn this whole continent into a greenhouse?"

Some of the red seemed to fade from Halloran's face. "Then that force would be in a position to hold the rest of the world hostage. The results would be a massive swing of global economic power over to it, political power too; for, in effect, the whole world would know where its next meal was coming from . . . or not coming from." Halloran hesitated. "But don't expect any of this to make things any easier for the boys and girls back home. The good old U.S. of A. would still be facing drastic economic realignment."

"Economic *what*?"

"Realignment. If a system doesn't work anymore, it's got to be thrown out and replaced. Regardless of what happens in South America, we'd still lack even the semblance of an economy as it's known today. No trading, no commodities, no stock exchanges, no banks as they function now, and cash itself would become increasingly worthless."

Then something suddenly occurred to Dogan. "But how could crops be grown in South America or anywhere else once the fungus is released? It would spread across the whole globe, wouldn't it?"

"Not necessarily. This fungus of yours could easily be engineered to be chemotrophic, meaning exposure to sunlight and oxygen causes it to gradually break down. It might have a built-in time clock of, say ten days—plenty of time to knock out the United States, Canada, and parts of Central America, while sparing South America and the rest of the world." Halloran ran another piece of crumpled paper over his face. "But don't worry because ten days would be plenty of time to plunge half our population into very real poverty. You'd see the evolution of a new two-class system divided simply into those who can afford food and those who can't. You'd need martial law, curfews, holding pens for the millions of homeless driven to live in the streets. There'd be more people unemployed than working, with the gap continuing to widen because the resources and capital wouldn't be available to reverse the trend. I could go on forever with this, but then so can you. Just use your imagination.''

Dogan had been doing just that for much of the flight, trying to see what the world would be like as Halloran described the Committee's vision. Now, as the 747 streaked for the runway, his mind turned to more immediate concerns. After he had spoken to Halloran, Dogan had initiated a series of calls through usual channels in an attempt to make contact with his own people apart from Division Six. None of the conversations had gone well. There was hesitance, uncertainty, contrivance in the responses of his contacts, and only one explanation was possible: Since Dogan had failed to comply with his orders, he had been quarantined. Field operatives would have been warned not to cooperate with him, especially those he'd worked with in the past. And if the quarantine order was restricted, as he fully expected it was, isolation was just the beginning. Qualified field agents would have an open mandate to take him out.

And there was more. Dogan tried to recall the final words of the woman he had killed in the shack overlooking San Sebastian.

The Committee is changing and there is nothing you can do to stop it. It's too late. You can't fool me with your words. I know they sent you.

The last sentences seemed to indicate a charge that *he* was part of the Committee. But if so, who did she represent? Perhaps a faction of the Committee had broken off. But what would such a faction have to gain? The operation was well underway. U.S. crops were going to be wiped out while the Committee began the process of turning South America into the greatest crop producer the world had ever seen. So why would there be need for change? What was it he couldn't stop?

The 747's tires grazed the runway. Dogan rejoiced to be back on the ground, ready to pick up the elusive trail once again. His trip had filled in all the missing pieces of Locke's story. He

257

recalled the college professor's rendition of Lubeck's final words on tape.

I'm in a position overlooking the fields now. It appears that . . . Oh, my God. This can't be. It can't be! I'm looking out at—

Lubeck must have been looking at the very sight the boy had described for Dogan in San Sebastian: a few fertile rows of crops standing amid utter destruction. The shock of that would have triggered his final, panicked words. Lubeck had known all along the key was food. He must have realized instantly the true significance of San Sebastian. And his report would have detailed it, but they had gotten to him. Yes, it made sense.

What didn't make sense was that on top of all this, something else was going on, as hinted at by the woman in the shack.

The 747 came to a halt at the terminal building.

The passengers started crowding into the aisles and he joined them. His isolation was a temporary matter. He would contact Vaslov with news of a shadowy terrorist group called SAS-Ultra. Its one-eyed leader had to be found and convinced to join him in attempting to destroy the Committee.

Locke would be waiting for him at the Rome Hilton. Dogan would begin the process from there.

Forenzo, the hotel manager, knew his old friend would be arriving sometime that night. Of course, the American could not be allowed to enter the hotel. The forces that had caught Locke were undoubtedly still about and discretion had to be observed. It would be a small matter to ward Dogan away and one that Forenzo would take on himself. His friend would be looking for him and Forenzo had already prepared the signal. The only other thing required was his presence in the lobby.

Night had already fallen when Forenzo returned to his windowless office. The hotel still had to operate and he was behind in his work. He opened the door to his office and limped inside, flicking on the light switch.

Nothing happened. The bulb must have blown, he figured. He had started to turn back out the door when he felt his shoulders grabbed and twisted. At the same time, the door closed all the way plunging the room into total blackness.

258

Forenzo was shoved viciously against the wall and was about to scream when he felt the burst of agony in his abdomen. All that emerged was a gasp and a gurgle as the blade was pushed in and drawn up, splitting his midsection in two. Blood poured up his throat but Forenzo was dead before it began to spill out. He slumped down against the wall drenched with his own insides.

Minutes later, after depositing the manager's body in a pile of dirty linen, Shang stepped into a room on the tenth floor and began the wait for Dogan.

Audra St. Clair held the receiver tighter to her ear.

"Dogan will be out of the way by the end of this evening," Mandala reported.

"And Locke?"

Mandala hesitated. "He slipped away from us again in Plymouth but he won't get far."

The old woman breathed a sigh of relief. She was playing with dynamite here, but a person did not reign over the Committee for a quarter century without developing a stomach for such things. Matters were out of hand, she knew that now along with the fact that Mandala was to blame. He was shrewd and cunning and would not be easy to best. She had defeated other worthy opponents, though, and he would prove no different.

"You learned nothing from Locke in Rome?"

"I'm afraid he's better than we thought. Displaying his son's finger should have gained us everything but, still, he held back."

"You underestimated him, Mr. Mandala."

"We all did."

"If you find him, you will bring him to me with no more of these childish games. It's time for Mr. Locke to join our crusade instead of fighting it. That means the release of his son is mandated. Understood?"

Mandala remained silent.

"I asked if my instructions were understood. I want the boy returned safely to America."

"As you wish, madam."

Mandala hung up the phone, hoping he hadn't hesitated long enough to make the old bitch suspicious of what was really going

259

on without her knowing. Her orders had puzzled him greatly. Not that they mattered, of course. Locke's son was to be executed just after midnight unless instructions were received to the contrary. And since he had no intention of issuing them, the boy for all intents and purposes was already dead.

CHAPTER 26

IT WAS PITCH BLACK WHEN NIKKI PULLED HER CAR TO A HALT DOWN the road from Bruggar House.

"You still haven't told me a damn thing about who you are or what your stake in this is," Locke said. "You are obviously part of the Committee, yet you acted against those who eliminated Burgess and his men at the Holiday Inn."

"If you know that, you know enough for now," she said firmly.

"But at the airport in Rome this morning, how did you know I'd use you the way I did?"

"I made myself available to aid your escape. You chose the proper strategy. I was impressed."

"Spoken like a true professional. . . ."

"It's going to take one to save your son's life."

That silenced Locke and suddenly he understood. Nikki was a killer, same as the dark man and Shang. The hardness of her eyes now was identical to theirs—and Dogan's—but the look didn't fit her. She should have been the smiling, happy girl from the airport. In the world he had entered, nothing could be taken for what it seemed to be. People became whatever best suited them at the time, revealing their true selves only rarely. Chris wondered if he was seeing Nikki's now. He followed her from the car.

They had discussed the plan on the way into Cadgwith Cove, going over and over it along the Lizard. She estimated four or five men would be inside Bruggar House. The key was swift and silent action. The men's orders would be to kill their hostage immediately if assaulted. They could not know an assault was underway until it was too late.

Nikki opened the trunk and handed Locke a pair of Mac-10 machine guns.

"Thirty-shot clips. Nine millimeter," she explained. "One for each of us but you'll have to carry both and stay out of sight until I get inside. I'd expect them to have a man watching the outside from one of the upstairs windows. That means you'll have to approach from the side. That's a lot of ground to cover in very little time."

"I can handle it."

"Once inside, your job is to protect my back. With any luck, my gun will be the only one we'll need."

Nikki grabbed a twin pair of sheathed blades from the trunk and stuck them on opposite sides of her belt. Chris noted their unique shape, blades circling off in near forty-five degree angles from the hilts.

"*Kukhri* knives," he muttered, "weapon of the legendary Gurkha soldiers from India. Where in hell did you learn how to use them?"

Nikki made no reply, just closed the trunk and started away. Locke followed in step toward the dark outline on the cliff that was Bruggar House.

The leader of the team holding the boy inside did not like working with Chinks. Too damn creepy for his tastes. The two they had sent him this time were better than most, but he still avoided turning his back on them.

He was a bear of a man with a pockmarked face and had reserved the duty of killing their hostage for himself. If the Chinks didn't like it that was too fucking bad. He would have preferred to be done with the job already, but the orders specified midnight and the damn Chinks always insisted orders be followed to the letter. He didn't want to push things too far with them. They were slippery creatures, these two, small but incredibly quick.

Now midnight was almost here and the leader was spinning

the cylinder of his Magnum. A long time ago he might have felt pity for the fair-haired boy with the blood-dried bandaged around his mangled hand, perhaps even regret at having to kill him. Tonight, though, all he felt was amazement at the job the damn Chinks had done on him with their knives, a surgical masterpiece.

Little bastards had been good for something, after all.

Locke split from Nikki halfway down the street and moved toward the cliff out of sight from Bruggar House. Nikki approached straight on. Chris kept her in view as long as he could, then stepped up his pace when she disappeared into the darkness.

Nikki moved right up the front walk without hesitating and rapped the brass knocker hard.

"Hey, is anybody home? Come on, I need help!"

Above her in a second-floor window, a shadow flickered. Obviously the lookout. She rapped the knocker harder.

"Come on, I know there's somebody in there."

She heard footsteps approaching but the shadow remained in the upstairs window. That was bad. If he saw Locke coming, the boy would probably be killed.

Nikki heard locks being turned inside the heavy door. Still no lights had gone on outside, leaving her *Kukhri* shielded by darkness. The door opened. From the dimness inside, a face peered out, inspecting her.

"You're not gonna believe this," she said, seizing the advantage, "but my car broke down and I don't know where the hell I am. I sort of got lost."

The door stayed open just a crack. "Yeah, well, we can't help you."

She made herself look innocent. "All I need is a phone."

The door opened a little more. "Ain't got one."

Nikki frowned angrily. "Well, can you at least show me where I am and how to get back to civilization?"

The man shook his head. "I'm bad with directions. Just beat it."

Nikki shook her head defiantly. She jammed her thumbs into her belt to facilitate drawing her blades. "Look, asshole, I'm not leaving this porch until I've got a place to go!"

The door was flung open. The man stepped out. An ugly hand thrust forward to shove her down the steps.

And then Nikki was in motion, dipping under the arm to make it look as if she was being yanked inside while she whipped one of the knives from her belt and swept it across the man's throat. The momentum of the blow and shape of the *Kukhri* carried it in and through, so the man's head slid obscenely to the side, held to the neck by only a few sinews of flesh and cartilage. For a second his eyes bulged crazily. Then they glazed over as a fountain of blood spouted from the gaping hole.

The action outside had seemed all wrong to the lookout in the upstairs window, and he had just reached the staircase when Locke sprinted through the front door, a Mac-10 in either hand.

Rapid footsteps pounded the steps and Chris saw a man rushing down. The man was aiming his gun as he moved.

Chris dived to the cold floor and rolled. A whistle split the air followed by a horrible gasp. Locke gazed up to see the man glancing dumbfounded at the *Kukhri* blade buried in his midsection. He rocked backward, then forward, crashing through the banister and tumbling to the floor.

"Damn," Nikki moaned, grabbing the Mac-10 from Locke, "the noise! We're blown!"

She took off for the staircase. Locke sped after her, finger against the trigger of his Mac-10. It was remarkably light but Chris knew its potential for devastation was incredible. Still, his bandaged left hand made grasping it difficult and he wondered what that might do to his aim.

On the third floor, the leader joined the two Chinese in the corridor. Footsteps pounded up the stairs. One of the Chinese pumped a shell into his twelve-gauge shotgun, tilted its barrel down, and squeezed the trigger.

The deafening blast blew out a good portion of the wall and showered Chris and Nikki with the splinters. Both went down hard, the fall saving them from the hail of fire that followed. Locke hugged the carpet but Nikki stayed in motion, firing her Mac-10 in a constant burst as she rolled. Bullets split the air around her, just missing. Nikki kept firing. From the top of the stairs came a scream and the sound of a thudding body amid the deafening roar of gunshots.

The leader watched the body of the Chink hit the floor, amazed at how the little bastard had managed to pump out three more rounds with his chest and guts blown apart. That made it two against two now, and the leader was thankful the guy on his side was another Chink.

Locke started up the stairs behind Nikki, gripping the Mac-10 as tight as he could with his bandaged hand, fighting to hold the barrel steady.

The leader slid out from behind the wall and fired three rounds down the steps, covering the second Chinese's move to a better position with his M-16. The Chinese tried to return the favor by firing a burst but it was too late. The leader's Magnum had clicked on an empty chamber, so when the figure rose before him he tried to duck away. He felt the hot pain burn his side and shoulder and crunched hard against the wall, sliding down to the floor. The figure was darting up the stairs now. It seemed to dance through the Chinese's hail of fire. A fucking broad, would you believe it? The leader's mind returned to his orders. Orders were everything, he reminded himself. Breathing heavily, the taste of blood thick in his mouth, the leader started crawling for the door. With a trembling hand he reached in his pocket for his final speed loader.

Nikki started her rush up the stairs just as Chris had almost caught up with her. Bullets blazed everywhere and he thought he heard her scream but he wasn't sure. The Mac-10's blasting led her way and out of the dimness a lithe figure darted down the corridor, firing a series of rounds behind him. Nikki took off after him, keeping her body low and tight against the wall, leery of turns and doorways. This was the last one left alive by her count.

The leader popped the speed loader home and snapped the cylinder closed. He had reached the door of the room holding the hostage, but the girl was too easy a target to let go. He aimed the Magnum as carefully as he could.

"Get down, Nikki! Get down!"

Locke was tugging the trigger of the Mac-10 even as he screamed the warning, spraying rounds toward the downed man holding the pistol. His bandaged hand couldn't control the barrel, though, and the bullets stitched a pattern in the wood above the figure as it pushed against a door and crawled forward into a room. Chris lunged after him, only to be tripped up by a bloody corpse that sent him sprawling to the floor.

Nikki, meanwhile, had gone down with Locke's warning, feeling the heat of the bullet pass just over her ear and dig into the wood above her. At that instant the lithe figure—a Chinese, she realized—rushed back toward her with his M-16 carving up the air before him.

Nikki swung her Mac-10 upward and fired in the same motion, catching the Chinese in the gut with a barrage of nine-millimeter rounds. Blood slid from the holes in his midsection. He slowed but kept coming, his finger clicking on an empty trigger, mad eyes clinging to life.

Suddenly a knife flashed in his hands in place of the rifle and Nikki fired the last burst from her Mac-10. The bullets tore much of his skull away, but still the blade was plunging down. Screaming, Nikki had risen to block it when the Chinese stiffened and collapsed atop her.

The leader knew he was dying but managed to raise the pistol toward his captive, pouring all his remaining strength into the effort required to pull the trigger. He started to squeeze.

"NOOOOOOOOO!"

The leader never heard the drawn-out scream as the intruder rushed into the room, machine pistol blasting away. He felt his own trigger give, heard the blast as life was stripped away from him.

Locke kept the Mac-10's barrel tilted at the sprawled body. The trigger clicked empty as he moved through the room.

Please let me be on time. Oh, God, please. . . .

Tied to a chair in the rear of the room was Greg, head slumped on a filthy blue T-shirt. Chris's heart sank in his chest as he crept nearer. The boy was dead. He had been too late.

Then he realized the T-shirt was moving, expanding regularly with Greg's breathing. He was alive! *Thank God!*

Chris hugged him tight, feeling with disgust the ropes that bound him.

"Greg," he said softly, almost sobbing, "Greg, can you hear me?"

The boy's face fell limply to his father's shoulder. He was unconscious, but he was alive. The beating of the boy's heart against his own chest was the most welcome sensation Locke had ever felt.

The tears of relief started to come and Chris let them.

Darkness was Shang's friend. His training en route to becoming the most dangerous man in China had dealt plenty with working in it, and now the giant almost preferred it to light. His eyes could adjust quickly and see things no other man could, which made the darkness his ally.

He huddled inside the door and waited. He had been waiting for some time now but the training had taught him infinite patience. He would kill the famous Grendel with his bare hands in the darkness.

A key turned in the lock outside. Shang tensed with anticipation. A wave of peace swept over him as the door started to open. Dogan's figure was entering the room now, his key still protruding from a gloved hand. His fingers felt for the light switch. Shang acted.

He grabbed his victim from behind at the head, hoping to snap the neck quickly and simply. But suddenly Grendel's hands came up hard, acting as a barrier as he twisted for a countermove. They faced each other in the darkness, each searching for an advantage on the other. A slight edge was all that was required to turn the tables.

Shang felt Grendel go for his eyes, a foolish move really because it forced him to overreach and allowed the giant to come under and find his throat. Shang shoved him viciously backward until Grendel's head smacked against plaster. Then, as Dogan writhed and clawed desperately, the giant joined both his hands beneath his chin and jammed it upward and back.

There was a crunching snap, Dogan's body going first rigid and then limp, his head sliding toward the middle of his back.

Shang let the American's frame slip down to the carpeting. Then he twisted the neck one last time just to make sure the job was done.

CHAPTER 27

"MAJOR PETE'S GONNA BE A LITTLE LATE, LOUIE," CALVIN ROY told deputy National Security adviser Louis Auschmann. "Some kind of emergency came up. We'll get started without him. You read my memo?"

Auschmann nodded. "You really think it's the Secretary?"

"Back where I come from, son, they say a bull carries his brains in his balls so it's pretty easy to tell what he's got for smarts. Same way with Van Dam. It all fits. Locke got himself fingered 'fore he even left Washington, way I figure it. And Van Dam was the only one in the department besides me and Charney who knew about the deployment."

"That's not a lot to go on."

"It got me started thinking, though, and when Charney's file got tampered with, I got downright pissed. Only somebody with control of a lot of strings coulda pulled that one. It was done too clean and all evidence of the tampering was knocked off the computer. That takes high-level clearance, Louie, the highest. It had to be Van Dam."

"Then you took a hell of a chance laying everything out for him."

" 'Cause he's part of somethin' much bigger, and if I'm gonna trap the rest of the maggots, I gotta have bait. This whole mess has been too clean from the beginning. Charney gets himself killed and Locke takes off all over Europe leaving bodies everywhere without getting himself caught or killed. He couldn't have gotten that far unless somebody wanted him to."

269

"Why?"

"That's what I'm hoping the Secretary will tell us . . . one way or another."

"What do you make of MI-6's report on picking up Locke?" Auschmann wondered.

"Shit stains don't wash out too easy, Louie, and that's what their story's got all over it. They had Locke and lost him. That somebody is tryin' awful hard to see he ain't caught." Roy started tapping a pen against his desk blotter. "They yanked his son and the boy's probably good as buried now, and I got me a feeling lots more people are gonna be joining him unless we get some answers real soon."

Auschmann thought briefly. "Van Dam won't talk."

"Yeah. So I already got the President to approve a detailed investigation into his movements in the last few months. Way I see it, he musta made a few stops on the sly at wherever this mess is centered."

"Those things take time."

"We're movin' extra fast. We've also got a tap on his private line and a couple men watching every move he makes hoping he leads us to the rest of the maggots."

The phone rang. Roy picked it up.

"It's Kennally, Cal," the head of the CIA said over the private line. "You'll be hearing from the President soon enough, but I figured I'd let you know first under the circumstances. You just became Secretary of State. David Van Dam's dead."

Roy wasn't surprised at all. "Shot himself, did he, Major Pete?"

"Not unless he held the trigger long enough to empty a dozen bullets into his gut. Somebody just assassinated him."

"Chris, we've got to get out of here."

Nikki's voice lifted Locke from his trance. He eased the still-unconscious Greg away from him and his eyes fell on the blood-caked bandage enclosing his left hand.

"Whatever happens, I'm not leaving the boy," he said. "Not again."

270

Her voice way strangely calm. "He needs medical attention and a safe refuge. We can't provide either."

"I'm not leaving him," Locke persisted.

"There's a doctor in the Devon countryside. I've used him before. He's reliable . . . and trustworthy."

Locke started working the ropes free. "Fine. Let's go visit him. But I'm staying with Greg the whole time."

"Then you'll be taking the very real risk of leading the Committee back to him. I can't protect you forever."

"Just another few days is all I ask, long enough to get us back to the States."

"You can't run from them, Chris. It's too late."

Locke swung toward her. "Wait a minute, you're part of the damned Committee. Or are you?"

"Yes. And no. Everything's changed. There's a splinter faction led by the man who kidnapped your son and tortured you. He's out of control. We're trying to stop him, but it's got to be done our way."

"Great. Be sure to send me a postcard and let me know how things turn out."

"His only chance to stay alive is if we win, Chris. Yours too. We need you."

"Why?"

"I . . . can't explain now. Just trust me. We'll take the boy to the doctor in Devon. He'll be safe there."

Chris felt himself wavering. "I want guards around him, lots of them."

Nikki shook her head. "No. The more men we alert, the greater the chances that your son will be found. The doctor will handle everything. He's well versed in these matters. You've just got to trust me," she repeated.

"You still haven't explained why."

"Everything will be clear in the morning."

"In the morning?"

She nodded. "We're going to Austria."

The doctor's house was nestled comfortably in the countryside of Devon, totally isolated from civilization. The doctor was an old man with a wizened face and flowing white hair. Greg hadn't regained consciousness when they arrived, nor did he during the old man's initial examination. He was a survivor of a German concentration camp, and he understood pain and the people who brought it. He would protect the boy with his life, he promised staunchly, and with the lives of his sons: a pair of brawny youths turned hard and strong by years of living off the land. Both handled guns quite well. Greg would be safe there and could remain as long as necessary.

Chris left detailed instructions on what to do with the boy if he failed to return. The doctor said not to worry, he would handle everything, though he said he could tell by Locke's eyes that he would return. Nothing was going to stop him, the old man claimed, he could tell from experience.

Chris and Nikki's next stop was a country inn ten miles up the road. They were both exhausted and in need of food. They registered as a married couple, and a large tip to the sleepy clerk who doubled as a cook gained them four sandwiches, which they gobbled gratefully. Nikki grasped Locke's arm tightly on the way to their room, resting her head tenderly against his shoulder. The facade ended as soon as they were inside.

"We can't take any chances," she explained. "We're sitting ducks here if anyone makes us. We've got to play the part of the married couple to the fullest. I know how the men after us work. We might be watched anywhere, anytime." She looked toward the room's single bed. "That means we sleep together."

"At last, the light at the end of the tunnel. . . ."

"That's as far as it will go," she snapped.

"Just joking, young lady. Christ, you're young enough to be my daughter. And this may surprise you but, that luscious body of yours aside, sex is the last thing on my mind right now."

"I didn't mean it that way," she apologized softly. "You just don't understand."

"*What* don't I understand, Nikki?"

She looked away, saying nothing.

"Who are you?"

"You know who I am."

"I'm not talking about names. I want to know who you are.

Your accent's clearly American but I've got a feeling you're not exactly a citizen.'' When Nikki made no response, Locke continued. ''Those *Kukhri* knives you're so adept with, you know how the Gurkhas used them in World War II, don't you? They were great warriors, almost mystical, I've heard. They used to sneak into German camps at night, right into a tent where two soldiers slept. They'd cut off the head of one—just one—so the other would wake up in the morning to see his buddy's head looking at him from his chest. Played hell with German morale, not to mention their sleeping habits. Anyway, no matter what steps the Nazis took, the Gurkhas still made their mark. You know when I knew the Falklands War was over? When it was announced the British were sending a boatload of Gurkhas into the battle.'' Locke hesitated. ''I guess I'm telling you this because you're like a Gurkha, aren't you? Cold and deadly. Nothing can stop you, or change you. I'm right, aren't I?''

''It doesn't matter.''

''I think it does.''

She turned toward him suddenly. ''Would you like to hear about all my years of training? Would you like to hear what I was doing while most girls my age were going to finishing school and worrying about boyfriends? I was fifteen when it started, almost twelve years ago. Training camps in the Soviet Union and Libya—that's where it started. Then came individual instruction from masters in some rather unique disciplines.''

''Deadly as well as unique, it seems.''

''Yes, deadly!'' she said, eyes narrowing. ''It was a question of beliefs. I felt what we were doing was right. I grew up with the ideals. Our actions were necessary. Sacrifices had to be made.''

''Sacrifices? Listen, lady, who the hell do you think you are? My son almost died today and as it is he's going to go through life with one less finger than everyone else. So don't talk to me about your damned sacrifices. More than two hundred people died at San Sebastian and lots of them were children too. Thanks for saving my life, but the people you work for are still animals. Only animals kill childen.''

''I agree,'' Nikki said softly. ''Times changed and we thought it was necessary to change with them. We went too far. We

273

recruited a man who was a specialist in organized terror and violence.''

"Good-looking dark guy with a Chinese ape for a pet?"

Nikki nodded. "His name's Mandala."

Chris held up the hand Shang had worked on. The bandage had slipped off and hung filthy around his wrist. The enlarged, poorly set fingers looked even worse than the day before.

"I've had the pleasure, remember?"

"Mandala, we believe, has moved out on his own," she told him. "He's taken Tantalus and changed it to his own liking. We're just starting to put things together now."

"The best strategy would seem to be canceling the operation altogether."

"It's too late. The operation's already reached the stage where Mandala was to take over. So we're going to try to beat him and salvage it at the same time. To abandon the operation now would have catastrophic consequences."

Locke jumped from the bed and walked to the dresser, his head starting to pound. "I don't believe I'm hearing this. You sound like your people are out to save the world, pure philanthropists. Well, that's bullshit. I've seen too much, heard too much to buy it. The Committee's only out for itself. We're talking about self-interest in its purest form."

"We're offering the world order."

"That's what the Nazis said, my girl."

"You don't understand, you're not even trying. Look around you, Chris. The world's being horribly mismanaged. People live only for today with no thought of tomorrow or the day after. Leaders are transients; their rushed, ill-conceived policies are never given a chance to work. People are poor, hungry, frustrated, and it's getting worse. In twenty years half the countries on Earth will have their own hydrogen bomb, and tell me somebody won't use it when the supply channels finally dry up and their people demand action. Tell me the time isn't right for the stability we promise."

"Stability is one thing," Locke told her. "What you promise is something else entirely. Don't forget, I know what Tantalus is all about. You're going to make yourselves the world's largest crop producer, aren't you?''

"It goes much deeper."

"Why don't you tell me how?"

"I can't. Not yet."

"Prefer to wait until your people have the world over a barrel?"

"It's called centralization."

"Blackmail is more like it."

Nikki shook her head. "You don't understand. Food's just the beginning, the very first step. Everything's laid out. Our people are everywhere, rising in positions of power. We're pumping money into campaigns across the world to gain control of parliaments and senates. Our policies have nothing to do with rhetoric. We believe in action."

"So you retained Mandala and look where that's gotten you."

"Tantalus was supposed to insure order. He saw it as a means to create chaos."

"I don't follow you."

"Everything will become clear in Austria."

"Your people set me up from the beginning, didn't they?"

Nikki nodded. "But I was always there when you needed me. I was even there in the park when you killed Alvaradejo and at Vaduz Mountain in case Felderberg's men took you down."

"Oh, my God. . . ."

"Without your participation we never would have learned about Mandala's treachery. He would have destroyed us all."

"You've destroyed plenty of people on your own. I lost my two best friends because of this. And don't forget my son. . . ."

Nikki's gaze grew distant. "We've all paid a price."

Locke's eyes sharpened. "All of a sudden you've got me wondering something, Nikki. Why you? Why this undying commitment to this cause since the age of fifteen?"

"Tomorrow," she replied. "You'll understand tomorrow."

PART EIGHT:

GENEVA AND AUSTRIA,
THURSDAY MORNING

CHAPTER 28

THE SUDDEN ASSASSINATIONS OF VARIOUS MEMBERS OF THE COM-
mittee's executive board had come as quite a shock to Audra
St. Clair. Of course, she knew Mandala was responsible but she
had never imagined he would be this bold. Obviously he believed
himself in sufficient control of the Committee's hundred-odd
direct representatives to take over once the others—and she—
were out of the way. It would prove a gross misjudgment on
his part and a fatal one, a fact that did little to provide a
sense of security for her now.

She leaned back in the chair at the head of the meeting table
and sighed. All her work, years and years of planning and
implementation, was being challenged. The Committee was not
made up of merely an executive board and body of the hundred
representatives from all major and emerging countries. It was
composed of thousands of others whom the Committee had set in
place in sensitive positions all over the world. Accordingly, Mandala couldn't possibly understand the true scope of what he was
attempting to control. Well, Audra St. Clair wasn't about to let
him. She felt certain he was on his way there to play his final
card. Fine. She had several of her own waiting for him. He
could not be allowed to leave Kreuzenstein Castle alive. It might
force the postponement of Tantalus, but she would deal with that
later.

To have ordered Mandala killed before he reached the castle
would have been a far simpler strategy, though an unrealistic
one. After all, she had to learn what damage he had already

done, what distortions of the original operation he had set into motion. There was no guarantee that his death would stop his plans, unless Audra St. Clair could learn the details prior to killing him.

The old woman tensed suddenly. In the emptiness of the old castle, approaching footsteps echoed, two sets by the sound of it. So Mandala had arrived, with his henchman, no doubt. She felt under the table for a small button. Once pressed, it would release a small canister of gas from a vent in the rear of the room. She would have time to grasp the gas mask from under the conference table even as the gas burned his insides apart.

It had been wrong to involve him in the first place, she realized now. The Committee had always been made up of reasonable individuals, and Mandala was anything but reasonable. His was a soldier's sensibility, the very thing the Committee was attempting to subvert across the world. But modernization had forced changes in strategy. The need for a man of Mandala's skills had seemed clear, and that need had cost them.

The double doors opened at the entrance to the conference room and Mandala entered. His Chinese giant closed the doors behind them.

"Good morning, madam," Mandala said, his bright smile glistening.

"Is that how you greeted Van Dam, Kresovlosky, and Werenmauser?" Audra St. Clair snapped.

Mandala feigned shock. "Old woman, I'm surprised at you. I have come here to strike an honest bargain and you accost me. That's hardly befitting someone of your manners."

"I do not bargain with murderers."

"But, old woman, I am the only one you have left to bargain with. All the others are dead or soon will be. I require the names of all those the Committee controls."

"You expect me to simply hand them over? What, may I ask, do you offer in return?" She had to keep him talking. Her finger stayed poised near the button.

Mandala moved forward with Shang shadowing him until he stood directly opposite Audra St. Clair at the other end of the long table. "Your life, old woman."

"At my age, I'm afraid you'll have to do better than that. I would have thought some token would have been more fitting. Allowing me to keep my chair of the Committee, for instance."

"You would never have believed such a promise, so I didn't bother to make it. I will spare your life, though, because you'll be in no position to harm me. I've cut you off, old woman. All your major contacts have been eliminated. Your time is done."

"You ask for much but offer little in return."

"Didn't I mention the life of your daughter?"

Audra St. Clair felt the blood rush to her cheeks. Her lips trembled.

"Come now, old woman," Mandala said, "did you really think you could keep it a secret from me? In any case, her life is in your hands now. She rescued Locke from my people in England. Sooner or later she will bring him here. I only have to wait with you as my hostage." His eyes swung back toward the Chinese giant. "Shang has a way of making things most painful for people. I'm sure you don't want to subject your daughter to that."

St. Clair felt the anger swelling within her. Blood bubbled within her ears. "We might be able to come to some arrangement," she said with forced calm. "But why is all this necessary? Why has all the killing been done?"

"To catch you totally unaware, I could say, old woman, but that would be only a portion of the truth." Mandala leaned forward over the huge table. "This operation has never been yours, it has been mine from the beginning. I have changed it to my liking."

"Changed it how?"

"I must compliment you, old woman, on the basic brilliance of this undertaking. Where dozens of countries and other organizations had failed, you succeeded in developing a means to neutralize America. I couldn't agree more with the necessity of that. But then you would have set yourself up in that country's place, utilizing genetic crops grown on the South American acres you've purchased. Also brilliant, but lacking because you would only be replacing one order with another."

"But our order would be motivated toward our own ends. The

South American harvests we would profit greatly from would allow us to build the Committee's position in governments everywhere, developing our people into ultimate leaders—planting the seeds, if you will, to reap a far greater harvest in the future.''

"It is still order, old woman," Mandala said. "And order is what I stand against. The balance of the world needs to be overturned, not just its leadership. We need a global revolution to utterly change the face of civilization. Tantalus provided the means.''

Audra St. Clair began to understand, and the shock so numbed her that she was unaware that her finger had slipped from the button which would release the gas.

"Food is truly the ultimate weapon," Mandala continued. "With their stomachs empty, people everywhere will revolt. Economic and political systems will collapse. No one will be able to keep the order you so desperately want for yourself. We will be looking at a world of utter chaos with room for only a few gifted men to unite the masses.''

"But how—"

"Isn't it obvious, old woman? Tantalus will not just be released in the United States and Canada. We will unleash it across South and Central America as well. And when the panic begins to peak in that hemisphere, we will turn our attention across the Atlantic and then to Asia.''

"My God," St. Clair managed, suddenly short of breath. "Millions of people will die of starvation.''

"Billions probably, old woman. A new world will emerge. Lines of nation and culture will no longer exist. People will turn to whoever can feed them.''

"But all the land, you're going to destroy it all." She found the button again and resolved to use it without grabbing her gas mask. She had to be sure Mandala would be dead, even if that meant she would follow him. She could take no chances now.

"Not all of it, old woman, just enough. And, you forget, all the genetically advanced seeds destined for South America are now in my hands to use as I see fit.''

"Why do you need the list of the Committee's rank and file then?''

Mandala moved out from behind the table and walked down its left side, eyes gazing out the window. He stopped halfway up and looked back at St. Clair.

"Because, old woman, any man able to plan for the coming famine would be in a tremendous position of advantage. A chain of individuals with a similar awareness stretched across the globe would assure total control. People will flock to men with the answers . . . and the food."

"You want control of the entire world," St. Clair muttered.

"Just as you did, old woman." Mandala moved closer, smiling wildly. "Aspirations to anything less would be foolish. But it would not be a world bearing any resemblance to the one we know now or even what you and your Committee envisioned. It would be the kind of world I was born to live in . . . and rule over. A world totally without order."

"Except yours," St. Clair shot at him. If she used the gas now, they would both die, it being inconceivable she could reach her mask and have it in place before the gas found her. But it didn't matter. Mandala had to die and so did Tantalus. For all the operation's brilliance, she had allowed it to be subverted. The Committee would go on, though. There would be someone to pick up the pieces.

Mandala ignored her with a faint smile. "My time grows short, old woman. My operation in South America will begin twenty-four hours after the American one begins on Sunday afternoon. I have much traveling to do, so please hand over the list. Call it up on one of your computer consoles."

"Go to hell," St. Clair spat out, and pressed the button, steeling herself against her own certain death. Mercifully, it would come fast.

Mandala started laughing. In the back of the room, Shang too broke into a smile.

Audra St. Clair hit the button again but by then she knew it was pointless. No gas would be escaping.

"Come now, old woman," Mandala teased, "did you think me a fool? I know all of your little tricks. I disarmed the gas canister mechanism before entering the room."

St. Clair leaned back, trying to look defeated. She still had an ace up her sleeve. Her eyes strayed toward a set of double doors just inside the entrance to the conference room. Any second now . . .

"It is over, old woman. With the life of your daughter at stake, I ask you one last time to hand over that list."

Audra St. Clair just looked at him.

"Why do you still resist? It is over for you. Now that Shang has eliminated Grendel, there is no one left to stop me."

"Locke will stop you," she charged defiantly.

"An amateur?" Mandala laughed.

"But you haven't caught him yet, have you? He keeps slipping away. You don't understand. You couldn't."

"Old woman, my patience is wearing thin."

"So is mine."

At that instant there was a crash in the back of the room. One of the closet doors slammed against the side wall and a white-haired bear of a man lunged forward. Clive Thurmond, British representative on the Committee's executive board and the man Christopher Locke had known as Colin Burgess, turned his Browning pistol first on Shang, who was rushing him. He fired five times into the giant's midsection.

Shang kept coming, his expression unchanged, the slugs slowing him a bit but not stopping his approach.

Audra St. Clair hit a second button beneath the table. This one worked, activating a secret door on the wall behind her.

Mandala was rushing toward Thurmond when he heard the noise and swung back toward the table's head, gun ready.

Thurmond had fired one more shot at Shang when the giant clamped a monstrous hand around his throat and lifted him effortlessly from the floor. Thurmond gagged for air, eyes widened with shock and agony.

Audra St. Clair stumbled on her way toward the secret door. She felt a jolt to her back and then a hot stab of pain. She started to pitch forward but righted herself as a second bullet burned into her side and a third into her leg. She felt the blood running from her, the sensation curiously like rainwater soaking through clothes. She knew she was dying but lurched ahead for the opening in the wall, crawling the final few yards as more bullets singed the air above her.

Finally she was inside the passageway. She hit a button just within her reach and the door closed, sealing her from her killers.

Shang lifted Thurmond higher. He squeezed harder and a crackling sound filled the room as the cartilage lining the big Brit's throat gave way. When it was over and his feet dangled limply, Shang tossed him away like a rag doll.

Mandala was already moving from the room. He had no time to waste in finding the old bitch.

"Come, Shang, it's over," he called to the giant. "Nothing she can do can stop us now."

Vaslov had been up most of the night pursuing some vital information from his suite in the Hotel Du Rhone in Geneva. Still, he looked none the worse for wear and was enjoying a light breakfast when a knock came to the door.

Right on time, the Russian thought, as he moved to answer it.

"Come in, comrade," he said to the figure standing in the doorway. "It's good to see you alive."

"I'm full of surprises," returned Ross Dogan, closing the door behind him.

CHAPTER 29

"YOU MUST TELL ME HOW YOU MANAGED THE TRICK," VASLOV SAID.

Dogan sat down and poured himself a cup of coffee. "Fortune's the residue of design, as they say. I had nothing to do with it. A man named Keyes was sent to dispatch me. He got into the room I was supposed to meet Locke in. Someone was waiting. The killer thought it was me and that was that."

"Keyes . . . the man you saved me from in Paris?"

"The very same."

"How unfortunate," noted Vaslov with no regret in his voice.

Dogan had called the Russian from Rome as soon as he learned what had happened at the hotel. They had set up this meeting. From the hotel, Dogan had gone straight back to the airport, where he boarded the next plane from Rome to Geneva. He had gotten in just thirty minutes before.

"You're certain our friends on the Committee are not pursuing you, comrade?" Vaslov asked.

"They probably still think I'm dead. Keyes was killed in the dark. We're almost the same size and shape. It's unlikely the killer had ever met me before, and there aren't many pictures of me floating around either."

"I have one," boasted Vaslov. "Showed it to my daughter last Christmas. She's quite taken with you, comrade." His face grew somber. "What of Locke?"

Dogan's eyes lowered. "I can't be sure but I think they got him this time. Their intelligence was too tight for him to slip through again. The body of my contact at the hotel turned up last night."

"Unfortunate. I would have liked to hear what the Dwarf passed on to our college professor."

"It couldn't be more than I learned in San Sebastian."

"Especially concerning this SAS-Ultra group. Last night I discovered that three agents from another KGB Directorate had infiltrated the group in an attempt to influence them toward our politics. It was from these I was able to learn the present location of this man Masvidal."

"Where is he?" Dogan asked eagerly, marveling at Vaslov's professional prowess. The man was a true master of his craft.

"You're not going to believe it, comrade, but he's here! In Geneva! Staying at . . ." Vaslov consulted a piece of paper he had scribbled notes on. ". . . the De la Paix across town. He must be here for the hunger conference, which will begin Monday. Perhaps he has an agenda of his own to present."

"But he can't go public with what he knows. He's a terrorist."

"What other choice does he have now, comrade? Perhaps he will have South American diplomats do his talking for him. Better yet," Vaslov theorized, "maybe he is planning to use his people to disrupt the conference. How ironic that he might be doing exactly what the Committee wants him to. . . ."

"No," said Dogan, "we were wrong about that. The Committee never did have a strike planned against the hunger conference. They want it to go on. They want the world's attention drawn to the issue of food, an issue so desperate that the United States and Soviet Union are about to join forces in dealing with it. Unless I miss my guess, the Committee's operation will go into effect early next week to coincide with the beginning of the conference. Suddenly in a world concerned about a means to better feed itself, reports will surface of massive crop destruction in the fields of the world's largest crop producer. A climate of panic will be created."

"The perfect atmosphere for the Committee to strike. . . ."

"And the crop destruction will continue unchecked even as the second phase of their operation—planting their rapid-growing crops in South America—gets underway. Within three months, they will be ready to start shipping, effectively taking the place of North America in the marketplace."

"At the time when the world has no alternative but to turn to them," Vaslov completed. "Brilliant. But what of the words of that woman you killed in San Sebastian? If there is validity to them, matters might be complicated considerably."

"There's validity, all right. The woman thought I was part of the Committee, which meant she must have represented a different part. And it's not her words that bother me as much as the presence of her and the other killers in the first place. They weren't dispatched to eliminate us, they were already in the area."

"Expecting your arrival perhaps?"

"More likely standing guard over San Sebastian."

"Dead towns do not require guards, comrade."

"There's something very much alive down there, something I got too close to. And whatever it is, it's tied into the part of the Committee those killers represented."

"So the Committee has become factionalized. What is it they say, divide and conquer?"

"Except this time we had nothing to do with the dividing and I'm not sure it'll make conquering the Committee any easier. That's why I have to speak with Masvidal. This is a war now and he has access to the troops we need. The problem is we're running out of time."

Vaslov raised his thick eyebrows. "I may be able to help us there. In the last thirty-six hours, a series of well-timed, brutally elaborate executions of important men have taken place all over the globe. The American Secretary of State was one, a ranking KGB scientific specialist another. The killings cannot be random. There must be a connection."

"The work of the Committee?"

"If you count killing off its own members, yes, comrade," Vaslov affirmed. "It's the only possible common denominator among the victims. As you said, the divisions in the Committee are already there. One faction, perhaps, is taking steps to destroy another. An old regime toppling, a new one emerging; we Russians are experts on such happenings."

"What does that gain us, though?"

"Precisely the question I asked myself last night. If these men were in fact Committee members, they would have had to meet somewhere together on various occasions.''

"Locke said Austria.''

"Indeed, and my computers are at work now, comrade, trying to narrow things down a bit. Men this important cannot simply vanish. There will be clues, references, patterns left to uncover. Mileage on rental cars, vouchers, arrival and departure times—everything is being analyzed. My experts assure me we will have an answer shortly.''

"We'd better,'' Dogan told him.

Masvidal returned from breakfast and inspected the electronic seals he had left on the door.

All the seals had been broken, evidence that someone had been or was still inside. Masvidal looked closer. The breaks had been recent. Yes, the intruder was probably still within. Only an amateur would have disregarded all his precautions. Masvidal yanked his pistol from beneath his jacket. Amateurs died the same way as professionals.

He unlocked the door silently and burst into his room in one swift motion, expecting to catch the intruder totally off guard. But he didn't catch the intruder at all because none was present in the room.

"Drop it'' came a voice from behind him.

Masvidal considered a quick turn and shot but the voice was too seasoned, too precise to challenge.

"I said drop it.''

Masvidal complied.

"Now raise your hands and turn around slowly.''

Dogan kicked the door closed behind him, as Masvidal turned and met his eyes. For some reason Dogan had expected someone colder. As it was, only the eyepatch gave the SAS-Ultra leader even the semblance of a sinister appearance. He looked more tired than anything, like a broken boxer who's tried the ring a few too many times. His face was littered with small scars and one long one that ran from his left jaw through his chin. His one eye was ice blue, almost hypnotic in its reflective gaze.

"I know you,'' Masvidal said, his one eye boring into Dogan.

"You were in the lobby this morning. At the front desk. If you came here to kill me, you should have acted while my back was turned."

"I haven't come here to kill you. I need you to listen to me."

"Except you have the advantage on me."

"The name's Dogan. And you can put your hands down. Slowly."

Masvidal lowered his arms, surprise showing on his features.

"The famous Grendel? I am honored. Who sent you after me?"

"No one. Now kick your gun over here."

Masvidal did as he was told. "You're free-lancing then. I didn't realize there was such a hefty price on my head."

"I'm no bounty hunter. I'm here because I need your help. I'm here about San Sebastian."

The color drained from Masvidal's face, but the long scar glowed red. "You know about . . ."

"I was there."

The man's hands clenched into fists. "I swore I wouldn't rest until we had revenge."

"Forget about revenge. You don't know what you're up against here."

"I know about a group calling itself the Committee. I know they were trying to destroy South America when we committed ourselves to destroying them."

"Be glad you got that far, but it goes much deeper. San Sebastian was a field test for two major experiments: rapid crop growth and even faster crop destruction."

"One of our people witnessed that the day of the massacre. He didn't know what it meant."

"The beginning of the end of America as a global economic power. Buying up the countries you're fighting for has given the Committee the land they need to take over the market."

Masvidal looked shaken. Clearly this was beyond anything he had considered.

"I learned about San Sebastian because an American agent also witnessed the massacre and sent a report," Dogan continued. "Another man was sent out in his place to pick up the trail he uncovered. London, Liechtenstein—am I making myself clear?"

"The man we tried to kill. . . . I had my suspicions about him from the beginning. His moves were too random to be professional. But he managed quite well to stay alive."

"Only because it suited the interests of the people actually controlling his movements, the same ones who were behind San Sebastian and the takeover of your lands. They needed to know where the leaks were. With Locke's help, they started plugging them."

"Were they aware of our commitment to fight them?"

"They must have known some organized group was standing against their interests in South America, and another of Locke's unwitting duties was to show them which. Since you're relatively new, and independent, they had no pipeline into you as they have into other similar groups. I would imagine you had them quite frustrated. But by now, almost surely, they've discovered it's SAS-Ultra who's their enemy."

"Then why haven't they struck at us?"

"They're waiting for the right time. The Committee never moves on impulse."

Masvidal's mind worked frantically, trying to assimilate all the information Dogan was passing on. It answered many of the questions that had so frustrated him for months. Still, he wasn't convinced.

"You said you needed my help," he said suspiciously.

Dogan nodded. "I've got an associate who's just about to come up with the location of a prime Committee stronghold, possibly even their headquarters. I want to storm it. I need men."

"Why not get them from your own CIA?" Masvidal asked with his one eye narrowed.

"Because all of a sudden someone on the Committee wanted Locke dead and I was assigned to do the job. I decided on my own not to. That got the wrong people pissed off. My own superiors had to punish me for not following orders and the Committee was worried I'd interfere with their plans. So I ended up under a restricted quarantine. My file's been deactivated. I don't exist anymore.''

"How convenient," Masvidal noted. "Your tale is quite convincing, almost too convincing. You didn't kill me before, Grendel, but if you had, the identities and location of my people would have died with me. So perhaps you concocted a story that would convince me to join you. That way, once my people were out in the open, yours could have us all.''

"I don't have any people.''

"So you say. CIA deep-cover agents rarely come to terrorists for help. You're asking me to take a risk that might threaten the entire existence of SAS-Ultra.''

Dogan shrugged. "If I were in your place, I'd feel the same way. No words will convince you. Maybe this will." He turned his gun away from Masvidal and tossed it to him. The terrorist snatched it out of the air with surprise. Then Dogan kicked the pistol on the floor back to him as well. "Now the roles are reversed. You have the gun and I am your hostage. All I ask is that you listen to what I have to say.''

Masvidal held the gun but didn't point it. "Go on.''

"You're here to attempt to expose what's going in South America at the hunger conference, aren't you?''

Masvidal made no response.

"You'll probably try to do it through diplomats you trust. You'll set up meetings, tell them everything you know in the hope they will bring these horrible injustices to the conference floor. So to expose the Committee you first have to expose yourself, and that's when they'll strike, possibly through the very diplomats you feel you can trust. They'll strike before you have the opportunity to resort to a more active form of disruption. The reach of the Committee extends everywhere. It's the way they work.''

"So basically you're asking me to trust you instead of these diplomats I was planning to utilize," Masvidal concluded.

"I didn't give you my gun out of bravery," the American told him. "I did it out of fear. I've escaped them several times myself but my luck won't hold out much longer. If I don't get them, they'll get me. But to get them, I need you . . . and your people."

"You already said we're no match for them."

"Not on their terms. We must make the terms our own."

"By raiding their headquarters? Terms that include suicide aren't acceptable."

"They won't be expecting an assault, nor will they be prepared for it. We've got to find out the details of the operation they're about to initiate. I don't think we can stop it altogether in Austria, but we can at least learn where and when it's going to start . . . and why San Sebastian is still important to them."

"San Sebastian doesn't exist anymore."

"There were armed guards down there two days ago, and I need your help in Austria to find out why. It might take an army to defeat them before we're through." Dogan paused. "*Your* army."

"You're mad, Grendel."

"So are they. We start out even."

Masvidal moved forward and handed Dogan back his gun. His features were softer, more reflective, but equally determined.

"I've been fighting this war for years," he said distantly, "even before the Committee, for as long as I can remember. We started as children, throwing rocks through the windows of capitalist invaders. When armed guards came to scare us off, we attacked them with sticks. Others have always wanted our land for themselves. They deny us an identity. We exist only to serve them. I grew up hating these men for their manipulations but I never feared them." Again the color drained from Masvidal's face, flashing only in his long scar. "The Committee frightens me, chills my very soul. They deny us not only identity but also our very lives. They stand against everything I have fought for these long years. I have seen evidence of their work for years but never do they leave more than a shadow for us to pursue. If you can turn that shadow into substance, I will help you any way I can."

Dogan breathed easier. "How long before you can call up your people?"

"For a trip to Austria, an hour. I have enough to suit our needs right here in Geneva."

Dogan started for the phone. "Let's hope we've got a target." He dialed the Du Rhone and asked for Vaslov's room, dreading the possibility that the Russian's computers had turned up nothing.

"How nice to hear from you, comrade. I was beginning to think Masvidal had gotten the better of you."

"We've reached a mutual understanding."

"With good cause, I can now safely say."

"You found it!"

"Kreuzenstein Castle, comrade. Did you ever doubt me?"

When Locke awoke that morning, Nikki had already showered and dressed.

"We've got to get moving," she told him. "Austria's a long way away."

Locke stretched. "Have you made the arrangements?"

She nodded. "We have reservations on a nonstop excursion flight. It should be jam-packed, so it will be easy to hide ourselves."

"And then?"

"From Vienna, we'll drive to the castle. Then everything will be made clear for you."

Locke didn't press her further. He would let Nikki lead him because he was sick of making the decisions for himself and so far they had got him nowhere. This was her world he had entered. She knew its territory and laws far better than he did. In the dim light of their room with the shades still drawn, she looked suddenly familiar to him. He knew her face, yet he didn't know it. The spell faded. It was time to get ready to leave.

They ate a quick breakfast and made the long drive to Heathrow, arriving at a peak late-morning time. Their flight was overbooked and delayed, and the gate was much too small to accommodate all the frantic passengers waiting to board. Chris had become quite frantic himself when he remembered his lack of a passport but Nikki swiftly produced one with a different name but *his* picture. He would have asked her how she managed it if the answer had mattered at all.

They were the last two people to receive seats and had to sit separately, he in the front and she in the back of the plane. That vantage point allowed her to watch for any people watching them. Chris had a seat next to an older man wearing a green porkpie hat who passed the flight doing crossword puzzles. Locke was grateful for his silence. The last thing he felt like was talking.

The plane landed in Vienna over an hour late. Locke rose from his seat, exchanged smiles with his crossword-playing neighbor, and headed out into the aisle after him. Waiting for Nikki inside the plane would make them stand out too much. Just because they had made it safely out of London did not mean Mandala would not have men waiting for them in Vienna.

She passed him as they moved into the terminal and smiled, as if at a stranger. Chris got the message and fell in comfortably behind her. He stayed always within sight as they passed through Customs, and finally caught up outside, crossing into one of several parking lots.

"You're getting rather good at this," Nikki said as she led him toward a dark-brown Mercedes. She inspected it very thoroughly to insure it had not been tampered with and, satisfied, she jammed her key in the door.

"How far to the castle?" Locke asked, climbing in.

"Twenty minutes," Nikki replied. "Far enough."

When they swept into the semicircular drive before Kreuzenstein, her hands tensed on the wheel.

"The guards," she uttered breathlessly. "Where are the guards?"

"Maybe they're—"

The crunching sound of tires spitting gravel buried Locke's words as Nikki jammed the brake pedal down. She screeched to a halt before a pair of huge doors and sprinted up the heavy granite steps. Chris kept up as best he could, feeling out of place and unwelcome. The doors swung open just before Nikki reached them.

"What happened?" she asked a butler standing just inside.

"It's bad, miss, very bad," he reported grimly. "She's waiting for you. She wouldn't let the doctor sedate her until she spoke with you."

Then Nikki was sprinting up the wide, carpeted stairway. Locke followed. He could feel the tension and despair in the air mixing with the ancient rusticness of Kreuzenstein itself. They had reached the third floor when Nikki veered to her left down a corridor and entered what looked to be the master bedroom. Chris heard her muttering to herself as she approached a bed containing an old woman propped up on several pillows. A man was moving a stethoscope over her chest.

"You're just in time," the doctor reported softly.

"Is he here?" the old woman asked Nikki, grasping blindly for her hand.

Locke moved into the room, noting the woman's ghastly pale face and empty stare. Obviously, she had been expecting him too, but why?

Chris stopped in his tracks, seized by a chilling realization of something both awful and incredible. His eyes fell on the woman in the bed just as Nikki's voice reached him.

"She's your mother," Nikki said.

CHAPTER 30

LOCKE FLOATED, UNABLE TO MOVE, BARELY MANAGING TO BREATHE. His whole body was tingling. He might have even passed out for an instant; he wasn't sure. He just kept staring.

"Come closer," the old woman beckoned him.

"You know who . . . I am?"

She managed a weak nod, the motion obviously a struggle for her. "And now you know who I am . . . or was."

Locke did nothing but stand there.

"Stop dawdling and come closer," the old woman ordered. "I'm in no condition to shout."

Chris found his feet and shuffled forward, stopping just out of reach. He could see the bandages covering the old woman's entire midsection. She looked so old and frail, such a contrast with the young and vibrant mother who sometimes came to him as a stranger in his dreams.

"I have little time, Chris," the old woman muttered through dry, cracking lips. "None to spare on apologies or explanations. There is much you have to learn and none of it concerns personal things. The past must be put aside, if there is to be a future for anyone."

Locke wanted to say something but there were still no words.

"It was all many years ago," the old woman said, eyes drifting, voice fading. "If I had it to do again, I would have changed much, all perhaps. I loved your father, I truly did. But times were so different then. We all had our duty, and that duty had to come first. He understood that."

"He never understood!" Was that his voice? Had he said that?

"It was not easy for me to leave him or you. And it was even harder never to contact you after my escape was complete."

"They caught up with you at a farmhouse."

"There was an escape tunnel that was never discovered. For me the war was over, for Germany too. I knew it; others didn't. I used the time to arrange for the requisition of funds. Years later, when the world was ready, that money gave birth to the Committee."

"You were its founder," Locke said.

"And only leader these many years."

Chris looked at his mother, wanting to feel bitterness, hate, sadness, anxiety, even affection. But he felt nothing. He stood there transfixed, feeling overloaded. Too much was coming in too fast.

"We searched for methods of control," Audra St. Clair said. "We sought from the beginning to succeed economically where the Nazis had failed militarily. We came close a few times—the oil embargo, the wave of international terrorism unsettling governments everywhere. But only with the latest operation did we see the opportunity to truly realize our goals."

"Tantalus," Locke muttered.

The old woman nodded weakly. "Food became our weapon. We would destroy America's crops and dangle our own grapes beyond their reach."

"And you used me to help you!" Chris charged. "From the very beginning you used me!"

"But the risks you faced were minimal." The old woman's dying eyes tilted toward Nikki. "Nikki was around to protect you. I had a brief love affair some years ago and from that she emerged. I was so grateful for the chance to have another child. Abandoning you had left a hole in my life."

Locke felt his knees wobble. "Then she's—"

"Your half sister." She struggled for breath. "Weeks ago, when we learned of your involvement from our Washington representative and elected to . . . use you, I dispatched her to keep you alive. With Nikki in your shadow, I never feared for your safety. She's quite good at what she does. I've made sure she's had the best training available.''

"You turned her into a killer."

"To survive, one becomes what one must."

Chris shook his head. "You want me to accept all this but I won't. I've seen too much, been scared too much these past weeks. My son, your *grandson*, had a finger chopped off and I couldn't even stay long enough to comfort him when he came out of shock. Not that I would have known what to say. All of you seem the experts when it comes to explanations."

Audra St. Clair's eyes moistened. "That was Mandala's work," she said softly.

"So was this," Locke told her, showing her his hand.

The old woman's features squeezed together in anguish. "Retaining his services was the one mistake I made," she said distantly. "But he was an expert in fields we needed covered. We hoped that through him we might avoid direct entanglements with authorities. He was our cover. The strategy seemed sound."

"Because it allowed you to keep your hands clean of the blood he spilled," Chris charged. His feelings confused him more than anything. He couldn't look at the old woman as a stranger, yet she was nothing more. Anxiety knotted his stomach.

"No, you don't understand," St. Clair said. "It was never meant to be like this. Mandala exceeded his parameters. I should have put an end to it earlier. I should have known what was coming after the massacre."

"San Sebastian . . ."

"It was the key to everything, but I didn't see that in time. He killed an entire town acting totally on his own. He loved death; we knew that and accepted his actions. We still needed him, you see. Something else was involved, though, something he had to hide. He had done more than subvert Tantalus. He had remolded it to fit his own goals. He was out of control. We had given him the rope he needed to hang us."

"And the United States."

"More than just the U.S.," the old woman said with a sudden burst of energy. "He's after much more now, and you and Nikki are the only ones left who can stop it."

"Stop what?"

"There are things you must hear about Tantalus before you can understand. Years of exhaustive and expensive research paid off some months ago with the discovery of a fungus that destroys all field crops in an amazingly short period of time. The fungus, through a toxin it produces, kills them almost on contact and is spread both through the air and the soil. It is swept over the earth remarkably fast by weather systems. If the jet stream cooperates, all American and Canadian crops would be affected within a week, dead within two at the outside."

"Oh, my God!"

"Nothing can stop the fungus once it's released. It's unkillable, a perfect organism. It regenerates and multiplies at an incredible level. We developed it in a vacuum. It contains qualities literally not of this world. The only way to destroy it once the spoors are active would be to deny it a food supply, roughly a hundred square miles for every ounce released into the atmosphere."

"Which explains why San Sebastian had to burn."

"Exactly. But keep in mind what I said about the potency of one ounce and then consider that nearly one thousand canisters containing a hundred and twenty-eight gaseous ounces each are going to be released over the United States. The whole country would have to be burned to destroy the fungus."

"*Over* America," Locke muttered. "The gas will be released by airplanes?"

"Cropdusters taking off from the center of the nation. A place in Texas called Keysar Flats. A chain will be set up through the country's center. Each set of cropdusters will handle a hundred-mile segment, then land and pass the remains of their canisters over to the next set. The switching process will not take more than an hour. In the course of little more than a single day, then, the whole of America's central portion, the nation's breadbasket and Corn Belt, will be infected."

"And the fungus will begin moving both east and west with weather patterns."

The old woman nodded weakly.

"But Keysar Flats is the key. If we can stop Tantalus there, we can stop it altogether."

The old woman was breathing hard now, her strength ebbing. She grasped the bedspread tight as if to hold on to life. The doctor hovered over her again, probing with stethoscope. She pushed him away.

"Not anymore," she managed. "Our plan was merely to eliminate field crops in the U.S. and Canada. That didn't suit Mandala. He has expanded the operation. Sunday is when the planes are scheduled to leave Keysar Flats. On Monday he will release the fungus in South America."

"But the Committee *owns* those lands."

"Mandala is not part of the Committee. We are a civilized body. Yes, our plan was to use genetic crop production to overcome the loss in the market caused by the destruction of crops across North America. The world would go on, but the United States and Soviet Union would be hostages to us." The old woman lost her breath, snatched it back. "Chaos would reign throughout the U.S. but our crops would be the linchpins of order through the rest of the world. It was the beginning of a far deeper plan."

Audra St. Clair hesitated as death reached out for her.

"With destruction of lands in South America, our order will disintegrate. Massive starvation will result. Economic chaos and upheaval will spread everywhere. We teeter on a tightrope. Mandala is going to push us off, even if that means spreading Tantalus . . . everywhere."

"He could destroy the world," Locke said.

The old woman nodded, face hardening. "But he can still be stopped. If North America can be saved, there is hope. His fleet of planes at Keysar Flats will be well protected but vulnerable to the right kind of attack." St. Clair reached out and grasped Locke's arm. He stiffened but didn't pull away. "You and Nikki . . ." She was fighting for air every two or three words now. ". . . two of you must go there, go to Keysar Flats in Texas and find planes. . . . Destroy them before . . . contents of canisters . . . is released. Only sure way to kill fungus . . . is while it lies in inert state. Planes . . . must be burned, blown . . . up."

"What about going to the American government for help?" Locke wondered. "They'd have to believe—"

"No!" the old woman ordered, fingers digging into his flesh. "Mandala's people everywhere. Government channels too open, take too much time to clear. Might . . . be walking right into him. Can't take risk. No time."

Audra St. Clair started to rasp horribly. The doctor started to herd the others out of the room.

"No," she commanded him in a voice that was barely a whisper, "not yet." Back to Locke now. "Mandala's dangerous. Avoid him at all costs. Avoid his giant." Her eyes dipped in and out of consciousness. She was rambling. "Bullets . . . can't . . . kill him."

Locke shuddered. "He's the one who broke my fingers. I shot him six times. *Six times* and he kept coming!"

"Thanks to space-age steel, not magic" came a voice from the doorway.

Locke turned and saw Dogan. "Ross!"

"It's good to see you, Chris, and quite a surprise."

Audra St. Clair's eyes wandered. "Grendel? Here? *Alive?*"

Dogan stepped forward. "I'm here, Madame St. Clair, and I'm very much alive."

She looked up at Locke. "Tell him everything I told you. He'll know what to do. He'll know . . . how to stop Mandala. . . ."

The old woman's voice tailed off and she slumped forward. The doctor rushed over and checked her eyes and pulse.

"She's alive," he announced grimly. "But it won't be long now."

Chris looked over at Nikki and noticed her tears for the first time. She was holding the old woman's hand tenderly. So many questions had been answered now, so much was clear. Nikki was his half sister! No wonder she looked so familiar to him. No wonder—

Dogan's hand grasped his shoulder, lifting him from his daze.

"Let's go downstairs and sort this thing out."

Locke started to follow him from the room. Nikki let go of her mother's hand.

"I thought you'd want . . . to stay with her," Chris said.

"You heard her last orders. My place is with you." Then, toward Dogan: "And him."

"Meet my guardian angel, Ross, and my . . . sister."

Then everything fell into place for Dogan. "The old woman's your mother, isn't she?" he asked softly.

Locke just nodded.

In the downstairs study, the three of them were met by a large, dark man with a black eyepatch. Both Locke and Nikki noticed a number of armed men standing around the perimeter of the semicircular drive before the castle.

"This is Masvidal," Dogan said, "who has graciously agreed to lend us his firepower."

"It must have been his people I saved you from in London," Nikki explained, "the ones who sent the old hag to take you out later in Liechtenstein."

"All that's in the past," Dogan cut in before Locke could respond. "We're all together now and that's the only way we can win. First I want to hear everything Audra St. Clair told you."

Chris related her words as best he could with Nikki adding elaboration on several key points.

"My God!" Dogan said at the end. He thought of the vague accusations of the woman in the shack before he killed her. She had been there to stand guard over the next phase of Mandala's operation. "Mandala's going back to San Sebastian."

"And taking his Chinese monster along, no doubt," Chris added. "What was it you said about space-age steel?"

"Our scientists—and others obviously—have been experimenting for years with a thin but virtually impenetrable alloy that can be molded to fit the body of a man. It would protect him from any shot other than a direct hit to the head or neck. This man Shang must make that kind of steel underlayer a regular part of his wardrobe." Dogan paused tensely. "But Mandala's our problem now."

Minutes later they were inspecting a map of Texas. They saw that Keysar Flats covered a surprisingly large patch.

"Christ"—Chris moaned—"it's the size of Rhode Island."

303

Keysar Flats was located in northern Texas, nearly two hundred miles east of Lubbock off Route 82. The North Wichita River was its central landmark.

"Those cropdusters won't be easy to find," Locke persisted.

"You'll have help," Dogan promised, and his eyes moved from the map to Masvidal. "How many men can you get to Texas?"

"Given two days, between a hundred and twenty-five and a hundred and fifty."

"Equipment and weapons?"

"I'll have them brought up through Mexico. A few helicopters should be easy to get. They should make the search for the planes far simpler."

"I'll say," Locke noted. "It'll be damned impossible otherwise."

"You'll need lots of explosives too," Dogan told Masvidal.

The head of SAS-Ultra smiled. "My specialty."

"How did you find us here?" Locke asked Dogan, who gave him a brief review of what he had learned in San Sebastian and from Vaslov.

"The Committee's planners are out of the way for good," he said at the end. "Mandala's the only thing we have to concern ourselves with." He looked at Locke closely. "Chris, you and Nikki will go straight from here on the fastest route to Texas. We'll have to come up with a rendezvous point for you to link up with Masvidal in or near Keysar Flats on . . ." He looked to the one-eyed man for the answer.

Masvidal calculated briefly. "I'll have to gather the men together at my base in Spain and leave en masse. Say Saturday afternoon."

"The operation is scheduled to begin sometime Sunday," Locke reminded him. "That doesn't give us much time."

"We won't need much," Masvidal said. "I have been waiting for years for the chance to destroy my greatest enemy."

"Then we're all agreed so far," Dogan concluded.

"Sure, boss," Locke snapped sarcastically, "except what am I supposed to do about my son?"

"I don't know what—"

"Mandala wanted some answers from me back in Rome. He thought showing me one of the boy's fingers might do the trick." Chris steadied himself, backed off. "Nikki stashed him with a doctor in Devon."

Dogan turned to Nikki.

"I've used him in the past," she explained. "Just me. Mandala doesn't even know he exists."

Dogan looked back at Locke. "Then your son's safer where he is for now. When this is over, the U.S. government will fly him home in *Air Force One*."

"Unless we fail and there's no one left to make the reservation."

"We won't fail, Chris. We can't."

"I'm going after Mandala," Nikki said suddenly. "No trips to Texas on my agenda."

"So you'll leave Chris to make it there on his own?"

She hesitated at that. "You saw what the bastard did to my mother. I owe him."

"And I'm the only one who can find him," Dogan told her. "But he won't be in Texas; that part of the operation has been planned like clockwork all along. It can easily proceed without him. Mandala will be in South America preparing to get the second stage of his plan underway."

"San Sebastian?"

Dogan nodded. "That explains the presence of those guards down there who tried to kill me. Mandala burned the town but he always knew he'd be coming back." He held Nikki's eyes with his own. "But all this is speculation on my part. There's no sense in both of us wasting our time on what might turn out to be a wild goose chase. You're a professional. God knows you've proved that much. A professional's place is with Chris. Leave Mandala to me."

"And his giant?"

"He's not indestructible."

"Where will you be while the rest of us are in Texas, Ross?" Locke wondered.

"Washington. Trying to pry some people off their asses."

"My mother said that would be a mistake," Nikki reminded.

"For you maybe, but not me. Up until last week, Washington

paid my salary. I'll find people who'll listen. I know the right buttons to push.''

Nikki nodded. "Insurance, right?"

Dogan said nothing.

"Ross, what does she mean by insurance?" Locke asked anxiously.

It was Nikki who answered the question. "I mean if we don't get the job done in Keysar Flats, he's going to try to have somebody standing by who can."

"They might supplement your efforts," Dogan said. "And there's San Sebastian to consider also. This whole thing's much too big for us to handle alone."

"Why not let me take my people to San Sebastian?" Masvidal suggested. "It is my territory."

"But Keysar Flats is the key, the *U.S.* is the key. We've got to concentrate our forces there. Both of us will have to succeed anyway if Mandala is to be stopped altogether." Dogan met the eyes of Nikki and then of Locke. "I should reach Washington tomorrow about the same time you reach Texas. I'll start knocking on doors immediately."

"And hope somebody answers," said Locke.

"Someone who won't put a bullet through your head," added Nikki.

CHAPTER 31

BEFORE LOCKE AND NIKKI DEPARTED FOR AMERICA, DOGAN GAVE them a number to call once they reached Paris. They would be speaking into a tape machine and need only state anything that had come up along the way. Dogan would need Vaslov's help in establishing the line, so he cautioned them not to bother calling it until Paris. It would surely be in place by then.

Next a site had to be found for the rendezvous with Masvidal and his people on Saturday. A guidebook provided them with a roadside motel just off Route 83 that would be perfect. Masvidal would arrive there with his men and equipment sometime after three but before five on Saturday. If he was going to be any later, he would get word to Locke through a messenger.

At Vienna Airport, Chris let Nikki take care of purchasing the tickets and obtaining their boarding passes. While she was at the ticket counter, he busied himself with watching the people. Airports were fantastically uniform locales. All cities in all countries featured the same luggage and the same people carting it in a rush to make their flight, nervously checking their watches as if their eyes might make the hands move slower.

Locke's attention was caught at a small café. An older man with little hair was seated at the counter. Chris felt a tingling in his spine, a warning of recognition. He tried to place the man, couldn't, and stared harder. The man swung round briefly and their eyes would have met if Chris hadn't looked away.

Nikki was by his side seconds later and when he turned back to the coffee counter the man was gone.

"Something wrong?" she asked him.

"No. I just thought I saw someone I recognized."

"Well, we've got forty-five minutes before the flight leaves," she said, placing their boarding passes in her shoulder bag. "A drink should settle those nerves of yours."

Chris went with her to the bar but ordered soda. They sat on stools at the end of the small bar, a vantage point that gave him clear view of the airport lobby.

"The flight has a stop-off at Geneva and then goes to Paris," Nikki was saying. "We'll be in by early Friday morning."

Chris didn't hear her. Something had caught his eye, a head, no, a hat—a green porkpie hat. The man from the coffee counter was visible only from the rear at a newsstand but the hat reminded Locke where he had seen him before. It was the man who'd sat next to him on the flight from London, the man who had spent the trip doing crossword puzzles. Locke slid from his chair.

"Chris?" Nikki called after him.

But Locke was already in motion, pushing through a swarm of debarking passengers crowding into the terminal and hurrying toward the newsstand. What was the man doing back at the airport? Had he been following them all along?

Chris reached the newsstand, but the man with the porkpie hat was gone.

A hand grasped his shoulder. Locke swung quickly.

"Take it easy," Nikki said. "What's going on?"

"The man I sat next to on the plane from London, I thought I saw him standing over here."

"Are you sure?"

"I don't know. Maybe."

"Same size? Height?"

"Just a hat, a green porkpie hat. The overcoat too, I think, but I can't be sure."

"You didn't get a good look at his face?"

"I was too far away. That's why I came over here."

Nikki didn't seem overly concerned. "I think all this is starting to get to you."

"It already has. I still think it was him."

"And what if it was? This airport is known for delayed and canceled flights. No one followed us to or from the castle; I'd bet anything on that. He's probably just a stranded traveler."

Locke shrugged. Nikki led him away from the newsstand back toward the bar.

"You could have stayed at Kreuzenstein," he said when they were seated once again on their stools. "You could have stayed with . . . your mother."

"She's your mother too."

"She was never my mother."

"But what Mandala did to her bothers you as much as it does me, doesn't it?"

"No, because I never knew her. And what I knew I didn't like. She was a specter from my past, a specter I loathed all through my childhood. I didn't just lose her, I lost my father at the same time."

"Chris—"

"No, let me finish. I never knew my mother, Nikki, and I never knew my father either. It isn't easy growing up that way."

"I know how you feel," she said honestly. "But it still hurt when your father died, didn't it?"

"It hurt. And what about you?" He looked at her sharply. "That was your mother we left dying back at the castle. But after shedding a few tears, you took a couple deep breaths and left for the airport with me. You know you'll never see her again, yet I can't see any change in you because of that. Doesn't it hurt for you?"

"Plenty. Feel enough pain, though, and you learn to control it. I've learned to deal with grief in my own way."

"What?"

"You don't want to hear it."

Nikki started to move away. Chris grabbed her arm. "Yes, I do."

Her eyes went cold. "You make it work for you, Chris, that's how you live with it. You turn the grief around and sprinkle your bullets with it. You dream about coming face to face with the person who caused it and that keeps you going, takes your mind off the pain. You dream about killing that person a hundred different ways and when you finally finish him the grief is lifted off your shoulders."

That left Locke speechless. Once again the coldness of the world he had entered hit him head-on. These people could live with death just fine. It was life that gave them problems.

Ten minutes later they passed through Austrian Customs and headed through the terminal for their gate. Chris stopped for a drink and snuck a look behind him.

"He's following us," he told Nikki as he fell in step with her again.

"Who?" She started to turn.

Locke grasped her at the elbow. "Don't look back. It's the man in the damn porkpie hat. Convinced now?"

"Enough to be glad I got my knives through security."

"You think he'll be boarding the plane?"

"More than likely he's just here to make sure we do. He knows we're headed for Geneva now. All he has to do is contact Mandala and there'll be a welcoming committee to greet us at the airport."

"What if we changed our plans?"

"Wouldn't matter. The man would just change his."

"And if we . . . took him out?"

If Nikki was surprised at Locke's suggestion, she didn't show it. "There could be others with him, probably are. Him we've marked; them we haven't. We watch him while he watches us. Stalemate."

"Which gives the advantage to Mandala."

Nikki's face was a mask of determination. "Only for now. We'll have the whole flight to figure out some way of slipping by them in Geneva."

Locke managed to keep a watch on the man with the porkpie hat as he and Nikki joined the boarding line for the flight. Their seats were in the front of the second cabin so they had a clear view of the entrance to the jet. People filed through one after another and found their seats quickly. The stewardess gave the usual set of instructions in German and then English.

The jet began to move. Chris looked out from his window

310

seat. The man with the porkpie hat was standing against the glass over the runway, watching, hands in his pockets. Locke could see him clearly only for a few seconds. But something about the man's stare was chilling.

"He was in the window," Chris told Nikki.

"It makes sense," Nikki whispered calmly. "He's absolutely sure we're on the plane now. Geneva can be alerted. He thinks we're trapped."

A chill seized Locke. "Why did he let us see him?" he asked suddenly.

"What do you mean?"

"He wanted us to see him, that's what I mean. He wanted us to think just what we're thinking, and he was standing there in the window to be certain we didn't try a dodge at the last second. It was worth risking exposure for him."

"What are you talking about?"

"They put a bomb on this plane!"

Nikki's head seemed to snap backward. She searched for a rationale to refute Locke but knew immediately that he was right. Mandala couldn't chance letting them reach Geneva. The man was a red herring sent to distract them, perhaps even to activate the bomb now that they were on board.

"What are we going to do?" Chris asked her, fighting against panic.

"I don't know. I've got to think. We've got time. The bomb won't go off until we're well in the air, past Zurich at least. No trace that way."

"We've got to tell them to go back and land the plane! We've got to tell them about the bomb!"

"They'll detain us, steal time away we don't have. We'd be sitting ducks for Mandala. He wins either way."

Locke thought quickly. "Then only one of us will alert them."

Nikki shook her head. "No good. If we go back to Vienna, we run smack into your friend with the hat again. He'll have others waiting with him, and it'll take all our efforts to stay out of their grasp. We can't afford that. Keysar Flats, remember?"

Locke felt the panic surging now. "What the hell do we do then?"

311

Nikki thought quickly. "There's a way out but it's risky. We'll have to wait until we're close to Switzerland. Another twenty minutes maybe."

"And what if the bomb goes off before then?"

"We'll have to take that chance. We can't risk going back to Vienna if my plan backfires."

"What are you going to do?"

"Hijack this flight."

The minutes passed slower than any Locke could ever remember. Finally Nikki leaned back and pretended to stretch, while she freed her Gurkha knives from their sheaths beneath her bulky jacket. A stewardess was approaching, wheeling a tray of beverages. Good fortune, because the cart would block the aisle and prevent any dime-store heroics once Nikki made her move.

"There might be security agents on board," she whispered to Locke. "If they get me, rush to them immediately and say I mentioned something about a bomb but you thought it was a joke. Understand?"

Locke nodded.

"And whatever happens, act as if you don't know me. Act terrified, dismayed, inconvenienced. Just don't look any different from everyone else."

The stewardess pushed her cart up even with their seats.

"Would you care for a—"

Nikki sprung over the hand rest, *Kukhri* knife gleaming in her hand as she grabbed the stewardess and spun her around, blade pressed against her throat.

"Anyone makes a move and she dies!"

Screams and cries rang out through the cabin. People ducked under seats or covered their ears and eyes in terror. No one dared intervene.

"You!" Nikki shouted at another stewardess. "Go to the cockpit. Tell them this plane is being hijacked. I want it landed in Zurich straightaway." Then, to the passengers who had grown silent. "I'm not alone in this. I've got partners. They won't show themselves unless someone foolishly forces them to."

Back to the other stewardess: "Take my message to the cockpit. Now!"

The stewardess ran down the aisle, whimpering.

Locke watched Nikki back up to the break between cabins with her blade resting dangerously close to her hostage's jugular. Her back came up against a steel divider, which would preclude attack from the rear. She seemed to settle down a little, waiting.

Chris couldn't settle down at all. His heart was thumping madly against his chest. He forced himself to think. If Nikki's plan was successful and the jet landed *safely* in Zurich, Mandala would be caught off guard. He couldn't have men with green porkpie hats waiting at every airport in the world. Chris would be free to make his escape from Zurich and get back to America by any route he could arrange. Nikki had slipped him plenty of cash to make the trip. The prospects of incarceration, prison even, didn't faze her.

"I've gotten out of these kind of scrapes before," she had assured him. "I'll be free again within a few days."

Minutes later the captain's voice came over the intercom, announcing that the plane was being forced to land in Zurich by an armed hijacker but that the passengers were not in any danger whatsoever. Everyone was asked to stay calm and the delay would be kept to a minimum.

When the jet had landed in Zurich, the captain coolly approached Nikki and her stewardess hostage, holding his hands in the air.

"What next?" he asked her in German-laced English.

She pulled the blade from the stewardess's throat, freeing her as she handed the knife over to the captain.

"I'm turning myself over to your custody. Get the passengers off this plane fast. There's a bomb on board."

Locke let himself be swept away in the rush that followed.

Chris broke free from the body of passengers and collected his thoughts in a men's room stall. Mandala might have men waiting at the jet's final destination in Paris, so that city was out of the question for him. He had to head for another, less traveled city, someplace less likely to be within the dark man's reach.

He made his way from the men's room and stopped at the TWA counter where a clerk provided him with the answer: a flight leaving for Madrid in ninety minutes. The wait was nerve-racking but necessary. He went to the gate early and sat facing the runways with his back to airport pedestrian traffic. He could see no one and no one could see him.

Hours later, from a phone booth in Madrid, he called the number Dogan had given him. It rang once, was answered, and a tone followed. Chris was brief in summing up what had happened. His first two lines, in fact, said it all:

"Nikki's out of it. I'm alone."

PART NINE:

WASHINGTON AND
KEYSAR FLATS,
SUNDAY AFTERNOON

CHAPTER 32

SATURDAY AFTERNOON, CALVIN ROY WAS WORKING ON VAN DAM'S files when CIA director Peter Kennally appeared unannounced in his office.

"To what do I owe this pleasure, Major Pete?" Roy said, looking up. He pulled his glasses off and massaged his tired eyes, then ran his hands over his bald dome.

"Depends on what kind of mood you're in, Cal. I'd like to keep my job when you get confirmed as Secretary."

"Got a reason why I'd put an ad in the paper?"

"One just turned up." Kennally moved forward but didn't sit down. "One of our agents was quarantined, a Division Six man named Dogan."

Roy mocked putting his hands over his ears. "I'm not supposed to hear stuff like that."

"This time you'd better. It turns out Dogan was in Liechtenstein at the same time Locke was, and apparently they were supposed to meet at a hotel room in Rome. And the quarantine order was restricted. That means somebody doesn't want Dogan coming in at all."

"How do you know all this?"

Kennally sighed. "Because one of our agents went to Rome and got himself killed in Dogan's place. That's what put me on to the connection in the first place. The hotel was the one our man in Locke's house received a call from. I did some checking. It seems Dogan's original assignment was to kill Locke."

"Where in hell did that order come from?"

"Executive sanction."

"Van Dam?"

"I might have started with him but the restricted status on Dogan originated at a lower level. Group commander, station leader—something like that."

"Christ," Roy muttered. "So one of our agents is ordered to kill Locke, probably ends up joining him instead, and then becomes the object of a kill order himself."

Kennally nodded. "I've lifted the quarantine but it'll take a while for word to filter into the field."

"Ever have a cow piss on ya while you were drawin' milk, Major?"

Kennally just shrugged.

"Well, that's what I think's happening to this country right now, and I ain't got the slightest idea where, when, or how." Roy hesitated. "Your men got shooting clearance on this Dogan, Major?"

"Some of them will certainly interpret it that way."

"Then let's hope they got bad aim."

Dogan was still awake when the sun came up Sunday morning. He wasn't hungry or thirsty. He just lay there hoping the phone would ring, because if it didn't he would be helpless.

The route he had taken into Washington had been long and tiring, for he had taken a number of precautions to avoid identification and capture. There had been several plane changes and brief trips by train and bus along the way. The worst stretch of the journey came in Lisbon, where a fogged-in airport stranded him for six maddening hours. Only a bribe assured him of passage on the first plane out. But it still took him until late Saturday afternoon to arrive in Washington.

The fact that Locke was alone again bothered Dogan only slightly. After all, by now the college professor would have linked up with Masvidal, and their raid on Mandala's Keysar Flats airfield was only hours away at most. Masvidal was supposed to contact Vaslov with confirmation of the rendezvous, and Vaslov, in turn, would contact Dogan. So far no call had come and Dogan found himself increasingly uneasy.

He had spent Saturday night on the phone tracing down old contacts and making new ones, channeling each call through sterile exchanges but keeping them short in case the ciphers had been changed. The end result was to gain him a series of meetings with government officials starting with the Department of Agriculture and moving on to Brian Charney's State Department bureau. He needed allies as well as evidence for the strategy he would implement later today even as Masvidal—and Locke—set out to destroy the canisters in Keysar Flats. If all went according to plan, Dogan would then be free to deal with Mandala personally at San Sebastian. Audra St. Clair's words had confirmed that another phase of Mandala's plan would begin there, one that would destroy South America's farmland as well. It would end where it had started, and Dogan would be the one to end it.

The phone rang, startling him. Only Vaslov knew where to reach him. The Russian's call had come at last.

"Yes?"

"Sorry for the delay in reaching you, comrade," Vaslov said, voice flatter than usual. "But there has been a complication and it has taken me this long to sort everything out."

Dogan felt his stomach sink. "What happened?"

"The Sanii Corporation's plant in Liechtenstein has been destroyed by several well-placed bombs. Many people were killed or injured. Everything is gone."

"It makes sense. Mandala's covering more of the Committee's tracks. He doesn't want the crop genetics research to fall into anyone else's hands and disrupt his plans."

"There is more, comrade. The perpetrators of the explosion have already been arrested. Officials are calling it a major breakthrough in the assault on terrorism."

Dogan knew the rest before Vaslov continued.

"Our friend Masvidal and over fifty of his troops were apprehended in Spain after a gun battle that claimed many lives. That final bit is right off the Associated Press wire. . . . Are you there, comrade?"

"Give me a few minutes to sort things out," Dogan managed.

"I'll call you back in a half hour, comrade."

Dogan hung up the phone dazed. Masvidal had not made the rendezvous in Keysar Flats. Locke was there alone.

But he didn't have to be. It was time to forget about precautions and procedures. None of that mattered any longer. He would make more calls and demand the meetings begin at once. He would keep calling until somebody listened and sent the marines into Keysar Flats.

Dogan had lifted the receiver from its hook again when the door to his room burst open and a flood of bodies poured through. He was in motion immediately toward the pistol hanging from the back of a chair, but he knew he'd never make it. The men charged forward, guns all black and steel, promising death.

It had been seven o'clock Saturday evening when Locke had given up waiting for Masvidal at the Ramrod Roadside Motel. He might have given up much earlier, when the messenger did not arrive as promised by five, but had no idea of what to do next. So he had stayed, hoping against hope Masvidal would materialize. He had no way of contacting Dogan, Nikki was gone, and now something had stopped Masvidal from coming.

It had been drizzling all day and by seven, when Locke finally returned to his room, the heavier rain had finally started, subsiding back to a drizzle around midnight.

The trip there had been long and unsettling. The man with the porkpie hat had reminded him to trust no one. Every person he passed was a potential assassin. Chris had spent much of the flight from Madrid to New York scrutinizing the half-filled cabin. He changed seats twice to avoid being near any one person too long.

Returning to the States made him think sadly of his family. He could only hope the real Burgess had been right about the government protecting the rest of them after Greg had been kidnapped. But the Committee could reach anybody. If he failed in Keysar Flats, what would become of his loved ones?

It hurt too much to think about, so Chris made himself stop. His mind swung back to Masvidal and a hundred possible explanations for what might have gone wrong. None of them mattered, though, because the one overriding fact was that he wasn't coming and neither were his people. That left Chris with two choices: Either he could sit and sulk or he could go out and do something on his own. Keysar Flats was a big place but he had lots of time, a whole night to drive his rental car around every road he could find. He was looking for cropdusters and plenty of them. They'd be well protected and that might make them stand out.

Of course, Locke had no idea what he would do if he found the planes, but he had to make the effort. He was well rested, having slept a full dozen hours since arriving at the Ramrod. And he had a full tank of gas in the car he had rented in Dallas.

Chris started for the door, the absurdity of the situation almost making him smile: if the Gods themselves had imprisoned Tantalus, how could he possibly hope to free him?

Pop Keller sat in the corner of the Lonesome Horn Bar and Grill drinking his second special of the young day, a sweet concoction that tasted like sugared prairie dust. Yesterday's special had been Jack Daniels straight up with a twist, and that had been much more to his liking. The day before that . . .

Pop Keller scratched his head. He couldn't remember what the special had been day before yesterday. Amazing what advancing age could do for you. . . .

Pop sipped his special and blessed the thin mist in the skies above the Lonesome Horn because it saved him the trouble of spending the day looking for a new site for his Flying Devils air show. The engagement had been scheduled to begin a week ago but then the rains came and on top of that they lost the only site in the Flats worth a damn. So Pop had sent his people out to enjoy the sights of Texas, hid himself in the Lonesome Horn, and started on the specials. Today was the sixth, seventh maybe. They were all starting to taste alike.

He might have stayed with his sugared prairie dust all day, except he was supposed to meet his people at their roadside camp at noon sharp. All this waiting around had the boys getting restless. Most had regular jobs they had already taken too much time away from.

The Flying Devils had once been the best in the business. They barnstormed the country with their World War II fighters, putting on mock air battles that thrilled their audiences. No jet-powered engines, no gymnastic circles in the air. Just plain old gutsy flying in reconditioned fighters.

The planes carried live ammunition in their front-mounted machine guns and real rockets under their wings. The highlight of the exhibition had often been Pop Keller himself putting on an amazing display of target practice at a thousand feet. He'd been able to shoot the horns off a bull . . . until his eyes went, that is.

He should have gotten glasses but they looked lousy under his leather flying goggles. Seven years back he had been squinting to focus when his fighter made a sudden dip and scraped the wing of another. At least it felt like a scrape. In fact, the collision tore the wing off his buddy's plane and a moderate crowd of 1,200 watched him crash and die in a nearby field.

Pop Keller escaped jail but not scandal. The insurance company laid into him heavy and there were so many lawsuits, he figured he might as well move a cot into the Superior Court. The Devils started to come apart. Pop's best fliers, the young ones, left for the Confederate Air Force or the Valiant Air Command and took their planes with them, leaving him with a ragtag unit of mostly old men who napped before and after performances. But flying was an important part of their lives and they didn't want to quit. And their pension checks took some of the strain off Pop Keller's barely solvent operation.

He had weathered the storm of the scandal, steeled himself even against the pranksters who changed the first "e" in his name to an "i" on billboards, proclaiming him Pop "Killer." And the Flying Devils had managed to hang together, keep their live ammunition, and change their show to include more mock air battles, which were strangely the most rehearsed and safest segments of their show. The younger fliers started coming back and the Flying Devils again became as good as any of their competitors.

But not many people seemed to care anymore. They had done only six gigs in the past nine months and no crowd had reached a thousand. They collected far less money at the gate than it took for repairs and reconditioned parts for the ancient fighters which, like Pop Keller, didn't know enough to give up. Pop was down to thirty-seven fighters, and there was seldom a day when more than twenty of them were able to take the air. Parts had been traded around so much that it was impossible to tell which had started where. Pop kept hiring mechanics to patch his fleet together with Scotch tape, Elmer's Glue, or whatever else it took. He was living off a dozen loans now. Before too much longer, though, he'd have to sell all his beautiful fighters just to get out of debt.

Pop had gotten in the World War II air show business early, before the Warbird craze caught on. He bought most of his fighters in the fifties and sixties at rock-bottom prices that didn't even approach their value today. But as they appreciated, so did his insurance costs until he had to sell off a few every six months just to stay above water. He started taking on pilots just to get their planes in the show, agreeing to pay upkeep, maintenance, and insurance on them just so long as they were ready to go at showtime. The compromises made his flesh crawl. Doctors, pharmacists, cesspool technicians—for a while the civilians had outnumbered the true fliers in the Devils. Bad times had forced most of them out now, leaving Pop with a nucleus of hardcore Warbirds who had lasted through a week of rain and a cancellation here in Keysar Flats.

Pop still owned a majority of his fleet, twenty-one of the thirty-seven planes. Regardless of ownership, they were all beautiful: six one-man Piper L-4s, eight T-6 Texas trainers, five P-51 Mustangs and the same number of P-40 Warhawks; four Corsairs, three F8F Bearcats, and a pair each of Spitfires, Trojans, and German Messerschmitts. He pampered them like children, taking great pride in the fact that several had been lifted literally off the scrap heap and reconditioned with his own hands.

Pop drained the rest of his special and watched the mist starting to break outside. He didn't have the spare parts anymore to make planes fly, and the men flying them were living out ancient fantasies in skies that didn't scorn them. It was nice when you thought of it that way. Pop could see the bitterness and despair disappear every time they took to the air. They would have been much happier in a real battle.

Keysar Flats, he figured, might be the end. Having their site yanked right out was a crippler, a total loss on the money he'd spent getting his fleet there. Looking for another site had started as a pain in the ass and then the weather fucked him sideways, so it probably didn't matter anyway.

Not surprisingly, then, Pop Keller could recognize a man in trouble because one looked back at him in the mirror every day. He knew he was seeing one in the nervous man swallowing coffee at the bar. They had the Lonesome Horn all to themselves, and Pop Keller didn't feel like being alone.

He pushed his ragged, arthritic bones from his table and slid onto the stool next to the stranger's.

"Mind if I join you?"

"Be my guest," Christopher Locke told him.

Pop Keller ordered another special and looked the man over. His eyes were drawn and bloodshot, his hair matted down by the morning rain.

"You look like hell, friend."

Locke almost smiled. "Believe it or not, that's the nicest thing anybody's said to me in quite a while."

"Been up all night?"

"Yeah."

"I figured as much. I knew I recognized that look. . . . Can I buy you a drink?"

"Just coffee."

"Some food?"

"I'm not hungry."

"Gotta eat, friend. I turned sixty-six last week and I ain't lost my appetite yet."

Locke stared down into his coffee, wishing the old man would go away. He was depressed and frustrated, and wanted very much to be alone with his misery. He had been up the entire night driving the roads of Keysar Flats, losing his way enough times to lose track of which roads he had been on and which ones he'd missed. It was no use. The airfield sheltering the cropdusters was too well hidden. It was over and he had lost. There wasn't a single soul in the world he could turn to for help.

"Sometimes it helps to talk things out, friend," the old man suggested.

"Not this time."

"Friend, I've had a load of trouble in my life and finding a sympathetic ear always seems to ease it. Let me try and help you."

Locke looked into the wizened, liver-spotted face beneath a sparse crop of white hair. "Unless you've got an army regiment or air force squadron waiting close by, there's not a damn thing you can do."

Pop Keller smiled.

Dogan was confused when the men who'd converged on his hotel room had not killed him. They roughed him up a bit, refused to respond to his questions, and then transported him handcuffed in the back of a van to what must have been a safe house over the border in Virginia. There he was locked in a small living room with steel-barred windows and plenty of guards beyond the door. Dogan spent the ensuing hours pacing anxiously. What was going on? What did the men have planned for him?

It must have been closing in on noontime when the door to the room finally opened and a small, balding man wearing a pair of steel-rimmed glasses entered.

"I'll tell ya, son," he said, addressing Dogan in a comfortable southern drawl, "somebody should dig up all the channels of this piss-ass government and plant new ones. Woulda been here sooner but word takes a damnable long time to travel." The figure stepped closer and extended his hand. "The name's Roy, son, Calvin Roy. Had your lunch yet? I don't know 'bout you, but I'm starved."

They drove north along U.S. 83 in Pop Keller's battered pickup.

"You sure they'll be at that airfield?" Locke asked him. "What did you call it?"

"Stonewall Jackson Air Force Base. Been shut down for fifteen years now. But the runways are still kept in condition and there's plenty of hangars, barracks, and large storage areas. I should know. I rented the fucking place four months back. Somebody canceled our show eight days ago. They didn't give no reason."

"You're lucky they let you walk away alive."

Pop's fingers tightened around the steering wheel. "Let me tell you something, friend—"

"Call me Chris."

"Yeah, Chris, I went through the big one: WW Two. I shot down lots of Jap planes and I walked away from every battle. I don't intend to break that streak now."

Locke searched for a clock in the pickup but found none. "How many planes do you have?"

"You're talkin' 'bout some pretty heavy flyin' here, Chris. My fighters got lots of guts but not an awful lot holdin' them together. Twenty's a reasonable figure to get up, give or take a few."

"I can't ask you to go along with this. The risks involved would be—"

"I don't give two shits about risk," Pop snapped.

"But your men, they—"

"My men feel like I do. We're all beaten old farts, Chris boy. We've all been dreamin' about fighting one last battle for years now. 'Sides, cropdusters ain't exactly about to offer much of a contest in an air-to-air battle with my fleet. Hell, I still got planes that'll go three bucks easy."

"They'll have taken other precautions."

"No sweat. We'll come in low and fast and the bastards'll never know what hit 'em."

Locke shook his head. "No, I can't let you do this. Just get me to this air force base and I'll take it from there."

"Alone, friend? Now that wouldn't be too smart, would it? Come on, you're doin' us a favor. Flyin' on weekends like a bunch of circus clowns has beaten the life out of my men. They all left their best days behind, and anything that helps them get those days back is okay for sure. They joined up with the Devils and stayed 'cause at least they can still fly and maybe pretend. Well, they won't have to pretend today."

Locke hesitated. "You're sure about Stonewall Jackson being the place?"

"I'm sure it's the only site in the Flats capable of sustaining the kinda operation you described 'cause I spent plenty of time lately lookin' for others. And what better reason can you think of to cancel my gig all of a sudden?"

Chris shrugged, knowing he had to give in to the old man for lack of any other alternative. "Just volunteers, Pop, we only take volunteers."

Keller smiled at him. "Wouldn't have it any other way, friend."

The Flying Devils had set up camp not far from the North Wichita River, fifteen minutes flying time from Stonewall Jackson Air Force Base. Locke stepped down from Pop Keller's pickup and felt as if he were stepping back in time. The trailers and storage trucks had been arranged in a circle surrounding a huge mass of green tarpaulins, which covered the fleet. It almost looked like the men of the traveling air show had arranged their vehicles to protect against Indian attack.

"Gus, get the boys together!" Pop shouted to a toothless, barrel-chested man hammering away at a stripped engine.

"What you say, Pop?"

"Hurry up's what I say, asshole! We got us a war to fight today!"

"Huh?"

Minutes later Pop Keller was standing on the roof of a trailer with the Flying Devils logo fading from its side. Fifty or so men gazed up at him intently as he recited his own colorful version of Locke's story. Chris scanned them, saw not hesitation and fear but determination and resolve in their faces.

"This here's the front, boys," Keller said, nearing his close, "and we're the last thing that stands between these murderin' bastards and America. Some of us knocked plenty of Nazis and Japs from the sky and others took out their share of Gooks a few years later. I say it's time to hit the skies for real again!"

"Yeah!" came the resounding chorus.

"Who's with me, boys?"

Every hand went up.

"Let's get to it, then!"

With roars of enthusiastic delight, the men of the Flying Devils headed toward their positions, each knowing his proper place. For them the preparations were probably the same as those for a show, yet Chris could not help but be amazed at the precision of their motions. In less than a minute, the tarps were all ripped from the planes and left to flutter in the wind. Locke looked at the ancient fighters and felt his heart sink. Somehow he had expected fresh, glowing Warhawks and Cobras shining proudly in the sun. What he saw instead was a squadron of battered, broken airplanes that looked as fragile as the balsawood fliers boys toss around their backyards. The Devils had done their best to restore each fighter's original paint job, but patchup work was so evident that not a single plane could boast a consistent shade.

Locke sat down against a trailer. For a while the sight of broken men readying broken airplanes for battle had an almost comic texture to it. Then suddenly Chris realized there was nothing even remotely comic about what he was watching. The Devils moved confidently, even as they spit tobacco and huffed for breath. Engines were checked, propellers oiled and greased, glass cockpit covers washed squeaky clean. Gun sights were set and huge ammunition belts for the front-mounted machine guns were snapped home. For those planes still capable of holding bombs, dark-green projectiles were loaded beneath the wings. Wooden blocks were yanked from under the fighters' tires and mechanics rushed crazily from one to the next, tightening a lug or fastening a bolt. When they wiped the sweat from their brow, they left a trail of grease behind. Their white T-shirts grew filthy from the grime.

Chris found himself rising involuntarily to his feet. The fighters were all being spun around now to face the same direction— toward the highway. A few pilots gunned their engines and taxied forward on their own. The ancient fighters seemed brighter now, more alive, as if they understood the role they were being called on to perform and were responding to it.

"We'll be off the ground in fifteen minutes, Chris," Pop Keller told him, the pain of his arthritis vanquished along with thoughts of unpaid debts and bankruptcy.

"What are we gonna use for runways?" Locke asked.

Keller's eyes gazed out at U.S. 83. "The highway, friend. We'll place trailers across to block off a big enough stretch. Yup, it'll do just fine."

Four prairie dust specials were starting to make themselves felt in his stomach, and Pop moved off toward the water jugs to drown the damn booze. Locke looked back at the fighters and watched the pilots donning their flying gear. Other men were still prepping guns and passing out parachutes.

Keller returned, dragging his sleeve across his lips. "We'll be able to get about twenty of them in the air like I said and about half are equipped with rockets."

"How many men per plane?"

"Most are outfitted to take two but we'll stay with one. Cropdusters ain't the fastest planes on the market but we'll still need to cut out as much excess weight as possible to be sure of catching them."

While the plane engines idled, all the men gathered together, and Pop Keller moved toward them. The average age of the Flying Devils looked to be about fifty-five, with variations twenty years in both directions.

"Boys," Pop Keller began, eyes plainly on his watch, "we ain't got much time. I ain't much good at speakin' so I'm just gonna speak my mind. It's gonna be dangerous for us on this raid. Our best bet is to strike fast and hard and take these bastards with their pants down. If it looks like none of the dusters have took off yet when we get to the base, both Red and Blue wings will go in blasting. If some dusters have made it up, and that's my guess, we'll use a different strategy." Pop Keller searched the crowd. "Mickey O.," he called out.

A burly, white-haired man wearing an oil-stained shirt stepped forward. "Right here."

"You'll lead Blue Wing on the air-to-ground assault while I

take Red Wing air-to-air after any of the bastards that already took off. Let yours and the other Pipers head the attack 'cause you each got six rockets and the best aim by far. We all gotta be careful," Pop went on, speaking to everyone, " 'cause catchin' them with their pants down don't necessarily mean they'll be holdin' their dicks in their hands. They'll be protected, boys. Make your ammo count and remember we gotta knock these dusters down before they can drop their stuff."

The men of the Flying Devils glanced at each other.

"Boys, I'm not much of an expert on this scientific junk but it's a plain fact that the scum we're goin' up against means to do a swift number on the old U.S. of A. Well, I fought the Nazis and the Japs to keep that from happening and I'll do it again today, tomorrow, or any other day it's called for."

The Flying Devils started hooting and hollering. Some of the men whistled through their parched lips.

"Ready, boys?"

A triumphant scream rang out.

"Then let's get to it!"

And with that, the Flying Devils scattered toward their fighters, or the trucks and trailers that would follow them to Stonewall Jackson on the ground. Members of the ground-based crew helped the leather-clad pilots into their cockpits and waited for the thumbs-up sign as engines were gunned and propeller blades spun to life. A chorus of sputtering followed, quickly drowned out by the sound of gunned engines revving again. The assault squadron was ready for take-off, with nineteen fighters, six of which were Piper L-4s carrying rocket-propelled warheads under their wings.

"Ain't gonna miss your own show, are ya, friend?" a voice shouted at Locke over the roar of the engines.

Chris turned to Pop Keller. The old pilot adjusted his goggles and then zipped up his brown leather flight jacket.

"I saved you the rear seat in my personal sweetheart," Pop said.

And together they trotted toward a red P-40 Warhawk with the gaping mouth of a shark painted on its nose.

330

CHAPTER 33

TWENTY MILES AWAY, ANOTHER PART OF KEYSAR FLATS WAS ALIVE with similar activity. Fifty eager cropdusters were approaching takeoff position on two runways at Stonewall Jackson Air Force Base. The canisters had been loaded and all had been ready for ten minutes now but Ahmad Hamshi, the man in charge, had his orders as to the precise schedule and under no circumstances would he deviate from it. Hamshi was Mandala's leading operations man in the Mideast and one of the few anywhere he trusted. He had brought the Arab to Keysar Flats specifically because he was a man intolerant of slipups. Hamshi would not disappoint him. So far things had gone off without a hitch and he wanted to keep it that way.

Once the cropdusters had begun their climb, Hamshi would dial a number in South America and give the go code, which would be relayed to Mandala in San Sebastian. Direct contact between them was impossible, as was further contact of any kind once the go code was given.

To insure total secrecy and complete control, Mandala had devised a plan he called Hop-Skip, whereby all canisters were loaded onto the initial squadron of dusters. They would empty their prescribed amounts and then rendezvous at the first "hop" point where the remaining canisters would be loaded onto dusters that would then "skip" on to the next rendezvous point. To have evenly distributed the canisters at the fifteen bases lining the center of the country would have meant far faster dispersal but would also have required the taking of far more men into his confidence. The physical logistics would prove more difficult under his Hop-Skip strategem, yet on the slim chance that one or more of the rendezvous bases were raided, there would be nothing for the authorities to find. Time clearly wasn't a factor because the fungus spread so fast that this method of dispersal would slow the rate of total crop contamination across North America by barely a day. Furthermore, if a rendezvous base was captured, the approaching dusters would simply proceed on to the next one.

Ahmad Hamshi checked his watch: one minute to go now. The pilots were revving their engines. Since each plane was weighed down with the bulk of the excess canisters, its climb would be slowed. It would take just over seven minutes from takeoff for the dusters to rise to their optimum dispersal altitude and spread out sufficiently, and not until then would they open the valves that would dispense their cargo.

Hamshi sniffed the air. The clearing skies had left things hot and humid, ideal weather for the fungus to procreate and spread. Mandala would be pleased to learn that even the weather had cooperated with them, as if Allah was behind their plan. He checked his watch again.

The time had come.

He made the appropriate signal to the men directing the planes on both runways, and immediately the first two dusters began to accelerate down the dust-blown strips.

Ahmad Hamshi saw them clear the ground. As the next two taxied into position, he moved inside his cobweb-coated office and adjusted the transmitter to the proper frequency. He gave his call signal and a slightly garbled voice answered with the according one.

"The birds are flying" was all Hamshi said, repeating it twice before he returned to the runways.

"We got two thousand horses under us, Chris," Pop Keller shouted back to Locke from the front of the cockpit.

"What?"

"There should be a set of headphones in front of you," Pop shouted louder. "Put them on!"

"I got them!" Chris yelled back, fitting the plastic over his ears.

Pop Keller's voice filled them immediately. "I said we got two thousand horsepower pulling us. I do some special stunts so I had the old Warhawk souped up a little." He tightened his own set of headphones. "You'll be able to hear all communications clearly now, friend." His eyes tilted down. "That's the base down there to our right. Enjoy the show."

The ninth and tenth cropdusters were climbing for the sky when Hamshi saw the planes coming. He shook himself, wondering if it might have been a trick of the brightening sun, then quickly realized it wasn't. Unless he had lost his mind, though, the squadron of planes swooping toward Stonewall Jackson on an obvious attack run was a mixed collection of World War II fighters!

He started running toward the twin rows of dusters, reaching them just as two more screamed toward the sky and the ghost squadron roared closer.

"Damn!" Pop Keller rasped into his headset. "Some of the cropdusters are already airborne. Blue leader, how many do you figure slipped out?"

"I count twelve climbing and spreading, Red leader," the husky voice of Mickey Ostrovsky came back. "Weighted down by the look of it. Climbing slow."

"Blue leader," said Keller, "take your Pipers down and knock out as many of the other dusters as you can. Have the other half of your wing wait to mop up the mess."

"Affirmative, Red leader."

Pop adjusted his headset and Locke felt suddenly dizzy as the bottom seemed to drop out of the Warhawk.

"Red Wing, this is Red leader. We're a little late, boys. Time to do some huntin'."

Ahmad Hamshi had just signaled the dusters to continue taking off when the wave of Pipers soared over the runways. He saw the shiny, oblong objects shot from their wings, heard the

333

rockets whistling through the wind, and hit the pavement just before they did.

The explosions came fast and loud, like thousands of pieces of glass shattering. Smoke clouded the start of the runways but as Hamshi climbed back to his feet he saw that miraculously only two of the dusters seemed damaged. Armed assault troops were pouring from the barracks by this time, rushing toward flatbed trucks that held heavy-canvas-covered, high-caliber machine and antiaircraft guns.

They were still yanking the covers away when the Pipers attacked again from the opposite direction. A dozen rocket-propelled warheads hurtled toward the ground. The resulting explosions sent huge chunks of cement into the air and disabled at least four additional dusters. As the Pipers swung into a steep climb, a pair of Bearcats dove under them and sprayed the runway area with machine-gun fire, scattering Hamshi's men.

The smoke made it hard for Hamshi to estimate the damage. This was crazy. He was watching the whole plan disintegrate around him thanks to a bunch of crazy men flying ghost planes. He started running toward the main body of troops, who had started to organize their fire, even as the truck-mounted big guns were tilted toward the sky.

"The planes!" Hamshi shouted. "Move the disabled planes out of the way! We've got to keep the runway free! The runway must be kept free!"

Already he was starting to consider how to make up for the loss of at least six dusters. Mandala's orders had been precise in the event of sudden mechanical breakdown. Well, this certainly fell into that category. The canisters were the key, Mandala had explained, and should be moved from disabled planes onto planes that could fly.

Sprinting along the runways, Hamshi noticed two more of the dusters had managed to take off and were climbing into the sky. Then he saw the streak of red, a Warhawk with a shark's mouth for a nose, screeching forward, and he heard its machine-gun fire. Both dusters dipped crazily out of control, swooning for the ground beyond the runway and exploding on contact.

The bastard had shot them down! Then Hamshi watched as

half the ghost fighter squadron broke off and soared higher in obvious pursuit of the dusters that had managed to escape the base. He glanced in the direction of one of the hangars and then bolted in a diagonal toward where the base personnel had gathered.

"We got the sons of bitches! You see that, Chris?"

Pop Keller pulled up from his dive and climbed almost vertically, his engine straining. Locke had seen all right but he couldn't believe it. The ease with which Keller had maneuvered the Warhawk and knocked the cropdusters from the sky was incredible.

"Two down, lots to go!" Pop screamed. "Heeeeeee-yahh-hhhhh!"

Keller leveled off and picked up the Warhawk's pace as Blue Wing was diving for another attack run.

Down below, the monstrous machine guns and antiaircraft cannons had finally been made ready.

"Holy shit!" Pop grabbed his headset. "Blue leader, this is Red leader, do you copy?"

"I copy, Blue leader."

"I just spotted guns, big ones, on the ground."

"I see them too, Red leader," Mickey O. acknowledged.

"They'll tear you to shreds! Have your team pull up, do you hear me?" Keller could hear the booming *rat-tat-tat* of the big guns and see the fire belching from their barrels even from this distance.

"Negative, Red leader, too late to pull out now."

"The bastard's crazy," Pop said to Locke.

Aren't we all? Chris might have responded but he was having trouble catching his wind.

"Red Wing," Pop Keller started into his mouthpiece, "this is Red leader. Assume attack formation. We'll take airborne planes from the rear. Let's go for it, boys!"

As in the steps of a complex dance routine, the planes of Red Wing—a pair of trainers, three Mustangs, two Corsairs, a Spitfire, and a Messerschmitt—fell in behind Pop Keller, whose Warhawk flew at the center of a wedge spread into a pattern of wide wings. The fighters stormed into the wind, cheating the currents in pursuit of the specks climbing, spreading, and drawing away from Stonewall Jackson Air Force Base.

"We haven't got much time," Locke said, finding his wind but not his stomach.

"Won't take much," Pop promised, opening his throttle a bit more.

Behind Red Wing, the battle was raging back at the base. Mickey O. lost one Piper and a Trojan in the first assault from the big guns. Not one of his wing's rockets, fired in desperation, had found its mark.

"Blue Wing, this is Blue leader. Remaining Pipers, follow me down for a run at the guns, 'specially the cannons. You others blast the runway to fuckin' hell."

Mickey O. swung his Piper for the big guns as the Bearcat, Mustang, and T-6 trainer roared for the runway. In World War II, the Piper L-4 Cubs had been used extensively for bombing runs on German Tiger tanks. A direct charge into those heavily armored monsters, of course, was out of the question. So the Pipers would make their runs by coming around the flank of a mountain or diving from the camouflage of a hill. Mickey O. tried that strategy with his remaining Pipers now. He swung in low beyond the barracks and cut a sharp angle back for the big guns, hoping to take them by surprise from the rear.

As he dipped into his approach, he saw the other three members of his wing had made a successful strike on the runways. Green-garbed men who had been pushing already disabled aircraft aside scampered frantically away. More of the dusters were blown onto their sides and set ablaze.

"Hot dog!" screamed Mickey O., who somewhere had left a wife and kids, several sets of them actually, scattered all over the country. He was sixty-two and cancer had for some time been eating away at his innards. Well, fuck these Commie bastards and fuck the cancer too!

Mickey O. released two more of his rockets as he soared over the big guns and watched as the other three Pipers did the same. One of the trucks blew up in a blaze of red, struck broadside by a pair of warheads. Guns from the other three kept blasting away, the other bombs either misses or duds altogether. Forty years ago Pipers had taken on Tiger tanks and often enough had won. But age had taken its toll on their sights, and Mickey O. should have known coming in this fast was a mistake. The enemy still had one machine gun and both its cannons.

"Pull up," he ordered his team. "Pull up and prepare for our next run."

"Blue leader, I'm hit! I'm hit!"

"Eject! Get the hell outta—"

"I can't! Fuel line ruptured. Trying to—"

The explosion swallowed the rest of the younger man's words. The big guns bore down on two more of the Pipers and just kept firing, orange flaring continuously in their barrels. The Pipers bled black smoke and went into a swoon, the only consolation being the sight of two parachutes floating toward the ground. That left Mickey O. with five planes now, including his own.

"Red leader, this is Blue leader, do you read me?"

Pop Keller's wing had almost caught up with the first wave of airborne dusters.

"I read you, Blue leader."

"Have encountered casualties, repeat casualties."

"Shit! How bad?"

"At least four planes destroyed. Two pilots dead."

"God damn! Gotta take out those guns, Mickey."

"Negative, Pop, we can't control these old birds sure enough to come in that low and fast."

"Then blast the runways from up high. Just don't let any more of the bastards take off! We'll finish our run here and come back and take them together."

In fact, no other cropdusters were even attempting to take off because Hamshi had ordered the functioning ones to swing away from the runway and taxi behind the protection of the three remaining big guns while canisters from the disabled planes were loaded onto them.

Up ahead of him, Pop Keller watched with dismay as the airborne dusters began widening the distance between themselves.

"Shit"—he moaned—"they're pulling out."

"No," Locke said. "They're approaching their dispersal altitudes. We've got to take them *now*!"

"I'll drink to that, friend." Hand on his headset again. "Red Wing, this is Red leader. Spread out and take 'em, boys, one to a customer." Then, to Locke. "Now the fun begins."

The Flying Devils had never performed better. They fanned out neatly and expertly in the trails of the various dusters, banking away from the wedge formation. The duster pilots fought for more speed as some of the fighters roared overhead in pursuit of the first few that had taken off.

Pop Keller drew his Warbird closer to one of the dusters in the rear.

"Gonna crawl right up his ass and give him a fuckin' enema to remember!"

Locke could see the old man tightening his gloved hands on the control stick and placing both thumbs over the red firing button that operated the twin machine guns. The 2,000-horsepower engine shook the old fighter forward like a jet.

"Here we go!"

Locke watched Keller press the button. Bullets pounded into the back and wing of the target and Keller pulled immediately into a climb.

The duster exploded beneath them, bursting into flames and dying right there in the sky. Still crackling, it slid through the air screeching shrilly and leaving a trail of black smoke in its wake.

"Hot shit! One down, eleven more to go," Pop announced proudly.

Another duster exploded to their right, and Red Wing's pair of Corsairs had successfully crippled a pair of dusters to the left.

"Double up," Keller ordered. "When you've made a hit, link up with the fighter closest to you and keep on huntin'." He turned to Locke. "If any other dusters get off the ground, they'll send them away from us in the other direction. We'll have to go back for them as soon as we've finished with these."

As it was, though, no other cropdusters had taken off. Mickey O. followed a Piper and a Bearcat down for a quick run to head them off before they reached areas of safety behind the trucks, but the big guns found a quick bearing on the two lead planes and fired, tearing the old fighters apart before they even got close. They just seemed to disintegrate in the air, taking their pilots with them. They were good men, Mickey O. thought, damn good men.

He swung into a climb quick enough to smack his teeth together, as his two remaining planes provided cover fire. He had another Bearcat and a Mustang left and both still had rockets, but their aim was unreliable. They were horribly mismatched against the ground-based antiaircraft cannons. There remained twenty, maybe twenty-five perfectly flyable dusters just waiting for a chance to take off. They had to be disabled. But how?

"Blue Wing, this is Blue leader. We'll circle around for a bit and regroup. How's your fuel?" Both pilots acknowledged they had plenty. "All right, here's the plan. . . ."

Mickey O. was about to go on when he heard a familiar sound that sent a shudder through his entire cancer-eaten frame. He looked down toward the hangar area in time to see four armored helicopter gunships lifting straight into the sky. Damn things looked like giant black insects with two twin machine guns mounted on either front side as stingers and rocket launchers aimed forward and back looking like antennae.

"Holy Christ . . ."

The helicopters had to be taken out. Otherwise they'd catch Pop and blow his entire wing to hell.

"Blue Wing, this is Blue leader. Go for the helicopters. Repeat, go for the helicopters. Hit 'em with everything you've got! I'm gonna draw the fire of the big guns so you can come in unhindered."

Mickey O. banked around the outskirts of the base and roared downward much too fast to even think of using his remaining three rockets over the big guns lodged on the truck beds. His teeth clamped together, and he was thrown back hard against the cockpit's shoulder rest, which snapped off from the impact.

He felt the bullets pound his wings and tail, and the Piper sputtered. The windshield shattered and glass blew into Mickey O.'s face, drawing blood everywhere and blinding one of his eyes. But he had done his job by drawing the fire of the big guns away from his fighters long enough to allow them to engage the gunships. He turned his remaining eye in their direction.

The Mustang and Bearcat were in the midst of a vicious air

battle, firing as they darted through the sky. The gunships, though, could match them in speed and easily outmaneuver them. Mickey O.'s pilots managed to position themselves for several volleys of fire from their machine guns. But only a direct hit in a vital area could cripple the gunships, and virtually all their bullets bounced off the choppers' armor.

The Bearcat streaked in front of one of the choppers and a rocket from the gunship blasted it into flaming oblivion. The Mustang settled into an escape run, but a second gunship drew near quickly and pounded it with cannon fire intense enough to tear the plane in half.

Mickey O. pushed for enough thrust to reach the choppers himself but the Piper handled listlessly, showing the effects of its wounds. The engine sputtered. He was drawing straight over the big guns again and tried desperately to drive the Piper into a lift.

It climbed a little but the big guns still found him. Mickey O. reeled as a piece of shrapnel thudded into his side and part of a ricocheting shell smacked his stomach. With the last of his strength, he pulled the dying Piper up and away from the big guns, and limped off into the hills, as the helicopters took off on Pop's trail.

"Red leader, this is Blue leader," he muttered through the blood starting to collect in his mouth. "Watch your rear. Big . . . guns . . . coming. . . ."

His radio, though, had been knocked out by the first rampage of bullets. Pop Keller never heard his warning.

On the ground, Ahmad Hamshi gazed happily at the helicopter gunships streaking away in the trail of the ghost planes. By his count there were still twenty-eight cropdusters waiting to take off, with ten destroyed and twelve airborne. Even if all twelve of these were destroyed by the ghost planes, Hamshi calculated that the remaining twenty-eight could still accomplish their task. There was no way of contacting Mandala, so he was forced to take matters into his own hands. The distribution strategy would have to be altered a bit, the range of the dispersal pattern modified. Little of Tantalus's effect, though, would be lost. The range would only be narrowed, the time for total infection lengthened accordingly by only a week, even less maybe. Mandala wouldn't have been able to do better himself under the circumstances.

Meanwhile Hamshi would not risk any more of the cropdusters until the helicopters completed their chore of destroying the other half of this ghost squadron.

It wouldn't take long.

Pop Keller and the Red attack wing were closing on the last four dusters, the first four that had taken off from Stonewall Jackson. They were all in sight of his fighters and coming rapidly into range.

"Fire when ready," Pop ordered as he pushed his Warhawk into range of the duster he had trained in his sights.

He had left this one for himself and assigned three of his fighters to the other three remaining dusters. There were a lot of low-flying clouds and the dusters had passed into them in the hope of shaking off their pursuers. This unnerved Pop slightly because it took him out of eye contact with his wing and that was something a squadron commander dreaded. He wanted to be done with this, link the wing together, and make tracks back for the base to find out what had happened to Mickey O. and Blue Wing.

A flood of black smoke stained a cloud to his far right.

"There!" Locke pointed.

"My Messerschmitt did that," Pop boasted. "You can make book on it."

More smoke billowed from a cloud to his left.

"That was the Spitfire's work." Pop beamed. He gritted his teeth. "Okay, you bastard," he said to the duster before him as the clouds broke and they flew together into sharp blue sky. "Get ready to join the fellows."

The duster could have released its canister contents there quite effectively but refrained, as the others had, because it would have required a substantial loss of speed. The pilot didn't realize that escape from Pop's 2,000-horsepower engine was impossible no matter what he did. Pop snapped his thumbs and tore into the plane's fuselage with machine-gun spray. The duster burst into flames.

"Straight to hell, asshole," Pop shouted after him as a similar orange ball erupted far to the right. A pair of Mustangs had finished the final duster.

"Red leader, this is Red Wing three" came a pilot's old, panicked voice. "Something's coming up on me from the rear. I'm turning to. I'm trying— Oh, God, it's—"

The volley of bullets came right over the headset into Pop's ears. Then nothing.

"Red Wing three, what the hell happened? Red Wing three, are you there?"

The trainer, which had taken up a position behind them, wasn't answering. Locke glanced back to his rear and felt his bladder weaken as the helicopters roared toward them.

CHAPTER 34

"OH, SHIT!" WAS ALL POP KELLER COULD SAY AFTER HE COMPLETED a wide turn that brought him face to face with the four gunships. "We got a bit of trouble here, Chris."

"Then why the hell are you—"

Locke's words were drowned out by the Warhawk's engine as Keller lifted into a sudden climb and streaked over the four helicopters. They turned effortlessly and continued their pursuit.

"Red Wing, this is Red leader. I've got four big bugs on my ass and I need some help fast. Reds three and four," he said to the Messerschmitt and the Spitfire, "come in from the rear and take them with your air cannons. The rest of you hang close."

"They're right on your rail, Red leader!" came a pilot's desperate voice.

"I know that, numb nuts," Pop muttered, and proceeded to drive the Warhawk up and over, defying gravity, diving fast with its shark mouth swallowing air to elude the gunships on his tail.

Two of them broke off and headed for the rest of the wing.

"At least we took out the dusters," Pop said simply.

"You didn't impress me as the kind of man who'd give up."

Keller's crusty features flared. "Who said anything about giving up? I was just stating fact."

A volley of machine-gun fire sprayed them. Pop dove, then climbed, fighting to stay out of the gunships' sights if not their range.

Up ahead, two of the gunships were bearing down on four of Red Wing's fighters that were acting as decoys for the strike by the Messerschmitt and Spitfire. Suddenly the decoy planes dove together, as the two assault fighters dropped out of the clouds and fell in behind the two gunships.

"We're on them, Red leader. In range . . . now!"

The air cannons blazed from the Messerschmitt and Spitfire.

"Hot shit!" Pop beamed. "Kiss those choppers good-bye!"

"Negative effect, Red leader," the Spitfire reported. "Achieved direct hit with negative effect."

Pop leaned forward. "They've got armor plating. Our shells won't cut through it. Go for the rear propeller."

A helicopter's rear propeller is its most vulnerable point. Knock it out and you strip the machine of balance and stability. The Messerschmitt and Spitfire, though, never got the chance to try. A pair of rockets blasted from the warships' rear launchers blew them into a thousand pieces that fluttered to the ground.

"Dirty bastards! I'll get you for that!"

Pop went into another climb, bringing him almost into the path of the two choppers. Their bullets pounded the side of the Warhawk, sending steel shards everywhere and just missing the fuel tank.

"Come on, old girl, hold together for Pop just a little longer," he urged his plane, tapping it tenderly. He went into a dive that took him between the four gunships. He spoke frantically into his headset.

"Form two wedges, boys. We'll take them from different angles. Reds seven through ten, try to get over them and use your rockets. Might score a lucky hit."

Pop knew the chances of that were virtually impossible. Perhaps, though, the sight of falling bombs would distract the choppers' attention long enough to allow a full frontal assault.

"My bombs are loaded with firecracker stuff," Pop told Locke. "Not as potent as the real thing but they'll still make a helluva mess. . . ."

With that, Pop swung into a climb that took him over the two gunships that had originally given chase. More bullets sprayed their rear and Keller had to dive again, ducking and sweeping like a crazed bird, fighting to stay out of the sights of the second pair of choppers.

"Fuck this strategy," Pop said. "I never went in for the sneaky shit anyway. Hold on to your balls, Chris!"

Pop went into a climb, then banked at an angle that brought him head-on with the two trailing gunships, his machine guns blasting away more for effect than anything else. The other two choppers veered off toward the approaching wedge made up of a pair of Mustangs, a Corsair, and a trainer.

"Get ready, Chris!" Pop grabbed the throttle tight.

A collision with one or both of the gunships seemed inevitable when Pop kicked in all 2,000 lovely horses of the stubborn Warhawk. As it climbed he released all four of his firecracker-loaded bombs. The gunships slowed suddenly, just as Keller expected they would, and at least two of his bombs exploded on impact against one. Glass shattered and metal gave way as a burst of Fourth of July colors sprang from the chopper's frame. The pilot fought frantically with the controls but black smoke and bright colors stole his sight away. The chopper's engine died and the machine went into a hopeless dive. Its crash sent more pretty colors flying outward.

Two of the remaining gunships were firing away at the first wedge and they disabled one of the Mustangs. The second wedge banked in front of them, machine guns spitting. Bullets poured through the windshield of one of the gunships, killing the pilot instantly and sending the giant insect into a dying spin. The second chopper escaped the fire by dropping beneath the attack. It tilted its laser-aimed rocket launchers upward and released a burst of four. The last trainer and a Corsair exploded in twin fireballs, while another of the Mustangs limped away, gray smoke pouring from its injured engine.

"Reds six and seven, get the hell outta here," Pop urged the battered Mustangs, and turned his attention to the spectacular aerial dogfight going on between the two gunships and his two remaining fighters.

Forty years ago, the Red Wing's last Mustang and Corsair might have made mincemeat out of the choppers, but their engines were laboring from the strain of the chase now and the planes moved sluggishly. Exchanges of fire were frantic, the two fighter pilots struggling to take aim on the slippery gunships, which were never in the same place for long. The final Mustang swooped down trying to take one of the gunships from behind. But the other chopper was equal to the task, dipping effortlessly and spraying the attacking fighter with its machine gun. The Mustang fell immediately, spitting black smoke. The pilot ejected.

"That makes it two against two," Pop reported grimly, driving the Warhawk forward toward a gunship's tail.

The gunship he was trailing seemed to drop straight down, under the Corsair that was banking into an attack run. The Corsair pilot kept enough cool to drop both his wing-mounted rockets, but the wind took them and they soared harmlessly away. He turned to link up with Pop's Warhawk but the helicopter fell in on his tail, machine guns blasting.

"They're on me!" the pilot shouted into his headset.

"Hang on," Pop commanded. "I'm coming."

"I'm hit! I'm hit!"

"Eject! Don't stay with the damn thing! . . . Do you copy? I say again, do you copy?"

There was no reply. The Corsair went into a death dive and spun to Earth.

"Just us against them now, Chris" was all Pop said.

The gunships fell in line and roared at the Warhawk together, gunners struggling to adjust their aim at Pop's daredevil dips and darts. For twenty years he had practiced such maneuvers to thrill fans and sell tickets. Now he was using them to save his and Locke's life but it felt little different, just a routine to follow and somewhere a crowd to please. He performed magnificently. But the 2,000-horsepower engine had been pushed to its fullest for too long now and the tach's needle was dancing crazily.

The gunships were gaining ground, letting their final target bob and weave to its heart's content. There was no reason to rush things. The old plane was moving away from the base, not toward it, and there were no more cropdusters in the air to protect. The gunners kept firing erratic bursts from their machine guns as they closed the gap on the Warhawk, down to two hundred yards now.

The glass surrounding Locke shattered and he felt something hot stab his shoulder with burning agony. His ears were exposed

346

to the rushing wind, the effect like twin sledgehammers pounding away on either side. With his free hand, he squeezed his wounded shoulder and felt blood soaking his fingers.

Pop knew the choppers were closing and started with more evasive maneuvers, swinging up and down, left and right, to avoid their fire. The motions hit Locke's stomach like a rollercoaster ride, but that was a hell of a lot better than being hit by the bullets pouring from behind them. He clung to the hope that the Blue Wing had successfully disabled the remainder of the cropdusters, blew them to bits, burying Tantalus forever.

There wasn't much chance of that, Chris knew, not with the gunships to consider. And then he noticed the blinking red light next to the Warhawk's fuel gauge.

"Wouldn't happen to have any gasoline handy, would you, friend?" Pop shouted back at him.

Ahmad Hamshi knew he had responded to the crisis brilliantly. The enemy planes had all been destroyed. He had managed to save twenty-seven of the cropdusters and all canisters from six more. The overall operation would be slowed but hardly wiped out. So when word had come from the helicopters that they were in pursuit of the final ghost fighter, Hamshi ordered the dusters to return to the runway and begin takeoff procedures again immediately. Keysar Flats was isolated but still too close to civilization for comfort. A prolonged aerial battle would certainly have drawn attention to the area, and with the dusters—and their contents—still on the ground, it was attention he could ill afford.

Men perched behind the remaining machine-gun and antiaircraft cannons watched the sky warily, anticipating yet another attack from the ghost squadron. The engines of the cropdusters, meanwhile, were revving, and the first two had taxied into takeoff position.

Ahmad Hamshi allowed himself a smile.

The smile vanished quickly at the sight of the battered blue Piper Cub roaring over the hangars, barely clearing them, coming out of nowhere.

"Heeeeeee-yahhhhhhhhhhhh!"

Mickey Ostrovsky was screaming as his Piper soared over the hangar. Parts of his guts had escaped from a gaping wound in his stomach and were hanging over his belt but he didn't care. The cancer had taught him how to live with pain, and he had only two months left anyway. He had another minute before it got to be too much, and a minute would suit him, just fine.

His Piper had almost crash-landed minutes before but he had managed to keep it whole, losing consciousness only briefly. When he came to, he pushed the fighter back into the air, feeling its wheels scrape against the hangar roof, and headed it straight over the big guns for the runway.

The men manning them struggled to change the big guns' angle but the best they could manage was to bring them directly overhead. Only the machine gun was able to get off any rounds at all as the blue plane screamed above them.

Mickey O. took a chest full of lead and felt the blood filling his mouth, but he wasn't about to let such inconveniences stop him. He was going out the way he had always wanted to and the rest of the world be damned.

He fired his three remaining rockets and followed them to the ground, crashing his Piper into the line of cropdusters at the front just as his rockets tore up the middle rows. The dusters were shoved back against each other, tumbling like dominoes, as Mickey O. grazed the ground and waited for the merciful explosion that would end his life. Enough of the dusters' fuel tanks had ruptured upon impact, and the flames from his final rocket blasts sniffed out the gushing gas and stuck to it. The explosions came fast and furious, belching black smoke and orange flames, consuming the last of the air before Mickey realized he couldn't breathe it.

Ahmad Hamshi rushed desperately about, hands flapping and signaling, ordering his men to salvage the canisters. His words were absorbed by the fire and the blasts, but he knew it didn't matter; there could be nothing left to salvage. His men were fleeing toward safety. He fled with them.

Mickey O.'s remaining eye found the sky he had loved one last time. Two bright flashes broke before him, coming straight from the heavens, angels no doubt sent to carry him up.

348

*   *   *

"I'm gonna make a fight of this," Pop said, breaking the red warning bulb with his bare fist. "Hang on, Chris."

With the gunships only seventy yards back, Keller swung up and over them, hoping to move in from behind and take them with his guns. But the battered Warhawk moved too sluggishly to gain him the advantage he sought, and he fired his guns at targets already swerving to the side, angling themselves in for a direct hit. His only advantage was gone now, Pop knew. He kept firing his guns until the hammers snapped on empty chambers, which was about the same time the engine began to sputter.

Chris watched the helicopters closing for the kill, dual guns blasting at the dying Warhawk as it started to drop from the sky. The giant insects hovered with it briefly, taunting their prey, then roared forward angling for a rocket shot.

There was a blinding explosion that shook Locke's eyes closed, and he opened them fully expecting to see a long tunnel extended toward the next world.

What he saw was totally different.

The remains of one of the gunships were slipping from the sky, shedding more parts of its carcass as it fell. Locke turned toward the second chopper just as a similar explosion shattered the air and turned it hot. He shook himself from what must have been a hallucination. In the cockpit, though, Pop Keller seemed to be jumping for joy as he struggled to hold the Warhawk steady.

A pair of F-16s roared over them and then circled back to render assistance. Chris felt the tears burning his eyes. The jets were the prettiest sights he'd ever seen, and he forgot about his injured shoulder long enough to wave at them.

"We ain't out of the woods yet, friend," Pop said grimly.

The engine sputtered one last time, then died out altogether. Pop had used its last spurt of fuel to level out the Warhawk's descent into the wind.

The ground came up fast. The last thing Christopher Locke remembered was checking to make sure his seat belt was fastened. Impact shook him forward, then quickly back so that his head smashed against the wooden railing. He felt himself being shaken violently up, straining against the seat belt, and imagined he had been catapulted outward into the warm air.

But he hadn't imagined anything. The brave Warhawk had broken up around him, and Locke had been thrown well into the air at a frightening clip. The landing knocked the wind out of him, and he felt himself rolling over again and again, crunching bones with each turn. The pain was everywhere at once yet still spreading.

Then darkness.

PART TEN:

SAN SEBASTIAN,
MONDAY MORNING

CHAPTER 35

ROSS DOGAN TIGHTENED HIS PARACHUTE BELT IN THE CARGO HOLD of the C-160. Around him 150 members of the army's elite Rangers were crowded together passing cigarettes and candy. The hold had been silent for ten minutes now. The jump was almost upon them and there wasn't an eye that strayed long from the red signal light, waiting for it to start flashing.

Dogan stared at the light intently, trying to fight against the exhaustion that threatened to overwhelm him. He needed to be in top form for the next few hours.

Yesterday Calvin Roy had heard his story, accepting his words with little argument and posing only essential questions. Roy had scrambled the F-16s to Keysar Flats but word came back that a mothballed air force base the cropdusters were using had been devastated before their arrival. The jet fighters merely finished the job, a mop-up operation. Incredibly, it seemed the participants of an air show had done the bulk of the damage but information was still sketchy, as was the fate of Christopher Locke. Dogan knew Chris had been behind the bizarre raid and prayed he had managed to survive it. He was astounded by the amateur's resourcefulness. Amazing how fast men learned when they had to.

Roy's first inclination was to launch an air strike over San Sebastian after reconnaissance photographs confirmed men and equipment were massing in the dead town. Dogan, though, had argued vehemently against that strategy. Yes, an air strike would successfully obliterate the canisters that were there, but who knew whether Mandala had more stored somewhere else. The only acceptable solution was a ground-based strike. Mandala would have to be neutralized. He could not be allowed to revive his mad plan another day.

Ultimately Roy had relented and set about getting the bureaucracy in motion to call up the elite Rangers for a foreign operation. The two C-160 cargo-personnel transports had left at nine the previous evening, allowing only a brief stop in Panama for refueling en route to their target in Colombia. By launching an attack from the hillsides surrounding San Sebastian, the Rangers could effectively surround Mandala's troops. Up till now things had gone miraculously without a hitch.

The red light flashed on. Wordlessly the Rangers shuffled to their feet. Dogan fell in step among them, taking a place in line. He was here under CIA authority but answerable to the Rangers' commander. His job was to get Mandala while the Rangers took care of the rest of the town.

Dogan swallowed as much air as he could. He had never enjoyed jumping even under the best of circumstances, so when it came to his turn he leaped from the ledge with feet trembling and eyes squeezed closed. The fall was swift and uncomfortable, the added weight in Dogan's pack making it harder for him to stay with the group's dive pattern. He angled his body to keep close, shifting his pack to ease the strain. It included a pair of Laws rockets, the army's miniature bazooka; a Mac-10 machine pistol with four spare clips; and Dogan's favorite handgun, the Heckler and Koch P-9.

He hit the ground and rolled to a halt. The heavy equipment was being released above, and the Rangers were already clearing the area for its landing.

It was an hour later—amazing time really—before everything was organized and the Rangers were ready to set out. They had come down a good thirty miles from San Sebastian to insure against being spotted in the air. Dogan wasn't expecting Mandala to be watching for them anyway; he had no reason to. There was no way anyone should have known the specifics of his private endgame.

The problem at this point was travel. The Iranian rescue had failed due to a combination of bad weather and equipment breakdown. Weather was not a factor here but walking the thirty miles was unthinkable given the time frame, which meant the transports *had* to hold up. And if the operation was to be a complete success, the trucks toting artillery and antiaircraft guns had to make it as well. The Rangers couldn't afford to let even one of Mandala's planes or its contents slip from their grasp.

Nor could they afford to alert Mandala to their presence at any time prior to the direct assault. Mandala would certainly have guards posted on the hillsides surrounding the town, and the Rangers' heavy equipment could be spotted easily from a distance of a half mile or so. It was Dogan who suggested what eventually became the unit's working plan, and now as they headed for San Sebastian under a hot and heavy sun he could only hope things would go as expected.

It took ninety minutes to reach the town's outskirts. At that time they abandoned their transports and covered the rest of the ground on foot. They made their approach to San Sebastian from three different angles, much of the last eighth mile with their bellies to the ground. All three divisions stopped perhaps fifty yards from where Mandala's first guards had been spotted. Dogan nodded to the bearded Ranger commander and started off alone, crawling on his stomach toward one of the hillsides overlooking the town.

Since his job was to infiltrate the enemy and destroy the planes along with Mandala, no assault could begin before he made a careful inspection of the area. Once satisfied, he would signal the Ranger commander and the next phase of the operation would begin. Dogan crept through the dirt and burned-out debris, almost to the first line of Mandala's defenses. Fortunately, the guards were spread out with far too much distance between them. And they each wore a different uniform, which provided Dogan with the final shadow of his plan.

He crawled closer and closer until he could almost smell the boots of an approaching guard. The man's eyes were locked on the town instead of the surrounding area. A lucky break. When the guard passed him, Dogan yanked his feet out hard and without any hesitation snapped the man's neck. Then he took the dead man's place.

Dogan pulled a pair of binoculars from the pack he wore over his shoulder and held them to his eyes. With a slight shudder he realized this was how it had all begun when Lubeck had occupied a similar position overlooking the town more than two weeks ago. He pushed that thought back and turned the focusing wheel, pretending to first look out over the wide expanse of land where the Rangers were pressed to the ground. Even with the binoculars he couldn't see them. Amazing. He turned the binoculars on the town beneath him.

Mandala's troops were everywhere, especially concentrated in an area north of the burned-out town where a makeshift airstrip had been constructed and a dozen small planes had lined up one after the other. No, Dogan realized, they weren't planes but small jets capable of carrying the fungus infinitely farther and faster than their counterparts in Keysar Flats. A dozen would be all it would take to do the job nicely, assuming refueling stops had been arranged, and Dogan was sure they had.

He shifted his binoculars toward the dead fields. More of the troops were at work there, handling shovels instead of guns. Silver canisters perhaps two feet long were being lifted from the ground and handed to men passing by in jeeps. No wonder Mandala had left guards behind in San Sebastian. His hidden canisters had to be protected from anyone who ventured too close. He must have buried them before the genetically advanced seeds had been planted, the precise agenda of his plan clear even then. The fields were an ideal resting place for his canisters, for who would ever expect him to burn the ground resting over them?

Dogan focused his binoculars next on the formidable arsenal, which included small tanks, small artillery lodged behind sandbags, and several machine-gun nests. The ground had been set up as if Mandala expected an attack, and Dogan had to give him credit for taking such elaborate precautions.

Satisfied that he knew the layout, Dogan pressed a button on his belt-held communicator, giving the Ranger commander the GO signal.

356

Two minutes later, two jets dropped out of the sky, belching white exhaust no more than a thousand feet over the town. Men began scampering frantically about, eyes locked on what looked like small missiles sliding toward the ground. The missiles burst upon impact and huge swells of thick, gray smoke stretched outward.

Dogan started down the hill, tripping and stumbling, panic on his features. He passed into the gray smoke and felt his eyes burning. The charging Rangers would have donned gas masks to protect themselves. But since Dogan had to pass through Mandala's lines to reach the airstrip, he had to appear to belong among his troops. That meant no mask for him. In addition to providing camouflage for the Rangers' charge, the smoke had the same effect as tear gas on the nose, eyes, and mouth. Dogan was coughing and wheezing horribly as he struggled forward in the direction of the jets.

Behind him the sound of gunfire was beginning. The Rangers would spare nothing in taking the town now. The advantage was clearly theirs, and they weren't about to squander it. Mandala's heavy guns and tanks pounded away, though, taking few casualties but slowing the Rangers' rush. Their own artillery weapons were motoring into position now, ready to shoot down fleeing planes.

Dogan rushed through the lines, staying low and shielding his mouth as floods of Mandala's troops charged by him. His nose felt as if he had sniffed ammonia and his eyes poured hot tears that obscured his vision. He kept moving as the gunfire behind him intensified, indicating the first wave of Rangers had reached the town and were engaging Mandala's troops directly. Dogan quickened his pace.

The Mac-10 was held tight in his hand now and he had fitted the Heckler and Koch P-9 snugly on his hip. His weighted-down pack still slowed him slightly. The Rangers were using a funnel strategy, assaulting Mandala's men from two sides and the front simultaneously, moving constantly inward to pin them into the smallest possible area. Dogan made for the runway as fast as he could, knowing that the line would be pushed back upon him before long.

357

The airstrip was located at the very edge of San Sebastian and the gas thinned as he got closer to it, allowing his eyes to clear slightly. The rapid gunfire, shouts, and screams were still behind him. He had turned all his attention forward just as a series of bullets hit the ground at his feet. He dove to the side, rolling with the Mac-10 blazing in the direction the shots had come from. Dogan rolled further, behind a parked jeep, and looked up to see a pair of machine-gun nests resting just off the side of the airstrip, guarding the small jets while men worked feverishly to finish the loading process. Already pilots were struggling with the controls, readying the jets for takeoff. The Rangers would be breaking through the enemy lines within minutes but that was too long and Dogan did not trust the accuracy of antiaircraft fire. The planes had to be stopped now.

Dogan ripped his pack from his shoulders and unzipped it. He pulled the three grenades free along with one of his two Laws rockets and sifted through twenty powerful bombs composed of plastic explosives for another machine-gun clip. He lifted the Laws rocket up to his shoulder and snapped up the sight. His target was the first of the dozen jets in line for takeoff. His object at this point was disruption.

He fired the rocket and the jet exploded in a roar of flames. The eyes of the men in the machine-gun nests were drawn to it long enough for Dogan to rise with the pins already pulled from two grenades. He was stripping the pin from a third while the first two were still airborne, not direct hits but good enough. The machine guns were neutralized, and his third grenade took out the troops rushing to defend the runway from another position. Men were fleeing the airstrip now, both troops and pilots.

The battle behind him was still raging, Mandala's men having regrouped somehow, as Dogan sprinted for the runway. He was in the open, but if anyone was there to take a shot at him, confusion prevented it. Here was a lone man sprinting toward the jets without a gas mask. He could be rushing in to provide reenforcement as easily as anything else.

Dogan slid behind one of the jets and checked the area. He hoped he could stay out of the Rangers' approaching fire and not get himself shot by his own side. The thick gas was blowing over the runway now, but he forced himself to concentrate on setting the detonators in place as quickly as possible.

Dogan rested his pack on the hardened dirt and extracted four small yet deadly bombs. Since his Laws rocket had disabled the first of the jets, he would need to set only eleven charges. He turned the timers to the four-minute mark and stuck the first one against a Lear's tail. The second and third charges wedged in tightly but the fourth wouldn't stick. Dogan checked the adhesive strip and had bent over to wet it when he felt the blow to the back of his skull.

Only the fact that he had been leaning over saved him from a direct hit and certain death. He turned to face Shang.

The Mac-10 was back with his pack, leaving him only the Heckler and Koch. He drew it quickly. It would have to be a head or neck shot, Dogan knew. Nothing else would have any effect on the Chinese giant protected by thin, bulletproof steel. He got off one shot with the world still spinning before him and missed. Shang was rushing him now and a second shot grazed the side of the giant's head, tearing his ear off but barely slowing him down. He was upon Dogan too fast for the pistol to be adjusted, and Grendel's next three shots hit the stomach, accomplishing nothing. Then the pistol was ripped from his hand and tossed into the gray smoke.

Shang went for him with a vicious swipe at the head. Dogan ducked and the giant's hand slammed into a jet's steel side, denting it. Shang went for another blow and Dogan ducked again. He backed away from the giant and they faced off. Shang smiled, almond eyes narrowing, as he beckoned to the man he thought he had killed in Rome.

Dogan charged, going for a leg sweep. But Shang anticipated the move perfectly and tripped Dogan up, then kicked at his head as he lay on the ground.

Dogan caught the foot and yanked, then thrust one of his own feet up for the giant's groin. He felt the thud of impact, but the steel had saved the giant from the effect of the blow and Shang was able to grab Dogan's foot with both hands and twist violently. Grendel felt his knee go and spun quickly onto his stomach, kicking free.

359

Another of Shang's feet caught him in the stomach and lifted him into the air, pitching him sideways. The pain was incredible but Dogan swallowed it down. Another foot leveled at him and he managed to grab it and yank hard. Shang lost his balance and staggered backward.

Dogan struggled to his feet and, pain exploding in his stomach and knee, faced off against the giant again. His pack rested ten yards to Shang's right. If he could get to it . . .

Shang rushed him. Dogan couldn't believe a man his size could move so fast. The giant was on him in no time and Dogan felt the massive arms closing around him. Shang thrust him back till his shoulders smashed into one of the jet's wings. Shang pounded him again. A knifelike pain surged through the area between Dogan's shoulder blades and he realized the giant had lifted him off the ground. He pounded the giant's head, especially the wounded side where the ear was torn off.

The giant grimaced and released his grip. Dogan slipped to the ground as Shang stumbled slightly, a fresh flow of scarlet pouring down onto his white suit from the hole where his ear had been. Enraged, he went for Dogan, but Grendel easily ducked under his attack and pounded the back of his head with an elbow. Shang slammed up against the side of a jet face first. Dogan threw all his weight forward into the monstrous frame and Shang's face mashed forward again.

The giant, blood painting his face, turned quickly with a wild swing. Dogan deflected it as it passed Shang's center and weakened, then followed in with a set of rigid knuckles into the giant's exposed throat. Shang gasped. His eyes bulged. Dogan went for another blow, a killing one this time, but the giant snatched his fingers out of midair with a massive hand and jammed them backward, sending Dogan to the ground howling in agony.

That could have been it, would have been if Dogan had given in to the pain instead of rising suddenly as the giant leaned over to finish him. He came up fast and hard, neck tensed as his head drove upward and slammed under the giant's chin. Shang's head snapped horribly backward, crunching his vertebrae together. Shaken, he lashed out wildly but Dogan was already under the strike, hitting him square in the gut with his shoulder and feeling his entire body tremble from impact against the steel. But the giant was forced backward, the back of his skull driven hard against a wing. Dazed, he could do nothing to thwart Dogan's outstretched fingers from rising for his eyes.

Shang managed to close them but Grendel's fingers still dug deep. The giant screeched in agony, clawing and striking blindly.

Dogan limped away, making for his pack as fast as he could.

Shang staggered forward, one hand still swiping at his eyes as he swayed from side to side. He righted himself and his free hand produced a massive, shiny knife from inside his jacket.

Dogan reached into his pack and came out with his second Laws rocket. He popped the safety off, extended the stock, and fought to steady the weapon in his trembling hands.

Shang mounted his final rush, the long blade glistening overhead.

Dogan fired the Laws rocket.

It blasted into the giant's midsection, through the steel body armor, and blew him apart, showering the immediate area with pieces of his flesh. Particles of metal fluttered in the air as well, no match for a rocket.

Dogan caught his breath but couldn't let himself relax. In the rising noxious mist he could see Mandala's men had succeeded in moving their line back against the Rangers, holding them off to provide the pilots with time to reach their Learjets. There would be no dispersing the fungus from these, Dogan realized. They were merely courier aircraft assigned to transport canisters to other areas across South America.

Dogan struggled back to his feet. He grabbed his machine pistol in his good hand and his pack in the twisted one. He had to finish the job of taking these planes out, even as a number of Mandala's troops were rushing toward them, hoping to clear the way for the pilots. Dogan fired a burst at them and darted from one plane to the next as bullets richocheted off steel around him.

The detonators he had already set had ticked down to the one-minute mark, so each explosive he jammed on the jets' frames as he ran would be set for only fifty seconds. He wedged two home, then a third, was handling a fourth when a bullet grazed his side and spun him around, bringing him face to face with three of Mandala's troops rushing from the end of the runway.

Dogan dove to the side away from their fire and he felt another bullet pound his shoulder. The warm soak of blood was spreading now and it felt almost relaxing. The three men rushed at him, and he turned onto his stomach and finished them with a single burst from the Mac-10.

Mandala's troops were being forced back by the Rangers into a narrower and narrower field. They were almost upon the runway when Dogan rose on his weakening legs and wedged another detonator into place, leaving him only three jets to go. He realized with terror that the explosions would begin in little more than thirty seconds, so he skipped the next two planes and jammed the three detonators set for thirty seconds onto the first plane in line.

The Rangers fired another burst of the thick, gray gas as Mandala's troops converged on the runway.

Dogan's wounds and desperation made him look enough like one of them for Mandala's men to ignore his passage off the runway and into the fields. His eyes darted back to the sight of several pilots working frantically in their cockpits to get their jets ready for rapid takeoff. The explosions would send steel rocketing everywhere. He had to get clear, had to—

The first four explosions sounded virtually together, swallowing the sounds of gunfire and sending all those still alive, including Dogan, to the ground. The next explosions, five in all, were separated by a few seconds but spread quickly to all the jets until the individual fires merged into a single bloody graveyard for men, planes, and canisters. Numerous secondary explosions erupted as fuel tanks ignited, helping the flames claw out and upward, stretching for the sky.

The explosions had carried most of the debris straight up, sparing Dogan and, he hoped, the Rangers as well. Mandala's troops who had retreated to the runway, though, had been almost totally wiped out. The battle was over.

But what of Mandala?

* * *

Dogan limped toward the approaching Rangers with arms clasped behind his head.

"Dogan, CIA," he announced breathlessly. "I'm with you."

Three of them moved near him suspiciously as the rest fanned out to continue herding prisoners together. One of the Rangers looked at him and nodded.

"I jumped from the plane just after you," he said. "Helluva job back there on the runway. I assume it was your work."

Dogan nodded.

"You spooks got all the tricks."

The Rangers' commander was moving among the wounded with Dogan limping at his side.

"He's not here," Grendel reported.

"We haven't checked the corpses yet," the commander said.

"It doesn't matter," Dogan told him. "He's not among the prisoners or the bodies. I can feel it."

"Then where the fuck is he?"

Dogan sat down against a jeep in the center of what had once been the town of San Sebastian and considered the question. The Rangers still had the entire area surrounded. No one had tried to get out and all stragglers had been captured and were being processed now, which meant Mandala must yet be in the vicinity waiting. *Waiting for what?*

If he could remain under cover until the Rangers left, he could mount his escape. But how? What was his plan?

A passing Ranger handed Dogan his canteen and Grendel gulped its contents gratefully. He had already been to the make-shift infirmary and the doctors were not at all pleased about letting him leave. The wound on his side was nothing but his shoulder would cause him problems for some time. The doctors had insisted on putting it in a sling, which Dogan promptly slipped out of, after making sure to get a large shot of Novocaine. None of the fingers on his left hand were broken but two were badly sprained and the swelling made holding objects virtually impossible. His knee, though, was the worst of all. The cartilage was torn and surgery would be necessary as soon as he returned to the States. Sudden motions, Dogan was warned, could result in further damage to the joint, and he should definitely stay off the leg altogether. Grendel shrugged and listened politely. There would be no staying off it until he had finished with Mandala.

What was his plan for escape?

The question hammered at Dogan's mind. He grabbed a set of binoculars from the jeep and scanned the perimeter of the town, moving from hillside to hillside, scanning all levels. He passed the area where the children's shack had been, where the direction of the wind had spared most of the flora from the flames weeks before, and froze on a plateau to the right of and above it.

He pulled his eyes from the lenses and wiped them. He had to be sure they weren't playing tricks on him. He refocused the binoculars, feeling his mouth go dry as the sight was confirmed.

Then he was back on his feet, forgetting about his pain as he searched for the bearded commander of the Rangers. He found him in the area reserved for the infirmary.

"I need four of your best men," he said.

"Care to tell me why?"

"A hunch."

The commander, a career combat soldier who had led the first unit into Grenada, had played many himself. He had orders from Washington to cooperate fully with this man, but even without those orders, Dogan's resolve impressed him and he would have done so anyway.

"You've got them. I'll need to know what you'll be doing, though."

"Hunting," Dogan replied.

"You're not in the best of condition, my friend."

"We're not going very far."

Dogan's battered body made him suffer all the way up the hillside. He was shot so full of painkillers that he could feel his motions were slow. Any fast ones that were required he would leave for the Rangers. Mandala he would leave for himself.

It would have been far simpler to have just told the Ranger commander what he had seen and turned the operation over to him. But Mandala *had* to be his. Otherwise he could take nothing out of all this personally. Too many people had died, too many lives had been ruined or marred. Mandala had to pay. Dogan had to make him pay.

The Novocaine had worn off by the time they reached the plateau and Dogan dry-swallowed two more painkillers. The Rangers' hands were tight on their rifles as the men watched out for a possible ambush. Dogan moved ahead of them.

The plateau looked different up close from what he had seen through the binoculars. He couldn't get his bearings. Might he have imagined the sight that had brought him here in the first place? The fatigue and throbbing pain made him question himself. It could have been an illusion, a trick of weary eyes. He tried to picture the plateau as the binoculars had shown it to him. Perhaps it had been a different one, a little higher up perhaps.

The wind picked up and a sudden brightness forced Dogan to squint. But the sun was behind him. Why, then, the glare? The sun must have bounced off something, something metallic.

Dogan moved slowly forward, the picture from the binoculars all at once clear again. There was a whole nest of thick bushes and branches concentrated right before him. He reached up into it and his hand touched steel. He yanked some of the bushes and vines away, revealing part of a helicopter's propeller—the metal the sun had reflected off and the sight he had glimpsed through the binoculars.

He stripped more of the camouflage away and the helicopter gained shape. It would have been hidden up there for Mandala's escape, weeks ago perhaps.

"Help me with this, will you?" he called back to the Rangers.

They had slung their rifles over their shoulders and started to approach when the rapid series of soft spits cut them down. Dogan was reaching for his machine gun.

"Don't, Grendel. I'll kill you just as I killed them. Turn slowly with your hands in the air and move to the side, out of sight from your friends below."

Dogan moved as instructed and then faced Mandala. The madman was holding a silenced Uzi aimed straight for his stomach. Ten yards separated them. Dogan flirted briefly with the notion of launching into a quick dive and finding his trigger, but

365

Mandala's advantage was too great to overcome, especially considering his own weakened condition.

"Very good, Grendel," Mandala said, stepping closer. "Now drop the gun to the ground holding the barrel with both hands."

His machine pistol clicked against the dirt.

"Now kick it aside."

Dogan complied.

"Turn around again, Grendel, and keep your hands in the air."

Again Dogan did as he was told and felt Mandala creeping up behind him. The madman slammed him in the lower back with his rifle. Dogan went down like a felled tree, pain exploding over his kidneys and intensifying in his already wounded areas. Somehow he ended up on his back. Mandala hovered over him.

"Someone must have seen you from below," Dogan squeezed through his grimace of pain. "You're finished."

Mandala kicked him hard in the same side the bullet had grazed an hour before. The agony squeezed his features into a wrinkled mask. He felt sick.

"No, Grendel, it's you who's finished. You're going to die, and I'm going to escape."

"They'll shoot you down before you get a mile."

Mandala kicked him again. "Not under the cover of darkness they won't." He stalked around Dogan, like a hawk ready to strike. "You really think my failure in Keysar Flats would have remained a secret from me? Hah! Calls had to be made from every checkpoint. When they didn't come I altered my strategy a bit." Mandala's finger thrust viciously toward San Sebastian. "Those jets you destroyed down there would have carried their canisters back to the U.S. with only a few left to unleash here in South America. When I learned of Shang's error in Rome, I feared you'd be coming, prepared for it even, but I still hoped I'd be able to get the jets off before your arrival. If not"—Mandala turned his eyes toward the camouflaged helicopter—"I had another plan arranged. I still have five hundred canisters of the fungus gas well hidden, along with the formula to produce as much more as I want." Mandala smiled. "And the research done at Sanii was not totally lost. When the time is right I will finish that part of the Committee's plan, but on my own terms, of course.''

Dogan's unfocused eyes caught a shape emerging from the area behind the helicopter. The figure moved lightly forward, a pair of knives gripped in its hands. *Kukhri* knives. It was Nikki! Dogan had to keep Mandala distracted long enough for Nikki to draw close. Tossing the sharply curved blades was too chancy, especially in this wind.

Dogan stared into Mandala's eyes. "You're full of shit," he managed, the pain racking him with each syllable.

"You will not be around to see yourself proven wrong," Mandala shot out furiously, "because today I am given the very great pleasure of killing you. If I had more time, I'd make it slow, Grendel, to make up for all the trouble you've caused me."

Nikki was just ten yards away now.

Dogan shook his head, the motion sending bolts of agony through his body. "You won't make it, Mandala. You're alone, isolated. Kill me; it doesn't matter because there'll be a hundred nations coming after you with everything they've got."

Just five yards away . . .

Mandala's eyes flashed eagerly, still locked on Dogan's. "Yes, Grendel, I think I will kill you." He stepped back and tilted the Uzi's barrel down. "I think that—"

The sound of a branch cracking behind him made Mandala swing fast, Uzi coming up and ready. Nikki was already upon him, *Kukhri* knives slicing into his throat on twin diagonal angles.

Mandala lost the Uzi's trigger, lost everything as he started to crumble, blood pumping from the gashes across his windpipe. Through fading eyes, Dogan watched Nikki pounce on Mandala's writhing frame. The blades plunged into flesh. She withdrew them and plunged them in again. There was little left of Mandala's torso and head when she was finished, trembling as she rose, a look of grim gratification etched upon her features. She let her knives drop over Mandala's mutilated corpse and moved toward Dogan. He watched her lean over him and he tried to ask her how she had escaped from Switzerland. But he could form no words and it didn't matter anyway.

Then Nikki was speaking softly to him but he couldn't hear her and everything hurt too much, so he closed his eyes and let her disappear.

Dogan was conscious of being carried down the hillside on a stretcher, the Ranger commander at his side.

"I guess this finishes it," the bearded man told him. "You did a helluva number back there on Mandala."

"Wasn't . . . me," Dogan muttered.

The commander turned to a doctor trailing just behind the stretcher holding an IV bottle. "What did he say?"

"Couldn't hear him."

"The girl," Dogan rasped, struggling for volume.

"What girl?" the commander asked. "We didn't find any girl."

Dogan smiled and surrendered to oblivion.

EPILOGUE

"SORRY I CAN'T OFFER YOU ANYTHING BUT ORANGE JUICE, MR. ROY."

"Call me Cal, son. We been through enough together to be on a first-name basis."

Dogan shifted tentatively in his chair on the patio outside the Bethesda Naval Hospital. His left leg was encased in a cast from the knee down and would be for another two weeks. Across the table Calvin Roy sipped his orange juice out of a paper cup.

"Thanks for stopping by to visit."

"Least I could do, son. Doctors tell me you'll be up and around in a month tops and I ain't surprised. Back home they say you can kick a bull in the balls but don't expect him to flinch."

"I guess I can take that as a compliment."

"I don't pass them out lightly, son."

Dogan folded his arms across his chest. "Tie up any of the loose ends?"

"Not many we could find. The girl who saved your life has dropped totally out of sight, and we received confirmation from our team in Austria that the body buried three days ago there *was* Audra St. Clair. No games this time. Let's hope Tantalus was buried with her."

"Five hundred canisters are still out there somewhere," Dogan said. "But it's my guess only Mandala knew where, and they're probably so well hidden we won't have to worry about anybody turning up with them."

"That's a comfort."

"What about the list of Committee members? Any luck finding it?"

Roy shook his head. "None at all, son. It's gotta be on some computer bank, and without the proper accesss code we can forget about it. That leaves lots of people, thousands even, out there still connected with all this—people in high positions everywhere. As long as they're out there, the Committee's still a threat, the way I see it."

Dogan shook his head. "I don't think so. They've been cut off from a central command. There's no one left to direct them and without that direction they're helpless. They'll go about their jobs harmlessly until they're replaced or voted out. Audra St. Clair was the key. Without her, the Committee's finished."

"There's still her daughter running around somewhere."

Dogan's tone became defensive. "We have nothing to fear from Nikki. Her only connection to the Committee was her mother, and it was buried with the old woman three days ago."

"Quite a resourceful girl from what I hear, though. Wouldn't mind havin' her on our side."

"She's been playing sides since she was sixteen. I think she's finished with that."

Roy eyed Dogan closely. "And what about you?"

"I doubt Division would have me back even if I wanted to go."

"I wasn't talking about Division, son. Word is the President wants me to take over as Secretary of State. I don't fancy that much 'cause you can only see so much bullshit before everything turns brown. I need someone to shovel it aside for me, to be my direct link with what's *really* going on in the field."

"Sounds like you're offering me a job, Cal."

"I'm offering you anything you want. Make that Russian Vaslov your assistant even. I don't care. I just wanna keep you on my side, son, on any terms you dictate."

"I'll give it some thought." Dogan paused, sipped his own orange juice through a straw. "Have you spoken with Locke yet?"

"Not directly but the right people approached him and handled the resettlement matter and name change for his family as soon as we brought his son back from England. We sent 'em all out to sunny California. Locke's got a position at Berkeley, as I recall. Charney detailed all the arrangements of their deal in a memo to me. We offered to arrange for both his novels to be published. But Locke said he didn't want it that way anymore. Said he'd rather write another and get it into print on his own."

"What about the old pilot who raided Keysar Flats with him?"

"Government offered to pick up where the insurance leaves off to rebuild his fleet, but he decided he'd rather start an aerial museum for relics like himself. Told my man he wanted to quit flyin' while he was on top."

"Who can blame him? He went through hell."

"So did you, son, running around the world with your own people trying to kill you. Wasn't hard to figure out what was going on even for a country asshole like me once we got an ID on the body in that Rome hotel room. Man named Keyes I hear you weren't too friendly with. Division's out of control, son, and word is somebody's doin' their level best to keep that restricted quarantine order in place . . . on you *and* Locke." Roy's eyes narrowed. "Something's gotta be done," he added, his meaning clear. "You had enough time to consider my offer yet?"

Dogan nodded. "I think so."

Four weeks later Dogan met Christopher Locke for lunch at a small café near Berkeley. The noontime rush was over but the place was still crowded with students. Locke arrived first, secured a corner table, and stowed his crutches against the wall. One arm was still in a cast, and it would be another several months before he would be without pain. In all, Locke's spill from the Warhawk had broken four bones, tore a network of ligaments, and cut wide portions of his flesh to the bone. Nevertheless, his recovery was proceeding well ahead of schedule. He had been teaching at Berkeley for a week.

Dogan arrived and limped toward the table. Chris pushed himself from his chair to greet him. The two men almost laughed at each other.

"Look at us," Chris quipped, "a couple of cripples." He

took his seat again gingerly. "You know, it all started for me in a restaurant. But that day it was Brian who made sure we got a corner table. Today it was me."

Dogan eased his chair forward. "You're safe, Chris. Nobody's going to touch you."

"That's what I keep telling myself, but I still hate turning my back on anybody. It never stops either. They used my family once. They might again. I won't let my kids take the bus home from school, you know."

"The paranoia will subside. You'll see."

"If you were talking to the man I was two months ago, I'd probably say you were right. But he's gone and here I am sitting in his place trying to live his life."

"Things aren't going well," Dogan concluded.

"That's just it, Ross, they *are* going well. L.A.'s only a bus ride away for my oldest son, and my daughter is being overwhelmed with boys as beautiful as she is. Your people set my wife up in a fantastic real estate job and well, the California life style, as they say, agrees with her. As for Greg, he's had the best medical care available. That man Roy arranged for one-on-one sessions between him and some professional ballplayers. They're showing Greg he can still play baseball even with a finger missing from his glove hand, and if he buys that he just might be able to adjust. But his childhood's gone, and they can't give that back to him, not even Roy."

"That covers all the members of your family except one."

Locke shrugged. "I just can't seem to put everything behind me. I lived in an academic fantasyland for fifteen years and all of a sudden I saw how violent and ugly the world can be. I met up with a mother I never knew and found out I didn't want to."

"She kept you alive, Chris, and in the end it cost her."

"She kept me alive because it suited her needs. And she sent Nikki out as my bodyguard, Nikki, who at Whitney's age was entering terrorist training school. What kind of world are we making for ourselves, Ross?"

"One a shitload better than the one the Committee envisioned."

"Maybe." Locke had to search for words. "You know what it comes down to in the end, Ross? The running. When you're running, everything you pass is a blur. I ran myself out in Europe. I can't run anymore and there's nothing left to run away from. So I've slowed down and everything's so damn clear. But I think I liked it better before. The blur made it easy to endure.''

"Then it comes down to pretending, not running, doesn't it?" Dogan challenged. "In Europe you said it felt like you were trapped in a labyrinth. Well, you made it out of that one only to land in another with just as many passages that lead nowhere. But this time the only way to escape is to accept that it's you that's changed, not your wife or your kids or even your job. It's not the world you've got to get used to again, it's yourself.''

Locke found himself smiling. "You ever get tired of spy work, we could use you in the philosophy department out here.''

"Let's just say I've been where you're finding yourself now. Trouble is, in my business do too much thinking and somebody will have your brains for breakfast.''

Locke tensed. "Now you've come to the real problem, Ross, 'cause how do I know that won't happen to me . . . and my family . . . tomorrow morning? I can't handle the fear, the doubt, the cringing every time the doorbell rings or a stranger meets my eye. We fucked with a lot of people out there who aren't used to being fucked with. You told me about that Division of yours. Eliminate the two of us and they walk away from this clean.''

Dogan stood up without ordering. "It's time I went back to work.''

The Commander sat in the shade at his usual table on the Champs-Élysées, sipping warm tea and toying with a basket of croissants. His ever-present newspaper was spread out and he read it mindlessly while awaiting the appearance of the two agents he had ordered to meet him. Division Six had to remain immune from standard government checks and balances. He had weathered worse storms than this, though. It was simply a matter of filling in certain holes now that the time had finally become right. Patience was everything, rashness a quality of the shortsighted.

The Commander heard the blind beggar's cup being rattled

before him and fished in his pocket for some change to drop in. Damn nuisance. Such human lice had no business ruining the scenery along the Champs-Élysées.

Glancing briefly up at the cup, he slipped a piece of change in and heard it jingle among the rest. Then he shooed the man away with his hand.

The blind beggar shook his cup again.

The Commander looked up from his paper to search for the café manager when he caught the blind man's face.

"Grendel . . ."

Ross Dogan winked once. Then he fired two bullets from the silenced Heckler and Koch held beneath his bulky brown rags. They entered the Commander's stomach, the impact pitching the older man backward and toppling him over. Waiters rushed over followed by the manager. When they saw the blood and the Commander's sightless eyes, they screamed for help. The Commander's men converged on the area, searching for the assassins, but they found only startled tourists, distracted shoppers . . .

And a blind beggar tapping his cane down the avenue.

ABOUT THE AUTHOR

Jon Land, twenty-eight, is the author of three previous novels: *The Doomsday Spiral, The Lucifer Directive*, and *Vortex*. He is currently at work on his next book.